Rosalind Miles has worked as a writer, journalist and broadcaster in the UK and throughout the world. Her career in broadcasting began at Oxford University, when she captained her college on the quiz programme *University Challenge*; her more recent work includes *Question Time, Behind The Headlines* and *Woman's Hour*. A contributing editor to *Cosmopolitan* magazine, Rosalind Miles specialises in the lives and careers of women, and has written award-winning non-fiction including *Women and Power, The Women's History of the World* and *The Rites of Man*. She is also the bestselling author of *Return to Eden*, based on the successful television series.

Rosalind Miles' work has been translated into many foreign languages and she was recently appointed a Fellow of the Royal Society of Arts. She is married with two children and lives in a sixteenth-century farmhouse in Warwickshire.

Also by Rosalind Miles

FICTION
Return to Eden
Bitter Legacy

NON-FICTION
The Fiction of Sex
The Problem of Measure for Measure
Danger! Men at Work
Modest Proposals
Women and Power
Ben Jonson: His Life and Work
Ben Jonson: His Art and Craft
The Female Form
The Women's History of the World
The Rites of Man

Prodigal Sins

Rosalind Miles

HEADLINE

First published in 1991
by HEADLINE BOOK PUBLISHING PLC

10 9 8 7 6 5 4 3 2 1

ISBN 0 7472 3649 6

Phototypeset by Intype, London
Printed and bound by
HarperCollins Manufacturing, Glasgow

HEADLINE BOOK PUBLISHING PLC
Headline House
79 Great Titchfield Street
London W1P 7FN

for
SJF
again

Our acts our angels are, for good or ill,
Our fatal shadows that walk by us still.
                              John Fletcher

Contents

PROLOGUE

Australia

Spring 1965

The young man ran down the beach, naked as a soul in bliss. The dawn sunlight clothed his lithe, well-proportioned body in streaks of fire, crowned his fair head with gold, and warmed his pale skin with the promise of the first hot day of the year. Oblivious to it all, he raced across the still-cold sand and with a shout of triumph threw himself into the sea. Ahead of him the pounding surf thundered into land, each wave as high as a house. But with the familiarity of endless boyhood hours and days in the water, he gave himself like a merman to the towering breakers and struck out fearlessly for the glimmering horizon.

'Robert! Rob! Wait for me, blast you!'

Behind him his companion was still struggling free of his clothes, his strong hands wrenching at his heavy working gear in all the frustration of haste. 'I beat you, Everard!' floated back to him off the gleaming surface of the sea. 'Fair and square – admit it! You lost!'

'You try doing a night's work first, then we'd see who'd lose!' With a howl of mock annoyance, Paul Everard tore off the last thread of his clothing and made a dash for the sea.

Far out now, the swimmer sported like a porpoise, leaping, diving, resurfacing with boundless energy and pure natural grace. At last he rested, floating on his back to watch the kaleidoscope of the tropical dawn as the sun raced up the sky.

God, how lucky he was! Was there a happier, luckier soul in the whole of Australia? To have all this – and all that was coming, coming soon. He laughed out loud at the thought of it; he felt like shouting from pure joy. As he did so, a muscular hand grabbed his ankle.

'Gotcha, Maitland!' growled Paul through a mouthful of sea water. 'Now we'll see who's beaten!'

Like every one of their contests since childhood, the underwater wrestling match ended, by common consent, in a draw. Afterwards they lay side-by-side on the sand in the companionable silence of exhaustion and perfect peace. Alone in the secluded bay, protected by the encircling rocks and the lofty sweep of white cliffs beyond, they could have been the first living things on the face of the earth at the dawning of the world.

Robert was the first to stir. 'Well, now that we've celebrated the rites of spring—' He stretched, uncoiling his long body like a tiger.

'Rites of spring?' murmured Paul lazily. 'So that's what it was. I thought you were just grabbing the chance t'see your old mate before he hits the sack – or else you just fancied a dip in y'birthday suit – a bit of back to nature!'

Robert flashed him a wicked grin. 'Well, now you're a working man – especially now you're on nights – you're not easy to catch up with, that's a fact. But as for back to nature – I'm leaving all that to you, mate!' he cracked back. 'Though the way you were with Janice Peaseley at the dance last Saturday, that wasn't natural – it was animal! You're sex-mad! Don't you ever think of anything else?'

'Hey, I was only trying t'show her a good time!' protested Paul. 'And y'know what? After I'd been all over her all night, she had the cheek t'tell me it was you she really fancied!'

'Me?'

If Rob had half an idea how good he really was, he'd be a killer, Paul thought, not for the first time, looking at his friend. He knew he was no slouch himself – already he had found that his tall, muscular body, filling out to its full manhood's breadth rather earlier than Robert's, his swarthy, almost gypsyish good looks and bold, bright, black eyes could pull the birds right out of their trees. But not always the best ones – not always the ones he wanted – and even then, he had to work for it. He'd never yet got anywhere with women, he reflected

6

grimly, without a serious amount of hard graft.

But Rob . . . glancing under his eyelids at Robert Maitland's broad shoulders tapering away to long, slender, well-shaped loins, his pale, golden skin, his handsome, strong-jawed face under its thick, smooth thatch of dusty fair hair, Paul knew again the ugly undertow of envy that he had been fighting ever since their schooldays. For whatever it was that women went for, this man had it – had always had it – probably had it in his cradle.

The only saving grace was he didn't know it. Even at school, the girls could be sidling round him like flies around a jam jar, hanging on his every word and batting their eyes till they almost took off, and he wouldn't notice. He simply didn't see that the way he listened to them – treating them like a cross between Kim Basinger and the Queen of Sheba – was just guaranteed to have them eating out of his hand. And he'd just go his own way afterwards, completely unconscious of every wasted opportunity.

Paul sighed. 'Yeah, you!' he said grudgingly. 'And she's not the only one. There's Noellene Foley, she always liked you, ever since kindergarten. And Joanne Mackintosh, she only asked about you the other day. Trouble is, you've lost touch with them all since you went away to college.'

'Well, how do you stay so closely in touch with them all when you're spending your working days – and even more your working nights, like last night – down the mine?' grinned Robert.

'Dedication, mate.' Paul smiled to himself. 'Constant dedication. The mine's only a job. The girls, now, they're my—'

'Horizontal recreation?'

Laughing like a hyena, Robert expertly evaded the punch that accompanied Paul's howl of fury. 'Bloody cheek!' spluttered Paul. 'I knew we should never have let you go off to college – I knew you'd get too big for y'boots!'

'I had to, Paul, you know that.'

In Robert's suddenly grave expression, Paul recognised one of the lightning changes of mood that distinguished his friend's mercurial character. 'Yeah, well,' he said awkwardly. 'It was different f'me. I never wanted anything else but Brightstone, the life here. 'Course, I was never as smart as you in the first place.'

'It wasn't about being smart. Oh, you know what I mean – my father–' He fell into a brooding silence, gazing out to sea with an expression Paul knew so well from countless discussions on this theme in the past. Then his natural good humour reasserted itself with a shrug and a broad smile. 'Still, I won that one! And I'm off again now, as soon as I can.'

'Off again?' Paul was aghast. 'But you've only just got back!' He bit back the ready reproaches that rose to his tongue: I thought you were here to stay, I thought it would be like the old times when we were boys, I thought you'd made your break, getting away before. He compromised lamely. 'I thought you'd done your degree, finished at college – that was it.'

'That was it,' agreed Robert, whose subtle intuition had missed none of his friend's feelings. 'But it's left me wanting to do more – see more – than I am ever going to here.' Imperceptibly his tone hardened. 'I've only been back a couple of weeks, and already I'm suffocating! I'll go mad if I have to stay much longer! I've got to get out, Paul – and for exactly the same reason I had to go before!'

Paul gave a nod. All he could offer was the silence of awkward sympathy. Once again Robert fixed his eyes on the horizon with a gaze of bleak aggression as he resumed. 'You've always been so lucky in your parents, Paul – particularly your dad. Oh, I know he was pleased when you decided you wanted to follow him down the mine, but I don't think he'd have tried to stop you, whatever you wanted to do. You or Claire – he treats both his children just the same. But my father – to him Joan is just the perfect daughter, and I'm nothing but the prodigal son!'

'Well, Joan's a great girl, y'got to admit that,' Paul put in urgently. He nearly added 'as good as a bloke', but wasn't sure how it would go down as a compliment.

Robert's taut face softened. 'Oh, I know,' he said fondly. 'And it's not her fault that she's so like him – any father's pretty well bound to love a chip off the old block. He never seemed to mind letting her do exactly as she wanted. But everything I've ever wanted to do, I've had to fight for. Including my freedom. And the fight's still on!'

Paul noticed the hard line of Robert's jaw, the unconscious lift of his chin, and could not help but admire the strength of the resolution that lay behind it. Young as he was, he could still sympathise wholeheartedly with the trials of another – and although man enough, in his own mind at least, to plunge enthusiastically into the most grown-up of sexual activities, he still could not imagine many things worse than being at daggers drawn with his own parents. 'So what'll you do?' he asked guardedly.

'Whatever comes up!' came the prompt reply. 'I've applied for just about everything going – jobs of all sorts – and scholarships, grants to do more studying. I'd love to get a crack at doing some research work – but anything, just anything, to get me out of here!'

A painful realisation was dawning in Paul's mind. 'Out of Brightstone?'

'Out of Australia, mate!' Paul had never heard Robert sound so determined. 'This island may be the biggest island in the world – but as long as my father's on it, it'll never be big enough for both of us!'

There was a heavy pause. Paul groped for something to say. 'What's he going to do when he finds out you're not going to take up the teacher training thing he's fixed up for you?'

An impish grin lit up Robert's handsome face. 'Stand by for typhoon Maitland!' he laughed. 'He may be a man of God, but he can lose his temper just as violently as any ordinary sinner. I guess you'll feel the hurricane down in the town just as soon as it blows off the Rectory headland! And I guess it'll be tonight, when he gets in. I can't put off tackling him any longer. You can thank your lucky stars you'll be safe underground!'

* * *

Why did he now call it 'the Rectory', not 'home' any longer, Robert wondered as he climbed the cliff path from the bay, and struck back along the headland. Because it's time to go, he decided. Time to hit the road – and that'll be my home, for a while at least – wherever I end up. The morning sun, riding high in the sky, warmed his shoulders and the back of his neck with its fierce caress. He could still feel the power of the breakers he had just left, could still smell the vast freshness of the ocean, taste the salt on his lips, sense the tang in the warm, lightly stirring air. He had never felt more alive. Suddenly he felt overwhelmingly confident, clear and strong. Nothing – not his father, not anything – could hold him back. His life was opening like a book, and no human hand could stay the turning of those leaves.

As he slipped into the kitchen through the back door, the tall, slim girl busy preparing breakfast read his face with a sister's quickness, and smiled her encouragement. Such was the understanding between them that there was no need to speak.

For theirs was more than an average sibling relationship. From her first sight of the huge-eyed baby with his long Viking limbs and downy fuzz of pale, gold-dust hair, still wrapped in his birthrags and lying beside her exhausted mother. Joan had worshipped, protected and depended upon Robert with more than a sister's love. When his precocious intelligence baffled everyone around him in his early days at school, it was Joan who insisted that Robert must be moved up a class because he was ready for a higher level of work.

Throughout their schooldays, their closeness, and Joan's championship of her brother, had persisted. When Robert had been told that he could not study the subjects he wanted and in a passionate fit of rebellion had threatened to drop out altogether, only Joan held him on course with her steadfast insistence that he should be allowed to do what he liked, in whatever combination he liked, if he was to have the chance to do himself justice.

In those days they had almost invariably been taken

for twins, since both had followed the rangy physique of their father. As a boy, too, Robert had lost no time in making up the three-year head start nature had granted to his older sister. Both had inherited their father's fair, well-favoured Nordic looks, upright carriage and open, level gaze, and without ever having the slightest consciousness of it, were the admiration or resentment of every other mother in Brightstone whose children were inevitably darker, stumpier or less prepossessing than the strangely other-worldly young Maitlands.

With the years, though, their natural differences had begun to make themselves felt. From her earliest infancy Joan had displayed what had later emerged as her central characteristic: a truly remarkable single-mindedness which no one in the family could ever deflect her from, let alone outdo. Whatever Joan set her hand to, they all affectionately recognised, she would finish, come hell or high water. Always clear about her goals, Joan had worked steadily throughout her schooldays, and never wanting anything more than Brightstone and the life she knew in the family she adored, had been well pleased with her place at the local college where she had been a well-regarded if not exceptional student.

Robert, by contrast, had been gifted from his cradle with the kind of versatility which can be a trial as much as a blessing. Good at most academic subjects, he hated to be pinned down to one. Enjoying the rough and tumble of the sports field just as well as the solitary peace of the study, and music or making things with his hands as much as either, he developed early on the eager, responsive nature which was both his strength and his bane. He craved hard work, a constant challenge, change and stimulus, and without them was like a plant starved of its vital nourishment.

Nothing could have been more calculated to aggrieve his father, a patriarch of old-style authority and rigid conviction. 'If only he wasn't always so sure he was right!' Robert blazed to Joan. 'If only you weren't!' she retorted. 'If only mother would stand up to him more!' he complained. 'Or you less!' she flashed back.

11

How had it all begun? It had never been an easy relationship. Strict yet over-anxious, pious and concerned, his parents had expected too much of both their children. But on himself, as the only son, an extra burden of unreasonable hope had always been riding, as he had always known.

He could not remember when he had first found himself at loggerheads with them, it had started so early – over his choice of activities at school, his friends, his attitude, his future, even the subjects that interested him at school. 'Philosophy? Why not theology? And what's wrong with the local college?' the old man had raged, quite unimpressed by the scholarships that had taken Robert away from the backward little mining town of Brightstone to altogether different worlds, introducing the son to opportunities the father had never sought, nor even desired. The more Robert flourished, the more the old priest had resented his son's success, secretly alarmed now at the fierce questioning of the young man's strong personality, and determined to resist what he saw as no less than an attack upon his faith.

So had begun the arguments, then the rows, when the old man had blindly demanded his son's obedience, and Robert had fought back with every fibre of his being. Mrs Maitland had taken refuge from the conflict in daily migraines and nervous attacks; Joan, who adored her father only slightly less than she did her brother, had laboured ceaselessly but in vain to reconcile these two determined opposites, and her own nature had been forged by her baptism in this fire.

At a glance now, Robert could tell that young as the day was, the Rectory had already seen stormy weather.

'What's up?' he demanded.

Joan shrugged. 'He wanted you to drive him to the Church Council meeting. You weren't here. So he went off in a huff.'

'But I offered to drive him last night!' Robert exploded. 'He turned me down, and read me a lecture that he was perfectly OK to drive, thank you very much!'

Joan did not try to argue. 'Mother's worried about

him again this morning. Says he wasn't well in the night
– had a bad turn.'

'One of those turns he always denies having, you
mean?'

Again Joan let it pass. 'He's got to go out again tonight
– with Mother – it's the Golden Years social. She got
him to agree to let you drive them there. It wasn't easy.
He's in a terrible mood today.'

Robert groaned. 'God, it's hopeless! And if he's so
unreasonable about these petty things, how's he going
to be when I tell him I'm leaving – that I'm running my
own life from now on?'

'Cross that bridge when you come to it,' advised Joan
in her best big-sisterly manner. 'Speak to him tonight –
I'll back you up. It probably won't be half as bad as you
think.' Her voice changed. 'Let's talk about something
more cheerful.' Suddenly her manner became very
casual as she turned her back on Robert and busied
herself with a pot of steaming coffee. 'That dance in
town on Saturday night – are we going to make up a
foursome again with Paul Everard and his sister?'

'Why not?' said Robert slowly, his hand reaching for
a plate of buttered toast, but his mind suddenly full of
a bright, pansy-like face surrounded by a cluster of dark
curls. 'Why not?'

By that evening, Robert had prepared himself as well
as he could, he thought, for the encounter with his
father. But nothing could have led him to anticipate the
fury of the old man's wrath when it arrived, almost
before he himself did, as the minister walked, unan-
nounced and without knocking, through the door of
Robert's room.

Tall and gaunt, his face set in a mask of Old Testament
outrage, the Reverend Maitland presented a formidable
sight. 'You! – you! –' He could hardly speak for rage.

Robert raised his eyes from the book he was reading,
and met the storm head on. 'Yes?' he demanded boldly.

'Swimming naked – in Eden Bay this morning! Don't
attempt to deny it – you were *seen* –'

Robert burst out laughing. 'Is that all? I was with Paul

Everard, we've been doing it since we were kids!'

'—you were seen – and recognised – by a lady parishioner, who has made a formal complaint to the Church Council! She was disgusted – shocked and disgusted!'

Robert bit his lip. 'Look, Dad, we didn't mean to upset anybody—'

But his father brushed him aside. From the livid greyish-purple of his complexion and the dull fire in his eyes, the old man had been building up to this confrontation for a long time, and would not be denied. 'The arrogance of it!' he rasped. 'To make free of God's universe, as if it had been created for you alone!'

'Come on, Dad!'

As always, Robert could feel his patience – all his good intentions – slipping away with every word his father uttered. 'It's not a mortal sin, you know!'

'No? Then I'll tell you one that is!'

To Robert's alarm, the old man was working himself up into even greater heights of fury with every moment. Trivial though the bathing incident was in itself, it had obviously triggered something deep in his father, deeper than either of them could know. The old man ranted on unchecked. 'You! My son! My only son! You're pretty pleased with your book-learning – but you're not going to win any prizes for your Bible knowledge, are you?'

Robert flushed. 'What do you mean?'

His eyes glittering, the old man begin to recite in a frightening, sing-song chant: ' "Whosoever shall break the least of these commandments, he shall be called least in the Kingdom of Heaven . . ."'

'Commandments? What commandments?'

'You're no son of mine if you can't even recognise the Second Commandment – let alone obey it!'

Robert fought for control. 'I know the Second Commandment,' he said quietly. 'And I do honour my father and my mother – I respect both of you, Dad – you know that. But "obey"—'

'A father should be obeyed!' thundered the old man. 'He knows what's best for his children!'

'When they are children, maybe.' Robert was breathing heavily now, but determined not to give way. 'But I'm not a child any longer. I'm twenty-one, and I've got to start making my own decisions. I've been wanting to tell you, Dad – I'm not taking up the course you fixed for me. I'm applying for jobs, scholarships – I'll be taking whatever I can, as soon as I can, then I'll be out of your way, out of your hair, and you won't have to worry about me any longer.'

In the storm that ensued, raging ever stronger as the night outside darkened the world to oblivion, Robert was a party to words and actions that he was to regret for the rest of his life. One by one his sister, then his pale, frail mother, ventured into the eye of the hurricane in an effort to restrain the old man, or at least to mediate the force of his frustration and fury, but in vain. In the heat of the engagement, no one, least of all the old man himself, noticed the bluish-purple complexion subsiding to a dull livid grey, nor the rasping breath becoming increasingly raw with every harsh word he forced through his lips, so powerful was the almost religious passion that drove him on.

Only Mrs Maitland seemed to have any intuition of what was to come. 'Robert! Robert!' she wept, in a cry that was to echo down the years. 'You're breaking your father's heart, can't you see that?'

'Oh Mother,' Robert groaned, 'he's breaking his own – and mine!'

Yet her soft pleas prevailed where the old man's tyranny could not. Choking back his anger, Robert tried to make the peace. Concerned now about his father, about both of them, he prepared to drive them to their evening engagement as arranged.

But his father would have none of it. Spurning the olive branch, he chose instead to play the outraged patriarch, and refused to listen to a word Robert said. And when he suffered a massive heart attack high on the headland outside Brightstone, plunging the car straight off the cliff to the instant death of both himself and his wife, it was that failure, as much as any other, that was to live with his son all the days of his life.

15

BOOK I

1970

Spring

Chapter 1

It was going to be a long, hard journey. There was no other way but right across the continent, through the night, through the dead red heart of the land. Bathed in an angry evening light the train nosed its way out of the station, cut through the city and outlying suburbs till it had left behind the last reaches of man-made civilisation, then headed west across the sunburned plain.

All day long, the heavy clouds had been massing on the far horizon as the winter equinox fought its last battle against the advent of the spring. Now, with the approach of night, the sky was alive with monstrous shapes of purple, blood-red, fire and gold. But the storm would not break just yet: the time was not ripe. The last rays of the evening sun invaded every carriage with the promise of the coming night as the passengers braced themselves for what was to come. Meanwhile, the train plunged steadily on towards the heart of darkness ahead.

The crowd slowly gathering the next morning at the dusty little wayside station was small even by Brightstone's standards. Nevertheless the tall, handsome woman who had arrived with them could not wait to shake off the rest of the group and stroll off down the platform to be alone. The early morning air was sweet and clean, and the wild oleanders beside the track were exploding in splashes of red and gold in the spring sun. But Joan had no eyes for the beauty all around her. Bloody Wilkeses, she brooded furiously, what the hell are they doing here? Just because he owns the mine doesn't mean he runs the town! Him and that stupid wife of his! They never knew Robert – never even met him!

'All right, Joanie?'

Turning, Joan smiled into the concerned face of the short, motherly woman behind her.

'Yeah, no worries, Molly.' She paused, her smile becoming tight and hard. 'Except – I could have done without *him* here.' With a bitter nod she indicated the stout, self-important man puffing busily up to accost the Brightstone station master, with his wife in tow.

'Robert won't mind, lovey,' said Molly sturdily. 'A minister's public property, y'know, we've got to get used to that.'

A minister. Yes. How strange it would all be – Robert a minister now in place of Father – in Father's very place . . .

'And a big man like Wilkes,' Molly went on, 'he could help Robert a lot with his work if he wanted to. Anyway, forget Wilkes! As long as you're here, you'll be all the family Robert wants.' Anyone'd be glad of a sister like Joan Maitland, she added to herself – not that Joanie's had it easy these last few years, on and off with that fella of hers, then everything falling through at the last minute . . . 'Blood's thicker than water, after all' she resumed quickly. 'He's got you, and you've got each other, no matter what.'

Joan nodded fiercely. It's true! she cried inside. But a lifetime of self-control had made her careful to observe the proprieties. 'He's got Claire, too,' she observed mechanically.

'Yeah, Claire.' Molly Everard's broad, work-worn face softened at the mention of her daughter. 'Well, I'm hoping they're going to start a family of their own, now that Robert's come into his own place – somebody better make a grandma out of me before it's too late! I'm sick of waiting for Paul to stop playing around! But a wife can't be the same as a sister. He's lucky he's got you both – especially since—'

'I know.' Joan turned away, and made a pretence of looking down the dusty red track into the distance for the arrival of the train, shading her face with the brim of her hat to conceal the sudden stinging behind her eyes. 'Robert was so desperate then to get away for good – I can't help wondering how he'll settle down here again now he's coming back. It's been years, Molly, years . . .'

She had packed for him herself after the funeral, and brushing aside all his concern for her, seen him off on the overland train. 'Don't look back, Robert,' she'd said. 'Never look back. You can never go back in life. But you'll never have to.' Her face and voice had been as steady as a rock, though the heart inside her was like Brightstone's own deep bed of death-black granite. And now . . . how would he feel *now*—?

'You worry too much, Joanie – always have.' The characteristic wheezing cough announced the arrival of Molly's husband George, a veteran, and lately a victim, of the deep-level coal mining that was Brightstone's sole industry and *raison d'être*. 'You and that brother of yours both. Worrying never solved anything. All it gets you is a one-way ticket to the giggle-house.'

'That's if *he* doesn't drive us all there first!' hissed Joan, staring over George's shoulder at the rapidly approaching Wilkes.

'Miss Maitland, good morning to you! You know my wife, of course. Morning, Mrs Everard, morning, George.' Even under the excitement of good news, the mine boss would not overlook what he called 'life's little courtesies'. He smiled patronisingly round the small group. 'I have just received the very latest information from the station officials. The overnight train is on time, in fact expected ahead of schedule. We shall be welcoming the Reverend and Mrs Maitland to Brightstone any moment now!'

There was a silence. Joan looked round. Her rising excitement gave way to disappointment as she struggled to sound non-committal.

'*Where's Paul*?'

Never go back. *Never* go back? Oh God, is that always true? The young woman passenger shifted restlessly in her seat as she wrestled with the sudden onset of an unexpected anxiety. Never-go-back, never-go-back, never-go-back, chattered the wheels of the train, in mocking echo of her thoughts. I'm hearing things, she thought with amusement, I've been on this train too long! The stuffiness inside the sleeper was unbearable, and an outsize fly buzzed remorselessly against the dusty window. Abandoning all pretence of reading, Claire Maitland threw herself into the furthest corner of the compartment and, tossing her book aside, reached for her handbag.

From his seat opposite, the man with her seemed to divine, without lifting his head, the flow of her thoughts.

'Tired, darling?'

Claire looked up from her make-up mirror and smiled tenderly at her husband. As ever, one glance at his handsome, sculptured features had her heart turning over inside her with a surge of passionate love. She could not remember a time when she did not know this man, first as a solemn-eyed, seven-year-old chorister in Brightstone's beautiful old church, when she herself had been too young to attend the services but was banished with the rest of the little ones to Sunday School in the vestry next door; then as the inseparable friend of her big brother Paul, the two of them nothing less to her than a pair of young gods.

Robert Maitland in those days had had the world at his feet – and half the women in it, she recollected ruefully, as least as far as Brightstone went. How wild she had been when he took any of the others out! And how little she had ever expected that Robert, of all men, would turn his back on all the worldly success he was promised, and the countless women who wanted to share it with him, to vow himself to the religious life, and to become her husband.

That in itself was a miracle to Claire, and no minor one either, she thought humbly. She did not know, had never known, that her pale, heart-shaped face, wide, thoughtful eyes and dark hair clustering against her porcelain skin had a flower-like appeal that lingered in the mind long after all the eye-catching Bondi blondes, tall, tanned and leggy, had been forgotten. She could not speak for love.

Suddenly she was longing for him, her whole being craving his touch, shuddering with desire. The smile in his eyes told her that he had read her mind and body together with his usual swift, subtle sensuality. Slowly, teasingly, he reached out a hand to draw her to him.

A piercing whistle cut through the silence between them. The train shuddered and convulsed as the brakes dug into the wheels and they began protestingly to slow down.

'Already?'

Robert's keen, mobile face lifted attentively and quickened with excitement. He bounded from his seat and threw down the window of the carriage, Claire fighting her way under his arm to lean out too. In the distance lay a dim huddle of houses and bungalows. Beyond them, dominating the town, was a massive outcrop of heavy machinery looming stark against the golden morning light, a futuristic fantasy of smoke-blackened, funfair-sized wheels, jutting chimneys and pit-head cranes. Even from afar the low clanking, grinding and hissing proclaimed that, like the travellers, the pit had also, as always, passed a sleepless night. Robert fixed his eyes on the mine with the hungry intensity of the wanderer returned . . .

'It's Brightstone! We're here!'

'At last!'

Further off, some way behind the mine, rose the slow swell of the headland where the great rocky outcrop whose rich seams gave Brighstone its coal plunged abruptly into the sea. Beneath the busy whine of the pit-head workings they could hear a deeper roar, low, but unmistakable, the incessant pounding of the South Pacific ocean breakers along the undefended coastline. Claire gestured towards the wild beauty of the horizon in joyous abandon, then leaned back ecstatically into Robert's arms. Looking down into the sweet face turned up trustingly to his like a flower to the sun, Robert's whole being was gripped with yearning, and his passion for her stirred as swiftly and fiercely as a boy's.

25

Overhead a flight of sunbirds, flashing past in a flurry of bright yellow and metallic blue, made way for a lazy, wheeling flock of Tasmanian gulls. Through the hot, dry air, the cool, salty tang of the sea reached them like a benediction. A lone gull cried overhead. Robert leaned down and gathered Claire's mouth to his in a long, searching kiss. 'Look at that! Look at that out there!' he said urgently. 'What can go wrong for us here, darling? We're back where we ought to be. We're *home*!'

'Well, will you look at yous!'

'Oh Mom! And Dad!'

'Steady on, Claire, love, I'm an old man now, I can't take too much excitement!'

The reunion party fell into two natural and happy halves as Claire tumbled weeping into the arms of George and Molly Everard, and Robert, impetuously tossing all their luggage out of the train into a jumbled heap on the platform, leaped out looking around for his sister Joan.

'I'm here, Robert. Right behind you.'

'Just like always.'

He folded her in his arms. They stood together in silent communion, their foreheads leaning lightly together, Robert's arms resting easily on Joan's familiar shoulders, comfortably of a height with his. He was back. There was nothing to say, nothing that needed to be said. She smiled into his eyes and knew that he, too, was quietly slipping back into their childhood closeness again. A fraction of her normally tense, guarded defensiveness relaxed within her. It will be all right, she thought carefully. It's going to be all right, if I'm here to look after him like it always used to be. It's a new start. Not like last time. We'll make it all right.

'Claire!'

'Hello, Joan!'

Claire wrapped her arms affectionately around the taller woman and showered her with hugs and kisses. 'My, it's good to see you! You never change, Joan, you know that! Oh, I can't believe we're all going to be together again after so long! But where is he? Where's—'

'Ladies and gentlemen!'

Quite enough time, Mr Wilkes's faintly disagreeable expression made plain, had been spent on family reunions and emotional exhibitions. Time for more important matters. 'Ladies and gentlemen, this is no inauspicious occasion which finds us gathered here—'

History was never to know how auspicious the occasion might have been had Mr Wilkes and his pearls of wisdom had the gracing of it. But a low hum in the distance had swollen to a roar as an open-top Dodge in an aggressive shade of metallic blue, racing frenziedly up to the station, cut daringly in through the station access itself and screeched up to the bemused group. The blare of its horn, sounded continuously for the last two hundred metres, silenced Wilkes and his speech into stunned stupefaction as it pealed off into an exuberant fanfare of welcome. As the car performed a lightning swerve and stop, it threw up a spurt of fine red dust all over Mrs Wilkes's flowered voile. Like an animal released from a cage, the driver bounded effortlessly out of the coupé without bothering to open the door.

'You rotten buggers! You're *early*, blast you! Trying to do me out of my rightful place as chairman of the reception committee, eh?' A roar of amusement filled the air as Robert and Claire fell on the unexpected arrival with wild hugs and jubilant horse-play.

'He's here,' said Joan weakly, overcome by the all-too-familiar surge of confused but powerful emotion. 'I knew he wouldn't miss it. Here's Paul.'

Chapter 2

The old blue Dodge roared away from the station in a triumphant cloud of dust as the driver raised his voice to make himself heard above the noise of the engine.

'I can't believe I almost missed you! The devil of it was I could see the train coming from miles away, heard the whistle and all! Only question was whether I could beat it to the station.'

'If you still drive the way you used to, you could beat the devil himself, on horseback,' grinned Robert.

Paul Everard threw back his head and laughed. His heavy, muscular physique and dark, now almost self-consciously flashy good looks could not have formed a stronger contrast with Robert's lean, graceful form and casual attractiveness. But there could be no doubt of the strength of the bond of friendship still existing between them. 'Stuff you, Reverend!' laughed Paul. 'Just because some of us have to work for our living – I only just got off the night shift!' And he punched Robert's upper arm affectionately with a playful but powerful fist.

In the back seat the two women broke off their own conversation to exchange a smile.

'He's a case, that brother of yours,' said Joan lightly. 'He'd be late for his own funeral.'

Claire laughed. 'He's not getting any better then?'

Her question was immediately answered as Paul, slewing the old Dodge dangerously round a tight corner, hooted cheerfully at two attractive young women as bright as flowers in their spring dresses, waving and accelerating at the same time.

'You know me, sis,' Paul threw back delightedly over

his shoulder. 'Rich cars, fast women – nothing changes round here.'

'You don't say,' murmured Robert drily. 'How can they tell?'

'Hunter Street, Macquarie Place, Tuggerah Park.' One by one Claire wonderingly ticked off Brightstone's few, familiar landmarks. Around her the small town revealed all it had to give: a huddle of low, dusty buildings, a handful of old-fashioned shops, a petrol station and a bedraggled-looking square with a cluster of ancient palms. 'It all looks exactly the same!'

'Well, you haven't been gone that long,' protested Paul.

They have, they have! Joan cried inside. Aloud she said, 'It's been a few years.'

'Tell you what, mate,' Paul continued cheerfully, impervious as ever to any undercurrents, 'you got your work cut out for you here, and no mistake. Problem was, the Reverend Patterson, poor old bugger, he only came in to help out, he was past retirement as it was. His wife was past it too, sick most of the time—'

'Oh Paul!' protested Claire. 'I'm sure he did his best!'

'Too right, sis,' agreed Paul, his expression hardening. 'Did his best for Wilkes and the mine management all right – if he could've prayed the men down the mines to work eighteen-hour shifts at a dollar a day, he would've done it!'

'Wilkes?' Robert's keen glance cut through Paul's badinage. 'Was he the official-looking bloke at the station?'

'That's him,' agreed Paul. 'He's the new mine boss, took over after you left. Pity he didn't get his chance to give you his speech of welcome just because the old Dodge and I showed up!'

'Mmm, a real pity,' murmured Robert drily. 'Though I have the feeling that I haven't seen the last of Mr Wilkes. But who knows? Perhaps he'll be as useful to me as he obviously expects me to be to him.'

'You'll make him an instrument to your hand, Robert,' Joan struck in passionately. 'You have a purpose here, and you're gifted with the power to fulfil it.

You could make anyone do what you want.'

'If only everyone had the faith in me that you do, Joan,' Robert responded lightly, 'my success here would be a foregone conclusion. As it is, I think I may have to work for it, though!'

'No false modesty, Rob!' protested Paul. 'Y'may be a reverend now, but y've still got to have the truth, in the family at least. Y'not denying you've got the gift of the gab?'

Robert burst out laughing. 'Trust you to bring me down to earth, Paul! Well, we'll see! Sounds as if there's a lot to be done here. I just can't wait to get home and get started on it all!'

The whole party fell into a silence of keen anticipation as the car cleared the outskirts of the town, circled the dark sweep of the mine and gained the coast road running straight up Brightstone's prominent rocky headland into the morning sun. Claire leaned forward eagerly. Slowly the laden car crested the rise.

'There it is!'

Outlined against the sunlight rose a church, not large, but so beautifully proportioned that it looked more imposing than it was. Beside it stood an old rectory, stone-built in the English style with bay windows, a low, welcoming porch and high gabled roof, shaded against the fierce Australian sun by cool verandahs all along the length of the ground floor. Behind the church lay a small, well-tended cemetery extending a little way back over the grassy headland to a neat fence. With a flourish, Paul accelerated over the last few yards and screeched to a halt beside the thickly clustered shrubs crowding around the little flight of stone steps leading to the front door.

'Ladies and gentlemen – the Maitland residence.'

Robert got out of the car like a man in a trance. Claire sat spellbound in the back seat. 'Oh Robert!' she murmured. 'It's just as beautiful as it always was!'

'And a lot cleaner too!' called Paul from the rear of the car where he was now energetically unloading the suitcases. 'The whole place has been given the once-over from top to bottom, inside and out.'

Claire moved to join Robert, who was surveying the gleaming paintwork with the expression of a man in the grip of a powerful emotion. 'Doesn't it look wonderful, darling? Who have we got to thank for this?'

Paul laughed. 'Who d'you think?'

Robert's gaze fell on Joan as she mounted the stone steps of the porch with a set of old and ornate keys in her hand. The rich scent of the frangipani trailing languidly along the warm stone wall was as heady as wine. Through the cool glass panels of the heavy front door, the house – his house – seemed to beckon him in. With a smile of triumph, Joan threw it open to him. 'How did you manage all this?' he asked in amazement.

Paul shouldered past them into the cool, sandalwood-scented hall with a suitcase in each hand and one tucked under his capable arm. 'Same way she does everything, mate – don't say you've forgotten! A bit of organisation and a lot of persuasion, that's our Joan.'

Joan cast a quick glance at Paul, and kindled instantly at his praise, her pale face flushing with pleasure. Self-consciously she looked away. 'Wasn't much,' she said with a shrug. 'I just got the paint donated, then organised a couple of work parties. Paul helped too.'

'What did I tell you?' Impervious as ever, Paul favoured Joan with the routine flashing smile of practised charm. 'A genius for domination, this girl has. Oughta take it up professionally. Keep all the men busy for miles around!' He dumped the luggage at the foot of the stairs and returned to the porch where Robert was still standing drinking in everything around him. 'Was I ever glad that she's your sister though, not mine,' he murmured *sotto voce* to Robert as he passed him. 'She's too smart for me! I like 'em a bit more playful these days, mate – know what I mean? And wherever they carry their brains, they don't need 'em in their heads, far as I'm concerned!'

'Robert?'

Joan's voice summoned them from deep inside the house. Robert took a deep breath and felt Claire's warm hand inside his. A flood of strong feelings swept over him. Stooping down he caught her in his arms, lifted her off her feet and carried her joyfully over the threshold. 'Welcome to the first real home we've had of our own, darling!' he breathed. '*Welcome home.*'

Inside the house there came surprise upon surprise and the renewed delight of further discoveries.

'The old dining-table – the chairs – and everything,' exclaimed Robert in wonderment, arrested at the door of the big front room giving out over the headland beyond. Excitedly he crossed the hall to the room opposite. 'Dad's study! Just as it was!' he murmured. 'And all his books.' In the big bay window stood an antique desk with a group of old family photographs, a venerable manual typewriter of ancient but still serviceable design, and fresh paper, pens and pencils at the ready. Beside them lay a Bible and the Book of Psalms.

'Your study now, Robert.'

He had not heard Joan coming up behind him.

'I thought you said it had all been sold, everything had gone?' he questioned, shaking his head in delighted disbelief.

'I kept Dad's books and his old typewriter, and as much of the other stuff as I could. Then when I knew you were coming back I went around to everyone who had bought anything of ours, and tried to buy it back. Got most of it, too. People were glad to help.' She paused, watching him carefully. 'They all wish you well, Robert.'

'I know.'

'And y'going t'need all the help y'can get,' she said, 'with everything to start more or less from scratch, and the Centenary coming up.'

'The Centenary? Oh yes, Claire's mother wrote to us about it—'

'Brightstone's one hundredth birthday! They're all so proud of it, they're determined to do something big. They're wanting a special service of commemoration, a church fête, a grand exhibition all about the town's history in the public library – and they're looking to us to organise the whole bang-shoot!'

Robert laughed in protest. 'Steady on, Joan! At least

let me unpack my dog-collar first!'

'Joan!'

Claire's delighted voice floated down from upstairs. 'You *are* a naughty girl! You've unpacked all the stuff that came in our trunks, saved me the most awful job! And I can see from here you've been busy in the garden too.'

'Hope you don't mind.' Joan moved into the hall. 'You can always shift it all around again when you've got settled. Anyway, I've enjoyed doing it. My landlady won't let me do a thing in her place.' Heaving a suitcase, she started up the stairs.

A beaming Claire came out of a bedroom to greet her, her hands full. 'I don't think I'll need to bother! You've done everything beautifully. You always were so much better at all that sort of thing than I ever was. Look, what do you think I ought to do with these ornaments? I thought they were so pretty when I bought them, but now I'm not so sure!'

Downstairs Robert stood for a moment, then moved to the window and threw it open. A wave of sea air rushed in to greet him and he gulped in deep breaths of it hungrily. He felt like someone rediscovering food after long starvation. He turned back to the desk and picked up one of the photographs.

Even as he looked on from the doorway, Paul recognised the tall, striking young military figure in the faded sepia portrait, with its spare, finely cut features, expressive eyes, and thick, springing fair hair so like Robert's own.

'He was a beaut bloke, your old man,' he observed gently, 'for all his faults. And your mum – a real lady, through and through, just like Joan.'

'This photograph used to be in their bedroom,' said Robert mechanically. 'On Mum's dressing-table. Taken when he was an army chaplain. Just before they got married and – came here to Brightstone.'

Paul studied the picture. 'What was he then, twenty-six, thirty? About the same age as you now – and he could double for your twin brother, 'cept for the uniform.'

'Except that he'd lived a whole lifetime at my age,' said Robert passionately. 'And he knew what he wanted after the war – just a quiet life and a good ministry in a small, peaceful town.'

'What's to stop you having that too? Isn't that what you came home for? Or did you just get homesick, you and Claire?'

'Claire?' Robert's surprise at the question told Paul how much his brother-in-law continued to rely on Claire's unquestioning love and devotion, and how little he ever considered that her needs or desires could be separate from his own. 'If Claire felt that way, she never said so. No.' He paused, feeling his way forward. 'We came back because we were chosen . . . and sent.'

'Yeah.' Paul chuckled warmly. 'Heaven-sent, mate. At least, that's what old Wilkes seems to think – and quite a few others round here, by the sound of things. Any rate, it's bloody good to have you both back, I can tell you!' He moved away to the door, embarrassed at what suddenly seemed too much like a show of raw emotion. 'I better finish getting the bags in, or the girls'll kill me.'

Sent . . . we were sent . . .

Robert's mind flew back to the fateful conversation which had come so recently out of the blue to turn his life upside down. 'You've done well here, Robert,' crackled the gravelly voice of his Archbishop down the still-burning wires of his memory. 'An inner-city parish is no easy billet for your first post, even in a city as modern as this one. What is it, a year? Eighteen months? You must be thinking of your next move, eh?'

Robert had been thinking of little else as his period of apprenticeship drew to its close. But he already knew enough of the church's way of working to realise that it was pointless to advance his own hopes and dreams. 'No, no, not really sir,' he said, drawing a deep breath. 'Perfectly happy here.'

The Archbishop gave a low laugh. 'Well, I believe I've found you a place where you and that charming little wife of yours will be even happier to live and work.

Rather a run-down parish, I'm afraid. Been without its own pastor for a few years now, but you'll soon sort that out. Mining town, north of Sydney a fair way, up on the coast above the Hunter valley coalfield. About two or three thousand souls, all told – it's wild enough for sure, but very beautiful, and ripe for the right man. Am I ringing any bells yet, Robert?'

Robert could not speak.

The Archbishop's voice was as dry as a bone. 'It's a good move, Robert. You'll be good for Brightstone, and Brightstone will be good for you. See what you can do with it, OK?'

'*Brightstone*? We're going back to *Brightstone*?' Claire's face had been alive with hope and delight. Robert turned away. 'Claire – I don't know if I can.'

'Can? What are you talking about?'

He leaned back towards her and took both her hands in his. 'Let's be honest – I'll never fill my father's shoes. I could never be even half the priest he was. It wouldn't matter if we were sent somewhere else —'

'Somewhere like a key post on the Archbishop's personal staff, or serving as one of the big cheeses in the Cathedral?' Claire loved Robert passionately, but she was not blind to his true nature. She knew just how much it mattered to him that his efforts should be recognised and appreciated.

Robert flushed, his face alive with enthusiasm. 'It's not a sin to be ambitious, Claire! And you know how much I've got to give! And Brightstone – if it were any other place in the world . . . *you* know . . .'

Claire looked at him with the steady, clear-eyed gaze that always went straight to his heart. 'I know that you've never stopped punishing yourself for what happened there, Robert.'

With his ready understanding, he had caught her meaning almost before she knew it herself. His face glowed with the excitement of a completely new idea. 'So you think – yes! – that maybe we're being sent back to Brightstone so that I can lay those ghosts of the past once and for all?'

Ghosts . . . All the spirits of the unquiet dead must walk until they are laid to rest, he knew that. Alone in the house that still seemed his father's, he dropped his head in his hands and lost himself in thought. Beside him on the desk lay his father's ancient Bible, battered through a lifetime of constant use. He caught it up and opened it at random. 'If thou shalt do this thing and God command thee so,' he read, 'then shalt thou be able to endure, and all His people go to their place in peace.'

Peace. Yes. The peace of God that passeth all understanding keep thy hearts and minds . . .

'Robert!'

Oh Lord, grant us thy peace . . .

'Robert?'

For the Lord giveth, and the Lord taketh away . . .

'Are you there, darling?'

To everything there is a season, and a time to every purpose under the heavens . . . A time to weep, and a time to laugh; a time to mourn, and a time to dance . . .

'Robert!' Claire's face, bright with happiness, came round the study door. 'Joan's made lunch, darling – the most marvellous spread. Are you coming?'

Chapter 3

'God, it's good to be back!'

'You said it, Rob!'

Hand in hand, Claire and Robert wandered through the Rectory garden, dispatched outside by Joan 'to get over the long train journey' as soon as Paul had offered to give her a hand with the washing up.

'It's like the garden of Eden – just paradise!' Claire continued delightedly.

Robert squeezed her hand 'Pity we don't have time to play Adam and Eve!' he whispered in her ear in his most seductive tones.

'What?'

Slowly Claire followed Robert's glance as he nodded over her head towards the tall, spare figure of Joan approaching over the grass. She looked tense, as if she had something important to say. 'It's all right, Joanie,' he called in mock-contrition. 'I'm not really slacking, I'm planning my campaign for the conquest of Brightstone! If I can just have this afternoon off, I promise to do my duty without any more escapism in the future!'

Joan gave a light laugh. 'Well, that's good news!' Intensely attuned as she was to Robert's moods, she still could not join in so readily with his playful teasing. 'Because I'm afraid it's going to be your duty to sort Brightstone out for everything from Sunday service to Harvest Supper!'

'Mmm,' said Robert reflectively. 'Sounds as if I'll have to build up a congregation first.'

'That's no more than Dad had to do,' countered Joan determinedly. Robert recognised the age-old, big-sisterly 'pull-your-socks-up' intonation in her voice, and smiled. 'Good job I've got his desk then – and his books and all his things.'

'Only just in time, Joan says,' Claire put in. 'Robert, if we hadn't come back, apparently, all the old books and things were just going mouldy'.

Robert threw Joan a questioning glance. The look which had been new to him when he arrived, but which he was beginning to recognise, hard, bruised, embittered even, settled on her face. 'Well, I had to keep them all in boxes in the shed at the back of the place where I'm living. It's behind the old pharmacy, you know where that is? Back of Macquarie Place, at the bottom end of town? It's been disused for years. Damp's awful there – and the roaches – but it was the only place I had. And it's handy for the library – not to mention the best I could do on a librarian's wages!'

Robert exchanged a look with Claire.

'It can't have been easy for you living like that, kid,' he said gently. 'We were – we were very sorry to hear it didn't work out with you and Phil.'

Joan's expression hardened. 'Don't waste your sympathy. He never really loved me – he just thought he did.' Almost absently she pulled at the head of a marguerite and began shredding the white petals one by one. 'And we'd been going together for so long – remember how Mother always pushed the business, in that quiet way of hers? I guess she liked the idea of a pharmacist for a son-in-law. Poor old Phil, he thought he ought to do the decent thing – 'specially after I was all on my own when Mum and Dad died, and you went away. But I knew all along I couldn't marry him. He just wasn't—'

She gazed out to sea, overcome by a kaleidoscope of impressions of a powerful masculine frame, sun-browned hands and shoulders, bold eyes and an electric smile, and had to fight down a sudden urgent physical longing.

'—he just wasn't my type.' Squaring her shoulders, she turned back with a defiant smile. 'So it looks like I'm destined to live happily on my ownsome till Mr Right comes along!'

'Not necessarily.' Robert's tone was warm and hopeful. He glanced at Claire for support, then turned back to Joan with a loving smile. 'We've talked about this, Joanie, and we want you to come back here – back to the Rectory – and live with us.'

A dark flush mottled Joan's neck and her eyes ached with dull appeal. 'Are you serious?'

'Of course.'

Across the grass the old stone house beckoned serenely, its deep double bays and all-embracing, wide gabled roof offering an immemorial welcome to all comers. Claire could feel the pull of Joan's need warring against her fierce innate pride.

'I could make myself useful.'

'You wouldn't need to.'

'I could do all your typing. I always did Dad's. I'm the only one who can work that old Underwood anyway.'

Claire put her hand on Joan's arm and felt the muscles clenched like iron. 'You've done so much already to welcome us back.'

Joan was oblivious. 'Y'going to be so busy, Robert, with the Centenary coming up,' she ran on. 'And the congregation to build up from nothing, just as Dad had to, starting from scratch, picking up where Dad left off . . . And Claire, you'll have your hands full, too, when you take up your teaching again – and somebody's got to look after Dad's roses, I found them all still alive in the back there, did you see, next to where I made the new herb garden . . .'

Gently Robert took her by the shoulders and gave her a light shake. 'It's all settled then!'

Joan's pale face was ablaze. 'It's the only home I ever had!' she declared passionately. 'The only one I ever wanted! I'll make it up to you, Robert, to both of you.' Suddenly conscious of giving herself away, she groped for her usual dignity and control. In a moment she was the older sister again. 'And with the right backing, we'll make a bishop of you yet, my lad, won't we, Claire?'

Robert laughed in delight. 'An archbishop at the very least, sis, or I'll think you've lost your touch! And as soon as possible, please – next year would be fine!'

'Hey, you guys!'

Paul stood forlornly in the porch of the house, his tall frame filling the doorway. 'If the party's moved outside, mind if I come out to play? Or are we going to get Claire back down to Mum and Dad's before they think you've kidnapped her all over again, Reverend?'

'How is he, Mum?'

With a quick shake of her head, Molly Everard threw Claire a warning glance, just too late to prevent a reaction from the group of men ahead.

'Not deaf yet, whatever else is wrong with me,' wheezed George defiantly as he led Robert and Paul through the tiny miner's cottage to the even smaller backyard beyond. Ruefully Claire caught up with her father and slipped her hand through his arm. 'I'm only worried about you, Dad.'

'Don't be.' George patted her hand. 'See m'garden? I c'n still manage a bit of watering every day – hose down a weed or two – and kick the cat every now and again, eh, Moll? This won't be the last spring I'll see, never you fear, chuck!'

Molly's careworn expression showed that she was in no mood for humour on this subject. 'That's about all he can manage now, love,' she said to Claire quietly.

But George was not to be deflated. 'Sit yourselves down, lads, it's great to see yous. Could be the last rest you get for a long time, Robert. They tell me you'll have your work cut out at St Jude's. Not too many paying – or should we say praying – customers up there these days.'

Robert smiled, remembering with a rush of affection George's penchant for drollery. 'Got any ideas as to how I can rectify that situation, George? Going to set the town a good example by turning out for me?'

George laughed as he eased himself into a capacious recliner with a sound like air escaping from a burst tyre. 'No use asking me, lad. Only way you'll get me to church now is in a pine box.'

Robert shook his head. 'That's no good to me, George. I want the ones that can still answer back!'

George erupted into cascades of broken laughter. 'Then I'll volunteer you a good 'un right here – my prodigal son! If ever a man needed saving, he does.'

'Who, me?' Paul's ready smile flashed with delight as he took up the game. 'Just because I like the ladies – you're only jealous, Dad! Anyway, it's not me they want, it's you! You've been an old reprobate far longer than I have, I'm only just beginning!'

'Y'right, son.' George chuckled uproariously. 'Well, one way or another, I'll be there. They'll all turn out for a good funeral – y'll fill the church then, Reverend!'

'Yeah, too true.' Paul's face and voice darkened. 'Had plenty of proof of that lately.'

'How come?' Ever-sensitive, Robert divined the deep concern between the two men.

'Miners getting killed,' said Paul laconically.

'Killed? How? Not—?'

'No, not lung disease.' With careful self-control, Paul avoided looking at his father. 'Fatal – and avoidable – accidents. Two in the last six months.'

Robert was horrified. 'But the loss – the suffering – and with modern mining methods, surely—?'

'Oh, we're going to change it, don't you worry.' As Paul spoke, there was a hardness and resolution Robert had never seen before.

'Mind you do, son.' George, too, was serious now. 'It's too late for me – oh, I know it's true, never mind that. But I want something better for you now, Paul. God Almighty!' The sudden flash of anger made him unconscious of Robert's presence. 'I never thought I'd find myself trying to turn a son of mine against a miner's life! But if it don't get better for you and the men, Paul, you get out. It's not worth dying for Wilkes and his cronies, you mark my words!'

Her heart lurching, Claire followed her mother into the kitchen. 'Oh Mum, he's much worse than I thought – much worse than he was!'

'Well, what did you expect?' Molly's face was a mask of suffering, surviving womanhood as she weighed expertly into the task of preparing a man-sized mountain of sandwiches. 'Old miners don't get any better, love –

you ought to know that by now. Give us a hand here eh? And don't let him see you're bothered. He's entitled to enjoy the rest of the life he's got.'

Out in the yard George, revitalised by company and indignation, felt better than he had for years. 'Yes, there's real problems round here, worse than I've ever known. It's management against men, and the mine against the rest of the town. But Paul there, he's the one to fix things, if anybody is. He's a big man now, y'know. Chief union official for the whole region. They all got to take notice of Paul Everard these days!'

Robert turned to Paul in delight. 'You didn't tell us you'd been made union leader!'

Paul waved away Robert's congratulations.

'Nar, don't pretend it's nothing, son!' George was determined to enjoy Paul's triumph. 'Wasn't no easy thing to cross Wilkes's plans, and budge that bugger Calder out of the job at the same time—'

'Wilkes?' He was hearing a lot about Mr Wilkes today, Robert reflected thoughtfully.

'Yeah, told you about him,' said Paul grimly. 'New man at the top, full of newfangled claptrap about "economic efficiency" and plain old-fashioned Bible-bashing, in equal proportions – all for the greater glory of Wilkes, of course. He's been dying for you to arrive, mate! He just can't wait to enrol God on the side of the bosses.'

'Who's Calder, then?' Robert had an uneasy feeling that the problems of the mine would ensure that he became all too closely acquainted with these men, all too soon.

'Calder?' An expression of sheer disgust crossed Paul's handsome face. 'Lower than a snake's belly, that one. Union boss for years. Corrupt as hell – and a nasty piece of work beside. In the management's pocket, and feathering his own nest quicker'n a kookaburra in springtime. Him and Wilkes between them, they're responsible for the low safety standards we've got now. Oughta be exterminated. I could personally volunteer for the job of taking him out myself!'

When had this come, this violent streak? Robert wondered sadly. This was a Paul he had never seen before.

'Yeah.' George leaned forward, fists fruitlessly jabbing the air between phrases as he struggled for breath. 'Going down for years, safety's been. No money – they won't spend money. Old shafts – need reinforcing – now they're working deeper and deeper—'

'And Calder sneaking round the back door trying to persuade Wilkes and the management that I'm just a pinko trouble-maker trying to stir the men up and give the company shit for the fun of it! Well, screw him! And I will!'

Again it was a new Paul, far from the laughing, charming boy of the old days, intent on nothing but cars and girls.

'But Paul showed him, didn't you, son?' George's pride was not to be contained. 'Took Paul to get him out. Filthy fight it was, too.'

'And he hasn't forgiven me for it !' A flash of the old Paul showed through in his thoroughly boyish delight of annoying the older man. 'Been gunning for me ever since. He'll have to get up early in the morning to fix me, though!'

'Sounds as if this is all good preparation for politics,' murmured Robert in fascination. 'Is that still the masterplan, to get out of mining and try your luck on the greasy pole?'

'First things first, mate,' grinned Paul, his good humour now restored. 'I want to get things right at the mine first, mop up the messes that Calder and his stooges have left us. Then I guess I'll be on my way out of mining.'

'Don't want to end up crook like yer old man, eh?' demanded George without resentment.

'Sure thing, Dad. And us Everard kids can't all marry reverends as our passport to respectability and the good life!'

'Hey!' protested Robert, laughing. 'I like to think your sister married me for myself!'

'And I like to think,' pronounced Claire entering on Molly's heels with a groaning tray of food, 'that after all my efforts, I worked my own passport to whatever it is, thank you very much. I'm a qualified junior school teacher now, I'll have you all remember. And if the future Prime Minister and the future Archbishop can come down off their pedestals, ladies and gentlemen, tucker is served!'

A huge tropical moon stood high in the pale springtime sky, the starry frame of the Southern Cross glimmering away to the west like fire in indigo. Further along the headland a cluster of old grey ghost gum trees kept a silent vigil over the moon-bleached cliff-face, the jagged rocks beneath rearing like primeval animals from the hungry, sucking surge of the waters below. God, how I love this country, thought Robert. Quietly he closed the front door of the house behind him and moved out into the warm, scented night like a swimmer taking to water.

All around him the night-time world lay as bright as day. Without difficulty he made his way to the cemetery and in a quiet, shaded corner found what he was seeking. 'SACRED TO THE MEMORY OF ROBERT GEORGE MAITLAND' he read, 'AND OF EMMA LAVINIA MAITLAND HIS WIFE' . . . Gently he touched the still sharply-engraved letters in the smooth stone, then dropped to his knees by the grave.

If only he had paid more attention to his mother's soft and anxious murmurings, whispered into his ear over so many long months. If only he had not been so inclined to dismiss her as a born worrier, so involved in his plans for his own future that he could not see what was going on under his nose. If only he and his father had not been so at odds – if his father had been less stubborn, less determined to be right – if only *he* had been! If only he had succeeded in persuading his father not to drive that day . . .

And the greatest regret of all . . . if only he had had time, had been given the chance to make amends. For the end had come with a cruel, brutal suddenness. The tragedy had cheated the family of the years they needed for love and reconciliation to make their healing head-way against anger and irreconcilable conflict.

Yet he knew, too, that he was not wholly to blame.

His father, as it later emerged, leaving the Rectory in a towering rage, had been driving like a madman. So the old man had given himself no chance of escape when his overburdened heart, whose warnings he had stubbornly ignored, finally gave way. From this came the death-plunge of the car over the cliff, and the final swift oblivion in the embrace of the black rocks below.

Immediately after the funeral Robert had got on the overland train with no notion of where he was going. His odyssey took him through many strange places until he found the direction he had so desperately sought. He knew he could never be free of the past until he had found a way to make the reparation which he craved. Once this became clear to him, so did his future course of action.

Taking advice from no one, he enrolled at a theological college on the other side of Australia and, beginning again as a lowly student, eventually qualified as a priest. By this he pledged himself to dedicate his life to God, to replace, as far as he could, the father for whose loss he felt so completely responsible.

'But Brightstone . . . here, where I sinned . . . Father, God, is this your will?'

Nothing but a vast silence answered the whispered words. But slowly, by degrees, as he waited quietly and almost without hope, tiny tendrils of the serene stillness began to wrap themselves around Robert's heart, and one by one to work their benediction. In the timeless bowl of the sky the stars hung motionless and the great moon itself seemed to stand still.

His vigil was long. But it was no less patiently observed by the small figure watching faithfully from an upstairs window. And when at last Robert slipped quietly back into the bedroom, he was not surprised to hear Claire's voice reaching out to him from the surrounding darkness.

'Come to bed, darling. Get some beauty sleep. You want to be at your best tomorrow for your public!'

Slowly Robert began to undress. 'What public?'

Claire drew a deep breath and stretched lazily, like a

cat. 'Look, I know the congregation at Brightstone has fallen off a bit in the last few years, but we're young, Robert, we can work hard, you can build it up. It's going to be all right, I know it is. The Bishop sent you here because he knows you're the man for the job—'

'The Bishop sent me here because he thinks I'm too young and too ambitious for my own good!'

She could not read his mood in the thick darkness. 'What do you want, Robert?'

She heard him laughing as his long, cool body slipped between the sheets. 'If only I knew!'

'You think you're too good for Brightstone, is that it?'

'Oh no.' His voice was very low. 'No – my fear is – I won't be good enough.'

'Oh, darling . . .'

He reached for her in a passion of sudden desire, impatient to have her naked as he was, to be close to her, to be at one. Almost roughly he divested her of her nightgown, his hands taking possession of her with the sure command that was always familiar, yet always new. Gripping her to him he kissed her again and again, claiming her mouth as hungrily as if he had never kissed her before.

His urgency was as stirring as a boy's. Laughing with delight, he schooled himself to a slower tempo. Tenderly he stroked the satin skin of her shoulders, flanks, and smooth, round hips, circling and returning again and again till she was moaning for him, melting into him. And when his fingers finally found her breasts he was rewarded with the message from her engorged nipples that she was aroused and ready for anything he wanted to do.

She called to him once, huskily, from the back of her throat: 'Robert!'. But laughing again, softly, playing her like a master-artist, he made her wait. For he knew the night was long. He knew, too, that only he could pace and satisfy that craving from her deepest being, which he knew so well how to arouse. And only when dawn burst like a fire over the horizon, gilding the whole of creation in shadows of white and gold, did they sleep at last, renewed in each other and in the promise of the coming day.

Chapter 4

Brightstone in the early morning lay like a flower opening to the sun. Every day now the air was warmer, the breezes off the sea a more welcome respite from the growing heat of noon. As Robert drove away from the Rectory, the church seemed to be extending its blessing to him, looming as strongly as the rock on which it was built over him and over the whole town. His heart filled with hope, even as his feet and hands struggled with the new car's unfamiliar controls. Don't worry about that! he admonished himself. Time enough to think about replacing the hired car with a bought one – time enough to think about how to afford it! – when he had made a start on the work to which he was called, the purpose that had brought him here.

Almost unconsciously his hand strayed to his neck, his long, sensitive fingers exploring the pristine and still unfamiliar dog-collar. In his work as a junior deacon in the inner-city parish where he had been sent immediately after being ordained, Robert had rarely been required to appear in the full formality of the priestly role. His task there had been to support the team of ministers who worked flat-out to sustain the miserable victims of twentieth-century city life, and not to alienate them by appearing in the guise of the establishment which had already let them down. To his parishioners then, Robert had appeared more in the light of a caring brother than as a Father vested in all the authority of God.

Here in Brightstone, he felt, his role would be very different. Here he was to be father, brother, spiritual leader, and, with the grace of God, guide and redeemer to a group of souls who, from what he had heard, had been sorely neglected. Ruefully he fingered the black shirt-front, the heavy, formal black suit which he knew would make him suffer from its weight before the day was out. Was he taking himself too seriously? Only time would tell. He made a mental note to review the whole question again at the end of the week.

The high street of Brightstone – to its disgruntled teenagers, the one and only street of Brightstone – unfolded before him like a ribbon as the road from the headland ran downhill. The low, red-brick cluster of shops, the small and dusty bank and further down, the scattering of tin-roofed 'supermarts' and snack bars huddling around the flea-pit picture-house at what his mother had always called 'the poorer end of town', filled him with the excitement of the challenge it posed for him. Brightstone! So be it, then! He parked the car, and checking the handouts and notices in his briefcase, stepped on to the pavement.

Early as it was there were people about, some on their way to work, some busy shopping. Without noticing it, Robert attracted many glances, as much for his casual good looks and easy manner as for the unusual sight of his clerical dress. Suddenly he was aware that a woman coming towards him was regarding him with the fixed stare of recognition. She was about his age, though with a voluptuous body that implied a greater maturity than her years would warrant, and her dress, that of a respectable career woman, did little to contradict the overwhelming impression that she had been quite a girl in the not-so-distant past. As she drew up to him, smiling, a flash of inspiration helped him to place her.

'Janice Peaseley!'

'You've got a good memory!' She laughed, showing a set of perfect, sharp white teeth in a tanned face, then ran a small pink tongue round the inside of her lips. 'But then, I haven't forgotten you either. I've often asked Pauly Everard where you'd got to – kept tabs on you, like.'

There was something more than faintly seductive about her manner. Well, well! thought Robert, with a mixture of embarrassment and amusement. For along with the memory of Paul's dogged pursuit of her all the way through high school had come also Paul's outraged complaint: 'It was you she fancied, after all!'

'Well, now I'm back,' he said kindly. 'And I hope I'll see you up at church, Janice – we're starting regular services again this Sunday.'

'Well, if anyone could get me there, you could!' She gave a hard laugh, her eyes raking him up and down. God, what a waste! she reflected. 'If you can't beat 'em, I guess you have to join them,' she murmured provocatively. 'And if we had to lose you to the ministry . . .'

'No loss, Janice,' he said warmly. 'My choice. Why not give me a chance to convince you? Look, it's great to see you. See you again in church, I hope!'

With a wave he crossed the street and entered the first building. At that early hour of the morning, the Paragon Milk Bar boasted no occupant but its owner, a lugubrious Greek immigrant known to all his neighbours and customers as 'Vic'. Years of boyhood exposure to the Greek Orthodox Church in which he had been forced by his pious mother to serve as an altar-boy completely against his will had left Vic with no love of religion, and he saw no reason to interrupt his morning tasks even when faced with the unfamiliar spectacle of what was evidently Brightstone's very own brand-new pastor coming to call.

'Good morning!'

With a curt nod, Vic continued his careful wiping down of the milk storage containers behind the bar, mentally checking the flavours as he did so – strawberry, raspberry, pineapple . . .

'Just a notice about the times of the church services up at St Jude's – all right if I leave a few with you?'

Vic nodded again. 'Just stick 'em onna bar, Reverend.' The least you argue with them, the sooner you're rid of them, was Vic's philosophy.

'Robert, please – call me Robert. You must get most of the young people in here – from the picture show?' Another nod. 'Well, if you could draw their attention to our notices, I'd be most grateful.'

'I'll tell 'em. My daughter'll maybe bring a coupla friends along.'

'Many thanks.' Robert turned to go. As he reached the door, another thought struck him, and he turned back again into the shop. 'If you need any more copies of our leaflet—'

At the back of the shop, directly facing him, stood a young girl. She had evidently entered so silently from the open door behind the bar that he had not heard her come in. Not much above medium height, but so slender that she seemed taller, she stood bathed in a sudden shaft of sunshine from the skylight above that gave the semblance of a halo to her pale, glistening hair. She had the beauty of a woman married to the innocence of a child, and like a child she was completely absorbed in what she had come to say: 'There's only one carton of crisps left in the storeroom now.'

Her voice was light and low, musical and oddly un-Australian. Suddenly she noticed him. Her eyes widened as they fell on Robert arrested in the half-open doorway. Her clear, steady, ultramarine gaze held his for a moment, then just as suddenly dropped.

'Y'betta order some more, then. Is 'at all, Reverend?'

'Ah – yes.'

She was oddly compelling – he could not take his eyes off her. Whatever was she doing here? She seemed so out of place. Vic had referred to his daughter – but surely any father would want a better start for a girl than this. Especially a girl like her. Maybe she needed his help . . . With an effort, he brought his mind back to the business in hand.

'If you could distribute those notices then . . .'

'Girl'll put 'em onna counter, OK?'

She was regarding him with a strange curiosity like a fawn disturbed in a forest, alert but not fearful. Despite her extreme fairness, her eyes had an almond lilt at the corners that seemed to suggest a more exotic origin than her Anglo-Saxon build and colouring. The steadiness of her gaze was disconcerting. But when she looked away, he could still feel her watching him out of the corner of those eyes.

'Yes, well . . .'

He was strangely reluctant to leave. 'Well, I hope we shall see you all up at St Jude's sometime soon. Every-one' – he looked directly at the girl and had the satisfaction of her long, sideways glance sweeping up to meet his gaze – 'will be welcome.'

She had the smile of an angel – an archangel.

'Yeah, OK, Reverend – good-oh.' Time you were gone, Vic's manner said more plainly than words.

How did such a clown, so dark, greasy and low, come to father such a creature? 'Oh – call me Robert – please.'

'OK, Rev – Robert, have it your own way. See yous, OK? G'day.'

The girl stood still, looking thoughtfully after the tall, black-clad figure until it disappeared from view. 'Vic – who was that?'

'Archbishop bloody Makarios. Now will you get them glasses up, and do some bloody work?'

The late afternoon sun hung low over the Rectory, cast-ing long shadows across the garden and filling all the rooms with mellow golden light. Standing among her pitifully small collection of worldly goods as she paid off the taxi from Brightstone, Joan thought it had never looked more beautiful. The familiar flight of stone steps overgrown with rioting viburnum, frangipani and fuchsia seemed to be inviting her in. Summoning her long experience of rigid self-control, she fought down the lump in her throat and tried to compose her features into their normal everyday expression as she approached the door.

'Oh, there you are! Let me give you a hand with your things. Come on in!'

Warm as ever, Claire darted down the steps and gath-ered up Joan and her belongings, sweeping her up the wide, welcoming staircase on a tide of cheerful chatter. 'It was your old room you wanted, wasn't it? Well, if you change your mind, take your pick – we're not exactly over-crowded!'

Tremulously, Joan put down her suitcase by the side of the narrow, iron-framed single bed and moved stiffly towards the old-fashioned dressing-table in the bay window. Beyond them lay the brilliant, dancing sweep of the Tasman Sea stretching out towards the horizon and infinity. Her eyes misted and lost their focus. 'I never thought I'd—' She paused, then tried again. 'You won't regret this, Claire, I promise you.'

'Joan!' Claire's peal of laughter took Joan by surprise. 'You silly girl, I'm already glad to see you! Robert came back from Brightstone in a dream just now, and he's buried himself in his study ever since, so am I glad of some company!'

'Robert?' Joan's watchful love was ever poised to spring into action. 'How is he? What's he doing?'

'Writing his sermon for Sunday. Big day, his first service! And he's fine, he really is. It's just as we hoped and prayed. Coming back to Brightstone seems to have laid those old ghosts for him – all that guilt . . . I'm sure that being here will be right for him – for all of us.'

'Yes, what about you?' Throwing open the first of her battered cases, Joan began swiftly to unpack as she talked. 'How did you get on today? Any chance of a teaching job round here?'

'A good chance, the Area Education Office says. There's one going as soon as the new term starts, over in Western Point.'

'But that's an awful long drive, Claire – it's way over beyond the headland.'

Claire perched lightly on the edge of the bed, looked down at her hands and fell to studying her small pink nails. 'I might not be doing it for all that long.'

A delicate silence fell between the two women. Joan cleared her throat. 'You mean—'

Claire's face was pink. 'Well, not yet, I don't think. But we've talked about it – a lot. I know it's the right time for us, Joan. After all, we've been married nearly four years. And you know, I'm not getting any younger now, and Robert's nearly three years old than me, so we don't want to leave it too late to enjoy it. But first he was studying, then we weren't sure where we were

56

going to be. Now we're here, though, it's the perfect time and place to have a baby.' She gave a surprisingly girlish giggle. 'Now you see why I was so keen to have you move in with us – when the time comes, I'm going to need all the help I can get!'

Joan's heart swelled with pride. Robert's son! Another Robert Maitland! Or possibly a baby girl first, an older sister – history repeating itself in the next generation. That couldn't be bad, she smiled to herself. Then after that, little Robert. Her pale face coloured to match Claire's. 'Be a fine thing, a baby. Fine for Robert, to be a father. For us all. I'll pray for you, Claire.'

'Well, if Robert goes on being as absorbed in his parish work as he is today, I promise you, you'll be the first to know,' laughed Claire. 'Honestly, when he came through the door just now and went into the study I swear he was so wrapped up, he didn't even see me!'

In the cool, still interior of the church, the old stones themselves seemed to give back a murmuring echo of the first hymn of the Sunday morning service:

> 'Dear Lord and Father of mankind
> Forgive our foolish ways . . .'

His face alive with feeling above the black column of his cassock, Robert stepped forward, the adrenalin coursing though his veins like a runner before a race. Had he been too hasty, he wondered ruefully, in his decision to begin regular services on the very first Sunday after his return? No time to build a congregation – no time to write a sermon worthy of the occasion – no time to write a real sermon at all, so hard he found it to settle down to work after that first morning visit to Brightstone at the beginning of the week.

Feeling the nervous tension running in sensuous torment like quicksilver throughout his whole body, he cast an angry eye on the notes bearing the apology for a sermon he had scrawled only an hour or so ago, before the service began. What was the matter with him? He had never had the slightest problem in concentrating before, never in all his life. Yet now, as he tried to work, to think, to plan, or to write, his mind incessantly reverted to the strange encounter in the Paragon Milk Bar. The girl there – Vic's girl – why did he keep finding her on his mind? And why was he disappointed that she had not turned up at church today? Even the best of priests never expected to win everyone to their side. An obscure thought seized him: I never even asked her name . . .

'Breathe through the heats of our desire
Thy coolness and thy balm,
Let sense be dumb, let flesh retire,
Speak through the earthquake, wind and fire,
O still small voice of calm,
O still small voice of calm.'

The hymn was drawing to a close and the congregation settling down for the sermon. With a last murmured prayer Robert rose to his feet, made his reverence to the great carved depiction of the Crucifixion behind the altar, and ascended the pulpit. In the deep silence that greeted him he could hear far below the headland the low, pounding roar of the ocean breakers against the cliffs, and nearer, though fainter, the light, regular metallic clanking and creaking of the mine machinery in its restless endless round.

Before him a scattering of faces dotted the old mahogany pews. Claire and Joan, George and Molly Everard, a handful of elderly people whom he did not recognise at all, a clutch of younger women which thankfully did not contain the problematical Janice Peaseley – and seated pompously in the front where he could be sure to catch the pastor's eye, the mine boss Wilkes, his feebly smiling wife arrayed in another creation of summer-flowered voile. Was that all? Suddenly, at the far back of the congregation, seated in the shadow of a pillar, he caught sight of Paul – a Paul almost unrecognisable in his miner's Sunday best, his black curls slicked into submission by the liberal application of brilliantine, the ever-smiling face for once completely serious, the brawny arms folded in an unaccustomed attitude of peace and submission as he paid earnest attention to the proceedings.

At the sight of Paul, a passion of feeling swelled in Robert's heart. With such friends, such loyal support, how could he, how *dare* he fail? His heart, mind and soul alike took wing. He took a deep breath. Calmly he discarded his crumpled notes, opened his Bible and began. His voice, full of emotion, colour and truth, filled the little church.

'Whatsoever things are true: whatsoever things are honest: whatsovever things are just: whatsoever things are pure: whatsoever things are lovely: whatsoever things are of good report, I beseech you, brethren, think on these things . . .'

Chapter 5

The congregation attending morning service at St Jude's, Brightstone, that sunny Sunday morning, may have been small in size, but those present more than made up for their deficiency in numbers by the warmth of their praise and appreciation.

'A very fine sermon indeed, Reverend, if I may presume to extend my congratulations,' insisted Mr Wilkes, resolutely pumping Robert's hand on the steps of the church where he waited to bid his parishioners farewell. 'I won't disguise from you that I had certain hesitations – in short, reservations – when your appointment was first mooted to the Diocesan Lay Council – on which, as you may or may not be aware, I have the honour and privilege to serve as honorary chairman . . .'

From behind the heads of the rest of the little crowd, Claire caught with an answering grin the happy twinkle of amusement in Robert's eye, instantly suppressed as he leaned forward with his usual impeccable courtesy to give his attention to the local worthy in full flow.

'I said at the time, I mentioned it to Mrs Wilkes, he's *young*, I said—'

'Oh, you did,' nodded the loyal swathes of voile. 'Very young, you did say so at the time.'

'And your dad's were big shoes to fill, from all I've been hearing about those days . . . but that's enough of that. By jingo, young man, if you can get the working men back to church for another blast on the Bible like the one you've just given us, I can promise you that you'll have my vote behind you for anything and everything you want to do!'

'Thank you very much, Mr Wilkes,' said Robert gravely, resisting a smile. 'I do have great plans for the church, and for Brightstone, and I'll keep you well informed at every stage. I have to plead guilty to the charge of being young, I'm afraid. But the Parish Council – and Mrs Wilkes, of course—' he nodded respectfully towards the voile now floating furiously in the morning breeze – 'may be relieved to know that I shall be doing what I can on a daily basis to correct that problem!'

'Ay, no doubt, no doubt,' agreed Wilkes, with an obscure sense that something was passing him by. 'Anyway, glad to see y'got one of the miners here – there's trouble-makers among them, and they need a stabilising influence, no doubt about that. You've made a good start getting their union man here. Keep it up, keep it up! We're counting on you!' And with a curt nod in the direction of Paul Everard who was just now emerging blinking into the sunlight, he gathered up his windblown spouse and left.

'Beaut sermon, mate!' enthused the approaching Paul, his normal ebullience restored as soon as he stepped out of the hallowed precinct and back into the real world. 'Didn't know you had it in you, I swear I didn't! You fair gave it to 'em, no messing, right between the eyes! And without notes, too! Now that does take—' he was about to say 'the gift of the gab', but hastily amended it to 'proper guts, fair dinkum!'

'You approve, then?' questioned Robert drily.

'Fantastic! Better'n a picture show. For one week at least. Mind you, it would have been worth coming just to see that old crook Wilkes' face when he saw me here.'

'He was impressed!' laughed Robert. 'But are you telling me that God and I are only having the favour of your company for one service – just for today?'

'Too right, mate,' Paul agreed, thankfully tearing off his tie and loosening the top button of his shirt. 'Don't want you to get carried away with the sense of your own importance. This is just a one-off, to get you launched, so to speak. Think of me as your temporary, self-appointed cheerleader for the God Squad. Oh, and also as your entertainments officer.'

Robert burst out laughing. 'What *are* you talking about?'

'Well, you don't think I'd've come all this way on my day off without anywhere to go afterwards, 'specially on a great day like this, do you?' grinned Paul, his dark face alive with mischief. 'It's all fixed. All we needed was the sun. Where're the girls? Claire? Joanie? Got the tucker ready? No arguments, Reverend. Even a man of God's entitled to an afternoon off. It's all arranged. Just get in your car and follow me, OK?'

Along the curved edge of the bay, a rising tide swelled the surf, and the light wind whipped the tops of the great waves into legions of white horses rolling towards the shore. The breakers were building steadily towards their full height, surging majestically towards the land with a sonorous slowness calculated to conceal from the rash or the unwary their true, elemental power. From the clifftop path, the natural shape of the small, secluded beach, its pure white sand glittered in the fierce light of the midday sun, revealed itself as a perfect horse-shoe. As they neared the ground, however, the jagged clusters of broken black rocks lying silently in wait on either side of the bay's narrow entrance to challenge every next surge of the sea, belied the innocent, sunlit promise of the afternoon with their hidden menace, and served as a constant reminder of how the place got its name.

Robert inhaled deeply, then breathed out a sigh of true happiness. He had always loved Broken Bay, not least for its peace and quietness. Although so near to Brightstone, it had never been the favourite of the young set, who had always preferred the bigger, noisier Sundown Bay next to Broken Bay along the coast. But this had always been the chosen venue of Robert and Joan as teenagers, and for years before there was the slightest hint of any special feeling between Robert and Claire, the young Everards – Claire always loyally chaperoned by big brother Paul – had usually found themselves here as often as not on the long, lazy, sun-drenched evenings and weekends of the endless Australian summer.

'Well, c'mon! Or have y'forgotten how to swim after

all those years in the big city?' Pausing only to set down the coolbox and beach paraphernalia he had humped down from the car, Paul was peeling off his Sunday best like a man who could not wait to be free of it, intent on beating Robert into the sea.

'You're on!'

Exchanging indulgent smiles the two women watched as the men raced down the beach towards the sea with all the abandon of schoolboys on the wag. 'Beat ya!' 'No, you didn't!' floated faintly up to them from the water's edge as they spread the towels, scattered the mats and cushions, and arranged the bags and the beach umbrellas, the food and the drink as women have done at the seaside from time immemorial. Settled at last, they were free to look around them.

'We haven't got the place to ourselves, then,' said Claire, as she disposed herself to sunbathe, her eyes on a couple of other groups of young people enjoying themselves further away on the other side of the beach.

'Mmmn?' Joan was looking out to sea with more than a passing interest, watching the two men as they crested the surf. Absently she applied suncream to her long, elegant limbs and slowly smoothed it into her skin.

Out at sea Robert was experiencing in one delighted moment of rediscovery all the joy of a powerful young body testing itself against the infinitely greater power of the sea. With a brief shock he realised that in all the time that he and Claire had spent in the city, he had never once even thought of swimming, or running, let alone keeping up his athletics or any of the sports he used to love so much; so intent had he been on nothing but work, work, work. 'Which makes Jack a dull boy!' he laughed to himself as another mighty breaker bore down on him, its huge top just beginning to curl lazily, threateningly, enticingly above his body braced for its fall. With a luxuriant grace and an unconscious, sensual abandon he gave himself to the slow, rolling thrust of the surge and rode its power in one triumphant swelling crescendo of sensation all the way in to the shore.

Robert always could do anything well, Joan decided, studying him with all the pride of her love. Dancing, swimming, playing any game, he was what they called 'a natural'; easy, lithe and graceful with an innate ability to make his body obey every command of his will. He was thinner, yes – she made a mental note to reintroduce some of his boyhood favourites into the Rectory menu. A proper breakfast every day to start with, she decided; then for dinner, nothing less than meat every day. Then maybe to follow, her own special rich ginger cake, for instance, or good old apple pie with lashings of cream – she'd soon do something about that boyish leanness, have him back in shape again.

But Paul – above and beyond the warmth of the early summer sun striking up off the sand, she felt the heat rising in her own body at the sight of his. Sketchily clad in nothing but the skimpiest wisp of black swimwear, Paul Everard was something else. Superbly built from the last few years of unrelenting physical labour underground, bronzed to the patina that only the lucky few can ever achieve, he was a man in the prime of his physical perfection, rejoicing in it like an animal at play. From beneath the cover of her sunhat and dark glasses, Joan watched with intense concentration as Paul dipped and dived through the waves like a dolphin, cresting every breaker like a champion surfer, his strength apparently equal to the power of nature every time. Once again, as so often before, the painful longing began to gather round her heart and hotly, shamefully, make itself felt between her thighs. Paul . . . oh Paul . . .

'I hope those two big kids are going to come out soon,' yawned Claire sleepily. 'I'm getting hungry.' Lazily she hauled herself to a sitting position and looked out across the shining sand. 'Don't say they're coming at last. Hey, who's that?'

Even from a distance it was obvious that the two attractive young girls running towards the water's edge were no strangers to Paul. Surfacing from a spent breaker almost at their feet, he leaped on them with exuberant whoops and shouts, laughing, dancing and splashing all around them to their evident outrage and delight. Only when they were both thoroughly wet did Paul tire of the fun and games, and with a final laughing goodbye tore himself away and came strolling back towards Claire and Joan.

'Who are those two?'

Joan's voice was cold. 'No idea. Not from round here, anyway.'

'Looks as if our Paul's going further afield for his lady friends these days, then,' said Claire ruefully. 'I wish he'd grow up and settle down! He's Robert's age, you know.'

'I know.' Better than you do, I wouldn't be surprised, said a small voice inside her.

'He always was a romantic, though,' reminisced Claire with a sentimental smile. 'Always said he'd never get married just for the sake of it. And he loves being in love! But I know Mum'd like to see him sorted out with a nice girl—'

'Doesn't have to be a girl,' said Joan distantly, busying herself with unpacking the picnic food. 'Someone a bit steadier, who'd be a real good homemaker, that's the sort keeps most men happy.'

'Well, she'll certainly have to be able to cook!' laughed Claire. 'Here they come now – and I bet you anything the first thing Paul'll say is "What's for tucker, you sheilahs?" '

The level sun was sinking in the west as Robert walked slowly along the edge of the quiet, darkening sea. The surging tide had swollen to the height of its afternoon fullness, turned, and was now ebbing silently with the remains of the day. It had all been perfect, just perfect, Robert thought, luxuriating in the feel of his body and enjoying every twinge of his aching limbs. Now, at the end of it all, he found himself reluctant to leave.

Turning away from the smooth-swelling, almost oily sea, its rough midday breakers now far off, rolling miles away across the surface of the sleepless ocean, he glanced back up the beach. As he looked at them, Claire, Paul and Joan seemed caught in a kind of old-fashioned tableau, frozen in an uncharacteristic moment of stillness, Claire seated patiently on the sand waiting for him to return, her arms hugging her knees, Paul trapped under the canopy of the beach umbrella as he grasped its central pole like Samson in the temple, and Joan leaning forward, her gaze fixed on Paul with a kind of hungry intensity. His heart went out to her – her secret, as she clearly supposed anything she kept locked up so tightly inside herself, had been no secret from him from the first moment he had seen her with Paul. If only those two could find the kind of happiness he knew with Claire!

All three of them now, and the little island of golden sand around them, were bathed in the deep amber glow of the late evening sun, like the thick honey glaze of old varnish. He felt as if he were seeing them from a long way off, caught and held for an undying second by a trick of the light, suspended in time as if they would never grow old. For the rest of his life he never forgot that moment, nor ceased to mourn its passing.

Instinctively he moved to rejoin that precious little group. His place was there, his life with them opening like a good book whose rich and satisfying story would hold him spellbound from now until the very last page. Yet something held him back. A moment longer for myself, he heard himself pleading, yielding to a wordless imperative welling up somewhere deep inside. I shan't be long, I'll join them in a second – just a few minutes longer to be by myself – to be myself.

Turning away from both beach and sea he struck off at random, making towards the broken rocks clustered at the foot of the cliffs whose fatal attraction for shipping in the olden days had given Broken Bay its ill-omened name. Deceptively low in the water, black and sleekly glistening by day and night, they lurked almost unseen on both sides to the entrance of what had been a fav- oured harbour of the first sea-farers to this undiscovered land, showing almost nothing of their hidden menace, their terror and their power to destroy. Unconscious of anything except the beauty of the evening, Robert drif- ted up to the base of a low, rounded rock formation known through the ages, because of its distinctive shape, after its even older Aboriginal name, the Mother and

Child. As he dreamily circled its smooth, rounded slope, he suddenly came face to face with the girl from the café.

She had evidently been approaching from the next beach along the bay, accessible to this one now only because the low tide had left a firm walkway of flat, wet sand between the two. So unexpected was her appearance, so startling the sight of this strange, slight creature in the fading evening light that he almost knocked her over. Instinctively he threw out his arms to catch her, but she recovered herself unaided with the natural balance of an athlete, and stood silently before him as if awaiting his recognition before she would consent to speak. The sinking sun irradiated her pale, almost colourless hair with shades of opal, fire and gold, and her eyes, those of a young Siamese cat, were fixed on him in some kind of unspoken appeal.

'I'm so sorry', he heard himself saying. 'I almost knocked you over.'

'I'm OK – no harm done.'

Once again his ear caught the strange lilting music of her voice. 'We met before,' he said. 'In the café. I'm new here—'

'I know. I know who you are – Reverend.'

'Call me Robert.' Why did it suddenly seem so important that she did? 'Please – I mean it.'

'Robert.' She turned it over in her mouth like a child exploring a sweet. 'OK – Robert.'

She was so near to him that he could inhale the fresh, childlike smell of the sweat and salt on her golden skin mixed with the breeze from the sea. She seemed shorter than he remembered, before he realised that on the beach she would be wearing no shoes. She looked up at him curiously, but sideways, out of the corner of her eyes in the same strangely disturbing way that she had before. How old was she? Eighteen? Nineteen? Too young! a voice cried somewhere inside, too young!

'Robert! Coo-ee! Robert!'

Far away across the sand the thin sound of Claire's call floated away on the night wind. His mind seemed incapable of phrasing a goodbye.

'Robert! ROBERT! You deaf, or what? Where the hell are you?'

Paul's aggressive cry pierced through the mist in which he seemed to hang suspended. He was seized with an inexplicable feeling that Paul must not come over here – Paul, womanising Paul with his contemptuous attitude to 'the sheilahs' could not, should not come into contact with this . . . this lovely young creature, this child-waif. He must protect her from that. He threw a hurried glance over his shoulder. Paul was already on his way, striding across the beach in the thickening dusk.

Out at sea the flaming sun was racing down the sky with all the wild impatience of a tropical sunset. For one first and last moment he met her glance full on in the last lurid light of the dying day, then moved swiftly away as the world was plunged into the thick night of darkness once again.

Summer

Chapter 6

By the next morning, the pleasure they had all taken in the glorious day on the beach of Broken Bay seemed mysteriously to have disappeared. Pale and abstracted, Robert sat at the breakfast-table refusing all Joan's offers of breakfast, or anything except strong black coffee. He hardly knew what was wrong with him. But he knew that something, somehow, was not as it ought to be. He should have been tired last night, after all the exertions of the day, all the surfing and swimming. But he had known, even before he went to bed, that he was far too restless to sleep. And when he reached for Claire, bearing down with an unaccustomed disregard for her feelings her mild resistance, her grumbles about being tired and having to go to work the next day, he had to admit that efficient as his body was in answering her needs and his, he might just as well have been a machine going through those motions as a man, let alone one who prided himself on being a loving, considerate husband.

He could not deceive himself about the cause of his feelings of unease. But why should the chance meeting last night with the girl on the beach have made such an impact on him? Why should she have the power twice now to trouble him in ways he could not even begin to understand? She had hardly spoken to him on either occasion, and he certainly had had little enough to say to her. She meant no more to him than any other of the female parishioners he had come to know – less, in fact, far less than many of them; than Mrs Anderson, for instance, one of the mine's many widows, anxious now about her only son who was desperate to become a miner in his turn; than Molly Everard, torn between her ailing husband and her wayward son; or even than poor old George himself, living from day to day and fighting for every breath. It was inexplicable – beyond rhyme and reason. Baffled almost beyond endurance, he lapsed into a brooding silence.

Across the table Claire threw a glance at Joan, who hardly needed to catch it to know what her sister-in-law was thinking. How wonderful yesterday had been, with Robert so free, so happy and relaxed, exactly like his old self in the years before the death of their parents had clouded their lives. And how short a time had lasted before the pressure of work, the inevitable responsibilities of his job, or simply all the demands on his time now seemed to have got him cornered again.

Almost imperceptibly a weight seemed to settle on the whole table. Claire looked heavy-eyed and downcast, Joan noted watchfully – she obviously had something on her mind, something serious, too, by the look of it. To Claire, who had awoken that morning to the disappointment of finding her hopes for a baby dashed once again, Joan's silent scrutiny was almost an invitation to open up her overburdened heart: she was still recovering from the realisation that Robert had been far too preoccupied with his own concerns, whatever they were, for her to share her sadness with him. But Joan's face had quickly resumed its everyday expression of hard and wary watchfulness, the 'nobody makes a fool out of *me*' look that had been nowhere to be seen when they embarked on the beach party of only yesterday. There could be no comfort there, Claire realised. Each one of them had to deal with their problems as best they could.

The silence was becoming unbearable. With a muttered apology, Robert hastily left the room and with a sense of relief crossed the hall to seek the sanctuary of his study. Seated at the desk, he plunged his head in his hands and closed his eyes. He needed to think. But almost before he knew it his hand was reaching for the phone.

'Hello – is that Molly?'

'Robert! How y'doing? How's Claire?'

'Fine, just fine. How's George?'

'Well . . . y'know. Doc says there's no use hoping for a miracle.'

'Yes. Yes, of course. Well, I really rang to thank you both for making such a great effort yesterday, turning out at morning service the way you did. It meant a lot to me. Claire too. We're both so grateful.'

'Aw, don't mensh!' Molly was not used to being thanked. Her warm embarrassment provided a ready opportunity to change the subject.

'There's something else you might help me with, Molly, if you could. I want to get to know the young people round here, to make sure the news of the church reopening has reached them just as much as their mothers and fathers. There's that daughter of Vic's, the Greek who keeps the café down the other end of town—'

'Daughter? Which one? Vic's got a big family!'

'Pretty young, about eighteen or nineteen, slight, very fair—'

Molly laughed uproariously. 'That's not his daughter!'

'Not—'

'Never in your life! She's no relation of Vic's, as you might imagine from that fairy look of her. That's Ally Calder. Daughter of the ex-union boss Jim Calder – Big Jim they used to call him – the one our Paully got slung out when he ran for office at the mine. She only works there for Vic a couple of days a week. Her old man won't hardly let her out of his sight otherwise.'

'You don't know—' Robert was overcome by an unaccountable urge to keep Molly talking, to get out of her whatever she knew '—you don't happen to know if this is one of her days?'

'Can't help you there, love. Paul might know, though. He knows pretty well everyone round here – everyone under thirty and wearing a skirt, that is!'

Paul? No! With his reputation, that would be the last thing an innocent girl would need. She already had problems with her father, by the sound of it – perhaps that was why he felt she was drawing him to her by some kind of mute appeal – she needed his help. And if she needed it, well, she must have it, he promised himself, suddenly exhilarated. He would find her, he knew. And not through Paul. He would find her some other way.

'Thanks, Molly, that's OK. It was just a passing inquiry while I was ringing anyway. Thanks again for yesterday. Take care of yourself – and that husband of yours.'

He put the phone down to the sound of Molly's comfortable chuckling laughter, and sat for a long time lost in thought. Brightstone was only a little town. It would not be odd or unnatural for him to call in to the Paragon for a cup of coffee in the course of his rounds. Sooner or later he would do that . . . sooner or later . . . maybe sooner . . .

> 'For there's nothing like a dame,
> Nothing in the world . . .'

Whistling tunelessly but rhythmically between his teeth, Paul drove slowly down the main street of Brightstone as the shops and banks were closing to signal the end to another working day. Slipping down the hill he chose his position, parked carefully to make sure he had a good view of the street, slipped a cassette into the Dodge's stereo, and waited. The opening blast of a hot rock number set his pulse and his sensuality instantly alight. 'Come on!' he muttered, his eyes fixed and intent. 'Come on!' Before one side of the tape had played its way through, his impatience was rewarded by the sight of two young girls coming out of the doorway ahead and loitering on the pavement deep in conversation.

One, obviously a working girl, was burdened with a battered old shopping bag full of food, while the other, although only around the same age, had a plump toddler in a pushchair who regularly made plain his objection to having to kick his heels while the girls continued their conversation. At last, when the child's litany of howls and screams became too much to bear, they said good-bye and went their separate ways, the mother and baby downhill towards Paul, the girl in the opposite direction up towards 'the better end of town'.

From the droop of her small shoulders, it would be a long and unwelcome walk in the heat and dust of another blistering day. Anyone'd be glad of a lift under those conditions, Paul told himself, let alone with a bag of shopping as heavy as hers. He caught a quick glance at his reflection in the driving mirror, slicked back his hair, and favoured himself with a wicked wink. Then grinning like a fox, he switched on the engine, engaged first gear, and cruised slowly up behind the struggling figure of the girl ahead like a hunter moving in on his prey.

'Hello, Ally.'

'Paul!' With a swift glance up and down the street as if to see who was around, she looked into the car as Paul leaned across the passenger seat, holding the door open invitingly.

'Just passing. You on your way home? Like a lift?'

She hesitated. 'Oh – well, OK – yeah, why not?' Painfully she loaded the heavy bag into the car.

'How y'doing, Ally? Haven't seen you around for quite a while.'

'I'm OK.'

The non-committal response told him nothing. But that sideways glance of hers through that rainfall of baby-blonde hair and the flash of golden thigh through the slit in her thin summer skirt spoke volumes to Paul – Christ, he could feel the start of an erection! Now cut that out! he silently admonished himself. Make some civilised conversation! Determinedly he tried again.

'You still only working a couple of days a week for Vic?'

A shadow passed across the smooth oval face. 'He reckons he can't afford me any more often. And even if he could—' She broke off resentfully.

'Your dad, huh?' Paul said sympathetically. Doesn't want to lose his little housekeeper, the selfish old bastard, he thought. Aloud he said, 'Maybe he'd give you a bit more rein if he thought it was a better position, a better chance for you. What about that job at the Shire Hall you were after – in the office there?'

She looked out of the window. 'Didn't get it. They said I'd got no experience.'

Paul clucked in sympathetic disgust. 'Their loss, hey, Ally? Smart girl like you.'

The features he had thought so gentle and unformed took on an expression he had never seen before. 'There's only one future for girls here, whether they're smart or not – and it's not for me.'

'What d'you mean?'

'You saw me talking to that girl outside the milk bar.'

He realised instantly that she had known all along that he had been waiting outside the café for her, and had seen through his story of 'just passing' for the fiction it was. He struggled to sound cool. 'The big girl in blue, with the baby? Yeah, what about her?'

'She was in the same class as me at school. She was the one they picked to sit for the university scholarship that time. We used to have such dreams – getting away to the city, a flat together . . . Look at her now. He's her second baby, Tom is. Her life's ruined.'

'Hey, steady on!' protested Paul in alarm. 'Lots of girls like babies, you know. A good bloke, a nice house, a nice steady routine – there's a lot to be said for it. And kids really can enrich your life, everyone says . . .'

Even he could feel the strangeness of this, coming from Paul Everard of all people. He had never thought any such thing in his entire life before – had always believed just the opposite, in fact, that marriage was a ball and chain for any decent bloke, and kids a nightmare to be avoided at all costs. What was this girl doing to him? He was supposed to be the hunter, women the hunted. Whatever it was, she seemed to know it, or at least to see into a part of him he did not know himself was there. At the unexpectedness of his tribute to marriage and motherhood, a faint flash of what looked like contempt passed across the Madonna face. Then she simply gave him her long, clear-eyed stare and was silent.

'So what are you planning to do with yourself then, Ally?' asked Paul, with a troubled sense that he was treading on ground he had never previously ventured on in his relations with women. 'What else is there for you here, then except maybe a little job, and then—' Fearing to mention marriage and babies again, he left it hanging delicately in the air.

'Everything!' Her normally slate-blue eyes were pale with fire. 'Paul – you've been to Sydney, haven't you?'

'Sydney! Hey, that's miles, hundreds of miles away—' He caught himself up. 'Yeah, a coupla times. Great place for a holiday.'

She did not reply.

'You planning a holiday, then?' he asked with a sinking sensation that he already knew the answer.

She shook her head. 'A new life,' she said very softly, 'that's what I'm planning. There's nothing for me here. As soon as I've got enough money, I'm away, out of it, gone! And I won't be coming back!'

Paul gripped the wheel, his mind working furiously. 'You sure you're not being too hasty?'

Again she gave him her direct, challenging stare. 'What am I waiting for?'

'Well—' He could not think of anything. 'You want some advice from an old bloke?'

'You?' she considered him up and down, again with that disturbing, calculating stare. 'How old are you?'

'Twenty-eight'. Nearly ten years older than you, he thought with an odd sense of distress.

'That's not old,' she said judiciously. 'What's the advice?'

'Give it till you're twenty-one. At least hang on for another year. A lot can change in that time.' Or be changed, he thought. 'Then you'll find it a lot easier to do what you want. You'll have saved a lot more money, too. It's no joke fetching up in a place like Sydney if you can't afford to live.'

'I suppose I can hang on for a bit. Can't afford to go yet anyway.'

'That's my girl!' He covered the words with an embarrassed chuckle, afraid of seeming to build too much on what was still after all only a young acquaintance. If he hadn't just felt like a soft drink that day on his way back home from the mine, instead of the usual cold beer . . .

But she had not noticed. 'Paul,' she resumed absently, her eyes far away, 'you know the new minister – the one that's just come to St Jude's, don't you?'

''Course I do. He's my brother-in-law, my sister's husband. What about him?'

The small sound she made might have been a reaction to this information, or simply boredom. 'Oh, nothing. He came into the café last week, that's all.'

'Now there you go!' With delight Paul seized on the sudden chance fate had handed him to strengthen his case. 'I told you things would change – and he's one of the changes round here! Full of new ideas, Robert is – he'll liven up the town for you, I'll swear to that. Um – disco nights up at the church and all sorts, I shouldn't wonder!' he improvised wildly.

'Disco nights?' She seemed distinctly unimpressed.

'Well, p'raps not discos. But he's a real goer, Robert is, a real smart bloke. And he's been in the city, if that's what you want. Had four years in Perth in a ministry there.'

'Perth!' He might as well have said Paradise, he saw.

'Yeah, Perth, Queen of the South. You'll have to have a word with him some time about it.' And I'll fix it up if need be, he told himself. Anything to keep the little lady here while I get a chance to show her the local lads aren't all duds and drongos. Could be an advantage after all to have reverend in the family! 'You'll have to meet him.'

'I'd like that.' She sounded as if she meant it, he noticed with approval.

'And if you're serious about looking for better work, a job that'll be more of a challenge, I'll put the word about. Got a lotta contacts through the union, you know. Shouldn't be too hard to find you something a bit more interesting than a milk bar!'

He was suddenly conscious that the journey to her house was nearing its end. 'You going to the dance on Saturday night, Ally? I could pick you up if you liked . . .'

'Don't think so. Waste of time. There's nobody there I want to dance with.' While he registered this backhander, she changed her mind, as casually as she had dismissed the dance in the first place. 'But if you're offering, I guess I might as well go. I'll meet you round the corner at eight o'clock. And you better drop me off there now, as well. I don't want my dad to see me—'

'I know, I know.'

'Well, he's not going to give a warm welcome to any man except the one he chooses – and he hates you like poison, ever since you took the union job away from him. He'd done it for thirty years, you know.'

Paul bit back the reply he was tempted to make, and drew in carefully to the kerb. Jumping out, he helped her to alight, and gave her a hand with the absurdly heavy shopping bag. As he did so, neither of them saw a car come up from behind and overtake Paul's parked vehicle, the driver registering both Paul and his passenger as it did so.

Pulling round the corner, Jim Calder swore long and viciously. Bloody Everard! So that was it! He thought Ally'd been quick back from the milk bar the last time or two. Had to be a bloke in the frame somewhere – a bloke with a car. But *Everard*!

The bitch. The two-faced little bitch . . . Looks as if I'm going to have to teach her a thing or two, that girl, he thought. But don't rush it. Not yet. Better get to the bottom of whatever's going on first . . .

By the time she reached the gate, her father was leaning over it with apparent casualness, but with a strange, unpleasant glint in his eye. 'Just wondering where you was, Ally,' he said, staring at her with a look she had not seen before.

He's loathsome, she thought, taking in for the thousandth time the beer belly, the huge, slabby, muscular frame and beefy forearms, the greasy unkempt hair, the black half-moons under his fingernails and the eternal sour smell of beer. 'I'm fine', she said shortly, attempting to march swiftly past. But he grabbed her arm.

'Expecting a visitor tonight,' he grinned. 'Mind y'cook up something nice. Mick'll expect a decent plate of tucker from a house with a woman in the kitchen, him being a lonely bachelor, like.'

'Mick? Mick *Ford*?'

'Yeah, Mick. What's wrong with him?'

What's wrong with him . . . nothing but his stubby, hairy body, his stupid, cheesy grin, his sweaty hands, his mean, crafty eyes, his friendship with *you*. 'Nothing,' she said.

'Man comes here to my house gets the best treatment, or I'll know about it, y'get it?' His face was uncomfortably near hers now, the threat in his voice and his twitching hand quite plain. 'Looking like that, acting like that, y'got the manners of y'bloody mother, bad cow she was! But I thought I taught y'better than that. And if I didn't, y'still not too old t'learn. *Y' get it?*' He paused, waiting.

'I get it,' she said.

He laughed a coarse laugh. 'Thought y'would. Away on in then, and get on with y'cooking. And while y're at it, remember y'can fly too high with your airs and graces, miss – and the only place it'll get ya is down to earth on y'backside with a bump!'

Chapter 7

From the end of the street, the little Everard dwelling looked like any of the other miners' cottages hastily thrown together in classic 'two-up, two-down' style by a callous mine management desperate for working men, but not too concerned about what it offered them in the way of accommodation. Walking towards it, Claire contrasted the grace and size of the Rectory, its spacious rooms and elegant yet comfortable proportions, with the way her parents lived, and felt a guilt she could hardly assuage. They had worked so hard, all their lives; they deserved something better now. Especially with her father so poorly off with the curse of all miners, the fatal lung disease. If only he could live high up in the clean, pure air of the headland, instead of down here in the heat and dust of the back streets!

'Claire! You should've told me you hadn't got the car – I'd've picked you up at the bus stop! It's getting far too hot for Shanks's pony!'

Claire smiled with pure love as she hugged the short, busy figure of her mother in her arms. 'No worries, Mum. A walk'll do me good. Robert's taken the car off on his rounds – he's off up beyond the mine today.'

'How is that handsome husband of yours?' Molly accompanied her question with a shrewd glance. To her female neighbours a few years ago, 'the parson's son' had been a fantastic catch for Claire Everard when he had first started showing an interest in her, back in his college days. But even then, Molly had been sure with all the conviction of her honest heart that marriage with young Robert Maitland, if it ever came about, would be no bed of roses for her daughter.

Nor had the cost of loving a man like Robert been Claire's alone. When Robert had departed from Brightstone after his parents' funeral, fleeing as if the hounds of hell were on his heels, George and Molly had borne the brunt of Claire's silent pining and loss of hope. When, a year later, he had abruptly summoned her three thousand miles away across the island to the other side of Australia to be his bride, Molly had helped to buy her bridal gown and seen her on to the overland train with all the unspoken feelings of any mother denied the chance even to attend, let alone to arrange in the most wonderful way she could, the wedding of her only daughter.

And now . . . it was not over, even yet. It never would be over, with a man like Robert. There was more, there would always be more to come, of that Molly was as sure as she ever was of anything.

'All well, then?' she probed gently, the hawk-eye of mother love picking up Claire's heavy look and subdued manner as soon as she walked through the door.

'Oh yes, Mum – we're fine. We're all fine.'

Molly took the bull by the horns. 'You don't sound very convinced, love,' she said, taking Claire by the arm and drawing her into the little kitchen. 'Here, let me make a cup of tea. Your dad's out the back, having his sleep in the garden. We've got time for a chat before I've got to wake him for his tablets.'

Claire accepted the cup of tea like the panacea it was. 'I'm OK, really I am, Mum. It's just that I've had another . . . you know, disappointment again this month. I really thought I was pregnant this time. I just felt so certain that coming back to Brightstone was right, I was sure that would do the trick. And now . . .'

'Ain't no trick to it, darling,' Molly said gently, taking her daughter's hand. 'It just comes when it's right, that's all. You've got to give it time. I knew a woman over in Blue Mountain Bay, waited twelve years before her first came along.'

'Twelve *years*? Oh Mum, have a heart!' Claire was laughing and almost crying at the same time. 'I think I'll die if Robert and I have to wait that long!'

'You won't die, love,' observed Molly gravely, 'but you'll surely grieve, and grieve hard. And that won't do any good. Grieving never got anyone a baby. Fretting's the very opposite of the way you need to be, to give the poor little thing a chance to take root and grow inside you.'

'Mum, what can I do?'

Molly paused for thought, her bright eyes fixed on Claire's clouded face. 'You got to give it time, Claire, you've just got to. Doctors won't look at you until you've been trying a good while anyway.'

'How long, Mum?'

'Six months – a year. How long have you and Robert . . . ?'

Claire blushed and laughed. 'Not that long, not yet.'

'There you are then! Getting in a state before there's any cause for alarm! It doesn't just happen when your husband hangs his underpants on the bed-post, y'know, pardon my French. You got to let nature take its course.'

'I will.' Claire sighed with relief, then haunted by a last shadow of doubt, sought reassurance again. 'But what if it doesn't?'

'If it doesn't, there's things they can do these days – they can do anything. We got the best gynaecologists in the world in Sydney, no worries,' said Molly stoutly. 'But it will. Nature finds the way. You got to stop worrying, that's all. Now give me a minute to give your dad his pills and his inhaler, then you can nip out the garden and see him. He'll be so thrilled – and he doesn't get many thrills these days, poor old darling.'

Robert was on his way to the mine even before he heard the siren. Drily aware that his rapidly growing congregation at St Jude's was enrolling considerably more women than men, he was keen to make contact with the mining fraternity as a way of redressing the balance. Disgruntled husbands of newly inspired wives and fathers of teenage daughters might grumble into their beer that if the new Reverend had been fat and fifty, the Word of God as delivered from the pulpit of St Jude's every week would have had nothing like so

powerful an appeal. But enough of their friends and
drinking companions were also beginning to feel the
impact of the new minister's personality for the jibes to
be kept very muted for the time being.

And afterwards, what would be more natural than to
stop off at the Paragon for a quick cup of coffee, see
how everything was going along there? His mind once
again returning to the girl, his body struggling with
another unfamiliar set of gears and controls, the result
of having replaced the hired car with a second-hand
vehicle of uncertain age and even more uncertain disposition, Robert was quite unprepared for the shock of
hearing the siren as its peculiarly terrifying and mournful
wail ripped through the still afternoon air. Immediately
he swung off his intended route, and headed for the
mine.

As he drew near he could see the frightened faces of
the people flocking to the mine to find out what had
happened, and the anxious knot clustered at the pit-
head growing from minute to minute. Prominent in the
crowd was Wilkes, the mine boss, from his harsh
expression and agitated manner a very different Mr
Wilkes from the self-satisfied Sunday version of Robert's
previous acquaintance. With him was Paul Everard, the
two men apparently locked in dispute. Beneath the
scream of the siren, the fire engines and ambulances
hastening to the scene wailed in a minor key, adding
their lamentations to the general sense of catastrophe.

Abandoning his car, Robert made straight for Paul as
Wilkes hurried away. 'What's happened?'

Paul threw him an angry glance. 'Couple of the blokes
copped it in a rock fall.'

'What? Killed?'

'They're still down there. Too soon to say. Several
more badly injured. We'll know more in a bit.'

'Any more trapped underground? In danger?'

'No, thank God,' said Paul, quite unconscious that he
was echoing the very phrase that Robert was fervently
uttering in the silence of his soul. 'But no thanks to
him!' He jabbed a vicious thumb in the direction of
Wilkes, who had taken advantage of Robert's arrival to

disengage himself from Paul's verbal attack. 'I've been on and on at him about safety up here – everything from the problems with the shafts to the men still getting lung disease—'

'The shafts?'

Paul sighed wearily, wiping a grime-covered fist across an even blacker forehead and pushing back his helmet to reveal the incongruous band of dust-free white skin along his hairline. 'We've had problems for years with the age of the mining shafts – they just haven't been renewed or reinforced in rotation, like they should have been. Wilkes says that the "current economic conditions" are against us. That's his bloody jargon for the fact that he's prepared to gamble with men's lives, while at the same time the shafts he's pushing us into are getting deeper and deeper all the time! Not that he's ever going to risk his precious neck down there – hasn't got the balls!'

The last remark was delivered in a tone loud enough to reach the officious little man who was standing nearby trying to calm a small, shaken knot of miner's wives. Wilkes's angry reaction showed that he had heard every word. Trust Paul! thought Robert, as he moved swiftly to head off a confrontation.

'Paul' he said urgently, 'why not introduce me to some of the miners' wives? And what about the two men who've been most badly hurt?'

As he hoped, Paul's practical mind switched instantly to the weight of matters in hand. 'Yes, Robert, you're right as usual. Be a great thing if you can help us out – always such a terrible shock for the women when a thing like this happens. The union'll take care of things as far as it goes for now for Nipper and Geordie – the two poor bastards down there. If they pull through, though, they'll be glad of a bit of company in hospital when you've got a minute. Them mining injuries take a powerful long time to heal, and you get so bored, they say, you almost wish you'd copped it in the first go.'

As he talked, Paul led the way through the gathering throng. Robert could not help noticing how well-known and well-liked Paul was on all sides, a mate and brother to the younger men, a son to his older colleagues, and obviously everything they ever wanted him to be to the women of the mine, married or single.

'Here y'are, girls,' he approached one group with confident familiarity, yet with just the right degree of seriousness for the occasion, Robert saw. 'Here, girls, let me introduce you to the new man at St Jude's, the Reverend Maitland. Rob, this here's Mrs Milligan, wife of Nipper. Nipper, y'know – he's—' Trapped underground, unaccounted for – the terrible phrases hung unspoken in the air. 'And Betty Bradley, Pete's mum; you know Mrs Anderson, the mum of young Johnny; then this is Mrs 'Spike' McGinnis; Franco Bellone's missus – don't speak much English yet, do ya Maria? but it'll come; and Tom French's wife, Ellen. I'll leave you to get acquainted. Need to have another word with Wilkes while it's fresh in my mind.'

The woman stood in silence, taking him in. He's too bloody good-looking to be a priest! ran through more than one feminine mind, despite the solemnity of the occasion. Returning their gaze, Robert was struck to the heart by the weight of dread, anxiety and sullen grief written in the worn faces and drooping shoulders of every one. What a life! To have to give their men to the mines and live every day in the fear of this very event! 'I'm glad to have the chance to meet you all,' he said gently, 'though I can't tell you how sorry I am that it's under circumstances such as these. I've just moved into St Jude's. I'm Paul Everard's brother in law.'

This last remark softened the atmosphere of hard and wary suspicion as nothing he had yet said had succeeded in doing. 'Oh, Paul!' 'Why didn't y'say, Reverend?' and 'Paul? Never!' all told him that he had won their instant acceptance.

'Reverend Maitland? Robert Maitland?' The speaker was the woman introduced to him as Nipper Milligan's wife, a woman of about forty, he thought, with faded hair, a pale, exhausted face and slack, over-used body.

'Yes.'

'I know you.'

He smiled. 'Yes, that's very likely. I used to live here before, some time ago . . .'

'I know. I was at school with you. Used to be Noellene Foley.'

'Noellene Foley! Of course!'

There was no 'of course' about it. The woman who, as he remembered, had been a only a year behind him in school and so was still only in her twenties, now looked at least middle-aged – not so much from her face, as he now realised, as from her whole appearance, which signalled her defeat in every muscle and bone of her body. She twisted her bony hands, perfectly conscious of what was going through his mind. 'O'course, I been working ever since I left the high school,' she said lamely, as if in excuse. 'And I've had a few kids . . . But if Nipper's copped it – if we're going t'lose him . . .'

She spoke as if her life were over, and as she spoke, she began to weep, softly and hopelessly. Instinctively he gathered her to his arms and comforted her, supporting her as she sobbed convulsively on his shoulder. Holding her there, Robert was filled with a sudden sense of purpose. I can help these woman! he vowed – not just for now, but for the future. His mind was racing with ideas: a trust fund for the injured miners, a crèche for their children, some relief for their wives, whatever form that would take. They need so much help, the women of this town, he thought passionately. And I can give it! Starting now! There is so much more to life than this – so much more than this narrow, wretched round so suddenly terminated by death. There is more – there has to be more – for all of them.

Gently, unhurriedly, he calmed the distraught woman. Noellene Milligan never forgot the smile he gave her. 'It's so good to see you again, Noellene,' he said – 'for all the world as if I was the Queen of England' as she later told her best friend, who also had not forgotten the heart-throb of her younger days. 'And I hope I'll have a chance to get to know you and your family a lot better. Now don't let's fear the worst. I hear the fall has been contained, and it's not as bad as they thought. There are no more casualties expected, so let's see what we can find out about Nipper and Geordie right now . . .'

Bad news – rock-fall news – travels fast in a mining town. By the time Paul and Robert got back to the Rectory, Joan was waiting for them with the hot water boiling in the pipes and fresh towels in the bathroom ready for Paul, and a spread of food on the dining-table that could have fed almost every miner in the town. But she had also lived in Brightstone among mining men for long enough to know that the first thing Paul would want would be the cold beer she had ready for his hand just as soon as he walked through the door.

It would take more than a beer, though, she saw with alarm, to cool Paul's rage. Grabbing the glass from her hand, almost unconscious of her presence, he paced up and down the study like a lion ready to strike. 'OK, so Geordie and Nipper didn't die!' he shouted furiously. 'But ten men injured, and the two of them critically! And still he talks economics! It's "economics", I suppose, to write off a dozen good men!'

'I think you made that point to him very forcibly,' said Robert, with grave understatement. Only his intervention had prevented Paul from almost coming to blows with the mine boss, who had showed the true ferocity that underlay his petty, obsessive nature with a series of vicious ripostes to Paul's renewed onslaught. 'I'm sure your best bet now is to take up the whole question of the mine's safety with the management through official channels.'

'Official channels!' snorted Paul in disgust. 'Fat chance we've got with those when Wilkes is still listening to crooks like Jim Calder and his stooge Mick Ford—'

'Calder?' interrupted Robert sharply.

'Yeah, Jim Calder,' snapped Paul. 'Told you about him before, remember? Used t'be the union official before I stood against him and got him out. Crooked as a dog's hind leg. Took one salary from the union, and another from Wilkes under the counter to make sure nothing that the union decided ever happened.'

'Calder,' said Robert, his mind working. This was the

name he had had from Molly Everard – it was the father of the girl at the café. 'Is he a local man?' he asked casually. 'Does he live round here?'

'Course he does, y'drongo, what's that got t'do with it? Point is, we wouldn't be twelve good men down right now if he hadn't been selling us all down the river for the last twenty years!'

Robert made the effort to collect himself. 'Do the men know all this? And the truth about the level of safety in the mine now?'

'Sure they do, and the company knows all about it, too. Wilkes knows all about it, more than we do in fact. But Calder's a canny bastard, there's nothing anyone can pin on him. And the kind of maintenance we need now would mean shutting down the mine for six months at least, with a loss of output, loss of work – and the men just can't afford that, not with families to keep. It's your blasted "economics" again!'

Paul's bitterness found an echoing toughness in Robert's heart. 'That's terrible,' he said heavily. 'Well, you're the union man! I'm afraid you'll just have to make the management sit up and take notice. I'll help you any way I can.' He smiled. 'A man's entitled to a little help from his friends.'

'Robert – be careful!' Joan had pledged herself not to interfere in this conversation of the men, but Robert's unexpected declaration drew the warning from her lips before she was aware of it.

'For heaven's sake, Joan, what are you talking about?' demanded Robert. 'We're dealing with men's lives here – the lives of their families, their women—'

'Whow – ee!' His mouth full of beer, Paul had taken a moment to react. Now his eyes widened in aggressive challenge as he turned to Robert. 'Watch it, Reverend, that's fighting talk round here. Your sainted predecessor, Holy Joe Patterson, he knew his place. The big bosses don't take too kindly to radical parsons. You'd better have a thought to that precious ecclesiastical career of yours before you plunge your lily-white hands into union politics!'

'Robert, think!' Joan could see which way things were

going, and the implications for Robert's future did not bear contemplation. She leaned forward urgently. 'Robert, there's no future in offending people! You know you've got it in you to do so much in the world – and you could do far more for the men – for everybody – from a really good position – Dean, say, or Bishop – than ever you could as just another local minister. And you don't want to stay here, stuck in Brightstone all your life, y'know you don't!'

Paul laughed sardonically. 'Well, well, well! Now it's all coming out! What d'you say to that, Reverend?'

'I know that you don't want me to stay here all my life, Joanie,' said Robert gently.

'So you shouldn't – so you mustn't take sides in this!' she concluded wildly. 'They're all at odds with each other – the town's split in two. What good do you think you can do?'

Robert drew a deep breath. 'It's not a question of taking sides, Joan. It's a question of showing everyone here that the church has a part to play – that I have a part to play – in what people call "real life", that my job here is not just a side show for Sundays!'

Paul laughed again in harsh amusement. 'This should be interesting! Glad I've got me a ringside seat! Look, Robert, you don't know what you're getting yourself into. Wilkes and the bosses used to have Calder, Ford and quite a few of the others in their pocket, and they paid them, paid them well, to keep the men quiet. But they can't keep the lid on it after this! Now they're going to have real trouble on their hands – and I'll be leading it, up to my neck in it, waving the flag all the way. You start sympathising with me, where d'you think that'll leave you?'

'Wilkes is your employer, Paul,' said Robert levelly. 'Not mine.'

'Oh yeah? How many bishops d'you think sit down to take their tucker with the miners? And how many get in the trough with mine-owners? Use you head, Reverend! And don't make pious noises for the sake of it!' He tossed back his head to throw down his beer in contemptuous dismissal of Robert's words.

'Pious noises!'

Robert was angry at last, Joan could see. Paul's barrage of insults had finally taken effect. Her gaze swung apprehensively between the two of them as Robert started to his feet. 'Robert . . .' she began with rising fear. 'Paul—'

The shrill voice of the phone seemed at first like another angry participant interrupting the argument. There was a long, painful pause. Then Robert grabbed the receiver.

'Who? Oh Molly – yes, hello. *What*?' He gripped the edge of the desk. 'Paul? Yes, yes, he's here. Look, hold on – we'll be there straight away.'

He put down the phone and looked at Paul like a man who has to impart the worst of news. 'Paul – I'm so sorry. It's your father . . . the doctor's on his way . . .'

Chapter 8

The small cortège wound its way slowly up the headland as George Everard made the journey to his final resting-place. In the leading car neither Molly Everard nor Paul shed a tear. Like so many widows who have lived out their husband's death a thousand times before the event, and found that there is only one thing worse than a death for which you have had no time to prepare, and that is the death you have already died. Molly had turned to granite. She sat between her children like a graven image, her bunched resignation and massive dignity expressing all the grief of all the women of the world.

Beside her, Paul was containing a fire of rage like nothing he had known in his life before. All his fury at the state of the mine, the cost of it in the lives of the men, of his mates, and now the death of a father whom he had never really expected to lose even through all these long years of slow decay – all this had conspired to put Paul in a strange and dangerous mood indeed. Only Claire, weeping silently but piteously in the corner of the huge black funeral car was giving way to anything like what Brightstonians would have regarded as 'normal' feelings.

As the hearse drew up at the gate of church, Robert was there to greet them. With a reverence towards the coffin, a formal gesture in which his own personal sense of George's loss could find only the hollowest expression, he bowed to the mourners and broke into the time-honoured words of the Service for the Burial of the Dead: 'I am the Resurrection and the Life, saith the Lord . . . We bring nothing into this world, and certain it is that we take nothing out . . .'

Slowly, like people moving in a dream, they entered the church and took their places one by one. Carefully the bearers laid the mahogany coffin on the trestles set ready to receive it before the high altar, and discreetly withdrew as Robert approached down the aisle with the words of the bidding prayer on his lips: 'Oh teach us to number our days, O Lord our God: for our most secret sins will surely see the light of thy countenance . . .'

The coffin lay before him laden with summer flowers, a heart-searing tribute to George's popularity and the love that had followed him all his life. Turning to face the congregation, Robert saw with a surge of excitement that for the first time since he had arrived at St Jude's, the church was packed. Behind the pitifully small family party in the first pew stretched a solid bank of men who, despite the good dark suits, the razor-sharp partings and impeccable grooming, were very obviously more accustomed to the filth and fury of the daily struggle underground than to occasions such as this. On the opposite side of the church he could see Wilkes and Mrs Wilkes, a body of what looked like mine management, and a number of families, evidently the Everard's neighbours from their forty years of married life in the same tightly knit community.

Robert's heart was aching. This was not his first funeral, that had come in his inner-city parish, where the old and the young, succumbing indiscriminately to age, disease or drugs, all seemed to die with unnatural frequency. Time had already taught him, too, that there are a thousand 'first' funerals in the life of a priest – the first time of burying a child, with the mother standing half demented with grief at the graveside; the first time of burying a young mother with her orphaned children's tear-stained faces mutely imploring him, 'Why, Father – why?' But this was the first time he had had to conduct the burial of someone who had been close to him – had been, too, even in the short time since their return to Brightstone, more of a father to him, he could not help feeling, than his own. He had prayed for the strength to get through it, and he made the same prayer again now.

> 'Abide with me, fast falls the eventide,
> The darkness deepens, Lord with me abide:
> When other helpers fail and comforts flee,
> Help of the helpless, Lord abide with me.'

The congregation were beginning the first hymn. 'A terrible, old-fashioned thing, Father, but he loved it,' Molly had said, 'and I reckon he's entitled to have what he likes this time anyway.' 'Of course he is, Molly,' Robert had said gently, though saddened and even estranged to find himself 'Father' now, and no longer simply 'Rob' as he had always been before, treated like Molly's second son.

It was almost time. Robert dropped to his knees and bowed his head in his hands. 'For you, George,' he whispered. 'This is for you.'

> 'Hold Thou the cross before my dying eyes:
> Shine through the gloom, and point me to the skies,
> Heaven's morning breaks, and earth's vain
>   shadows flee,
> In life, in death O Lord, abide with me.'

It was time. With a last prayer, Robert mounted the pulpit. From above he looked down at Claire in the front pew, trying to put all his love for her into one glance of sympathy, all his feeling for her grief, which had been very terrible. He opened his Bible, but did not need to read the words. Taking a deep breath, he began.

' "Blessed are they that mourn," the Bible tells us, "for they shall be comforted." In these words of God we find the clue to the life of George Everard, a man who was himself a comfort to all around him. I can remember when I was growing up in Brightstone the fascination I felt for the mine, how curious I was about the life of the men underground, and how impressed I was by the miners themselves: for the more I got to know about them, the more I respected their daily courage, their faith and their endurance. George was just one of many who spent their entire working lives so far from the sun and the precious light of day, so deep in the earth that they must sometimes see themselves more as denizens of that underworld than inhabitants of our own. They know darkness, they know hardships, and they know ever-present danger – danger like that we have just been all too painfully reminded of, in the near-disaster at the mine only last week.'

Wilkes stiffened. How had that come in? Surely the Reverend was not going to try to make political capital out of last week's cave-in? He'd seemed dependable enough. But you can be wrong about those intellectual types . . . too clever by half, some of them . . .

'The life of a miner, as you might imagine,' Robert was continuing, not unaware of the perturbation disturbing the peace of the mine boss in the pew below, 'is one to depress even the most cheerful spirit. But I have never in my life heard a miner complain. They are the pure breed of men who risk all, give all, and remain cheerful, even humorous, kind and dependable, all the days of their lives. Such a one was George Everard. George said to me once, "A bloke ought to give more to his life than his paid labour." And George lived by those words. He gave and gave.'

Wilkes relaxed. False alarm. What was politics to do with religion anyway? Let alone at the funeral of an old bloke who'd been retired for years. This young fella knew which side his bread was buttered on, if he could read him right. Going places, this one. Smart. Ambitious. Wouldn't want to foul his nest before he had any chance of leaving it!

On now about wife . . . family . . . all good stuff. Wilkes breathed deeply, and almost signed off. Suddenly he was wide awake again with a snap.

'But above all George gave to the job he loved, to the life he loved, to the men he loved, his fellow-miners. It is a tragic irony that the man who worked so hard to improve the lot of mining men should himself have succumbed to the tragic and quite avoidable disease known to us all as "miner's lung". George's death is a reminder to us all that there is still a long way to go before our mines are worthy of the men who work in them. No man must suffer disease and danger underground – no man must die – to serve the profit and convenience of those whose only idea of mining is to stay safely on the surface out of harm's way!'

In the family pew Paul was sitting bolt upright, eyeing Robert with passionate interest and a new, tough respect.

'This is the lesson of the Bible – the word of God. If Jesus taught us anything, it was that the defence of the Pharisees, the declaration that you can observe the letter of the law and not the spirit, will not pass muster in the eyes of the One above, He who sees all. For God sees all our sins, both of omission and commission, and sooner or later, He calls us to account. Those here today who are responsible for the lives and safety of the men in the Brightstone pit must examine their consciences, should ask themselves if they are ready to meet their own day of judgement, that great judgement that George is facing now, even as we must all – or if they should begin to set things in order before it is too late.

'The life of George Everard was dedicated to this end, and to no other. He fought for what was right, and his legacy will live on. Now his son Paul steps into his father's shoes in the post that as a young miner himself, so many years ago, George once held in his turn. Paul, I know, will work tirelessly to be worthy of his father's name. George, as you all know, was a modest man. But his one source of pride was the knowledge that Paul had taken up the position – the position and the struggle – that he himself had given his life to. I feel certain that Paul will be as successful and as respected in this important work as George was. In memory of George, we offer our support to his son. And what a fine legacy of George's life and work it would be if this could, please God, be the last untimely funeral of a Brightstone miner here in this church.'

To a deep, hushed silence he descended from the pulpit and bowed before the altar. 'Father, hear the words of our mouths and sanctify the thoughts of our hearts to Your eternal will and purpose . . .'

'O God our help in ages past,
Our hope for years to come,
Our shelter from the stormy blast,
And our eternal home . . .'

To the strains of the final processional hymn, six of the burliest miners moved forward, with Paul at their head. Carefully they shouldered the heavy coffin, and walking in slow time behind Robert, moved out towards the cemetery. Standing in the pew, head bowed to the final snatches of prayer floating back to him down the aisle, Wilkes ground his teeth with an almost audible fury.

'You know, O Lord, the secrets of our hearts . . . raise us from the death of sin that we might live . . .'

So that young fella thought he'd have a go at mine safety, did he? Wanted to mix it in union politics? Couldn't keep his brother-in-law's nose out of his own church business? We'll have to see about that, he promised himself vengefully. Whoever tries to fix me, gets fixed himself, m'lad. You're not going to last here, not now I know which side you're on. Well, well, he consoled himself as he struggled to regain a semblance of composure to make his exit, the morning's not been wasted. We've given old George a good send-off anyway. And sorted out the little matter of allegiances up at St Jude's. With a sense of Christian duty perfectly discharged, Wilkes jammed on his hat, gathered up Mrs Wilkes, and left.

On the steps of the church Robert had bidden a painful farewell to Molly and Claire, then turned back with Paul to the task of greeting and thanking all those who had come to pay their last respects. Paul had been the first to express his appreciation of what Robert had said and done for his father during the service. All he had said was 'Thanks, mate', the brief tribute accompanied by a truly bone-crunching handshake, but the depth of his gratitude was unmistakable.

Others were more forthcoming.

'Y'done him good, Reverend,' murmured one old-timer as he left.

'Yeah, that was the way he was all right, old George,' agreed his companion, a much younger man.

'Thank you.'

Robert could not pretend otherwise – he was deeply pleased and relieved. Every comment, even the simple aside, 'best funeral I ever been to', all showed Robert that his highest hopes had been fulfilled – that he had done justice to George in the way he had so hoped he might. Another handshake, and he murmured another thanks in return: 'Thank you for coming . . . so glad you thought so . . . thank you . . .'

Suddenly there was a change in the atmosphere, like an inexplicable drop in the temperature. Before him stood a mourner obviously intent on breaking the quiet flow. A big man, powerfully, even intimidatingly built and still burly though running now to seed, he had obviously been a champion miner in his day, Robert thought. But now he was somehow lacking in the upright carriage, the neat, tight, physical look that even the oldest of the working miners usually kept. Worse, there was something horrible about him, something repellent. Firmly Robert began to withdraw his hand from the newcomer's unwelcome and protracted grip – he felt instinctively that this man was his natural enemy, the enemy of everything that was good, kind or worth defending.

But the new arrival was not to be shaken off. 'Y'done old George proud, Reverend. Good on ya, that's what I say!' He grinned around him expansively, a knowing, head-on-the-side leer that emphasised his heavy, meaty jowls.

'You knew him then, Mr –?' queried Robert, trying to keep the cold edge of disdain out of his voice.

'Knew him?'

The other man's eyes widened in mock astonishment, and he swung a humorous punch at Robert's shoulder. It was all Robert could do not to floor him. 'Knew him? I should say so. Him and me, brothers, we were. So to speak,' he added judiciously. 'Down the mine for the best part of thirty-odd years side by side, we were.

'Course, we didn't always see eye to eye . . .'

A sick certainty began to gather somewhere around Robert's heart. What was it Paul had said . . . ? 'You were a colleague of George's then, Mr –? I'm sorry, I don't know your name.'

'Why should ya, Reverend? It's Calder, Jim Calder.' Rumbling with false laughter he looked behind him, and reached a long groping arm through the little cluster of people on his heels. 'And this here's my daughter – my only daughter – Ally. She was christened Alison, but everybody calls her Ally.'

She was before him again, dragged unceremoniously through the little press of people, yet strangely still and watchful, unruffled by the indignity of her companion and her surroundings, just as she had been in the milk bar. She lifted her head and pushed back the silver-blonde fall of bright hair with one hand. He saw the pale sweep of her neck, the curve of her small ear. Her eyes were – what colour? Or none – simply unfathomable. Her slender shapeliness seemed more tantalising, more pronounced. She stood before him like a young woman now, not like the child-waif he had taken her for. And she was even lovelier than he remembered.

'Was glad t'come here, as one of George's old pals, I was,' Calder was saying sententiously. 'Always turn out f'one of our own, us miners.'

'It was a lovely service.' She took his hand. 'Thank you.'

Her hand was warm, small, surprisingly hard. Her touch was electric. He did not want to let her go. 'Thank you, Miss Calder,' he said softly.

Calder snorted. 'No need for that, Reverend! Don't want to give her ideas, get her above herself, do ya? Just you call her Ally, like everyone else.'

'Ally? Is that what you like to be called?' he asked in a low voice.

'I told ya, Ally's her name, Reverend! Tell'm, Ally!'

She threw him one quivering glance, then dropped her eyes. 'Everyone calls me Ally,' she returned in a meaningless monotone.

'Yeah, Ally,' mouthed her brute of a father, his good

humour instantly restored by her submission. 'M'daughter Ally. And more to me'n a daughter, Reverend. Been on our own, Ally and me, ever since m'wife left us, eight or more years ago.' A twist of still-vengeful memory distorted his features. 'I ask you, Reverend, what kind of woman would leave a little girl – her only child?'

And what kind of a woman would stay with a man like you? Robert wondered in disgust. Aloud he said quietly, 'I can't imagine, Mr Calder. Now if you'll excuse me—' He waved a hand at the press of people waiting to say goodbye.

Calder grinned. 'Righto, then, we'll be on our way. See y'round, Reverend.'

'I hope I see you – and Miss Calder – here in church as soon as possible,' said Robert firmly. He knew now that he would see her again, and the sooner the better. But he knew, too, that she had heard what he said, and his heart soared as he saw her nod ever so faintly before obediently following her father out of church.

The awe and sadness natural to men in the face of death is nearly always followed by a renewal of the spirit of life. Nowhere is this more so than in the veins of men who already live their lives strongly, fiercely even, jousting with death every day of their working lives. The crowd of miners gathered together for the wake of George Everard that night at Brightstone's one and only pub was not disposed to be restrained. Nor was there any reason, in the minds of any man there, to hold back on the liquor. A wake was a wake, a send-off was a send-off, and old George was going to have the bloody best of bloody both!

At the centre of a group of the older miners, leaning against the bar which by this stage was doing more to hold him up than his own legs could manage, Paul was holding forth. 'So the boss says to him – the boss then, before the days of that bastard Wilkes, this was "I'm not disposed to listen to proposals from you or the men, Mr Everard" – and quick as a flash, m'dad comes back to him, deadpan-like, "That's all right, Mr Ferris, sir – I wasn't proposing to you!" '

The gale of approving laughter found no echo in another corner of the bar, where Jim Calder, in the company of his inseparable side-kick Mick Ford, had drunk himself through the thin surface of his normal pretence of *bonhomie*, and was spoiling for a fight. Rising to his feet, he swaggered drunkenly towards the group around Paul.

'He was a beaut bloke, your old man – beaut, he was,' he informed Paul aggressively. 'An' I'll buy y'a a drink on the strength of that!'

Owlishly Paul surveyed him. 'I must be drunk,' he enlarged to the laughing group around him. 'I thought I heard Jim Calder offer to buy me a drink!'

'I did an'all,' growled Calder, furious at being made a laughing-stock. 'Set 'em up, Faye!' he shouted to the barmaid. 'This young fella and I's gonna have a lesson in union rules.'

Paul's eyes narrowed. 'I'm not only drunk, I'm hallucinating!' he roared. 'Jim Calder's going to teach *me* about union rules?' Contemptuously he turned his back on the older man. 'Go piss in y'hat, Calder. Y'couldn't teach a fart t'find its way out of a colander! Get lost! Y'not welcome here. Go home.'

'Now you listen here, sonny, and listen good.' Calder was breathing heavily now. 'You think you're so bloody good – why, y'just a rank amateur, flexing your muscles! Just try your theory about closing the pit for safety measures on the men, let alone the management! How many buddy-buddies d'you think y'll have then?' He paused, sweating heavily, then moved in for the kill. 'They're all just wasting their time with you, anyway. Y're just a stupid kid. Y'know nothing, you aint nothing, an' you'll never amount to nothing! You'll never be half the man or half the miner your father was, if y'live t'be a hundred!'

There was no doubt in the general opinion of Brightstone's mining community where the honours lay at the end of the ensuing brawl. Paul had in fact only unleashed one punch in the direction of Calder before reminding himself, and being forcibly reminded as he was held down by others, that it was hardly a fair fight when his opponent was old enough to be his father and drunk as a skunk besides. But it was a hammer-blow, straight to the side of the head, and when Calder came to every morning for the next fortnight, he awoke to the daily reminder of his humiliation and defeat, an offence to his manhood and status he was not inclined to forget.

Chapter 9

Robert often felt that he loved the church in the aftermath of a service almost more than during the service itself. When the last members of the congregation had all departed, when the last notes had been wrung from the very bottom of the bellows of the old organ or the often equally old throats of the warbling worshippers, when the last prayers had been whispered, the last remembrances made, the last 'amen' breathed, then both church and priest could be briefly at peace, a luxury almost never to be enjoyed at any other point of a working week that unlike others, never permitted the uninterrupted prospect of a real day off.

Yet this Sunday, as he had to admit to himself, the usual sense of peace and release was not forthcoming. Moving among the pews, collecting hymn-books and restoring hassocks to their proper places under the pews in front, he had to confess to a restlessness, a feeling of being on edge, that had dogged him now for – how long? Oh, days – weeks. And it was worse this Sunday, after the service, when he had to accept that the hopes he had been building through the week were once again to be dashed.

For the girl had not come. She would not come, he was beginning to think: she had never intended to come. Twice now he had issued an invitation to her to come to church, and she had, so he thought, nodded her agreement. Every Sunday so far he had been living by the promise – or was it just the hope? – or seeing her again in church. And yet she had not come.

God, it was hot! And it was not yet midday: it was going to be as hot as hell before the day was over.

Finishing his tasks, he locked up the church and instinctively turned right to seek the cooler air of the headland, instead of left back to the Rectory. He needed to think. Why had he been wanting to see Ally Calder again? Why was she so much in his thoughts?

Something about her bothered him, that much was clear. He tried to track it through. She was out of place in the job she was doing, anyone could see that – a girl like her could not possibly be happy working in Vic's café. It was equally clear that she had no one to help and guide her. From all accounts, in fact, that father of hers was not only useless but worse than useless – a selfish brute who cared for nothing except himself, and would not scruple to force anything on his daughter that suited his own purposes. She needed help, that was indisputable. And helping people was his job – his reason for being here.

Yet that was not all. He trudged along, his mind working so furiously that he was oblivious where his feet were taking him. The sun beat down on his back with lascivious abandon, and the warm air off the sea, sharpened with its eternal tang, flirted with his senses. Why did he feel more aware, more intensely alive, more himself – and yes, there was no denying it, simply *happier* – when he thought of her?

He could not explain it. It was like nothing else he had ever experienced in the whole of his life. That in itself was unusual, he knew. And was it a warning, an indication that he should tread carefully? More carefully? Claire, always cautious, would certainly say so, he knew that too. Claire . . . Sunday lunch! He would be late! Recalled to reality by this random association of thoughts, he stopped in his tracks, turned at once and began to hurry home.

'How's the chicken?'

'Almost ready. When are they due?'

'Not till one. It's good of you to do all this, Joanie – you know I didn't want Mum to be on her own today of all days.'

In the Rectory kitchen Joan and Claire, having

108

hurried away as always as soon as the service was over, were almost done with their preparations for Sunday lunch. With Paul and Molly due to join them in unspoken recognition of the fact that a month to the day had elapsed since George's death, and Claire did not want her mother to be on her own, there was a great deal to do. They worked as they talked, in the harmony that two women who know and respect each others' methods can so easily develop in a working partnership.

What Joan had just heard, however, had provoked some interruption in her steady rhythm as she chopped the beans.

'But are you sure you want a stranger in the house – what did you say – for two or three days a week?'

'Well, it's not a complete stranger,' Claire returned vaguely, her mind on the dessert she was trying to conjure up in rather too short a time. 'And as Robert and I are both in and out, it's not as if we'll notice very much, really. Could even be useful to have someone here to answer the phone during the day.'

'Strangers in the house soon get to know all y'business,' muttered Joan, chopping furiously. She did not know why this news disturbed her so much. She only knew that she did not like the sound of it.

'What business?' Claire gave a laugh that fell somewhere between the wistful and the sardonic. 'A minister's public property, you know that from your father. I'm beginning to realise how little I can expect to have my husband to myself. And we've no secrets – from each other or from anyone else, Robert and I. There's nothing to know.'

'Still . . .' Joan was not appeased. 'They're not a very good family, y'know. The mother was a – oh, a chorus girl or something.'

'A *chorus-girl*? In Brightstone?' Claire's laugh was genuine this time.

'She was touring – with a troupe,' said Joan defensively. 'Just passing through. Met a few blokes here, decided to stop. Couldn't stand it in the end, though. Missed all her rackety old ways and bohemian-type

109

friends. Ran off again and left them soon after. And the *father—*'

'Yes, I know. I heard all about him from Paul. We wouldn't have to have anything to do with him. It's just to have an extra pair of hands up here to help Robert with all the work for the Centenary. You know how much the Church Council wants us to organise – a fête, a big display in the Library, history of Brightstone and all that – and we've been so busy settling in, we've made no progress on it at all. I know I've been much less of a help to Robert than I meant to be. And if the baby comes along, I'll be doing even less.'

With a little lurch Joan realised that Claire had taken now to saying 'if the baby comes along', instead of 'when'. How long had that been going on, she wondered? It had crept up so quietly, she couldn't remember. She stole a look at Claire. She was paler, yes, and thinner, but that had come with George's death; it was only natural. There was something else, though – a new hardness round the corners of the mouth, corners that were tending to turn down these days as a matter of habit, instead of up as they always used to.

Poor Claire! A rush of pity and love swept over Joan and she clenched her whole body in the effort to resist it. No good getting sentimental, after all. And the baby was Claire's business, hers and Robert's – it would never do to pry. It would have killed Joan to have to ask Claire any question about the apparent failure to have a baby, in order to be able to show her sympathy and understanding. But by the same token, it almost killed her not to.

'How is Paul?' she tried instead, though realising too late even as she did so that in terms of all the feelings she could not discuss, it was out of the frying pan into the fire.

'Paul? Oh, he's fine. Taking his union stuff very seriously – he'll probably bore us all to tears with it all through lunch.'

'It doesn't bore Robert,' observed Joan, whose jealous love missed nothing.

'They can talk to each other, then,' said Claire listlessly. 'Here they are now, all arriving together. I only hope with Paul here, we've got enough food to give him.'

Nobody who opened a milk bar in a town like Brightstone reckoned to make a fortune, Vic knew, least of all on a Monday at the end of a long, hot summer. But the guy sitting at the end of the bar had made one milk sundae last for best part of an hour, and had shown no inclination either to finish it up, or to order another one. Good job he was clearing out now, with the girl. He'd tell her tomorrow: no boyfriends! Not unless they were going to bring a whole gang of her admirers and drink him out of every pint of milk in the place.

'Y'ready! Thank God for that!'

Wearily Paul uncoiled his muscular limbs from the pathetically inadequate little plastic chair he had been balancing on, and grabbed Ally's bag. Together they walked outside where the 'Blue Streak', as Paul proudly called the Dodge, waited for them in the last warmth of the afternoon sun. Paul could hardly wait to engage gear and roar away from the precincts of Vic's.

'God, I hate milk! Bloody girls' drink! Why can't he sell beer, like any other decent bloke?'

She smiled, a cynical smile, accompanied by a tantalising look. 'So why d'you come?'

He dropped his voice and threw her a look. 'Why d'you think?'

She gave him a swift, flirtatious half-glance, then turned her head away. She'd have to get out of the car if he was going to be boring, and she didn't want to do that – not with another huge bag of shopping, and the long walk home all the way uphill not getting any shorter, or the days any cooler. She brushed the moment aside.

'I've got that thing I was on about, that job, did I tell you? The one you put me in for?'

'Yeah, I heard.'

'It'll be a real new start,' she enthused. 'Better'n the Paragon, any day of the week. Vic thinks it's a real laugh. He says I won't stick it for more'n a week. I will, though. I really need the money. And I'm ready to work for it, you'll see.' She paused, then set off on another tack. 'Paul – you know the new minister – Mr Maitland?'

Paul swerved expertly between two much slower cars. 'Yeah, what about him?'

'Oh, nothing.'

She fell silent again. What was bothering her now?

'New job, eh?' he enthused. 'Told you you'd get your chance! You'll make a success of it, Ally, I know you will. And you'll be worth every penny of it to them.'

'I know.' There was a curious shine in her eyes that made him uneasy.

'Huh! Getting keen on yourself now!'

She did not rise to the bait. 'I know I can be good at something,' she said slowly, frowning as if trying to make sense of what she was saying. 'I don't think this'll be it – because I know it won't be here. But I know I can do something – and I'll do it one day soon. You'll see.'

He felt, painfully, that he probably would. 'But it won't be here?' he echoed.

'Brightstone's nothing,' she repeated. 'It's just a mining town.'

'Full of miners?' said Paul bitterly. He had never imagined for a second that he could ever be made to feel ashamed of what he did – and by a young girl, hardly more than a kid, who had done nothing at all with her own life yet! But perhaps that was why her strictures hurt so much – she saw and spoke with the casual cruelty of a child – and maybe she spoke the truth. 'So you can't wait to shake the dust of Brightstone off your feet, is that it? Get away from it' – he nearly said 'us' – 'all?'

'That's it,' she agreed simply.

Angrily he revved the engine, crashing the car up through the gears and accelerating wildly round corners. She glanced at him. 'Oh, Paul,' she said provokingly, 'just because I don't like living in a mining town doesn't mean I hate miners.'

Moodily he shook his head. 'I know you've got your reasons for wanting to get away, Ally, and I've got to say that they're pretty good ones too – one bloody good one that's bigger'n all the rest anyway! But setting your dad aside – if you can – Brightstone's not such a bad place – there's a lot of good people round here, if you can take the trouble to find them.'

She nodded impatiently, 'I know that. Don't preach to me, Paul.'

He was angered again by her dismissive tone. 'What have I got to do to get it through to you, Ally?' he ground out. In a rage he threw the car to a full stop against the kerb, and turned to face her full on. 'You're just ready to rubbish the whole town because of your stupid dad! Well, he's not the only man in this town! There's others here—' He wanted to say, 'who love you, care for you, want you.' But he pulled back – he could not say it. Despite his almost legendary success with women, Paul had never, in one sense, made love before now. He had never had to 'be nice', as he saw it, to attract women, of 'sweet-talk' them. Hearing the call of his unselfconscious animal sexuality, feeling the lure of all that he represented, they came to him these days like birds to a feeding-table, without any effort on his part. So he had taken his pleasures carelessly, selfishly even, as and when he wanted, without commitment and without guilt. He had never pleaded with a woman in his life before – he had never had to. He had never even really talked to a woman before – his idea of an opening gambit was a hand on the knee, or the casual unbuttoning of the front of a dress. Now he realised in one of those moments of revelation after which nothing can ever be the same again, that he had never been truly, hopelessly, devotedly in love – until this moment. And he didn't know the words, or how to say them. At last, still conscious of the unfinished sentence hanging like a sword between them, he compromised in confusion, petering out lamely on 'people – who'd miss you if you left.'

She gave a sideways flick of her almond-cornered eyes, but nothing more in the way of encouragement. 'And I'd miss you, Paul. And lots of other people here, if it comes to that. Now will you get me home? Or I'll be missed there a lot sooner – and have a lot more explaining to do, too – than you've got the faintest idea about, no matter what you say.'

Wretchedly he started the car again and drove away in silence. As the distinctive blue Dodge passed uphill through the main street of Brightstone, neither passenger noticed that as they passed the library, Joan Maitland was just emerging half-hidden behind a huge pile of heavy volumes devoted to the history of the town which she had tracked down for the Centenary preparations; or that at the end of his leisurely afternoon's drinking while watching the world go by outside the town pub, Mick Ford was able to return to his meagre bachelor pad with a piece of information good enough to invite himself round to Jim Calder's for supper on the strength of it.

It had been a whole night of loving, a night of sensuous abandon and deep, deep need. And still he was not sated, not tired of the body so close to his in the wide, welcoming bed, nor weary at all in his own. And he wanted her again, he was ready again. It's a miracle, he thought as he felt his sex stirring lazily but purposefully under the soft ministrations of a small but determined hand. For she wanted him too, so much, he had never dreamed how much. Her appetite, her longing, her love, matched his step for step, move for move, and she would not be denied. It is a miracle, he thought.

Tenderly she ran a hand through his hair, stroking his temple, the angle of his chin, the soft hollow at the base of his neck. Reaching his shoulder, she began to circle the muscles up his upper arm and chest in slow, sensuous sweeps, relaxing and tormenting him at the same time. In the thick darkness he felt blind, helpless, like a new-born child, but his body responded to her like a man. He felt her above him, showering his face with a rain of butterfly kisses as her hand circled down and down, caressing his hard, flat belly and the smooth bony joints of his hips. Half groaning, half laughing with delight, he disciplined himself to endure the exquisite teasing hand, abandoning himself to the skill and sureness of her control.

Finally she satisfied herself that the moment she sought had come. Rearing up, she straddled his prostrate form, gripping him with her warm soft thighs. With careful assurance she readied him, then slowly, deliberately, she lowered herself on to him, laughing softly in her throat as she did so. He fought back a cry of joy, the sensation was so wonderful, better than anything he had known in his life, or could have dreamed of.

Dark, dark, all dark . . . the little hands were on his chest now, the thumbs and forefingers playing with his nipples, sending wave after sensuous wave through his whole frame. He could feel his pleasure mounting, accelerating out of control. Reaching up his hands found her breasts with all the joy of age-old recognition, yet with a strange shock of unfamiliarity – small, round, the nipples delicate and tipped like spring buds, they did not have the well-known weight and fullness in his hands. Wonderingly he explored the satin skin, the tender aureole, the sweet, tiny tip budding to his touch. She called again from the back of her throat, a sound he did not know. Dark . . . so dark . . . if only he could see . . .

The pace was rising now, he could hold it no longer. Grasping her firmly, he half rose on the bed, and flipped her over on to her back, easily overmastering her resistance. Greedily, hungrily, he drove into her, and laughing, crying, gasping, came in an explosion of need and joy. As he did so, the sun rose, and the room began to fill with light. Looking down, he saw a slender, golden-brown body and tangled mass of fair hair. Trembling, he brushed it aside, and found himself looking not at Claire, but straight into the face of a stranger.

Shivering, drenched with sweat, Robert awoke with a violent start. It was all he could do not to cry out. To dream of sex – and sex with a stranger, a perfect stranger! He fought to still his wildly beating heart and calm his shattered nerves.

One thing was true – the dawn was breaking. One by one the fingers of dark amber light stole into the bedroom until the whole room was bathed in gold. His pulse still racing, he struggled to orient himself. Beside him lay the huddled mound that was undoubtedly Claire, her dark curls barely showing above the sheet, her whole body curled up like a little furry burrowing thing. How could he have been unfaithful to her, even in a nightmare?

And yet . . . and yet . . . Was it a nightmare? He could not remember anything horrible in the dream, nothing frightening or even unwelcome. And it did not have the acid test of the nightmare – he knew, even before he acknowledged it to himself, that throughout the whole course of this dream, he had not once wanted to wake up . . .

Shuddering, he tried to pull himself together. What day was it? Tuesday? Tuesday always meant the return to what he thought of as 'serious work', after the semi-relaxation he tried to allow himself on Monday. After that first – and it had to be admitted last – glorious day on the beach with Paul, Joan and Claire, Robert had conscientiously tried to apply the lesson he had learned then, promising himself that he would never again so immerse himself in his work that he was denying the legitimate health and pleasure of bodily exercise. So he had adopted the habit, whenever he could, of taking long lone walks along the cliffs or over the rocks on any Monday when he could spare the time; to recharge the batteries, as he saw it, for another strenuous week.

The second day of the week, though, saw him ready for action again, all the keener for his short break. This week, he had resolved, he really would get down to making plans and arrangements for the great forthcoming event of the Brightstone Centenary. Already the townspeople were beginning to talk of it with great excitement. But in reality nothing had yet been fixed or even agreed, and Robert knew that only getting down to it would remove the faint but growing feeling of guilt he was beginning to experience every time anyone even mentioned the word.

Today it was, then. He had communicated his resolution to Claire and she had readily agreed, promising with some excitement, he thought, that she would have everything ready for him that morning. Claire! His heart contracted with the shock he had felt before – how could he have so betrayed her, even in his mind?

How, how, how? he demanded of himself in merciless interrogation. How, and why? Of course it was only a dream. But our dreams are messengers, he knew that, sent to tell us something we are unwilling to see. He'd dreamed of a girl? What girl? He did not know any girls!

Except one. Could it be – surely not – the girl from the café, Ally Calder? No, surely not! He did not think of her – in that way. His mind flinched away from it, it was too horrible. A young girl, so young – and one of his parishioners besides – even if he had not been a married man – and a priest . . .

He had been thinking of her too much, that was all. Busy, overstrained, burdened by George's death and the problems of the mine, he had allowed her to prey on his mind. Well, no more! His mind reverted to his earlier notion – this was a warning, clearly a warning, that in his mind, if nothing else, things were getting out of control. He could not allow this girl, this one person among all those he had a duty to care for, to overbalance his mind, his life, his judgement, his control, his dignity and even decency like this. He would not see her any more – he would not seek her out – he would avoid all occasions when he might bump into her. Clearly she was not to blame. Nor did he really believe that he had either consciously or unconsciously done anything wrong. But a responsible man – and a man of God – took care, of other people and of himself. Time to take care – to take great care.

Slipping out of bed in the dawn light, he showered vigorously, his resolution confirmed with every moment. Making a light breakfast, he spent some time on the preliminary planning for the Centenary, then slipped across to the church. There in a long session of prayer and meditation, he laid everything before God and struggled to clear his heart and mind of the cloud that had come upon him so darkly and unexpectedly in the still of the night.

At last he made his peace. Rising from his feet he felt refreshed and renewed, and above all re-confirmed in his decision to avoid the girl entirely, to put temptation – if temptation it was – entirely and completely behind him. Feeling clear, bright and strong, he turned his mind happily to the day ahead. Returning to the Rectory in the wake of the postman, he picked up the letters from where they lay on the old oak table beside the door, and made his way in the direction of the study.

'Claire!' he called as he went. 'Claire! Are you ready? I'd like to begin on the Centenary work now.'

He stood in the hallway, uncertain of where she was. 'I'm in here.'

Her voice was coming from the dining-room across the hall at the back of the house. He opened the door and went in. Claire was standing in front of the old mahogany dining-table which, big as it was, was already groaning under the weight of all the ancient volumes of local history, books, letters and files of papers for the Centenary celebrations. Her smile was innocently mischievous, and her whole air was that of someone who has contrived a delightful surprise.

'Robert,' she began, looking at him quizzically, 'You know I've been thinking that we couldn't manage all the work for the Centenary in time, all by ourselves. And I was worried that if we didn't do something, we might let everybody down, when they've been counting on us. Well, I asked Paul if he had any ideas, and he's come up with something – someone – someone I'm sure you'll think is a good idea. He's fixed us up a co-worker. Another pair of hands.' She laughed. 'Attached, of course, to a very nice young person.'

She stepped aside. Behind her at the table sat the girl. She had apparently been looking at a book and taking notes, and from the small pile of papers beside her she had already begun to make an impact on what she was supposed to be doing. She looked perfectly calm, perfectly self-possessed, perfectly . . .

'Robert dear, this is Ally, Ally Calder. Her father used to be a miner with Dad, she says. She's been looking for secretarial work in Brightstone, but there's hardly anything going and her father thinks she's a bit young yet to leave home and strike out for herself.'

The girl got to her feet. She came towards him, holding out her hand, smiling, as it seemed, right into his eyes. 'Hello – Reverend,' she said.

'Oh, Robert – you must call him Robert!' said Claire enthusiastically. 'Everybody else does. He likes it, too, don't you, Robert? He thinks "Reverend" is a bit too stuffy for him – and too old!' Claire laughed happily.

In the early morning heat her face, her arms, seemed to glow. She was wearing a light cotton slip of a dress, pink like her lips, like the soft hollows inside her smoothly rounded arms. He could smell her young, fresh scent, the scent of summer flowers, pink like her . . .

Numbly he extended his hand. 'Glad you could join us, Miss—' he saw Claire's face and hers at the same moment '—Ally. We really need someone to help us out here with all – this. I hope you'll enjoy the work, and being with us. I'm – glad you could come.'

'That's all settled then,' said Claire with evident delight at the success of her little surprise. 'Why don't I go and make us all a cup of coffee while you two get to know each other? I told you, Ally. I told you Robert would be pleased to have you here. He's so glad you've come – aren't you, dear?'

'Oh, yes.'

So glad you've come.

Glad . . . glad . . . glad . . . you've come . . . at last.

Chapter 10

'He loves you, yeah, yeah yeah . . .'

'Yeah, yeah, yeah, yeah . . .' she sang. The simple words and phrases wove themselves in and out of her head, and into the rhythm of her work. 'With a love like that, y'know you should be true . . .' She paused, her light voice reaching for the climax: 'Yeah, yeah, yeah, yeaaaahhhh . . .'

They were a bit old now, the Beatles, but they knew what they were on about all right. Totally secure in the comfort of her own room, Ally Calder busily folded away all her clean underwear from the ironing she'd just completed, while bopping away in time to the music to her heart's content. If only they'd come to Australia, the Beatles! Or what if she could go to England? That wasn't so daft, lots of people did. And that's where it all was. Her soft, peony mouth hardened, and the song died away in her throat. Anywhere was where it was in comparison with Brightstone!

Brightstone. She could hardly breathe the name, even in her secret thoughts. What a hole – what a fucking hole. She knew her father would kill her if he even thought she knew that word. But she'd heard him say it often enough with his drunken cronies when he thought she was asleep. Asleep? How could even a deaf girl sleep when he had one of his horrible boozy evenings, the racket him and Mick Ford and those other creeps – what does he call them, can't even remember their horrible names – make when they get a few tins inside them. Asleep?

Sometimes she thought she'd been asleep all her life, like the Sleeping Beauty. Not any more, though. She was on her way.

'She's got a ticket to ride . . .' sang John Lennon.

She'd got a ticket to ride all right. Single ticket, one way, no messing. She wasn't going to finish up like Barbara, two kids before she was twenty, and another on the way. 'He won't use anything,' Barbara had said, in a hopeless way that made her want to scream. 'He says it spoils his pleasure'. *His* pleasure? Since when was a girl like Barbara put on the earth for *his pleasure?*

Men – they were all such pillocks. That was another word her father didn't know she knew, and never would know she'd learned from him. Pillocks. That's what they were. She turned the word over in her mind, savouring the weight and the feel and the taste of it. Especially him. Pillock number one. Pillock-in-chief. Captain Pillock. She laughed, but the laugh was older than her years. Thank you, Dad. Thank you, God, for giving me such a pillock for a father.

Be fair, though. They weren't all like Dad. *He* wasn't. He was different. He wasn't like anything . . . anyone . . .

He was . . . what? Her hands suddenly still among the wisps of nylon and lace, she smiled her oddly calculating smile, then lapsed into a happy memory of the day she had just spent. He was more than all right, just for starters. He was a real looker, hunky but not beefy like Paul – more smooth, more film-starry. Great body, not that he seemed to know it – eyes, hands, that hair, that way he had of looking right into you – oh yes, he was really something, something special. She felt something growing, something stirring, deep inside her, a warmth spreading from her deepest core. Oh yes. Yes.

And he wasn't a pillock. Not in any way. He was so considerate: 'Are you sure you're not tired, Ally? You've done so much today.' He was so appreciative: 'This really is tremendous, just what we need, it's marvellous to see the programme taking shape like this.' He

122

was so courteous: 'please excuse me, I just have to make a very quick phone call, and I'll be with you again.' He was so . . . He was so . . .

He was so everything she'd never been accustomed to, never even dreamed existed, or could exist. And his eyes – the way he always seemed to be listening to you, whatever you said. Even if it wasn't great at all he made it seem so, the serious way he took it up. 'That's a good point, Ally,' he'd say, as if you'd just said something really clever. Mind you, that wasn't hard. Not much competition up at the Rectory in the cleverness stakes. His wife, Claire, she was nice, but she wasn't really on the ball, and she obviously had a hundred other things on her mind. And his sister Joan – she laughed softly to herself. Silly old bag! Thought she was so terrific! Watching everyone like a hawk and no idea of how daft she looked herself!

With an unconscious, resentful twitch of her shoulders she brought herself back to reality. Come on, Ally. Get this washing put away, then see to those sheets on the line, then the dinner. Then with a bit of luck, she'd be free to get back in here, play a bit more music, dream a few more dreams, do her weekly sums – Brightstone Escape Fund, current balance of – not that she didn't know it by heart, but it was great to see it slowly building up, and then . . . and then . . .

'Ally? *ALLY*!'

She hadn't heard him coming like she usually did. She flew to the window and looked out. From her corner room on the ground floor of the bungalow she could see the front door and her father just letting himself in. Behind him was Mick Ford, his offsider from the mine. Mick Ford! That slimy creep! She'd give anything – anything – to get away from this. And after a lovely day like today . . . to come back to this . . . It wasn't fair. It just wasn't fair.

'Ally! Blast ya, girl, where are ya?'

'She's maybe out, Jim. Young girls, they like to be out and about.'

'Out? Our Ally? Not without me knowing where's she's out, y'can take that from me, I'm telling ya.'

'Y'can't keep a young girl in all hours, now can ya?'

'She's here, I tell ya. Ally! *ALLY!*'

A thunderous lurch against her door, and her father was there, in her room, without knocking. 'What d'y'want?' she demanded, her back against the wall.

'What do I want?'

He was drunk to the gills, he always drank more in the hot weather, and still he didn't seem to think he'd had enough, for a six-pack dangled now from each meaty hand by way of evening reinforcements. Still, at least he couldn't hit her with his hands full. Unless he took a swing at her with the beer . . .

'I'm coming, Dad. Y'dinner's on the way.'

Dropping her eyes, she slipped past him as fast as she could into the hallway.

'Hello, Ally! *Wey-hey-heyyy!*' Mick Ford might have been greeting Marilyn Monroe. 'Whoo-ee! Y'looking good, girlie! Are you ever lookin' good! What a girl! Where y'been? I come here night after night hopin' t'see ya, an' all I get's y'old man here f'company.'

He was uncomfortably close, and she could smell the sweat of his heavy body. As he blocked her way to the kitchen, her father came up behind.

'Mick's been looking f'ya, Ally,' he announced portentously. 'Where y'been?'

Casually she flattened herself against the wall and started to inch past him towards the kitchen. 'You know where I've been. Up at St Jude's. Working on the Centenary celebrations with Mrs and Miss Maitland.'

'How y'doing up there, then Ally?' grinned Mick fatuously. 'All right? Y'doin' all right?'

''Course she's doin' all right! What y'on about, all right?'

They were both completely drunk. Well, what else would they be? She looked away. 'Yes, fine, thanks.' What a stupid conversation – an apology for a conversation – after what she'd had this afternoon – long talks, someone who listened to you, who actually cared about what you said . . .

'Why didn't y' tell me where y'was?' insisted Jim. 'I can't be expected to remember all y'comings and goings.

Y' should've left a note. I'm still y'father. I'm entitled t'know what y'doing.'

With one clean move she make it round the corner of the hall into the kitchen. 'Just getting the dinner, Dad, OK?' Swiftly she threw open the back door, and started getting pots out of the cupboard and banging them about.

'Hey, Ally!'

It was her father again. She closed her eyes.

'What?'

'Come out here when Mick's wanting t'talk t'ya!'

She threw some pasta into a pan and ran some water over it, lighting the gas with her other hand. 'Busy in here, Dad. Can't talk while I'm cooking.'

Mick Ford was at the kitchen door, his hot eyes fastened on her, his brown slug of a tongue crawling round his lips. Throwing back the pale fronds of hair over her face with one impatient hand, she turned her back on him and ignored him.

'Mmm, food! Y'sure know how t'look after a man, Ally.'

Ostentatiously she busied herself with grabbing tins from the cupboard, assembling different items and sorting the utensils for the meal.

'I come round t'see if y'want t'go up t'the pub with us after. Few of the lads getting drinks in tonight. Young Garry – y'know Gazza, big lad, one shoulder higher than the other – he's gettin' married t'morrow, so there'll be a few bevvies goin' down tonight.'

She looked at him. His little eyes were gleaming. She knew without even having to think about it what the evening's entertainment would be like.

'No thanks. I'm not much of a drinker.'

'So they're all piss-artists up at the pub, is that it?'

Jim had deposited his six-packs and followed the sound of the conversation into the kitchen, where it immediately became apparent that he was in a less than sociable mood.

'I didn't say that, Dad. I just don't want to go up to the pub, that's all. Prefer my own company.'

She concentrated on the pasta on the stove, praying

they'd go away. In the tiny kitchen she was trapped again, though the open door at least did something to alleviate the stale, sick smell of the beer on the pair of them. But the summer was almost gone – there was a chill in the air already – and then the Centenary celebrations would be over and she'd have no more job at the Rectory, and no reason to go up there – then she'd really be trapped . . . trapped . . .

'Too good f'miners, are ya?'

'Steady on, Jim, she didn't say that.' She could feel him, smell him, coming up close behind her. 'Got nothing against miners, have ya, Ally?'

As his hands snaked down across her hips, she rounded on him, the ladle from the pasta she was stirring leaving an arc of boiling drips across his shirt front. 'You want this in your face?' she hissed.

He pulled back, angry but afraid. 'Aw, be nice t'a fella, Ally!'

A stinging cuff caught the side of her head and sent her reeling. 'You watch y'mouth when y'talk to any friend of mine!' shouted her father, his face bulging with fury. 'Y'got t'learn a bit of respect, miss, f'the visitors t'this house, or I won't be bringing any more home t'keep y'company in a big hurry!' Another swinging blow caught her other ear. 'I c'n see I'm going t'have t'learn ya the hard way, just like I had t'learn y'bloody mother.' Snorting heavily, he rolled his shoulders like a boxer readying himself for the next round.

'Hey, come on, Jim.'

Mick was not quite so drunk as he looked. 'Tell y'what, let's go'n sit out the back while Ally finishes her cookin'. Y'never told me yet what happened when y'saw Wilkes today.' Grabbing the older man by the arm, he steered him through the back door out into the yard beyond, bestowing a wink on Ally as he went. 'Be all right if I stay f'tea then, Ally, OK?'

In the Rectory kitchen the uneasy silence between the two women clearing away and washing up after breakfast was the very opposite of their normally peaceable working mood. Joan's anxiety betrayed itself in the knotted knuckles of the hands furiously scrubbing down an already clean cooker, while Claire's expression had lapsed again into the reserve that was becoming more and more characteristic of her once-lively face. Determindly Joan returned to the fray.

'I just don't like it, that's all.'

'But you can't tell me anything you've got against her,' said Claire wearily.

Joan bit her lip. It was perfectly true. She could not tell Claire, could not even begin to hint to her, any one of the thousand things that were making her feel so resentful and uneasy. So she'd seen Paul driving Ally Calder in his car? He might have been just giving her a lift out of sheer neighbourliness. And how could she tell Claire that she instinctively scented Ally as a potential rival, when she had no claim on Paul in the first place, when he had never yet, despite her best efforts, taken the slightest interest in her in that way. She could have cried with frustration.

Doggedly Claire pushed on. 'And you don't seem to give her credit for what she can do, Joan. You know she's taught herself practically everything she knows – to cook and to sew; she made that pretty dress she was wearing yesterday, all by herself, I found out. She's very capable. About the only thing she doesn't know is how to drive. I said I'd see if I could get Robert to teach her. Or Paul.'

Robert. Or Paul. Alarm bells that had been buzzing in the back of Joan's mind ever since she had heard of Claire's plan to bring Ally Calder into the family circle rose to a screaming crescendo. 'Teach her to drive?' She tried to keep her voice calm. 'I don't know that that's such a good idea.' She attempted a laugh. 'You know Paul and cars – put him behind the wheel and he's a real Jekyll and Hyde . . .'

'It'll have to be Robert, then. He's getting on so well with her now. He was a bit stiff at first, but he's really pleased to have her around these days, I can tell.'

Robert? Why does it have to be either of them, Joan wanted to ask. But she could tell that Claire's mind was not really on this at all. 'Listen, Claire,' she tried again.

'Don't you think Robert's got enough on his plate without trying to teach her to drive as well? She's only come to work here, you know. You don't have to adopt her!'

'I wish I could.'

Claire's quiet riposte took Joan completely unawares. 'Adopt her! But she's already got a family!'

'She hasn't got a mother.'

And you haven't got a baby! Of course! Oh no, thought Joan in anguish, no! It's too cruelly neat, it's the filthiest trick fate could play. Her mind raced back over the girl's last visit: Claire receiving her at the door, fussing over her comfort in that loving, motherly way of hers, so like Molly Everard with her brood; bustling into the dining-room with a plate of mid-morning sandwiches and a glass of milk, her full, dark form hovering around the girl's tender, infantile fairness like a mother hen with only one chick . . .

Oh no. Joan's heart constricted. Claire never mentioned the possibility of a baby of her own these days. Instead, Joan knew, there were surreptitious visits to the doctor, and muted hints of a referral to a specialist before too long. She felt the force of elemental nature at work, and recognised its superior strength and inevitability. She bowed her head. 'Yeah, well . . .'

With a quiet goodbye, Claire left the kitchen, and soon afterwards Joan heard the car driving away. Finishing the washing-up, she went into the hall and picked up her coat and bag. The days were shortening now; the evenings, when she came out of work, suddenly much colder. She turned into the dining-room. Ally Calder was seated at the dining-room table, carefully pasting old newspaper clippings into an outsize cuttings book destined for display in the Centenary Exhibition. A pile of papers to her left showed how effectively she had been working.

'I'm going now,' said Joan, unconscious of the rudeness of her greeting, which had ignored anything like 'Hello.' 'When you've finished that, leave the book on the table. I'll check it over when I get back from work.'

'Yes, Miss Maitland,' she replied coolly. Check all you like, you know you won't find anything wrong with it, her eyes said as she stared Joan in the face. You know you're only doing this to put me in my place. Well, it ain't working – Miss Maitland.

Joan flushed. 'You've got to keep it all in order, you know,' she said stridently. 'It's important to get it all right.'

'I know.' The eyes were dark now, hard and cold, much older than the soft child's face, unmarked by any of the trials Joan knew had robbed her of her own bloom years ago – not that she had ever had anything like this girl's . . .

'Mrs Maitland won't be back till lunchtime, but you'll be finished and on your way by then, won't you?'

Another level stare. 'I don't think so.'

'Well, you should be if you don't hang around, dilly-dally and waste time like all you young girls, spending all your time on the phone!' She knew it sounded stupid, like a miserable old spinster schoolmarm, even as she spoke.

'Miss Maitland—' there was something sarcastic even about the way she used the name, slapping it down between them like a gauntlet '—I don't make phone calls here. I don't need to use the Rectory phone.'

'Yes, well—' Joan was furious with herself, but even more furious with the girl. 'Just get off as soon as you can, no need to hang around! And remember to slip out by the back door like I told you at the start. You don't want to disturb the Reverend Maitland in his study. He's got to have peace and quiet, you know!'

The Reverend Maitland! If she knew how pompous she sounded, taking about her own brother – talking about Robert – like that. Robert. She savoured the name. He'd decide if he wanted to be disturbed or not. And whatever 'Miss Maitland' decreed, she rather thought he might.

'Yes, Miss Maitland.'

She dropped her eyes. That's all right then, thought Joan grimly. Put her in her place, just got to be firm, show her what's what. It might still be all right. What was she worrying about, anyway? Paul had had thousands of girls; why should this silly chit be any more

129

than just one more in the line? And Robert – why was she fretting about him? He'd seemed a lot happier and somehow calmer this last week or two than he was before. It'd be all right. It had to be! She turned to go.

'Oh, Miss Maitland—'

The girl was regarding her demurely, the innocence of a baby angel shining out of her face.

'Just thought you'd like to know that your slip's hanging down at the back – and you've got lipstick on your teeth.' She smiled winningly. 'Just thought you'd like to know . . .'

From the study Robert felt the whole of the ground floor of the old house shake as Joan slammed the door on her way out to work. With Claire gone, too, he had the house to himself.

Or almost.

Rising silently to his feet, he padded across the study and opened the door. Diagonally across the hallway he could see straight into the dining-room, a corner of the table with its piles of books and papers, a small pair of hands busy with scissors and paste, a neat round head bent over its work, a rainfall of silvery hair . . .

Noiselessly he returned to his desk, leaving the door ajar. It was extraordinary how easy he found it just to be around her, how comfortable he was in her presence. And after all that fuss he had made to himself, resolving to avoid her, never to see her again! It was all right, and it was going to be all right. It was amazing the way things turned out. He had been worrying about Claire, when it was Claire herself, his beloved Claire who had, quite unaided, seen that there was something special in the girl, something worth taking an interest in, and had brought her into their lives without a moment's hesitation.

So it was all fine. And now she was here, he knew he could take his time, take time to get to know her, find out her story, discover the ways in which he could be of use to her, as her pastor and as her friend. There was something there, he knew, something going on in her life, that he did not yet understand. Several times now

130

he had caught her looking at him with a strange, deep regard, and even under normal circumstances, he felt, she was watching him, watching him intently. Whatever was troubling her, he would have to find it out, however long it took. Yet he felt, too, an unaccountable urgency, a deep impatience, as if he had already been waiting all his life for something . . . for what? Whatever it was, it was something to do with her.

But it was not a physical urge, he felt sure of that. She was attractive, yes – more than attractive, simply lovely, in every natural unspoiled line and movement of her being. He loved to see her about the place, and marvelled at the brightness she seemed to bring to every room in the dull old Rectory as soon as she came in. But he was her employer, her priest, a much older person, a happily married man. She was safe with him. He could enjoy her God-given, life-enhancing beauty without feeling the slightest temptation to take advantage of her. Anything else was simply unthinkable, beneath excuse, beyond contempt. He had proved that to himself every day she had been here. He could prove it again now. On an impulse he threw aside his work and went into the dining-room.

She had heard him coming with that strange, almost animal alertness of hers, and her deep blue eyes were already fixed on the door as he came through. Defensively she moved to switch off the transistor radio which he was suddenly aware was pulsing away rhythmically in the background. 'I'm sorry, was it disturbing you? I thought I'd got it turned down real quiet.'

'No, it's all right.' He smiled. 'It's not bothering me.'

His eyes were so kind, so clear, and when he smiled like that, the way his face crinkled up was really sexy, she decided. If only he wasn't – everything he was . . . He was still talking 'No, I was – I was just going to make a cup of tea. Wondered if you were interested?'

Her answering smile, coming from that small, guarded face, was like the sun coming out. 'Oh yes,' she said. 'Sure. Yes, I'm interested.'

Autumn

Chapter 11

The scent of her was so clean, she could have been bathed all over in Johnson's Baby Lotion only half an hour ago. In the close confines of the car, he felt very near to her, mentally as well as physically. The straight fall of shining white hair eclipsed the side of her face, but he knew from memory the expression she was wearing – one of fierce concentration, her arched eyebrows drawn together in a straight line, the pointed tip of her small pink tongue just visible between her tightly-drawn lips. He found himself smiling, and had his work cut out not to laugh out loud from the sheer fun of it. Whoever would have thought there could be so much pleasure in teaching someone to drive!

'Relax, Ally. It's only a motor, not a wild animal. It won't run away with you, you know.'

'It did before.' Her voice was stronger than usual, her manner more open, even bold. She was obviously going to make the most of the occasion.

'What d'you mean?'

'When I was learning to drive before.' She looked at him sideways, obviously trying to work out what his reaction would be to what she was about to tell him. 'The car ran away with me, didn't it? Ran into a tree.'

'Ran into a tree? When was this?'

'Just before I left high school. One of the boys there had his own car. I managed to persuade him to teach me to drive.'

Never mind how, she thought. He's too high-minded to wonder about that, anyway. 'Didn't work out, though. First time I got out in it I lost control and went off the road. Car was a write-off.'

135

'Oh, poor Ally! That must have been awful for you!'

She considered it, head on one side. 'Nah, not really. Wasn't my car. I was just worried after that I'd never be able to drive, that I'd always run into things.'

He laughed. 'Well, if that's your problem, all you've got to do is to aim at the next tree, then we'll be sure to miss it!'

She laughed, too, a low, unexpected sound, and as he had hoped, relaxed her fierce grasp on the wheel.

'You're doing very well,' he said reassuringly. 'You're no problem to teach. I've never known anyone pick things up as quickly as you do.'

Another sideways, almost provocative glance. 'Yeah, well . . . I'm a fast learner. All I need is . . . someone to teach me – someone to show me the way.'

There was a pause. Suddenly he felt strangely uncomfortable, at a disadvantage. If he didn't know better, it came to him suddenly, he'd have thought she was flirting with him, stringing him along. He frowned. He must control the situation more carefully – it was his responsibility, no one else's. He looked away.

Swift as a barometer, her mood changed with the sudden change of his. Some of her bold assurance vanished, to be replaced by a sullen resignation. 'Yeah, well,' she said inconsequentially. 'Yeah, well, that's it, isn't it?'

He still had not got used to her disconcerting habit of picking up something he had said, and dropping it again only half answered.

'What do you mean?' He seemed to be saying that to her a lot these days.

'I've got to learn quick, haven't I? Because I've got so much to learn. But I can learn from you – can't I?'

Her knuckles were tightening again as she spoke. Again he was conscious of the nearness of her presence, the tiny fine gold hairs on the back of her forearm, the outline of her thigh under the thin cotton of her skirt. Summer was dying now, every day it was growing colder, duller – how much longer would this lovely creature, this flower-child, be with them? For the first time he contemplated a future in which this light form, lightly clad, her garments revealing every curve, every hollow of her girlish form, would not be coming into his life, into his home, three or four times every week. He was conscious that everything seemed to be racing towards them rather too fast. The tension in the car was almost palpable. He moved to take control. 'Slowly – slowly on the accelerator there. No need to rush.'

'No need for *you* to rush.'

'What do you mean?'

Why did he have to keep saying that? Why did she make him feel like a stranger in an unknown land, struggling with a language he had never spoken before and could not understand?

She steered the car carefully round a bend in the road and took time over her answer before replying.

'Why would you need to rush? You've got somewhere, you've done something with your life, you're here, fixed, settled.'

He felt a chill wind blowing somewhere at his back at the very feel of that, even as she said it. Fixed? Settled? Was he? He shivered a little, and felt a surge of resistance. Maybe trapped was a better word. But what was he talking about? He had chosen this life if not this place, he was following his vocation. Of course he had to agree! Fixed, settled, yes! What was wrong with that? It was a fine thing to be, a thing countless people longed to be. 'In a way, yes. I suppose you're right.'

''Course I'm right. You got a position – you got a job! Me, I've got nothing.'

'Oh come on, Ally!' he protested. 'You've got—'

'What? What've I got?'

Her voice was quite devoid of self-pity. Her stern face showed, too, that she would be equally pitiless in scorning any facile consolation he might be tempted to offer. Here in the privacy of the car, he noticed, away from the Rectory, she had completely dropped the formality of their previous acquaintance and approached him on a basis he had never experienced before. Now she seemed to be communicating with him soul to soul, speaking to him without concealment and without defence. Once again he felt the urgent tug of the desire to help her, to heal her, to hold that little wind-blown bird of her being for a while in his hands before releasing it again to the sky.

'You have a home, Ally, and a family – people who love you.'

'People who—'

Her mind threw her back to the night of Mick Ford's last visit to her father's house, when the two men had forced her to stay with them all evening, getting them food, supplying them with drinks, emptying ashtrays, and above all listening to their unbelievably stupid, increasingly filthy talk till they both finally passed out.

'People who love me . . .'

Furiously she tossed back her hair. He did not know if he was supposed to see the angry tears in the corner of her eyes. She tried to slow down for a junction, and crashed the gears in hopeless confusion.

'Clutch in – slowly – find the gear you want. No, that's reverse. Try second.'

'I can do it! It's just my foot that slipped.' She was defiant again now.

'No worries. With the age of this car, your foot is probably not the only thing that slipped! Clutch out again, slowly now.'

The car was rapidly picking up speed again, but he did not want to comment or seem to criticise. This was the moment.

'Ally – you know you've become more to us – to both of us – than just someone who comes into the Rectory a couple of times a week to help out with the administration. If you have any problems – any problems at all, whatever they are – I hope and pray that you would feel able to come to me for help.'

The car wobbled. 'Yeah, well . . .' The small fists gripped the wheel. He could feel her mind working, feel her thinking her way forward. 'Thanks, Robert. Yeah, I know you care about me.' He could feel the tension between them again, faint, imperceptible, but building, building. 'And I would come to you for help or anything. I will. Just you wait and see!' She gave him a smile of what looked almost like triumph, then stamped her foot to the floor. The car lurched forward and picked up speed once again.

End of another summer – always something miserable about that. What you've had can't ever come back – and what lies ahead doesn't look so good. Rather surprised to find himself entertaining such philosophical thoughts, Paul strode down the cliff-path with what they all knew would be the year's last summer pilgrimage of beach chairs, sun umbrellas and laden coolboxes. Behind him came Joan, then Claire, both equally burdened down. On the clifftop Robert, making up the rear after having had to lock up the car, paused for a moment looking out to sea. Before them lay the perfect bowl of Broken Bay, and beyond, mile upon mile of anonymous dune-land where the headland ran down to the shoreline on either side. For the first time in his life it struck him as a melancholy desolate scene – anyone could get lost out there . . . die undiscovered . . . never be missed . . .

Well, at least Robert seemed a lot calmer and more settled these days, Paul reflected grimly. Good job some-body was getting their act together! Turned out it'd been a brainwave all round to get Ally fixed up with that job at the Rectory. She'd got the Centenary stuff all sussed out in no time at all, knew just what she had to do and was getting right on with doing it, taking all the worry off the others' shoulders. Maybe that was all Robert's problem had ever been, just having too much to do, and no one to delegate it to. Well, he'd got his Girl Friday now, and courtesy of the Everard Employment Agency, one of the best. She'd made all the difference to him, and it really seemed to show in every bone of his body.

Claire liked her, too – he was pleased about that. She'd sort of adopted the kid, even taking her shopping for clothes now, giving her a few ideas on how to make her money go a bit further. Could be just what Claire needed if kids of her own weren't in any rush to come along; he wondered what was happening about that. And Ally was happy there, he knew. She'd really blosso-med, got more confidence, had even started speaking differently, more openly now she was spending so much time with them and didn't have to watch every word that came out of her mouth. He was happy, too, because now he had such a good excuse to see her, just in the normal course of dropping by the Rectory to call on his sister, or bring her up messages from their Mum.

Only Joan wasn't too pleased, you could see that with half an eye. He laughed quietly to himself as he watched Joan ploughing doggedly over the sand towards the place he'd chosen to set up their umbrellas and chairs. Well, she wouldn't, would she? Not many spinsters of thirty would welcome a little beauty of eighteen or nineteen, right slap-bang in the middle of their patch! And especially around her precious brother!

Pity, though. He surveyed Joan surreptitiously but critically as she deposited her things, and with a sigh of relief and pleasure slipped off her sundress and stretched out her arms towards the sun. She was a fine enough girl all right, tall, and she had a bloody good body, which was still in bloody good shape. Good cook, too, and homemaker, and with Robert's clear-cut profile and Nordic looks, she'd be an ornament to any man.

There was something about her to hold a bloke back, though. Even after all these years he couldn't put his finger on it, but he'd been aware of it ever since they were kids. Man who married Joanie Maitland'd have to like living in a knife-box – and playing second fiddle to her brother all his life, was about the nearest he could get to it. Still, you could do a lot worse. The right man'd soon take the cutting edge off her – the right kind of loving, hot and strong, and plenty of good sex; that'd soon put a smile on her face and fill out those elegant but unseductive angles in her fine, long body. She wouldn't be the first woman that all she needed was to be warmed through by a man. If she'd been anyone but Robert's sister, he'd have tried it on with her years ago. Waste of time now even thinking of it – when all he seemed to have on his mind night and bloody day was bloody Ally Calder, who still hadn't given him so much as a by-your-leave in the way of encouragement. Ah, bugger them all!

'Paul—'

Joan turned to him with a winning smile. But he was gone, fleeing down the beach to the sea as if running for his life.

'Do they want the food now, or later, d'you think?' Claire dropped the rugs she was carrying and collapsed on to the sand.

'They'll tell us soon enough – or rather their stomachs will,' observed Joan resentfully, as she settled down to comfort herself with sun lotion and a good sulk.

From above, as he began the long climb down, Robert had a perfect view of the beach. It was more crowded than he ever remembered it, as everyone from miles around seemed to have signalled to one another to grab this last, late, peachy day of summer, before the warm days flew away again leaving them nothing but the grey desolation of winter.

Out at sea the flags were flying in two perfectly straight lanes, warning the swimmers to keep within the safety zone or risk their lives against the danger of the rising equinoctal tides. On the sand, parties of young people frolicked and ran away, stopped and doubled back, threw balls and dropped them, and ran races towards the sea, all to the accompaniment of distant, wind-scattered laughter like the soundtrack of an old film. He felt a sudden violent stab of envy. To be so physical – so free – so young – it must be fantastic. Had he ever been like that? He couldn't remember. Where had it gone, his youth and freedom? Was all he had now to look forward to nothing but middle-age and slow decay?

At the water's edge a gang of young men had gathered around Paul, some of them known to him from round the town, all of them miners by their build. They were looking out to sea, all their attention fixed on a single point. Far out in the bay a lone figure was body-surfing, head down, torso pointed like a spear, cresting the biggest of the breakers with serene self-absorption. From the intense attention of the men and the flash of pure white costume against the brilliant green and blue of the sea, he knew it had to be a woman. Gauging the track of the surfer's flowing flight inshore, the men laughed and fought, kicked and splashed, until they had

141

positioned themselves directly in her path. As the last of the breakers on which she was riding broke on the shore with a final burst of ferocity, the surfer was tumbled aground at the feet of the young men. Coming up from the foam, pulling at the front of her costume as she did so, she found herself struggling to rise amid a forest of burly male legs.

He could see from half a mile or more away that the swimmer was Ally. Laughing uproariously, Paul scooped her up in one smooth throw and tossed her to his neighbour. With shouts and howls of amusement the gang of men played with her like a doll, picking her up and throwing her back into the water, splashing her and each other, tossing her from one to another, sometimes catching her, sometimes not. He felt himself suddenly in the grip of a wave of powerful emotion. First came envy again, a wild jealousy that they could touch her like this, make free with her body, play like boys and make her their plaything.

Yet for her sake, thinking of her, he was overwhelmed with fury. But what was he angry about? They were all probably her friends; this could be a weekly ritual as far as he knew. He had no reason to believe she was in distress – he could not tell if she was enjoying the situation or not, could make out nothing either one way or the other, for although their cries and exuberant shouts were ringing loudly round the bay, he could not hear a sound from her. Would her low, rather childlike voice, never in his hearing raised above a quiet remark, carry this far anyway? And why shouldn't she have fun with a group of – whatever was wrong with this – young men of her own age? What was the matter with him?

Slowly he made his way down the cliff-path towards his own group, his eyes never leaving the scene at the water's edge. As he did so he saw Ally, with one swift flick of her body, break away like a dolphin from her tormentors and swim strongly back out to sea. Leaning on the back of a beach-chair he watched her cleave through the waters, her sea-darkened hair streaming behind her like a mermaid, swimming and swimming till she seemed no more than just a speck in the distance.

* * *

'No honestly, Joan, that was great – fantastic. But I couldn't eat another thing.' Carefully Robert packed up his plate and the remains of the picnic, and looked up at the sky. The sun was low now, and much less warm – they had maybe half an hour to an hour of the afternoon left.

A melancholy sadness enveloped him: another summer gone – another year – and what did he have to show for it? How many summers would he be washed up here, on Brightstone beach, lamenting the loss of his youth and wondering what became of his dreams, his hopes, his promise of a better day? Painfully he contrasted his feelings now with the happiness of the previous day that he and Claire, Paul and Joan had all spent together here on the beach at Broken Bay. He was too honest to deny what had happened. He knew that seeing Ally with those men – even with Paul, being played with by Paul – had spoiled the day for him before it had even begun.

He shook himself lightly. God, he loathed himself in these self-pitying moods! Must snap out of it, before I inflict it on anyone else, he warned himself sternly.

'Time for a last stroll, I think. Anyone for a walk? I'm just going over the rocks to stretch my legs.'

A chorus of murmured negatives told him that the others were too comfortable, too full of food or too preoccupied with their own concerns – the byplay between Paul and Ally had not gone unnoticed by Joan, he noticed sadly – to be bothered to move. Trying to shake off the mood that had drowned his spirits with all the suddenness of a fall of summer rain, he walked briskly towards the sea, then strode out along the water's edge until he reached the rocks.

Above him and to his right loomed the Mother and Child. Beyond it, trailing down to their sinister hiding-place below the surface of the sea, though exposed now by the low tide, were a series of lesser rocks which had been christened by the European settlers – from their distinctive shapes and scattered formation – the Fallen Angels. Carefully he picked his way over them, finding flat sand where he could, and rounded the headland into the next bay. Up where the dry sand began, tucked into the lee of a big rock, sitting on a beach towel with nothing but her little transistor radio and a beach-bag for company, was Ally.

Her eyes gave him the best welcome he had had all day. Without waiting for an invitation he dropped down unceremoniously beside her. 'All alone, Ally? Did you know we were here, over on the other side of the rocks in Broken Bay? You could have joined us.'

'I knew you were here.' She looked all white, pink and gold in the evening light – a fallen angel, he thought inconsequentially – and was breathing shallowly, like a little cat. 'I saw you when I arrived. But I didn't know if you'd want me. And I wanted to be on my own anyway – if I couldn't be with you.' She looked at him with a gaze startling in its intensity.

'You didn't want to be with your—' he chose the word as carefully as he could – 'friends?'

Her eyes flashed. 'They're no friends of mine! They're just miners – ignorant pigs they are – all they want to do is get drunk and grab hold of you. That's not my idea of a good time!' Furiously she leaned forward and started brushing sand off her legs in slow, circular sweeps. Suddenly he was reminded of the dream, when he was making love to the unknown girl whose hand had circled like that, caressed him like that . . .

He was mesmerised, transfixed by her presence, her every move. Her legs were long, slim and brown, dusted now with salt and sand, her small hands brushing rhythmically up and down between her thighs as if her life depended on it. Again she looked him straight in the eyes with her open, abandoned, trusting stare. 'If I can't be with – the people I want to be with – I'd rather be on my own.'

He was aroused; he knew it. Firmly he detached his gaze, wrenched his mind away. 'But at your age—'

'At my age,' she interrupted him with another level stare, 'I bet you liked being on your own, too. Trouble is, people won't let you.'

It was true. 'And I still do,' he admitted, feeling for the umpteenth time that this girl somehow constantly caught him out, exposed his attitudes and beliefs for what they were, oddly hollow, unthought-out and untrue. 'Of course, I have a lot to do in the study right now. But that's only because I'm new to the church and the parish, I think. Also this is my first full ministry that I have to run alone, and that needs a lot of thought; it's a very great responsibility. Reading up on all the old minutes and files, planning ahead, all that sort of thing . . .'

Again it sounded false – not a lie as such, but simply not quite the truth or the whole truth.

Ally looked at him. 'It's just nice to be on your own, think your own thoughts,' she said simply.

'But we all need others, Ally,' he said, determinedly conversational. 'To help us in life – to teach us things. Take your driving lessons, for instance. You're coming on well there. Soon be able to take your test, and pass, with flying colours I expect. That's how people help each other!'

'Not all people.' She leaned towards him. 'Just you. I could learn anything from you.'

He held his breath. What did she mean? If it had been Janice Peasely, or even Noellene Foley, he'd have begun to suspect she was making a pass – but Ally . . .?

As if reading his mind, suddenly she became a child again. She grinned at him and pointed at her bag. 'Want a grape?'

He looked at her. Rummaging around, she produced a bunch of grapes and opening her mouth, sucked one off the bottom of the cluster. 'Go on – they're great!'

'Thanks.'

Her arm and shoulder, her fingers as she broke off the grapes and pressed them into his hand, were all a golden, silken brown, covered with the finest dusting of hairs like fine gilt mesh. Her face was streaked with salt and her normally fine fair mane hung thick and heavy in a wet rope down her back. She smelled of the sea, but of her baby self also. He felt something he could not name gathering round his heart, and a stirring, a physical stirring of something he could not trust.

'D'you like being a priest?'

145

The question was hard, and brutally unexpected. It seemed to wind him, like a kick in the stomach. He looked up. Her eyes were chips of slate, and there was no evading their interrogation. He tried to think. 'I don't know. It was my own free choice – but I don't know if – if liking is quite the right word . . .'

'It doesn't seem like a real job for a man – if you don't mind me asking?'

He had to think again what the truthful answer could be. 'You'll never learn anything, or understand anything, unless you ask, Ally,' he managed at last.

'Here's another one then.' She paused, weighing up how far she could go. 'Are priests like other men?'

'Of course. Just like other men.'

She laughed derisively. 'What – tattoos and booze, swearing and lies, the quick backhander when they feel like it – "just like other men"?'

Her scorn caught him on the raw. 'We're not miners, Ally, if that's what you mean. But we're not perfect either. And just because we don't have to suffer the stresses and strains of life underground, doesn't mean that we aren't what you'd call "real men"! Beneath the dog-collar and the long gown, a priest is as human as the next man. If we're honest, we don't even pretend to be any different! We're flesh and blood like the rest of you, you know – perhaps even more so because of what we know first-hand of human weakness and wickedness. We're sinners, too – only flesh and blood!'

She was silent. Embarrassed by his outburst, he watched her covertly out of the corner of his eye. She leaned forward deep in thought, clasping her arms round her knees in a touchingly girlish gesture. He could see the rise of her softly rounded shoulders, the womanly movement and swell of her breasts, every soft contour of her slim body as she leaned forward in the clinging bathing suit.

He felt very peaceable now, very close to her. The golden skin of her legs seemed to glimmer in the last warm rays of light. He thought she seemed the very perfection of God's creation, and marvelled at the wonder of her all through the long silence that followed.

146

And even after she had whispered her light goodbye and drifted away up the beach, he remained there locked in wonder at the beauty of the turning world, and the grace of the gifts that the Almighty in his love had seen fit to grant to mortal man.

Chapter 12

It was colder now, no doubt of that. No more summer beach parties this year! And no hope of a baby this year either. Feeling the familiar drag of sad resignation, Claire let herself in through the back door of the Rectory and immediately felt her spirits revive at the comfort of being home. And a house was only a home when there were people in it, she thought. Oh, it was lovely to have a young girl round the house, there was no doubt about that – especially when Robert was so taken up with work these days, spending every waking moment with Ally on the plans for the celebrations, so preoccupied with the Centenary that he hardly had a word to say to her or Joan. Someone to look after – someone to fuss over and care for . . . And someone who soaked up all the love and attention you could give like a flower deprived of water for most of its life . . . Smiling in anticipation of the smile that she knew would greet her, Claire pushed open the door of the dining-room and went in.

On her knees on the floor, surrounded by mountainous piles of old newspapers, Ally was sorting and stacking little fluttering clumps of yellow cuttings into predetermined piles. She lifted her face as Claire entered, expectantly, as she always did, but not speaking till she was spoken to – she always did that too, Claire realised. God only knows what her home life must be like! No wonder she wants to be here all the time with us, no wonder she's so devoted to Robert she hardly lets him out of her sight! We're probably the nearest thing to a family the poor child has ever known!

Claire pulled up a chair beside the table and dropped thankfully into it. 'My goodness, you've been working hard here, Ally, while I've been out,' she said warmly. 'You've certainly made an impact on all that. Honestly, I thought it'd take you weeks!'

The girl smiled, the wary, waif-like expression she always wore softening visibly at the unexpected praise. 'I really like doing it, Mrs Maitland. Best job I've ever had, this is. And it's really interesting. I never knew any of this stuff about Brightstone – how the first pioneers got it going, then what a struggle the settlers had to build the town – it makes it all seem different here somehow.'

'It's true,' agreed Claire. 'You know, I was born here like you, and I really thought I knew the old place – but I didn't know the half of it. I really think we've got something to celebrate here come June – and thanks to you, we're going to be able to have a proper celebration and plenty to show all the Brightstonians about their history when they come to the exhibition.'

'Can I make you a cup of tea, Mrs Maitland?'

'That's sweet of you, Ally, but I really came in to say I don't think we should keep you any longer today. Look at the time! It's after six o'clock, and now the nights are drawing in, I don't want you to be having to make your way home on your own in the dark.'

'Yes, I s'pose so,' agreed Ally without enthusiasm. She never wanted to leave the Rectory these days after her work was done, Claire noticed with another quick shaft of pity – never wanted to go home.

As if reading Claire's thoughts, the girl turned again to the pile of papers on the floor. 'I don't like to leave all this – but I'll have to go soon.'

'Soon? I'm afraid you'll be late now! And I don't want your father to think we're overworking you.' Or to have any excuse to take it out on you, Claire thought firmly. 'So I'm going to ask Robert to run you home. Perhaps he can give you another driving lesson – he says you're coming on wonderfully well, Ally. You're a great pupil, one of the best, it seems!'

Robert. To run her home. And her his best pupil . . . it made her feel strange to hear Claire talk about him like that. 'Oh no, don't trouble him, Mrs Maitland, there's no need,' she protested. But Claire had gone.

'Darling?'

He knew from her expression what she was about to ask him the moment the curly dark head came round the study door. 'Robert, darling – will you be a love and run Ally home? She's been delayed here finishing off, and I don't really want her going down the headland on her own in the dark.'

'Ally?'

He remembered the last time they were in the car alone together, when he had been trying to teach her to drive. Then there had been the time on the beach, when he would have been hard pressed to say what he thought she was up to – or what he had been feeling either . . . He had to be careful; he had to keep telling himself that. He just had to keep out of her way. He looked at the papers scattered about on the desk before him as if he was too busy to leave. 'Can't she—?'

'Oh Robert!' Claire was shocked at his callousness. 'You know how that father of hers is! Paul says—'

Oh God. Paul. Any minute now Paul would be roaring up in the Dodge to offer her a lift – it was odd how Paul's visits to his sister so often coincided with the end of one of Ally's days at the Rectory. Paul. No, he couldn't have that. He hastened to retrieve the situation. 'Of course, I'll drive Ally anywhere you like, Claire. Just give me a second . . .'

Out in the hall Ally waited, a little nervously, it seemed, clutching her bag and looking at him with unnaturally large and darkened eyes. Doesn't want to go home again, poor lamb, and who can blame her, he thought, with a surge of compassion. Paul had been telling him about Calder's reputation for violence, all the fights and assaults he'd been involved with. Oh God – truly the sins of the fathers are visited upon the children.

He smiled at her as warmly as he could. 'Let's go, Ally', he said lightly.

The strange atmosphere that she was creating between them persisted as he led the way out of the house and across the drive to where the car was parked. It was a

151

glorious evening, almost magical, with a huge moon hanging low in a clear, pale sky. Beneath the trees the shadows were dense, black and deceptive.

'I'd like to give you another driving lesson,' he said humorously. 'But I'm afraid that you might drive me into a tree in the dark!' She laughed. 'And I'm sorry to say that the poor old car isn't what she used to be when I first bought her. Of course, she was already second-hand – or a hundred-and-second-hand! Lately, she just keeps threatening to give up the ghost altogether!'

To his relief the engine started first time, and once they were underway, as the car rolled out of the Rectory drive and struck off across the headland, he could feel her mood changing again; as if like the tides, she ebbed and flowed with the moon.

'Look,' she said at last, her voice husky with some deep, unacknowledged feeling, pointing out to sea. 'There's a ship out there, way out on the horizon.'

Together they watched as the low sleek shape of the liner, a dark blue smudge hardly visible against the darkening world beyond, slid over the luminous line of the horizon and vanished out of sight.

'Where's it gone?'

'Where? Well, to Sydney, I suppose. Melbourne maybe. Even to England—'

'I didn't mean that. I mean, where's it gone? I could never work that out when I was a kid.'

'Work what out?' Her voice was husky, almost seductive. He was on guard again, alert for her every nuance.

'I mean, if the earth is round like they say it is, how come it looks so like a straight line out there – where the edge is?'

'I don't know'. So many things he didn't seem to know when he was with her.

He doesn't know anything, she thought. He doesn't even know I'm sitting here thinking about . . . 'I didn't either,' she resumed dreamily. 'Not for years. Worked it out in the end, though.'

He thought of Galileo, Herschel, Einstein, all the great star-gazers of the past – and Ally Calder, her quest for knowledge, her struggle for self-expression no less fierce, no less important, than theirs. Yet even with the best of minds, in a body like that – how would she ever be taken seriously? That body . . . he fought to keep himself and the conversation on line. 'How did you do that, Ally?'

Shè was warming to her theme now, fired by his attention. 'One night, I sneaked out of the house – m'dad would have killed me if he'd known. I went down to the beach, and watched the moon come up over the sea. I watched all night – I didn't sleep, that would've ruined the whole thing – and then the next day, there was the sun, creeping up over the horizon. So then I believed it.'

'You believed it.' He could see her small pink hand resting on her thigh, so close beside him. A sudden, almost unbearable urge gripped him to pick it up, raise it gently to his lips, and bite the soft fingers between his tongue and teeth, one by one. He dared not move, in case he broke the spell.

'Yeah, I did. And then it all made sense, you know? The pictures in the books with all the spheres, and all – it all made sense, for the first time really. And you could see that the earth, our earth was just one of them – so there's nothing special about us – and how huge it all was, yet how little really . . .' A soft hush fell between them. 'So we might as well all do just what we want, when we want,' she picked up, her voice changing again. 'We're not here for very long. And there's a lot of infinity out there. I want to have some fun before I die!'

'Fun?' he queried in a dark, troubled voice. 'What do you call fun?'

She wanted to scream at him, to punch him, to shout abuse, to make him take notice of her. Why don't you wake up? she howled inside her head. Why can't you see what's right under your nose? Why can't you touch me, hold me, kiss me, why can't you . . .

'What a conversation,' he said in the same forbidding way. 'What a conversation to be having! I'm sure we can think of better things to talk about!'

She was torn between anger and acceptance. 'You

know I never talk to anyone else like I talk to you! Never talked like this in all my whole life before! Yeah, you're right! What a conversation!'

He smiled, his heart full of tenderness. 'No rules about conversation, Ally'.

Her sigh came from very far away. 'Not in your world, Robert.' He noticed now that for the first time she had used his name completely naturally, not awkwardly, nor with aggression, nor because he had insisted she did.

'If there are, then there shouldn't be. You said it. We're not here on earth for very long. We should speak the truth.'

She did not reply. Her eyes were still fixed on the far horizon, where the view from the headland gave out over the panorama of the wide, quiet sea, now fading into purple, grey and black as the night descended. She seemed calmer now, more at home with him, more at peace with herself than he had ever known her. Was the time she was spending up at the Rectory beginning to have some good effect? Were these odd snatched conversations of theirs making her feel that she was of value as a person in her own right – that her well-being, her future, were of value to him, as her minister, as her friend?

'Once I came right up here on my own at dead of night, way up the top of the headland,' she resumed in a pale, dreamy voice. 'I could see miles out to sea, the night was so clear. There was a pattern of lights sort of hanging above the water – and music – little snatches of the most beautiful music – like magic – coming to me in bits and pieces.'

'Music.'

'Yeah. There was a liner out there, one of them big cruisers. They must have had their own band, I think – and lights – just like fairy-lights on a Christmas tree. It was so beautiful – it's hard to describe how beautiful it was—'

'I remember. I used to watch them myself, from the Rectory.'

She was suddenly wide awake and yet another, different self. Her sideways glance found his again through

154

the gloom. 'Bet you didn't cry to be there, to be on board, to be one of the rich people, dancing to the music! Bet you didn't pray to be out of this, miles away, anywhere but here!'

'No,' he said slowly, his heart heavy for the child she had been.

'Well, I did! An' you know what?' He knew before she said it. 'I still do! I still want some life, something before I die! And to get it, I know for sure I'm getting out of here!'

He did not want her to go, he knew that. But he also knew that he must not say so. 'There's a wide world out there for you, Ally. You must take it, grab it with both hands. You're a woman now. You have to make your own decisions. And the people around you will have to get used to that. There's a lot to do in life. We mustn't waste it. The sooner we make a good start, the better.'

'Yeah, but what about *you*?' Her voice had changed again.

'What about me?'

'Have you got a lot to do? Or is this it for you, here, now?'

'Oh, Ally!' How could he burden her with his hopes, his dreams, his fears, his frustrations?

'Go on. I've told you all my secrets. You got to tell me yours.' She was a child again, stubbornly insisting on 'fair's fair'. But the question had been a woman's question, and it deserved a man's honest answer.

'I do want to do more,' he said slowly, 'to be more than I can be here in Brightstone. I know I have so much to give – and I long for a wider arena than this.'

'A wider arena.' He could tell the phrase pleased her, and that she was squirrelling it away for future use. 'But as a priest? Still as a priest?'

'Oh yes.' Here at last he was on solid ground. 'Always as a priest. If God in his wisdom'll continue to have me, that is!'

They were running down the headland now with the town lying waiting for them at the foot of the bluff. She stole a glance across the car at him as they entered the town, the street lights shining in from the side etching his profile in orange neon. Covertly she eyed his strong-jawed face, his fantastic mouth, the thick lock of ash-blond hair falling forward on his lightly tanned forehead. God, why did he have to be a priest? That was something for old men, for old fools like Holy Joe, St Jude's late and unlamented last incumbent. What a waste! He could've been a film star, Robert could. Telly, at least!

As if he could read her thoughts, Robert gave her one of the sweetest of his crooked smiles. 'You mustn't worry about me, Ally. It's you we've got to get sorted out – it's you we've got to help as much as we can.'

As he spoke, a car approaching from the opposite direction recognised them and began hooting wildly to attract their attention. A second later the blue Dodge pulled up alongside, and Paul stuck his head out. Robert drew his car to a stop.

'I was just coming up to the Rectory, Ally,' called Paul. 'Meant to see Claire, and thought I'd be in time to give you a lift home. See you've saved me a journey. I'll go on up to the headland, then. See you up there, Robert?'

'Not necessarily,' groaned Robert. As he had feared, the enforced halt had proved too much for his ailing vehicle. As Paul had been shouting above the noise of the Dodge's souped-up engine, Robert's had coughed, spluttered unconvincingly for a beat or two, and then died. Paul chuckled in unsympathetic amusement. 'Just let me park the old Blue Streak, and I'll come and give you a hand. In the meantime, if you want to make yourself useful, I suggest you start praying for a miracle!'

With resignation Ally reached for her bag from the floor of the car. 'I can walk home,' she said.

Robert was genuinely hurt. 'O ye of little faith!' he cried. Jumping out of the car, he threw up the bonnet and started poking about. Ally came up behind his shoulder. 'You haven't got a clue, have you?' she teased. She was delighting in his discomfiture, and didn't mind if he knew it.

'Oh Lord,' he groaned again. 'Give us light in our darkness!' He stood there, resisting the un-Christian urge to give the car a god-almighty kick. 'Devil only knows what's wrong with it!'

'And he's not going to tell you!' She was loving every second of it, he realised – and why not? How much fun had she ever had in all her girlhood, he wondered? No brothers, no father to play with her – no wonder she was enjoying herself now.

'You know what you're looking for, mate?'

Paul was shouldering him out of the way with the expertise of one who had been fixing cars since he was ten years old.

'Of course.'

Paul's eyes widened. 'What?'

'Help and assistance. In this case, yours!'

'You cheeky bastard! Saving y'reverence, Reverend, of course!'

But the exchanges of humour, however welcome to the passengers, had no effect at all upon the car. Nor did anything else that Paul could try. Waiting uncomplainingly by the roadside, Ally was beginning to shiver in her thin cardigan. Eventually Robert's fears began to get the better of him. He drew Paul quietly to one side. 'Look – could you run Ally home, d'you think? Only reason I was bringing her was that she was already late, and Claire was concerned about her father's rotten temper. I don't want to get her into any more trouble.'

'Sure thing! I'll have her there in no time, and get straight back to you. Don't you try anything in my absence, mind – unless it's the power of prayer!'

Delighted with his parting shot, Paul drove away, Ally at his side. 'I hope he'll be all right', she said with an undisguised longing and concern. 'I don't like to leave him like that, all on his own.'

Paul was faintly unsettled. 'Robert? He'll be fine, why shouldn't he be?'

'Why can't they give him a decent car?' she burst out. 'He deserves something better than that – a man like him!'

'He's only a small-town parson, y'know, not the Pope!'

Nettled, Paul spoke more sharply than he intended. But he did not like the turn the conversation was taking.

'Only bishops get decent cars, and that's a fact. He's lucky he's not still a curate – he'd be riding a bike around the town! As it is, they give him an old heap for his pains.'

She fell silent, brooding, and refused all his attempts to make friendly conversation. Only when they were drawing near to her house did she show any signs of coming back to life. 'Aren't you going to drop me round the corner or away down the road?' she asked in alarm.

'What about right outside? You've done nothing wrong, Ally.' You've never so much as let me lay a finger on you, he wanted to say, but didn't. 'Well, you tell me where to stop, if you like. But sooner or later, you got to stand up to that old man of yours. And you've only come straight from the Rectory, after all. Not much to get nasty about in that!'

'Yeah.'

Her mind was working, fast, but very clearly. She could hear Robert's voice, see the truth and warmth in his eyes as he said it. 'You're a woman now, Ally, you have to make your own decisions, and they should be respected.' Robert, yeah. He knew what was right. He knew how it ought to be.

'Outside, please, Paul.' Her face was bright and hopeful. 'Drop me off outside the house. I've done nothing wrong. Time he got used to that.'

But Jim Calder had no intention of getting used to anything that had to do with Paul Everard. The first blow caught her as she stepped into the house, before she had even taken her key from the door.

'Y'lying little whore!' he hissed, in a voice more terrifying even than his normal screaming rant. 'Y'lying bitch!' Another ferocious blow found the side of her head, sending her spinning across the hall.

'Dad – I didn't—' Weakly, half dazed, she lifted a hand to try to protect herself.

'Don't y'threaten me! Lift y'hand t'y'father, would ya, y'filthy little cow?' With great deliberation, pausing to take aim, he gave her a slap on the face that made her teeth rattle.

'Dad!' She knew that pleading would not save her, would only add to his enjoyment of what he was doing, but she could not stop herself. 'Dad – don't – *don't* . . .'

'I seen y'coming up here t'the door of my house in that bloody car of his, bold as brass – I seen ya, Ally, y'can't lie y'way out of that!'

She was sobbing now, less from the pain than from the hopelessness of it all.

'There's nothing t'lie about!' she whimpered. 'He's not my boyfriend, he's not anything, he just gave me a lift.'

'Y'lying, Ally.' His voice was horrible quiet again and her flesh flinched away from him in every part of her body. 'Y'lying, I know y'are. I seen that car and him in it, sneaking away from m'own front door.'

'I'm tryin t'tell y'if y'll only listen!' she moaned. 'I was at the Rectory, and the Reverend was bringing me home—'

Carefully he steadied her face in his left hand, and delivered a punch to her eye with his right.

'Y'lying again,' he cooed. 'Just like y'mother. A bit more of this'd've kept her straight – if she hadn't run off. Said she couldn't take it. You c'n take it Ally, can't ya?' With the same deliberation, like an artist putting the finishing touches to a masterpiece, he punched her other eye. 'There's a good girl.'

She was on the floor now, and he was bending over her, huddling into her, his hot breath coarse on her neck.

'Y'don't understand, see, Ally, 'cause y'just a bit of a girl, and y'don't know about these things. He's using you t'get at me, Everard is. He don't care nothing f'you, y'just another tart t'him. It's me he's after. But I seen through his plan.'

He paused, his snorting breath slobbering into the side of her face now. 'Y'know what he's fixing t'do. He's going t'give y'one, get'y'up the spout, then dump y'like rubbish, leaving me t'raise his spawn and see m'own flesh and blood tainted with his filth. That's his plan.'

He was burrowing away at her now like a dog at a bitch. 'But I fixed him. Din't I, girl? There's a good girl.

Y'always was a good girl, Ally. Y'still Daddy's girl? Like
y'used t'be? Still y'daddy's good little girl?'

Chapter 13

The second she saw it, shivering a little as she opened the door to the postman in the early morning chill, Joan recognised the letter for what it was. But with her habitual reserve and iron control, she would not, could not pry about its contents. Without comment she handed all the letters in a bundle to Robert, who shared them round the breakfast-table as he normally did.

'Here you go – one for you, Joanie – and Claire.'

The silence was broken by a small sound from Claire, halfway between a cry and a moan.

'Oh no! I don't believe it!'

'What's up?'

Claire flushed. 'You know that – that appointment with the specialist I've been waiting for? To go into hospital and have all those – you know, those tests? They've sent for me to fill a vacancy – they've had a sudden cancellation – they can take me in on Thursday. But I'd have to leave tomorrow – no, today! And how can I go off to Sydney for a week or more right now, and be away for the very weekend of the Centenary?' She let out a wail of frustration.

They looked at each other, lost.

'I just can't go, that's all there is to it,' Claire said at last, her face pink with emotion.

Joan voiced the thought troubling them all. 'But if you cancel it, how d'you know you'll get another appointment?'

'Joan's right,' said Robert heavily. 'You've waited long enough for this one, darling. Another six months . . .'

. . . would kill me! Claire wanted to say. She knew he was right.

'First things first,' continued Robert firmly, but wanting to make light of Claire's dilemma. 'After all, Brightstone has a centenary every hundred years! For you, this is once in a lifetime.'

'For us, Robert, for us!' said Claire angrily. 'This isn't just something I'm doing for myself, you know.'

'I know, darling.' Robert hastened to soothe the ruffled feathers, and introduce something that had come to him very forcibly as soon as Claire first spoke. 'I know how important it is. I think you should go – and I'm coming with you.'

'You?' Claire's eyes widened in shock. 'Robert, you can't!'

'Why not? They don't need me for the opening ceremony, nor for the exhibition. Everyone will be perfectly capable of admiring Ally's handiwork without my hovering over them to point out every last detail. And they won't miss us at the dance on Saturday night – they'll all be far too busy having a good time!'

'There's the service, Robert – the service of commemoration on Sunday, you can't miss that!' Joan's voice was anxious. 'No one else could do it except you!'

If only Joan was not so convinced that he was the best in the world, and therefore indispensable! He could see at once that Claire would never agree to his plan now.

'Oh yes, the service, Robert! Joan's right. That's the whole focus of the weekend's celebrations. You can't pass that over to anyone else. And I couldn't make you miss it, when you've worked so hard to build up the congregation and organise the whole thing.'

'Claire, I'm coming with you. You're more important to me than anything else!'

'Well, you're more important to me, too.' Claire's face was set in an expression of resolution he knew only too well. 'I can't let you do this, Robert. If you insist on coming, I simply won't go, that's all.'

They looked at each other, deadlocked.

'I'll go.'

Joan's intervention took them both completely by surprise.

'I don't think you should be on your own, Claire, for such a long journey.'

And for such a miserable, humiliating set of tests as you'll have to face at the end of it, she thought privately. Of course any man would want to support his wife through this. But if she could take Robert's place this once, there'd be no more talk of him going – which would mean him letting down the whole of Brightstone, not to mention ducking out of the big service, his showcase, his opportunity to shine in the eyes of the whole community, the diocese, the Bishop himself. Even the Archbishop had hinted that he might be able to attend, if his diary was not too full. No – Robert must take that service!

'I'd be glad to go along with you, Claire, I really would. I've got a bit of holiday due – and we could do some shopping in Sydney, make a little break of it . . .'

Claire looked at her sister-in-law, torn between guilt and gratitude. 'Would you, Joan? I can't pretend I wouldn't be glad to have you along. I know you want to be here for the Centenary too, but there's no one else I could ask. Mum's just not up to it since Dad died, and her legs had been so bad recently as well . . . and it would mean that Robert could take the service . . .'

For both of them, Robert knew, nothing else mattered. If he did not agree to this, Claire would cancel her appointment with the gynaecologist and uncomplainingly let herself in for another six months of waiting and hoping, with its slow drip, drip, drip, of constant disappointment. In the waiting silence, a verse from the Book of Proverbs floated through the spaces of his mind. *Hope deferred maketh the heart sick: but when the desire cometh, it is a tree of life*. So be it.

'You must go, dear,' he said gently. 'And if Joan will go with you, we should be thankful for her love and generosity, and accept that this is the way it's meant to be.'

Claire smiled, halfway between relief and tears. 'You're so good to me, Robert. So good. I'll be as quick as I can, I promise you. We'll be back before you know we've gone! And I'll phone you every day. I'll miss you, darling. We both will, won't we, Joan?'

The rest of Tuesday passed in a blur of frantic packing, phoning, making travel arrangements and hurriedly remembering final details of the arrangements for the Centenary weekend.

'We can't get sleepers on the overland train, Claire, but I booked anyway – we can sleep when we get to Sydney—'

'Mum, it's come – my appointment – Yes, Sydney – tonight, on the overland train—'

'Robert, the Archbishop's secretary's due to phone on Saturday to tell you if he's going to make it to the service – and don't forget to tell that Ally Calder she'll have to get the stuff down to the exhibition all by herself, now I won't be here to oversee her, OK?'

Then they were gone, and the house was oddly quiet. Oddly, but blissfully – as he wandered through the silent rooms dozing sleepily in the autumn sun, he felt the deep joy of being himself, being all by himself, that his chosen way of life so rarely afforded him. 'Better not let this become a habit!' he thought ruefully. 'Not that there's much chance of that!'

And he would not be lonely, not even really alone. He would have company. Wednesday morning, he knew, was one of Ally's days. He rose early, and was surprised to find himself whistling and singing in the shower. He would have to go down to Brightstone later, so he dressed with care, and spent more time than usual before the mirror. She would tease him about it, he thought happily, and looked forward to seeing her face as she walked through the door.

A heartbeat after 9.30, he knew there was something wrong. She had never been late before: such was her delight at coming to the Rectory, she had always been early to work. At 10.30 he rang her home – and once an hour thereafter throughout the day. There was no reply.

164

In the late afternoon he loaded all the cuttings books, the old photographs of Brightstone so carefully mounted, all the old deeds and documents of the early days which had been prepared by Ally for display, and took them down to the town where the organisers were waiting to set up the exhibition. As soon as he had delivered everything he had for them, he got back in his car. He knew he had to tread very warily if he was thinking of challenging Jim Calder on his home ground. But that was no reason not to try. Bracing himself for the encounter, he drove straight to the Calder bungalow.

'Hello?'

Rather to his surprise, Jim himself came to the door, the small eyes in his gross face instantly wary at the sight of the visitor.

'Oh, good evening, Mr Calder. Forgive my bothering you. I'm just inquiring about Ally. She was due at the Rectory for work today, and she just didn't show up.'

'No, well . . .'

Robert could almost hear Calder's mind working as he fabricated what he was going to say. 'She's sick, Reverend. Couldn't come.'

'Sick? What with?'

A pause. 'Cold. Got a bad cold.'

'Look, Mr Calder, this is a very bad time for us. There's so much to do for the Centenary, we were really counting on Ally.'

'Yeah, well, there y'go. Affairs of mice and men, as they say, Rev.'

Robert wanted to attack him, to beat some truth out of his hollow throat. 'Let me talk to Ally, Mr Calder.'

'Y'can't do that, Reverend. She's – in the bath.'

'I'll call back later.'

'Not much point in that, Reverend. She – she was going straight t'bed. She'll be asleep in two shakes of a kanga's tail.'

Silence. Stand-off. Blocked at every turn. 'Well, will you please tell her I called? I very much want her to come to work tomorrow morning. As it is, that only leaves us Friday to do everything we have to do before the celebrations begin. Will you tell her that?'

'Sure thing, Reverend, sure thing. Rely on me. Tell her the first minute I can, y'bet y'life.'

He was lying, Robert knew. Early next morning, after a troubled night, Robert found Ally once again obsessing his mind, dominating all his thoughts. It was stupid, he knew, self-indulgent even – especially with so much to be done. There were a thousand good, ordinary reasons why a young girl wouldn't come to work for one day. 'For God's sake, pull yourself together!' he ordered himself sternly. But even as he spoke, a dark foreboding gripped him that it was already too late.

Too late for what? If only he knew! What should he do? What *could* he do? He had tried to make contact, and failed. He could not simply go back to the house, defy Calder, call him a liar, and demand to have Ally produced for him. If he went back to the house, as he had been so strongly tempted to do yesterday, he could have no guarantee of seeing her, and might even make matters worse. If only Claire had still been here, or Joan! It would have been so much easier for one of the women to just drop in while they were passing – and a woman would not be so likely to trigger Calder's bullying, violence or insane possessiveness. But they were in Sydney for the duration. He had to handle this alone.

With a heavy heart he made his way slowly across the hall towards the study, and forced himself to try to work. Around noon a soft sound from the front of the house disturbed his concentration and made him open his door to look out. A solitary letter had come by the second post, he saw – the postman must have dropped the envelope on the oak plate when he found the front door unlocked and no-one in. Recognising Claire's writing, eagerly he tore it open. It was only a note: 'Just arrived, journey OK, clinic fantastic, all well.' That's one relief, anyway, he thought. At least Claire's OK and in the right place. Now what about Ally . . .

His ears caught a low, unidentifiable sound. There was someone in the dining-room. He strode across the hall and threw open the door. On her knees on the floor, bent over the piles of papers still littering the carpet, her back towards him, was Ally. He felt like a complete fool for fretting about her as he had done. He did not know whether to laugh or cry.

'Ally! Wherever have you been? I've been worried to death about you!'

She burrowed even deeper into her task, her long curtain of hair falling forward and completely concealing her face.

'No worries.' Her voice was level and controlled, and quite devoid of emotion, her hands flying briskly through the piles heaped around her knees, her unwillingness to talk to him or even look at him quite plain. 'Had a cold, that's all. I'll just get on with this, sort out what's left for the exhibition, then take it all downtown on my way home.'

He hesitated on the threshold, feeling uneasy but unable to say why. 'Look, Ally – I've been thinking that one of us should have called your father the other night, told him that you'd be late home and explained the reason for it. As it is, I—'

'No worries. It's all fine, no problem .'

Again he felt he was being put in his place, dismissed from her presence. It angered him. 'Well, I was concerned for you, Ally. And when I see your father, I'll mention it.' He turned to go.

'No!' The cry seemed to be wrung from her without her knowledge. 'No, don't! Don't!'

In two strides he was before her, thrusting the rubbish she had surrounded herself with out of the way, gripping her shoulders, looking into her eyes. As he shook back the long fall of hair from her face, he could not repress a cry.

'Good God! Ally, what's happened to you?' A fury began to sear him, to burn into his very bones. 'Who the *hell* has done this to you?'

Only her eyes were recognisable in the bruised and battered face, though even they wore a beaten, hopeless look he had never seen before. They stared out at him from sockets obviously swollen and puffed up from repeated blows. One cheekbone was grazed as if she had connected with a door or wall, and the other was split by a neat cut that could only have been made by a man's signet ring. Her lips were bloated, bee-stung and blue with bruises. He wanted to weep.

She was weeping already, silently and hopelessly, like a beaten child.

'He can't get away with this!' He had never felt so angry. 'I'm going to the police, Ally. I'll have him put behind bars – for life!'

'Oh Robert.' Even her voice had changed. She sounded older than time itself now. 'What good d'you think that'll do?'

'What do you mean?'

'He gets like that – when he's drunk. Says I'm like my mother.'

'Your *mother*?'

'She was a dancer – with a troupe on tour. They came here from America, but she was English.' So that explained the voice that had tantalised him since she first spoke, the un-Australian lilt in her intonation that he had found so appealing. 'He fell for her, offered her a home. But she couldn't stand him. She found another bloke, and ran away. He's never forgotten or forgiven it. He says all women are born liars, born whores, and the only way is to beat it out of them.'

'But you, Ally? *You*?'

You're innocence itself, he wanted to say. How could he even think of punishing you, beating you . . . He was shaking with fury, his whole being invaded by a murderous rage. He knew without a shadow of doubt that if Jim Calder had walked into the room at that moment, he would have killed him. That a man could do this . . . 'Oh Ally – you poor little girl – poor, poor darling . . .'

His senses were whirling, and the whole world seemed to be giving way beneath his feet. Her pain was overflowing now, the grief pouring down her poor, bruised face. His pain answered hers: he felt invaded, made raw, laid open inside as if by a great wound. She could not look at him, she was so ashamed of the beating she had taken, as if it were all her fault. He wanted to help and heal her, to take her to his soul. He could feel her small body trembling in his hands, smell the sweet, baby smell of her hair mingled with the harsher scent of her distress. With infinite tenderness he took her into his arms. She came into the circle of his body as if she had been born there. Holding her, he pressed his lips to the top of her head, stroking the smooth, fine hair. Then he turned up the crumpled flower of her face, and kissed her on the mouth.

It was a moment out of time, above time. Joy suffused his soul, and seemed to echo and re-echo through his whole being, then spread away beyond him through endless space. He could not have said where his life, his spirit, his physical reality ended, and hers began. She was making small, unintelligible sounds, timid animal murmurs and whispers of tremulous delight, turning her face to him for his caress like a flower seeking the sun. He kissed her again, taking her more fully, more completely to him and rejoicing in her closeness, her body, her very self, now laid open to him like a virgin land to its conqueror and king. The pulsing heartbeat, the warm, aroused flesh, the smooth skin of her back which the sundress she was wearing laid bare to his hands, the womanly swell of her hips, were his – his to command, his to adore, his to—

Realisation came to him like wildfire, and with it fear such as he had never known before – not for himself, but for her. Instantly he loosed his hold of her and stepped back. 'Ally! My God! What am I doing? God, God, oh God!'

Her eyes snapped open in sudden dread. 'Robert! What's the matter?'

'Oh Ally!' The groan he uttered came from the depths of his being. 'I shouldn't be doing this!'

'Why not?'

Her battered face was set, her small chin tilted as if for a fight. He was completely at a loss. 'Why not—?'

'Why not – if I want you to?'

'Ally, can't you see . . . ?'

'Robert, hold me, kiss me – *please!*'

She was torturing him, torturing both of them. He had to stop her hurting herself. 'Ally, I mustn't! I have to make you understand – why I can't—'

She broke away from him, her face flaming. 'I understand one thing! You don't give a damn about me, about how I feel! I'm nothing to you, nothing!' Turning on her heel, she raced from the room.

'Ally, no! It's not true! Listen to me, please *listen*—' Galvanised into action, he took off in pursuit.

But she was too quick for him. All he heard was the distant sound of running feet and the slam of the back door as she whirled away from the house. Head bent, he shuddered from head to foot, and flinging back into the study, he gave himself up to the punishment of his thoughts.

So this was what it had all been about, all along! His efforts to help her, his desire to be her friend – all, all exposed now for what they were. Was it his arrogance that had made him so self-deluded? Or simply his disregard for his own human nature, his animal instincts, his flesh and blood?

When did you first fancy her, Reverend? taunted his evil demon. When did you first think you'd like to get between those slim young thighs? Tried to be a father to her, did you? What kind of father, Father, wants to screw his own daughter? Saw yourself as working for God, expressing His will and purpose on this sinful earth? You were closer all along to the old Adam, the first of the sinners, the first man of flesh and blood – and what a sweet piece of flesh she was, right there, had her in your hand, didn't you? And you could've done anything with her, couldn't you, anything at all . . .

He groaned aloud in torment. His body could still feel the impression of her slender frame pressed the length of his, his hands on the silky hollow of her back, his every muscle remembering the quickening pulse of hers. Along with the memory, he fought down the answering stirring of his own flesh. To take advantage of her like that! And now, of all times – now when she was battered and bruised, turning to him for safety and consolation, only to find that he was just like any other man and couldn't keep his hands off her, that he could not even try to comfort her without sex making its vicious

170

approach. He was no better than her father – he was worse!

He could not think, he could not pray. Hours passed as his mind, like a tortured animal tied to a wheel, stumbled round and round in the same track. He had never known such pain. He had to get away. In a fury he flung out of the house, determined to walk until he dropped. The sun was setting, the afternoon almost gone as he struck furiously up over the headland, away from Brightstone and towards the sea. Approaching from the far side, he plunged almost unconscious of his surroundings into the long reach of dunes leading up to the headland above Broken Bay. Dune after dune lay before him, a series of endless bowls of white sand as empty as his mind. Not a soul stirred, not even a bird, for miles around. He might have been the last human being left alive in the universe.

Except for one. As he crested the furthest and deepest of the dunes, he saw her huddled kneeling in the hollow of the sand, the very picture of desolation. He froze. Bathed in the last low rays of the evening sun, she turned and looked at him across the shining sand.

'Ally—'

He leaped towards her. Her eyes were locked on his, her whole body called him to her. As he drew near, she rose to her feet and held out her arms. 'Robert!' she called softly, low but wild. 'Robert!'

He moved towards her blindly: nothing could have kept him from her side. Their bodies connected with the quivering shock of expectant flesh, their minds meeting, too, in the exquisite release of acceptance, trust and love. They kissed, their first real kiss, the first in true knowledge of each other as woman and as man. He stroked her hair, and kissed the purple bruises again and again, kissing her tears away as he did so, tasting the salt of them even as his own tears of joy began to flow.

'Robert, I'm sorry . . .'

'Darling, there's nothing to be sorry about . . .'

'I didn't mean to run away—'

'I would have come after you. I would have found you.'

'I tried to tell you, Robert – I wanted you to – to—'

'Ssshhh . . . I know, Ally darling, I know . . .'

Tenderly, worshipfully, he drew her down into the hollow of the sand. Kneeling before her he slipped off the thin straps of her sundress and exposed her breasts, bending his head to adore each small pink nipple with his lips and tongue. 'God, you're beautiful!' he murmured. 'You're so beautiful!' He slipped off his shirt and spread it on the sand, then carefully, carefully, as if she would break, he laid her down on her back.

Her breasts were perfect, small and sweet, the nipples showing the unspoiled shell-pink glow of the woman who has never borne a child. Wonderingly he circled each small, gently textured aureole, and felt her quiver and warm to his touch despite the chill in the night-approaching autumn air. Her eyes closed, her head thrown back, her whole body arched with anticipation, she gave herself as trustingly as a child to his every caress. With infinite patience, tenderness and skill he readied her. Then murmuring words of love, he began to draw down the folds of fabric from her waist and the lower part of her body, as yet hidden from his view.

She was ahead of him. Flexing her back, with a shrug of her hips she freed herself from the clinging cotton of her dress and stretched herself out again on the sand. The wonder of her body – its satin sheen, golden length and unspoiled innocence offered to him, only to him – almost dazzled his eyes. In a moment he lost all anxiety, all the pain and fear he had been carrying, it seemed, since they had met. He needed to be naked too, like her – like the first man and the first woman in the first garden, before time began. Shrugging off his clothes, he matched his soul and body to hers in all the purity of love, knew her for what she was, and claimed her for his own. Afterwards he said only, 'Come home, my darling – come on home.'

172

Chapter 14

In bed, they found their home. Alone together in the warm, whispering darkness where souls can be as naked as bodies, they shared at last the sweetness of complete discovery. Tenderly he cradled the long, slim mermaid body, smoothing the tangles in her long, silken hair even as he soothed the knotted anxieties of her heart.

'Oh, Robert!' she sobbed into his chest. 'A man like you – and someone like me—'

'Ally darling,' he murmured in reply, 'there is nobody – nobody in the world – like you.'

Then her joy grew along with her confidence and she had to share it, or die. 'I saw you first!' she exulted, the childlike boast at odds with the womanly body whose deep, hungry longing he knew he had hardly begun to explore, let alone to satisfy. 'In the café! I saw you then, and I—' Abruptly she broke off. This was no time to make him think she had had designs on him all along.

But drunk with love, he did not care. 'You what?' he teased. 'You saw me and you loved me – tell me, Ally!'

She hesitated, then gave a small nod, her face buried in his chest. 'I wanted you!' she confessed, her voice muffled against him, her breath warm against his skin. He laughed with delight.

'Let me tell you, darling, not half as much as I wanted you! And I've wanted you ever since!'

In disbelief he ran a wondering hand over the soft bones of her shoulder-blades, the deep, smooth hollow of her back, her long flanks and the soft swelling of her buttocks as she lay at peace against him. Responding instantly to his touch she wriggled closer and raised her mouth to his. Already her kisses were stronger, more demanding and yet also more satisfying, he marvelled – yet with the eternal paradox of the body's demands, more satisfying meant also more searching, more stimulating, more, more, more . . .

His left hand finding her breast, he reached over with his right and began to stroke down over the smooth globes of her backside and between her legs, his fingers playing over the smooth-as-satin skin at the top of her thighs and flirting teasingly around the circle of her sex, advancing and retreating in the age-old dance of desire. Almost immediately her breathing changed, becoming lighter yet huskier by the minute. He could feel her growing moist again to his touch, feel her heart fluttering against his, feel her kisses change from a light rain to a passionate storm.

He was learning, he realised with a rush of joy, not only what pleased and excited her, but her pace, her every rhythm, the meaning of her every breath. And she was learning too – her caresses in return were already less those of a novice, more of a longing, loving partner. She clung to him, more and more aroused, the shape of his shoulder moulded by the cup of her hand, her hand which played on down his body, her thumb pausing to punish his nipple in delicious torment before finding the ultra-sensitive hollow of his hip, then moving deep in the coarse triangle of hair at the top of his legs, already stirring at her approach.

'Ohhh . . .'

With a sigh of deepest joy, deeply controlled, he flipped her over on to her back, and leaning over her, expertly teased up her sexual rhythm to keep pace with his. Soon she was crying for him from the back of her throat, from her deepest core – 'Robert, please! Oh Robert, *please! please! please!*' Carefully, for she was yet new to him or to any man, he entered her again, feeling once again all the power of the conqueror, enhanced now by the sweet tribute of ecstatic love which is always the due of the longed-for liberator.

Afterwards they slept, he could not say for how long.

Suddenly she was wide awake and stiff with tension in his arms.

'Robert, what's the time?'

'I – God, Ally, I don't know!'

'*What's the time?*'

She was out of bed now, scrabbling for the lamp switch and trying to gather up her scattered clothes at the same time. He reached out and grasped her wrist. 'Ally, what's the matter?'

'My dad!' she panted, squinting at her watch. 'Look at the time!' Feverishly she fought her way into wisps of underwear which looked as if they would hardly withstand the unequal struggle. 'He'd kill me if he knew . . . if he even thought . . . !'

'Hey, hey, hey!' He swung out of bed. 'Calm down, Ally, calm down! How's he going to know? Think, darling – who's going to tell him? You will, though, if you insist on charging down there like that – he'll know something's happened as soon as he sees you! Look, we've got to *think*.'

He frowned. Smiling at his fierce expression, she began to collect herself.

'Look,' he went on, 'How about this? Why don't you just go home as normal, and tell him you were delayed? You can say we had a lot of work to do, and then I asked you to fix me something to eat as Joan and Claire are away.' He looked at the bedside clock. 'It's not so late, anyway, it's only eight o'clock.'

'Yeah, he'll go for that!' Her small face lit up with relief. 'And once I've fixed his dinner, he'll be fine!'

And then what . . . ? She was almost dressed now, almost on the point of leaving. He felt a hollow, a dread starting to form in the pit of his stomach. Don't go! his whole body besought her, don't leave me now, don't leave me like this . . .

'Ally,' he said slowly, 'if you've got to go, I'll run you home. OK, OK, I'll drop you off at the foot of the headland, I won't give him the slightest excuse to make trouble for you – but I can't let you go just like that. However you manage it, however late it is, I want you to promise you'll come back to me again tonight. I want

you, Ally, I want to be with you, I want to make love
to you again and again and again, I want to eat with
you, drink with you, shower with you, I want to sleep
with you, I want to wake up with you. I want you. So
Ally, darling Ally – come back – come home to me –
soon – just as soon as ever you can.'

That was Thursday. She returned to him that night, and
the next day, and the next night, slipping away only with
the dawn to be back at the bungalow before Jim awoke.
Days and nights, nights and days, wove themselves in
and out of one another in a world without time, a world
above time, a world above the world itself. No one
bothered the minister, knowing that his wife and sister
were out of town and that he was up to his eyes with
the details of the Centenary arrangements now that the
great event was upon them. At some early point Jim
Calder was bluntly told that he'd have to fend for himself
for the duration, as events at the Rectory had reached
the stage where only his daughter's full-time attendance
would do, and he took it with grudging pride as a tribute
to the importance and indispensability of the Calders
wherever they might be. Early on, too, a female hand
took its own private occasion to dislodge the telephone
receiver, disabling the line for any outside calls. Not that
their absence was noticed. Not on Thursday, nor all day
Friday, nor Friday's long night, nor Saturday morning
when it broke bright and early over the two sleep-
entwined, love-exhausted forms in the great, wide, welcoming Rectory bed.

The overland train rarely stopped at Brightstone, and
the little town boasted no such luxury as a taxi service.
But the two women disembarking with their luggage that
morning had already made their plans.

'I'll call Robert,' said Claire. 'He must have had the
phone fixed by now. I know it's early, but he's usually
up and about around this time. And I know he'll just
be so surprised and pleased to see us!'

'Yeah, it's fantastic we're back in time for the fête
and everything after all,' agreed Joan. 'I was so worried

176

about that Ally girl! – if she'd've remembered to type out the notes to all the stallholders, seen to the orders for copies of the old photos, checked with the caterers – there was still so much to be done when we had to leave—'

Driven as ever, Joan was still running through her mental lists when Claire returned from the phone. 'That's odd', she said with a puzzled air. 'The phone's still making that engaged tone, as if it's out of order. I rang and rang, and I just couldn't get through.'

'P'raps he's in church,' returned Joan absently. 'Taken the phone off the hook.'

'Not this early.' She thought for a moment. 'Ah, no worries. I'll ring Paul. He'll just have time to pick us up and run us home before he starts on the morning shift.'

Paul was delighted to see them back. 'Amazing you'll be here after all for the dance!' he enthused. 'Going to be great, that is – I can hardly wait!'

'It's not the only event of the weekend, you know,' observed Joan tartly, as she saw all her months of hard work and organisation taking second place – as things so often did with Paul – to the pleasure principle.

Why did she have to be so dry and harsh? 'Ah, give us a break, Joanie,' he protested. 'A bloke's not going to spend his precious one day off a week traipsing round that old exhibition. The lads just want to have a bit of fun.'

'Yeah, I'm sure'. Joan's sardonic agreement was lost in the excitement of arriving back home at the Rectory.

'Thanks for the lift, Pauly,' cried Claire, favouring him with a sisterly kiss. 'See you at the dance tonight, if not before!'

Together Claire and Joan mounted the shallow flight of steps to the Rectory's front door.

'He's slept in!' said Joan dismissively, picking up the milk bottles languishing on the doorstep in the already powerful rays of the early morning sun. They entered the hall. Immediately Joan's laser-beam glance fell on the telephone. 'Well, there's your "out of order",' she said, replacing the receiver in its cradle. 'I'll go and see about breakfast. You'd better go and wake Robert, or we'll never be ready for the start of the events.'

Smiling, Claire thankfully deposited her travelling bags and mounted the stairs deep in thought. How lucky she and Robert were in Joan, really! Such a good heart, so loyal and always so ready to turn to and organise things. She entered the bedroom, easing off her shoes as she did so. Oh, it was good to be home! The bedroom was empty, and the bed, dreadfully rumpled, looked as if wild animals had slept in it. God, Robert must have been having some dreadful nights while she had been away!

Was something wrong? She moved around the bedroom, faintly disturbed. Something was different. There was a faint, sweet smell in the air – what from? Could someone have been here? One of the Brightstone congregation popped in to clean? But who? She forced a laugh. This was ridiculous! What could have happened? She was imagining things – nothing that wouldn't have happened if she'd been at home, that was for sure! Suddenly she heard the sound of the shower – and was that a laugh? Robert laughing? In the shower? He never did that! Going out on to the landing again she approached the bathroom door, knocked, and called, 'Darling? Robert, where are you? We're home!'

The whole of the upper floor seemed to resound with a silence that lasted for a long time. At last she heard the bathroom door opening, and Robert stood there, clad only in a towel. 'You're home,' he said dazedly. 'You're home.'

'Yes, we're home!' agreed Claire, laughing. 'But you don't look very pleased to see us! We caught the overland train back. I tried to phone, but we couldn't get through. Anyway, I wanted to surprise you!'

'You – you surprised me.' Robert drew a deep breath. He was fighting for words, fighting, too, for the control to prevent her from noticing his state of shock. *How* had she come back here like this? And why *now*? All unnoticing, Claire rattled on, her own overriding concern taking precedence in her mind over everything else.

'I've got to go back again, later – probably for surgery,

the doctor thinks. The problem – my problem – it's so basic, it came up on the first day, in the very first set of tests.' She tried a smile. 'That was on Thursday. Seems there's not much point in anything until I can get that sorted out. So as soon as they told us, Joanie and me thought we'd be better off back here, helping you with the Centenary and all, rather than kicking our heels round Sydney, spending money we can't afford.'

'Yes. Yes of course.'

Why hadn't he gone up to her, taken her in his arms, greeted her with a kiss as he normally would have done? Get a grip, man! he warned himself savagely. Unless you want to blow the whole thing sky high right now, that is! Oh God! What a mess! Forcing himself, he stepped forward and folded her to his chest. The feel of her now-strange body was terrible, another shock, almost a betrayal. Yet who was he betraying? Oh God! God! God!

'Are you all right, Robert?' He looked terrible, Claire thought in wonderment as she stepped back – hunted, driven and so pale.

'I would – I would have met you at the station,' he said tersely. 'I wish I'd known you were coming.'

'Robert'. The clear eyes pinned him down in cool appraisal. 'What have you been doing?'

'What? What have I—'

'Look, I can tell—'

'I don't know what you mean!'

He looked dreadful now, she thought, ashen face matching the dull lowlights of his tousled ash-blond hair. 'I know you, Robert. You can't fool me. I know what all this is about.'

'Claire, please!' He could feel himself getting angry.

She smiled peaceably, and sighed. 'All right, don't get mad with me! It's just that you've been working too hard, haven't you? Trying to sort everything out on your own, because Joan and I weren't here? And not eating or sleeping properly ever since we went, at a guess? No wonder you look as if you'd seen a ghost!'

As an answer to her charge, he gathered her again into his arms and crushed her to his chest, covering her with kisses. 'Oh darling,' he muttered brokenly into the hair on top of her head,'forgive me? Will you forgive me?'

'Oh Robert!' She gave him a loving, reassuring squeeze. 'If you're going to be as sweet as this when I come back, I should go away more often!'

It was gone half past ten – nearly eleven. Why hadn't he phoned?

Why hadn't he phoned?

He'd said he would. He'd promised.

No, he hadn't promised, not in so many words. But he hadn't needed to. The way he was – the way things were, the way they were together just as a man and woman in love, when she slipped away earlier in order to be home at her father's before he woke up – he hadn't needed to promise, and she hadn't needed to make him.

He'd just said he'd phone – as early as he could without arousing her father's suspicions. Around nine o'clock, anyway – to fix up about seeing her today, now the Centenary was here. And he'd said he couldn't bear her to go, didn't want her to be away from him even for an hour, he'd said . . .

Of course he'd be a bit tied up while all this was going on, that was only natural. But it was only for a couple of days. Then she'd have him all to herself again for ages – at least until his wife came back. *And after, too,* she promised herself, *or my name's not Ally Calder. He's mine now. He loves me, I know he does, I'd know it even if he didn't keep telling me all the time. He's mine. I'll get him, no matter what it takes, it's me he loves, not her, nor that horrible old sister of his . . .*

But why hadn't he phoned? What was he doing? What was he thinking? How could he do this? How *could* he . . . ?

'Bloody awful racket going on in here this morning!' snarled Jim, lurching into the kitchen like a bear with a sore head. 'What's going on?'

Your hangover's going on! she wanted to scream. With the Red Army dancers doing a clog dance inside your skull, you stinking old soak! She busied herself

180

with a few more bangs and slams. 'Nothing,' she said.
'Nothing?'

He snuffled up to her suspiciously, like a pig after
truffles. 'Y'don't look like nothing, girl – y'look like
something the cat's dragged in. What's y'problem?'

She dropped her eyes and shrank from his coarse,
probing interrogation. 'Nothing,' she repeated in a low
voice. 'I'm telling you, nothing.'

He hawked and spat, ejecting a thick spume of fluid
into the sink where she was washing up. 'Making enough
noise about nothing, then,' he grumbled. 'Put a sock in
it, will ya? Man's entitled to a bit of peace and quiet on
his day off.' He moved to the door, then a thought struck
him. He peered into her eyes, assessing the remains of
the damage she had suffered at his hands, still visible
even to the most casual scrutiny. 'And mind y'ready on
time and all pooned up f'the fête this afternoon – put
something on that face'v yours – a bit of make-up or
something . . .'

Her silence resounded round the kitchen, till even he
heard it.

'I know y'might think y've got a bone t'pick with me,
Ally,' he began in that mixture of bluster and guilt she
knew so well. 'But I got t'look out f'ya! Y'dad's got a
right t'look out f'ya, and keep y'on the right path. I'm
only looking after your own interests, Ally, 'cause I been
around and you haven't. Y'might think I'm too tough
on ya, but it's f'y'own good. Y'never knew y'mother,
and what she was. And y'don't know nothing about the
ways of the world!'

She finished washing up, folded the dishcloth neatly
on the side of the sink, and turned to face him. Her
eyes were the eyes of a zombie, blank and dead, but
sparking to life with a seething hatred and contempt as
she looked at him. 'And whose fault is that?' she hissed.
Then she walked past him and into her room.

Standing in furious disbelief in the kitchen, he heard
the bolt slide on the inside of her door. He flung himself
against it in a rage, beating at the flimsy panels. 'Ally!
Ally! Listen to me! Open this door, blast ya, and listen
t'me! I want t'talk t'ya, miss. Open this door, will ya?

Or, God blast ya, I swear I'll – I swear – *open this
bloody door!*'

'Reverend, how y'doin'?'

'Mrs Milligan – good to see you – everything all right
at home? Oh, Molly – how are you? Claire's over there,
just gone to start the cake stall.'

'Grand do, Father, lovely fête! Can't remember anything like it before, not in all my time in Brightstone.'

'That's great, Geordie – glad you and the family are
enjoying yourselves. Hope we'll see you later on at the
dance?'

'You bet y'life! The missus has been lookin' forward
to it f'weeks! Wait'll y'see her new frock! Cost me a
week's wages!'

All around the grounds of the church and Rectory,
the Centenary garden fête was in full swing. Swelling
with delight and innocent civic pride, the Brightstonians
were passing from one stall to another in the last of the
autumn sun, trying this, declining that, with a sense
that they were sharing an occasion that few had been
privileged to see, while even fewer would survive to any
equivalent celebrations in the future.

Moving among them on public display, his face and
body going through the motions while his nerves were
screaming with suppressed tension, Robert was suffering
the tortures of the damned. Where was she? *Where
was she?* She had to come, she simply had to be here
somewhere. How else could he see her, speak to her, if
she did not come?

What was she thinking, what must she have thought
when he did not phone her first thing that morning, as
he had promised? After all that had passed between
them – after sweet days and nights of love, joyful, murmured truths and the relief of explanations, revelations
on both sides of feelings long cherished but never
realised till that very moment – she had wound herself
around his heart so tightly that not seeing her, even
since this morning, was like a physical pain. He loved
her, he knew that now, had known it all along.

Yet what kind of love could it be that dared not show

182

itself, had to skulk and hide, dodging prying eyes? That had to share itself with another instead of giving wholeheartedly the one pure gift of love, an unblemished, uncommitted self, soul, heart? What could he offer to Ally that was not already mortgaged, pledged and given to Claire? Claire! He almost groaned aloud. What was he doing to her? And why had he refused even to contemplate what would happen when she returned, so allowing this nightmare to descend on poor Ally's undefended head!

She had trusted him, and this was how he had repaid her. Could she forgive him? Why should she? What kind of love was he offering her, when he found himself so hopelessly in the wrong, trying to juggle his love for her against his responsibilities – to her and to others – oh, Claire! – to one other above all, one he had loved before, and could not now simply abandon or deny. Poor Claire . . . but Ally, oh Ally . . .

Restlessly he scoured the Rectory garden and grounds, searching for her between the crowded, gaily-coloured stalls and booths with increasing desperation. Yet at the same time, he could not simply switch off the world all around, nor his part in it.

'Homemade cakes, Mrs Greaney – yes, they look wonderful. No, I won't just now, if you'll forgive me – I seem to have been eating all day . . .'

'Is this all your own work, Mary-Lou? Well, there aren't many girls of your age who can crochet these days, let alone as beautifully as this. It's tremendous that you're giving your time and effort like this – simply tremendous . . .'

'Mr Maitland! Mr Maitland! Mr Wilkes wants to know, when does he have to make the draw f'the Grand Tombola f'the big prize f'the charity raffle . . .?'

'Hey, Robert!'

From a truck parked beside a garishly striped booth, Paul was unloading barrels of beer and rolling them up to a bar kept by an attractive woman whose knowing wink indicated that this was not her first acquaintance with the handsome miner.

'Oh, Paul.' Something stirred at the back of Robert's

mind. 'Got a message for you. Joan's over on the other side of the field, on the refreshment stall. She said if I saw you to ask as soon as you had a chance, could you get over there and lend a hand? She'd love to see you.'

'Yeah, well.' Paul looked down at his feet with the air of a man who has only just discovered that his legs ended in such interesting appurtenances. 'I'm a bit tied up over here just now, helping Freda here' – another wink from the well-favoured one – 'but tell you what, I will if I can, eh?'

But Robert had gone, unconscious of everything but his restless search. She had to be here somewhere. She just had to be!

At the end of the line of booths he was scouring, through a heavy press round a hot-dog stall, he caught a glimpse of flaxen hair. He sprang towards the little crowd. A firm hand closing on his arm checked his passage.

'Good turn-out, Reverend. Very good turn-out, after all, don't y'think?'

Trying to contain his anger, Robert glanced down at his interrogator.

'Oh – Mr Wilkes, And Mrs Wilkes, how are you? Enjoying the fête?'

'So far. So so.'

Wilkes had not yet forgiven Robert for the unwarranted intrusion of politics into his funeral address for George Everard, and wanted him to know it. On the other hand, this was a bloody good show and no mistake. No point in denying that. Point was to try and build on it, encourage the Reverend to see the error of his bloody pinko Commie ways. So moderate praise was in order – but nothing too fancy.

'Church'll get some good out'v this, you'll see,' he opined weightily. 'Not t'mention what it'll mean f'the church coffers when what all these stalls are making finds its way into St Jude's bank account.'

'Yes . . . I suppose you're right.'

What was the matter with him? fumed the irate mine boss. Planned all this, spent six months or more getting it all together, and now he was sounding as if couldn't care less if they'd spent a million and finished up with half a dollar? And why was he staring around all the time, looking over their heads as if he couldn't be bothered to hold a proper conversation – let alone say a word to Mrs Wilkes! Determined to avoid even the shadow of a slight to the plump spouse bobbing away at his side in yet another voile concoction even as he spoke, Wilkes made another, sterner attempt on the conversation.

'I must congratulate you, Reverend, on last Sunday's roll-up. Must have been fifty there in the church for Morning Service, and y'got about the same for Evensong, I heard. Good smattering of miners there, too. It's important that – y've got t'get the working men in. They've got to realise—'

'Will you excuse me?'

And he was gone. Bemused and furious, Wilkes watched him carve his way through the crowds towards the hamburger stall, hesitate there for a second, and vanish from view. A deep, resentful misgiving settled in the soul of Mr Wilkes, and took root. 'That young man,' he predicted darkly to the faithful voile, 'he thinks he's going places, and so he may. But they ain't any places that I'll be holding the keys to, not unless and until he learns a bit more manners and a lot more common sense!'

She was there. He had seen her.

He knew she was there.

She had to be.

Another glimpse of her hair, shining again at random among the mass of people, had brought him shooting from Wilkes's side like an arrow from a bow. But as the crowd around the hamburger stall parted, swirled around and reformed, he saw with a bitter shaft of disappointment that the flaxen head was not hers, was nothing like hers, was not even a girl's but that of a Germanic-looking boy of about her build and height. Losing direction, he stood there mechanically engaging in passing snatches of conversation . . . Hello, there . . . Yes, a very good day for it considering the time of the year . . .

Yes . . . no . . . I'm sure you're right . . .

What was that?

This time he saw her, out of the corner of his eye; he knew he did. Yet he also suddenly knew she was here without seeing her. All he had to do was to find her.

Rounding the last stall in the line, he came face to face with the stallholder opposite, whose practised eye immediately spotted an easy mark.

'Roll up, roll up, Reverend, try y'skill at a game of hoopla, all good clean fun and proceeds to a good cause, as you'll well know – how about it?'

Trapped again. With as good grace as he could muster, he approached the stall.

'And you, lady, have a go, keep the Reverend here company, don't let a man of the cloth play a game all on his lonesome.'

Robert turned round. Behind him stood Ally, her eyes fixed on his face, her shaking hand, palm forward, simultaneously trying to silence the showman. His heart lurched, and he had to force himself to stand still, not to race forward and crush her in his arms.

'Don't give me no, lady. I c'n tell from the look of you you'd give any man a good game if y'was in the mood, eh? Now what d'ya say to a quick game with the Reverend here – he'll put up a dollar f'you t'play, won't you, Reverend?'

He fumbled to comply. White-lipped, she stood beside him at the stall, and received her handful of hoopla rings.

'Try y'skill,' pattered the showman. 'See what y'can do. Y'never know that till y'try, do ya?' Every phrase, every word struck Robert like some kind of sexual innuendo, and went through him like a knife: feeling so abused by him, he thought, she must be dying inside at every line of this cheap talk. 'Lovely prizes, all worth a heap of dollars. Win something nice f'the lady now, Reverend, won't ya? See what y'can give her to take away from here? All in a good cause!'

He turned away to adjust the items on the stall. Seizing the moment, Robert leaned forward. 'I didn't know they were coming back this morning, Ally!' he said in low, urgent tones. 'You must believe me! I would never have done this to you otherwise!'

'Oh yeah?' Her eyes, though heavily powdered, betrayed hours of weeping, and her face was set in a mask of bleak betrayal. Squaring her shoulders and chin, she shrugged him off in open contempt as the showman turned back to them. 'Off y'go then, little lady! Show the Rev what a gentle female hand can do!' He sniggered.

She ignored him. Wildly, recklessly, she hurled her rings in quick succession, and missed. Then she stood waiting, staring at him in a silence more unnerving than any speech of reproach. How could he show her – prove to her . . . ?

With the utmost deliberation he scanned the shelf of goods, cheap vases and teddy bears, dolls and cigarette-lighters, a world of fairground tat. Then he raised the first of his rings, took aim, and projecting it through the air to the top of the pyramid of gifts, secured the prize he sought.

Surprised and not a little disgruntled, the showman handed it over. 'Here y'are, guv, best thing on the stall, that. Lovely present f'a lady. Genuine opals, them are. Sapphires, anyway. Real sapphire necklace for a lady's neck.'

In silence he handed it over. She took it, her face blitzed of all emotion save a deep, buried anger, her eyes wide as if open on to a field of pain. The showman had switched his attentions to the next set of hopefuls, and they were alone. He tried to speak. But she forestalled him, twisting the little chain of blue beads furiously in her hand.

'You think you can buy me off, is that it?'

'No!'

'Pretty cheap, huh, for a weekend's entertainment, and not even a "goodbye and thank you" at the end of it!'

Her bitterness was scalding him like acid eating into his soul. 'Ally – listen to me, please listen! I – wasn't expecting them back for another week – at least.'

'Yeah – *and what would have happened then?*'

Her expression might have been carved in marble.

187

There was nothing he could say. He said it anyway. 'Ally, I love you. I've never loved anyone as much as you in all my life . . .'

He was still saying it to her back as she walked away.

Chapter 15

Brightstone Town Hall, a low, brick-built bungalow in the centre of town, shone like a beacon in the night as they approached. Strings of fairy-lights garlanded its otherwise rather humdrum façade, and banners streaming from the flagpole on the roof across the width of the main street proclaimed 'Brightstone Centenary – Grand Commemoration Dance – All Welcome!' Up above, and shedding a thin light of its own, a late, sad, end-of-autumn moon hung low in a ragged wintry sky. Robert could not imagine how he was going to get through the next few hours, let alone a lifetime without her love, without her touch, without the nearness of her body – *without her*.

Moving like an automaton, he shouldered his way through the crowd round the doorway as he followed Claire and Joan on their way in. Although it was still early, the hall was already filling up: no one wanted to miss what promised to be the major social event of Brightstone's history. Robert was glad of the diversion that the dance seemed to offer. For he dared not allow himself to think.

'Claire! Mum was just asking where you were – she's inside by the wall, with Geordie and his wife. Why, you're looking a picture! And you too, Joan!'

Paul's greeting betrayed his high spirits, and the obvious effort he had made with his much-slicked-up appearance was a poignant indicator of his hopes for the evening. Claire surveyed him with warm approval.

'Well, you're looking pretty good yourself, if a sister's allowed to pay a compliment to her big brother!'

'Yeah, well, I'll have to take pity on you, and give

you a turn round the floor later on, if that sobersides old husband of yours is too busy with his parish obligations,' said Paul magnanimously. He was sure of seeing Ally later on – no one, but no one for a hundred miles around would miss this dance of all dances – so he could afford to be generous. 'You too, Joanie.'

'Thanks.' Another of the countless pangs Paul Everard had cost her pierced Joan's heart. The immaculate turn-out, the joyful anticipation, the flashing animal grin, she knew they were not intended for her. Who then? Not – ? Not the Calder girl, surely?

Inside the hall the small but professional band were already smoothly into their stride. As they came in to join the buzzing throng, the bandleader was just announcing the next dance.

'Ladies and gentleman, a waltz for you now – one of the all-time favourites.'

> I'll be loving you,
> Always,
> With a love that's true,
> Always . . .

'Oh Robert!'

Claire was gazing up at him with shining eyes. 'Robert, where are you? You look as if you're miles away! Oh I do love this song! Robert, could we? Can we have this dance?'

'Of course.'

Mechanically he took her in his arms and they moved out on to the floor. Her familiar perfume rose to meet him – the familiar weight and feel of her body recalled all the times they had ever danced, held each other, made love. Her small, well-covered frame, less plump now since her father's death but still sturdy, seemed twice as heavy as it had before. In a dream of pain he lost himself in the echoing memory of another body, a lithe, lissom, golden-brown length, a head which fitted so sweetly right underneath his chin instead of being so far below him, a face nearer to his when he turned it up to kiss . . .

And her body . . .

Dear God, her breasts, her thighs, her perfect back, perfect in its nakedness from head to heel . . . God had created her, this daughter of Eve, fashioned that form for pleasure and delight – how could that be a sin? How could anything be wrong that felt so right?

A wave of distress shook him. He could not think, he could not pray. He moved on round the floor.

> Not for just an hour,
> Not for just a day . . .
> Darling, hear me say,
> Always.

At the far end of the dance floor Paul was circling sedately with Joan in his arms. That means no one else has arrived yet, Robert thought; no one Paul's prepared to dance with, anyway. The cynicism of this thought shocked him, but only dimly: he felt numb to all feelings, especially his own.

At the far corner of the hall round the bar a cluster of excited youngsters jigged about, laughed and played, all in the highest of spirits.

'Hey Pete!'

'Geddoff!'

'Who's a big baby, then?'

Two girls were teasing a boy, pretending to find out how ticklish he was. For the pleasure of being the focus of their attentions, not to mention receiving a barrage of their teasing touches and pats, he was submitting to being tickled in all the regions, both orthodox and unorthodox, that public decency would permit. Robert watched them dully as he steered Claire round the floor, his body going through the motions with one woman while another dominated, indeed drained his mind. This is what she should be doing, he thought, having fun with her own age group, enjoying the uncomplicated pleasures of those early years like any other young girl, instead of . . . all this . . .

Would she come tonight? He had prayed that she would and he had prayed that she wouldn't. Both prayers, he knew, were equally hollow. How would he talk to her, in front of the whole parish, in front of his wife, his wife's brother, his mother-in-law . . . But how could he not talk to the woman who, as he now sat with all the clarity of extreme pain, had summoned something from him, found something in him, that no woman – oh Claire, no woman! – had ever come anywhere near before?

'Robert!'

'Oh – I'm sorry.'

He had stumbled blindly on through the end of the music and all over Claire's feet. 'Sorry, miles away,' he mumbled.

Fortunately something else had happened to draw Claire's attention. 'Good heavens!'

'What is it?'

'And in a suit and tie, too! You'd hardly recognise him!'

He followed her glance in the direction of the door. From the darkness outside Jim Calder was making an entrance, swaggering through the crush of people as if he owned not just the dance hall but the whole town. His large and powerful body was encased in a new and obviously expensive suit, his hair combed, his heavy jowls shaved and gleaming. But the ugly thrust of his jaw and the menacing sweep of his gaze round the hall indicated more clearly than words that he had not come with peaceable intent. He was clearly trying to put on a show of force for someone's benefit, and spoiling for a fight. With a bleak flash of insight, yet another dimension of the situation he was in struck Robert a hammer-blow. How marvellous, he thought with a savage self-disgust, to have run the risk of exposure to this! How to destroy your wife, your sister, by shaming them in front of the whole town! Nice work – Reverend!

But Jim did not hold the attention of the assembled company for long. Behind him, stepping out like a champion filly into the show ring, came Ally, looking as he had never seen her before – as he had never even imagined her before. She wore a short, black, strapless satin dress which fitted her slender body to perfection and made the most of her elegant curves. Her hair was piled up on top of her head, showing off her delicate, well-shaped neck, and brilliants in the shape of stars blazed at her ears. Her face, heavily made up, was shaded and redefined to a new level of sophistication by the lavish use of blusher, eye-shadow, mascara, eyebrow pencil and brow lightener. Only God could tell how she looked, or what she was feeling, behind that mask. Strutting boldly on a pair of the highest heels Brightstone had ever seen, she made her way into the room.

From his vantage point propping up the bar, Mick Ford was the first off the mark. At one sight of Ally, he set off towards her, his small eyes hot with interest. But he was not the first to reach her side.

'Would you care to dance, Ally?'

Paul, having by chance escorted Joan at the end of the previous number to a position at the edge of the dance floor not far from the doorway, was ideally poised to swoop, and swoop he did. Was it Robert's imagination, or did Ally step into Paul's arms with her chin cocked as if at the whole world, but perhaps with the merest shadow of a glance at him?

'Why, Paul!' Her cry of delight certainly reached his ears. Was she deliberately trying to torment him?

'Oh, isn't she lovely?' Claire's innocent warmth turned a knife in his heart.

'Yes.'

'That dress! And the shoes! My, she's giving Brightstone a fashion show and no mistake!'

'Yes.'

He knew he was watching her too closely – she was flirting with Paul to punish him, he was sure of it! He strove to find his normal voice.

'She looks – tremendous. It's – quite extraordinary. We've never seen her in anything like that before.'

'Well, you'd hardly expect her to come to work in a ballgown, would you?'

'I wouldn't even expect her to possess one.'

'Oh, it's all her mother's stuff, she told me. She was wondering whether or not she ought to wear it. She obviously decided to in the end. Let's just hope the local lads appreciate it! Look, darling, that's Mum. Let's go and say hello, then I guess you'd better start doing your duty with some of the older ladies. I know there's at least half a dozen in the parish who will never forgive you if you don't take at least some of the lucky ones on to the floor!'

> What'll I do
> When you
> Are far away
> And I
> Am blue,
> What'll I do?

Lending an apparently fascinated ear to the President of the Brightstone and District Mothers' Union, Robert could watch Ally in her brilliant progress round the floor almost every step of the way. She was hardly ever out of his sight, and every glimpse he had of her was pure torment. All night long she was in and out of other men's arms, for she was never without a partner. Undeniably she was the belle of the ball, as men to whom she had never before been anything more than 'Big Jim Calder's kid' queued up to salute her emergence from the chrysalis of childhood into a rare beauty of a young woman.

Among her partners, though, two jousted constantly for her attention: Paul Everard and Mick Ford. Jim, who had from his own purely selfish promptings of a mixture of pride and guilt encouraged Ally to 'make something of herself for the dance', had not reckoned with Paul's open and persistent courtship of his daughter in the full view of the whole of Brightstone, right under his very nose. He had convinced himself that his enemy was only interested in sneaking round Ally in parked cars and night-darkened streets, and was equally convinced that once Ally saw the previously-despised Mick in all his Saturday-night splendour, that a match there would be as good as made. Paul's determination, and even more his success with Ally, as time and again he cut in on Mick Ford, rescuing the girl from the embraces of the miner to her obvious relief, gnawed at him like a rat strapped to his chest. And as the booze made its effortless way down his throat during the course of the long evening, memories of his last public encounter with Paul Everard and his humiliating knock-down at the hands of the younger man began to fester dangerously in his alcohol-darkened brain.

Jim Calder was not the only one watching Paul with all the stunted fury of thwarted love. Joan Maitland was, in the eyes of the Brightstonians, 'having a good dance'. Like Ally she was rarely without a partner, single woman being at a premium in any mining town – and like Ally again, she was looking her best in a deep cornflower-blue gown with off-the-shoulder sleeves setting off her smooth pale neck and back, and contrasting strikingly with her ash-blonde colouring and handsome, compelling face. 'Y'looking good, Joanic' – 'Looking great tonight!' – 'My, you're a sight for sore eyes!' – she could have picked up compliments by the bucketful if she had wanted. But not from him! her soul mourned. Not him . . .

Now, watching him with Ally, she knew for sure she had no hope with Paul – had had none ever since Robert's return had first led her to hope, thinking as she did then that if only she and Paul could be thrown more together, she would at last find the way to let him know the feelings she had been nursing in silence for – oh, for how long? For too long, as it now seemed. Yet could this really be it? Could Paul, man as he was, have any more than a passing interest in such a kid – and a kid like her?

'Excuse me!'

Daydreaming on the side of the floor between dances, she found herself swept into the next dance by Mick Ford. 'Haven't see y'round f'a bit, Joanie,' he grinned. 'Missed ya, y'know. Always had a bit of a thing f'the parson's daughter. But I never see y'round these days. How y'been?'

'If you ever came to church, Michael, you'd have seen me on a very regular basis, I can promise you!' Furiously she tried to keep her eye on Paul as Mick whirled her round with all the show-off panache of the short fat man determined to cut a dash on the dance floor.

He was quite uncrushed. 'Nah, I'm not a churchgoer meself – leave that t'the clever buggers like y'brother there. But y'looking good on it, I'll say that f'ya – and that's more'n I can say f'him!'

He nodded at Robert, who was just passing them, the redoubtable weight of Molly now on his arm as he escorted her slowly back to her seat. Joan followed Mick's gaze. Robert was staring over Molly's head, his eyes, haunted by an expression she had never seen before, fixed on Paul further across the dance floor.

Paul? Why should Robert be watching Paul? Covertly she tried to trace the line of his gaze. As Paul swung his partner round, Ally Calder came into view. She was bright and animated, leaning into the circle of Paul's strong arm and laughing up at some humorous sally of his as she did so. Within seconds it had all changed. As she looked across the floor she caught Robert's glance, his eyes piercing hers with a desperate, beseeching gaze. She quivered as if she had been stung. As Joan watched them, their eyes locked in some terrible, unfathomable communication. Then Robert stepped on to the dance floor and tapped Paul on the shoulder.

'Excuse me?'

He took the girl in his arms. They stood motionless, transfixed, deaf to the music, lost in a world of their own. The outer casing of reality melted away from them in that moment of suspended time. All they knew was a great, echoing silence and the beating of another's heart that was closer than their own.

'Hey!'

The silence fractured, shattering around them like the broken pieces of a mirror. 'Excuse *me!*'

Roaring with delight, Paul scooped Ally from Robert's arms. 'If you ain't going to dance with her, Reverend,' he laughed, 'I reckon I'm entitled to have her back!'

But he had reckoned without the girl herself. Quivering, she turned on her heel, broke away from Paul, and ran weeping from the room.

'Hey, Ally!'

Baffled and alarmed, Paul hastened to follow. But as he reached the door, the burly form of Jim Calder barred his way. 'What y'been doin' t'my little girl, Everard?' he growled. 'I'll have ya – this time I'll have ya, I swear t'God!'

Paul stared at him in disgust. 'You're drunk, Calder! Don't tangle with me! I said nothing to upset Ally. I'm just going to find out what did!' He brushed past and ran outside. 'Ally!' he called. 'Ally! Where are you?'

Through the darkness of the car park he could just make out the glimmer of her hair and shoulders pale against the night. He ran to her side. She was weeping, her bold make-up coming off in streaks, the colours mingling with the dull blotches of her skin underneath. He tried to reach her with a feeble joke.

'Look, Ally, I know I'm the world's worst dancer, but—'

'It isn't you. It's nothing to do with you.'

'So what is it?'

Silence and tears.

'Look, I can help you, Ally – I'm your friend – I really want to help . . .'

Tears and silence.

'Let's walk a bit, eh? You want me to run you home?'

'You ain't running her anywhere, Everard! I'll run you out of town first!'

Calder was upon them, fists flailing, ugly, fighting drunk. With a moaning sigh, Ally turned and fled into the night. 'Ally!' Paul cried in anguish, 'don't go! Not like this!'

People were streaming out of the hall now: some of the men would soon be here to break it up. Ducking and weaving, Paul did his best to dodge or fend off Calder's attack. God knows, he had no stomach for this fight – he'd felt guilty enough last time he'd flattened the old sod, even though he'd been severely provoked! If only he could get to Ally . . .

'Well, come on, come on!' taunted Calder. 'You've been asking f'this, and y'going t'get it. Wassamatter, y'afraid? Y'going t'get it either way, Everard, fight or no fight, and now's as good a time as any!'

He was floundering now, losing breath as much through his oaths and threats as through his wildly scattered blows.

'Get this through your thick skull, Calder, and get it good!' ground out Paul. 'I'm not lookin for a fight with you, or anybody else!' Pushing Calder off with a powerful blow to the chest, he appealed to the men gathering uncertainly round the edge of the struggle. 'Give us a hand here, will you! He's pissed! I can't fight an old drunk!'

'Come on, Jim!'

The ever-ready Mick Ford was at hand, his head thrusting under Jim's arm, his own arm round the older man's waist in an iron band. 'This way, come on now, one two.' Dexterously he steered the rambling, mouthing heap of a man to his own van parked a little way away and in one smooth movement loaded him into the open sided vehicle. 'Now y'll be sure not t'fall outta m'van on the way home, Jim, won't ya? We don't want any more murder done tonight!'

> You made me love you,
> I didn't want to do it,
> I didn't want to do it . . .

Back in the hall the band was playing smoothly on, taking no heed of the sudden crisis. But there was little inclination among any of those left to get back on the dance floor. Cold, sensing the chill of impending winter, they huddled in the porch at a loss what to do.

'What'll happen to Ally?' demanded Claire in anguish. 'Robert, I really think you ought to go round to the Calders and make sure that she's all right.'

He did not speak, Joan noted with cold abstraction. But Paul was ready with his answer.

'I'll chase after her in the Dodge, pick her up, make sure she's OK. She can't have got far.'

'Well . . .' Claire was doubtful. 'Don't you think that might be asking for trouble, the way her father feels about you?'

'Aw, he'll be drinking with Mick Ford for hours yet. No, I'll get her back OK, and see if I can get to the bottom of whatever's upsetting her so badly.'

'Don't worry about that, Paul,' Robert's voice had a cutting edge they had not heard before. 'Just get after her and make sure she's all right. And ring me at the Rectory afterwards – however late it is – just to let me know how she is, will you?'

Winter

Chapter 16

Something was wrong – badly wrong. In all their life together, Joan had never seen Robert like this before. A bleakness seemed to have entered his very soul. With the experience of a lifetime of loving and watching over this man, she could feel the answering ache in her own heart. But never before had she felt more powerless to help him. If only she knew what the trouble was! If only she knew how to help him as she had always done!

'More coffee, Robert?' she tried.

'Mmmn? – Er – no.'

Claire came into the breakfast-room, loading books into her bag for the day's work ahead. Her gaze fell on Robert sitting blankly at the table over a cup of black coffee long gone cold. 'Good Lord, Robert, are you still here? I thought it was your morning for the hospital – to see the miners injured in the rock fall.'

He fixed her with a cold, almost abstracted stare. 'I think you can leave me to run my own appointments, Claire, thank you very much.'

There was a painful pause.

'I just thought – I thought you might have forgotten,' Claire ventured after a tremulous hesitation.

But he had gone.

'Haven't seen you in a good while, Reverend. You musta been pretty busy with the celebrations an' all. Betcha glad it's all over now, eh? At least for another hundred years! Cuppa coffee, is it?'

'Yes, thank you, Vic.'

He had to see her. He had to risk it. Anything was better than this inactivity – all it brought was pain, and more pain. But to come to the café so openly like this – was that the best way? What was he doing here? Especially as he could see from the street, even as he had pushed open the door, that she was nowhere to be seen. Perhaps out the back . . . ?

'Is good coffee, this, Reverend, the best. Best in Brightstone. Y'll see, try it.'

'Thank you.'

'How are ya these days, how y'keeping? Y'don't look s'good, if y'don't mind me sayin' so. Y'aren't sickening f'something, are ya?'

Robert pulled up a bar-stool at the counter, accepted the proffered cup of coffee, and tried to smile. 'No, no, I'm fine. Nothing wrong with me that a cup of your famous coffee won't cure!'

In the booth at the back of the café a group of Brightstone's older ladies were catching up on the week's news. Bound to be a parishioner or two among them, he thought dully. All I need is to be seen chasing after a young girl . . . perhaps it's as well she isn't here. Surely this had been one of her days, though? He could not remember.

'Y'make them give it t'y'just like I said?'

'Yes, Vic.'

His back was to the street, and he had not heard the door. She was coming into the milk bar, walking abstractedly behind the counter with a bag full of change from the bank. 'All the coins y'asked for, just the way y'wanted them – here.'

She turned and saw him. As their eyes met, she flinched, and all the golden warmth drained from her face. Then the anger he remembered so well from the fête flared up and with it the violence of her resentment. She turned her back on him and stalked away to the back of the shop.

'Hello, Ally.'

She did not reply.

Vic was absorbed in counting the change Ally had brought. 'Hey, din't I give y'ten dollar?' he demanded irritably. 'Where'sa resta d'money? An' give the Rev some more coffee!'

Moving like a robot, her face expressionless, she picked up the coffee-pot from the hot plate, and approached him from behind the bar. He threw a glance at Vic. The café-owner was completely absorbed in the contents of the small bags of change.

'I have to see you!' he murmured urgently.

She gave him a glance of pure hatred. 'Get lost!' she hissed.

Vic looked up. 'Well, what y'standin' there for, girl?' he snapped. 'All them things t'do out the back?'

She moved away. He could see her going, leaving him, walking away. It was like watching her drown in slow motion.

'You swim much, Vic?' he cried in desperation. 'I like to go to the headland, walk along the shore, swim if I can. Getting a bit cold for it now, of course, but I usually manage to get out there most evenings.'

'Y'don't say.' Vic could not have been less interested.

'Yes! Almost every evening! Around sunset's the best time, I find!'

He had raised his voice in the effort to make it carry to the back of the shop, and he was almost shouting now. Yet he had no idea whether she had heard him or not. Vic was staring at him now in surprise and some alarm, as if he had taken leave of his senses. Perhaps he had. Oh, God, what was he doing, trying to make a secret assignation with her like this . . . ?

'Robert!'

It was Molly Everard. He fought to contain the shock. What had she heard? How much had she understood?

'I was just having a gossip with the girls in the back there and I heard your voice. Whatever's up? What are you doing here?'

'Oh, just passing – fancied a cup of coffee.'

'You all right?' Molly was not convinced. 'You don't look very—'

'I'm fine! Fine! Only needed a quick coffee to pick me up. Well, I must be off now. 'Bye, Vic. 'Bye, Molly, see you soon.'

Molly looked after the retreating figure and laughed. 'Well, that doesn't say much for your famous brew, Vic!'

Together they stared at the cup of coffee lying abandoned and completely untouched on the bar.

Swimming again? In this weather? Some afternoons there could still be a couple of hours of sun, still a little lingering warmth, even at the start of the Australian winter. But by sunset, no; definitely not. Swimming it was, though. Every evening this week. Claire shook her head uneasily as she crossed the Rectory hall. Something wasn't right. Wonder if Joan knew anything – if he'd confided in her at all . . .

To her surprise, the normally busy Joan was sitting motionless in the bay window of Robert's study, staring out to sea. 'Joan?' queried Claire. 'Why don't you have the light on? Sun's going down.'

'I'm all right. You off now?'

'Yeah, down to Mum's. Don't know when I'll be back – don't wait up. Robert's out swimming.'

'Yeah, I know.'

Claire paused. 'It's funny, this swimming craze all of a sudden, don't you think?'

'Oh, I don't know.' Joan gave a shrug. 'I guess it's just a passing thing. He'll have forgotten about it by next week.'

Claire smiled. 'I expect you're right – as usual. Bye, then.'

'Bye.'

Swimming.

Again.

And Claire – even Claire, so tied up in her own sad, endless quest for the child who never came, had noticed it now.

Or if not swimming – walking. Long tramps for two hours and more over the headland, expeditions that brought him back exhausted in body, but as troubled as ever in mind, if his unnaturally bright eyes and short-fuse temper were anything to go by. Thank God Claire did not seem to have noticed anything very much. She had had another of her now regular monthly disappointments, Joan knew, and each time she seemed to undergo a little death, necessitating its own period of mourning. And Claire so obviously missed having the girl around the house now the Centenary was over, she'd admitted she did. But sooner or later, even Claire must notice – must notice something serious . . .

But what? From behind the bay window in the front room, Joan watched Robert striding away across the headland as if the devil himself and all the hounds of hell were snapping at his heels. For the hundredth time she tried to piece together and make sense of what she knew. Robert was facing some crisis, she could not be deceived about that. She had seen him watching Paul and the girl at the dance. That was when she had first noticed how strangely he was behaving. It had to be something to do with that.

Of course, that would have been the first he knew about the way Paul's feelings were going. And he could not want his brother-in-law, Claire's brother, to get involved with a girl like that. The kid had talked to Claire, Joan knew, about her mother and her whole background – or lack of it! brooded Joan grimly – and Robert was well acquainted with her dreadful father now, from all Paul had said as well as from his work up at the mine.

He must know something – that must be it! – something so terrible against the girl or her family, some awful secret or skeleton from her past, that it was making him feel badly concerned about Paul getting mixed up with the whole thing. And of course he couldn't talk about it, least of all to Paul, until he had found out if Paul meant anything by the attentions he was paying her, or if it was just another one of his long line of flirtations and conquests leading straight to a dead end for the female in question.

Then there was Claire. The bloody girl was mixed up in that, too, Joan realised with another rush of fury. Any man would be concerned about his wife's feelings as she grew to face the fear that she might never have a baby. When the girl had been there, Claire had been happier, there was no escaping that. It had been Claire's idea to have her there in the first place – I never wanted the little tart! Joan vowed vengefully – even though – yes of course! it was Paul who had put her up to it, recommended her and got her in at the Rectory with them all . . .

So everything had been fair dinkum when she was around. Now she wasn't. Was Robert brooding about how to get the girl back again somehow, to be with them on a regular basis to cheer Claire up? How to arrange it, or how to afford it, the problem of money being no less pressing after all the expense of the trip to Sydney, all the quarterly bills coming up again at the change of the season, with the long winter ahead and the car getting more and more unreliable with every day that passed?

It could be any of this – or all of it. But that was not all. She knew there was something else. A small cloud of fear gathered on her mental horizon. The Sunday service for the Centenary had been a great success, everyone had said that. It had been superbly conducted by Robert, as ever, and the choice of hymns, the new prayers he had composed for the occasion, and in particular his fine, powerful, moving address had held the congregation spellbound. But the Archbishop had not come. And the Bishop, although complimentary, had arrived just in time for the service and stayed hardly any time after it was over before rushing off to his other concerns. And since that Sunday night, Robert had been so depressed – so tense and irritable.

Yes, that was it! That must be it! She knew only too well – no one better – Robert's real ambition, his longing for promotion, for a better church, a wider arena, a bigger audience, a more elevated platform for his faith and work. She knew it so well because it was what she wanted for him too, all she'd ever wanted. He had felt spurned, passed over by the two great men on whom his future depended. He could see only darkness ahead, another five, ten, even twenty-five years in Brightstone like his father before him. And his soul had descended into its own dark night in return.

Joan's lips closed in a narrow line as her eyes stared unseeingly into the fading light of the low, glimmering sun. Robert was losing faith, in himself and in his future. But he must not be allowed to falter now, or fail! She would hold the line – hold him up to the mark she knew he was capable of attaining: she would secure for him what she knew he could achieve. Success lay waiting for him, if only he could see it. All he needed was a firm faith, in himself and in what lay ahead. He needed spiritual guidance and consolation, such as he freely poured forth for others from the vials of his own generous soul, but which was not so easy for him to come by for himself.

But I can do this for you, Robert, she promised him. I can be there for you as I have always been. You do not have to wrestle alone. God will send you your own guide and comforter – now – in your hour of need. I will come to you – I will be with you – as I have always done.

The sun was sinking. There was no time to be lost. Having reached her decision, Joan turned and left the room. A moment later the back door of the Rectory banged softly as the tall, lean figure slipped quietly out of the house and struck off in the wake of the earlier night-walker across the headland and out towards the sea.

She was there, he knew.

Out beyond Broken Bay, at the foot of the dunes, tonight she would be there.

She had to be.

In a fever of excitement he strode across the coarse level grass to the edge of the high coastline, scarcely conscious of his hurried footing along the cliff and the jagged, gaping rocks lying in wait for the unwary so many metres below.

Tonight she would be there. No matter that he had made himself this promise every night for the past week. No matter that he had been unable to go out on Sunday, tied as he had been to celebrating Evensong, though every moment of the calm majesty of the service, every word and note of the serene speech and music had been a torment to his beleaguered soul. She would have

209

known that he could not be there that night. She would not have gone to meet him on Sunday. Tonight she would. He knew she would come. She had to.

He came to the dunes. Bowl upon empty bowl they stretched before him for miles, completely deserted amid the desolation of winter and the death of the year, lying open to the great bowl of the sky in a silence like the end of the world. She was here somewhere. Fighting for breath, he began his search.

Of these tens, no, hundreds of great hollows of sand stretching for miles along the shore, which of them had been the special place where they had first come together? If only he knew! There she would surely be. He simply had to find her.

On he floundered, and on. Breasting the rim of every dune, he tasted again and again the bitter gall of disappointment rising like bile at the back of his mouth when time after time, nothing but an empty hollow rose to meet his eyes, echoing with the mocking whisper of the sea. But beyond each dune lay another, and beyond that, another again, each with their separate promise of hope, each with their own terrible betrayal . . .

On and on he went, the bleakness of the terrain beginning to bite into his soul. She was not there.

And on, and on. She had not come. He was alone, abandoned. My God, my God, why hast Thou forsaken me . . . forsaken me . . .

Before him the dying sun was sinking into the ocean. The light had almost gone, and a thin, cold breeze off the sea wrapped itself around him and pierced him to the bone. Sinking to his knees in the cold sand he dropped his head and buried his face in his hands. Ally, oh Ally! Where are you? *Where are you?*

Time stood still. Suddenly she was there, oh God she was there, her warm arms round his neck, her lips kissing away his grief with a thousand murmured words of sadness and regret.

'Ally! My love – my little love!'

Their kiss was the kiss of lovers famished for each other's touch since time began. Then she pulled away.

'Robert—'

Her tears were the tears of a child, but her face was dark with an adult's determination. He gripped her fiercely in his arms. 'I know, Ally, I know. But you've got to understand one thing. This is not just an affair for me, "a fling", whatever they call it. I love you, darling Ally and I can't let you go. I don't know what's going to happen – how I'm going to sort things out. But don't you ever—' holding her by the forearms he gave her an angry shake – '*ever* – think that this was just a weekend's amusement for me.'

In response she lifted her face to him and took his head between her hands. Hungrily he explored her mouth, the sweet, soft lips, the urgent, responsive tongue. Her hair felt like spun silk to his fingers, the back of her head nestled into the cup of his hand as if it had been made just to fit. She wrapped her small arms round his neck as tightly as a child. 'Don't let me go, Robert,' she whispered. 'Just don't let's ever let go!'

In answer he pulled her to her feet and wrapped her in his arms. Lovingly, langorously, he stroked her shoulders, her sides, the deep, smooth curve of her back. His hands found her buttocks and exulting in the beauty of her body he cupped their firm roundness, his thumbs at the same time circling the tender hollows inside her hips at the front. She moaned, and laid her head on his chest. He could feel the pricking of her nipples through his shirt, and his soul took flight.

Standing before her he drew her tee-shirt over her head, and unbuttoning her flimsy cotton skirt, let it fall to the sand. Naked beneath her outer garments, she stood prepared for love. Her slim figure gilded by the last cold rays of the paling sun she seemed to him like Venus newly risen from the sea. Fumbling at the buttons he tore off his shirt and laid it down on the sand. Then shrugging off the rest of his clothes, he placed her tenderly upon the improvised bed.

She clung to him, in love, in fear, in both, he could not tell. Gently, patiently, he readied her, soothing her agitation with whispered words, soft caresses and a wild, sweet rainfall of kisses on every inch of her body. To touch, to feel, to possess her fed a hunger of his soul so deep he had never known it was there. In every kiss, every caress, he poured the pent-up love of a lifetime's starvation. At every touch she quickened, her breath coming in light, short gasps until at last she opened her arms and cried for him from the deep heart of her own hungry young body and soul.

'Robert!'

To his rejoicing ears, as he entered her, it was the cry of a soul in bliss, a bliss that echoed and exalted his own.

But to the silent watcher who had followed him from the Rectory to the clifftop above, it was the howl of a devil-woman come from the burning fiery furnace to catch an unwary sinful man and drag him down to hell.

Chapter 17

'I love you.'

'I love you.'

All the oldest, simplest words of lovers came again and again as they lay together in each other's arms. But then came other, darker phrases and fears. 'What are we going to do? Oh Robert, what's going to happen? What are we going to *do?*'

'I don't know.'

'You'll think of something.'

He groaned. It was getting colder every minute, and she was shivering in his arms. He should take her to shelter somewhere . . . shelter against the winter storms ahead . . . He took a deep breath and held her even closer. 'I never expected anything like this to happen, Ally. Before you – before this – there's only ever been one woman for me. I never loved anyone in my life except Claire – my wife.' Lying in the circle of his arms she stiffened with resentment at the mention of Claire's name, but he plunged unknowingly on. 'I never thought there would be anyone for me but her.'

The small voice was muffled against his chest. 'Is Claire all you think about?'

'Of course not! Of course I think about God – His service – His demands. Since my parents died I've only had one ambition – to serve Him – and now—'

'What about me? You said you loved me!' Furiously she pounded on his chest with her hard little fist.

'I do! God knows I do! More than—' He bit his lip.

'More than anything?' More than *her?* she wanted to demand, but dared not. 'Because that's how much I love you! And I won't give you up, Robert! Don't ask me to, because I won't!'

'No, Ally, no.' He felt himself losing his grasp on the situation, and fought to be strong for her sake, if not for his own. 'I've tried to look beyond the present, Ally – and I will. I must think of you – think for you. Since I – we—' he had to say it, there were no other words ' – fell in love – I've been living with the fear that this is so wrong. I'm sure you feel the same way too.'

'How can it be wrong when it feels so right?'

Her words, his thoughts. He had no answer.

'We'll find a way – won't we? Won't we? I can't give you up, Robert, I won't! I love you!'

'Oh, Ally!' He groaned again.

'And you love me. I know you do.'

'Oh—' Love? Love was far too weak a word. 'Ally, I see you everywhere – in the street, in my mind, in my sleep. I think of you – endlessly.'

'You love me too, then.' A fierce glint of purpose shone in her face, lending a metallic gleam to the slate-blue eyes. He was hers, then! And she would have him, Claire or no Claire! She caressed his face, his neck, his lean, hard body. If any man was worth fighting for, he was! 'If you love me, we can work it out. I want you, Robert. And I know I'll never want anyone else till the day I die.'

'I know. Just give me time . . .'

'There's no time! I can't stand this any longer, I want you now! And what if my dad finds out? He could find out any time!'

Time . . . time . . .

Feverishly Robert rehearsed his options as he hurried back to the Rectory. If he . . . no, that was impossible. Perhaps then . . . no, he couldn't do that, Claire wouldn't stand for it anyway. What if . . . no, no, no! cried the stone walls all around him whichever way he turned. You're trapped! Trapped! There's no way out! No way out! And no time!

At the sound of the Rectory front door Joan came

out of the dining-room. Her eyes were hard and very bright.

'Had a good swim?'

'What? Oh yes.' He hastened to the foot of the stairs. 'Must shower and change.' But Joan barred his way.

'A bit ridiculous, don't you think, swimming out to sea on a cold dark night like this? And don't you think it could be – dangerous?'

He tried to concentrate. 'Well . . . it's good exercise. Relaxes me. I haven't – I haven't been sleeping well lately.'

'Don't you think you're taking this exercise business a bit far?'

A finger of fear, then a hand clamped itself around his heart. 'Maybe. I'll just shower and then you and Claire and I can sit down to dinner—'

'Claire isn't home. She's at her mother's. Just as well really.'

Her pale face was mottled with strong emotion, and her eyes were glittering now like a snake's. A black foreboding descended on him with a sense of doom.

'What in hell's name do you think you're doing, Robert?' she ground out, every syllable seeming to cost her terrible pain. 'You! You of all men, Robert Maitland! Not simply married – not just a man who ought to be above – above all that – that filth! – but a minister of the church – a man of God!'

His anger leaped to match hers. 'Joan, this is none of your business!'

But she was lost in the labyrinth of her own fury. 'How could you do this?' she raged. 'After everything that's happened! After all I've done!' She was plucking at herself in her desperation, wringing and pinching the flesh of her forearms as she spoke. 'Do you know what you could be throwing away?'

'Joan, I—'

'Do you?'

'I—'

'*Do you?*'

Her scream echoed round the old house.

'And for that – that girl! Oh, butter wouldn't melt in

her mouth when she was up here smarming round your wife. "Yes, Mrs Maitland, no, Mrs Maitland".' Her face was distorted with rage and savage mimicry. 'When all along she was fixing to become the next Mrs Maitland! The little tart! She's just a scrubber, man-crazy, like her mother was! How many men d'you think she's had as well as you, you poor sap!'

A darkness overtook him. He managed to arrest his bunched fist only inches from the side of Joan's face. 'Don't you dare to speak of her like that!'

'Do! Do!' she gloated, raging with a madness like his own. 'Go on, hit me! You'd like that, wouldn't you? One good hiding and it'd all be over? And so would she. That's the kind of man she likes, can't you see that? Brutes like her father?'

'No!'

'Oh yes, laddie, oh yes! And that's what she'd make of you, if you weren't too mad to see it!'

'Joan—'

'Don't "Joan" me! I'm nothing to you now, nor never again, if you choose her. You're finished!'

He could feel his anger surging up again, and made one more attempt at reason and calm. 'Joan, you don't understand!'

'Oh yes I do!' She was flushed and panting, her face and neck an ugly purple, but the light in her eye was that of the runner who has seen the end of the race and the promise of victory. 'I understand everything – much better than you do.' She paused and gripped his arm, her nails biting into his flesh. 'If you don't give up this tatty little tart – this madness – right now! – you're finished! Your marriage, your career, everything! I'll tell Claire. I'll tell the Bishop and the Archbishop. I'll tell Molly Everard. And I'll tell Mr Wilkes. I'd like to see what you'd make of your ministry in Brightstone – or anywhere else on the whole of this island – after that!'

She had his heart, his soul, his manhood in a vice, and she was enjoying turning the screw. 'Joan, for God's sake, will you *listen?*'

She looked at him with inhuman contempt. 'You heard what I said. And you know I'd do it.'

He knew. 'But what'll happen—?'

Again the withering stare. 'Nothing'll happen. I can keep my mouth shut when I have to. Nobody'll hear a word from me, I won't tell a soul. And neither will she!' She almost spat the word. '*She* won't be wanting to spoil her market with the other lads! She'll make sure she doesn't harm her chances elsewhere! Not with Paul Everard hanging round with his tongue out for her!'

So that was it. A thousand clues, small, insignificant signs, rose before him and he cursed his past blindness. Even in the depths of his own agony he caught the reek of hers. Poor Joan, and her hopeless, slighted love. His anger melted into pity. Poor, poor Joan. At least Ally was his, not in love with another!

'Joan, I know how it looks. You think I haven't thought about this, about what it means? I can't think about anything else! I can't sleep for thinking about it – about her—'

She glanced at him in sneering silence. He gathered all his courage in his hands for what he knew would be the greatest, the most important throw of his entire life.

'But one thing I know, I can't give her up. I'm going to work it out – find the way—'

'You can't! Because there isn't a way! You're fooling yourself, Robert, and you never did that before, not in all your life! No matter what you dirty devils of men would like to think, there's never been a way yet found for a man to have both his tart and his wife, and everyone in the world happy about it!'

He could not speak.

'You haven't a clue, Robert, or you couldn't come out with such rotten rubbish! You just don't know what you're doing, do you?'

'Time, Joan – that's all I need. Give me some time!'

'You haven't got time! You haven't got any time. You don't expect me to lie for you, cover for you, sit at the same table with you and your wife and turn a blind eye while you make up your mind, do you? No chance! There's only one way. My way. Or I'm telling everyone – starting with Claire, the minute she walks through that door!'

Claire. No. He could not put her through that. For himself, he knew, he could risk anything. But he could not play with Claire's life, happiness and peace of mind.

He would have to agree – for now, anyway. That was the only way to buy the time needed more than anything else. But he was in hell. And he would never, he felt, from now till the end of his life, be out of it.

A sallow, vengeful smile curved Joan's lips as she scented victory. And to the victor were the spoils. 'From now on – from this minute – all contact with that girl is over, finished, done. You don't speak to her, you don't see her. If she rings you, you put the phone down. If she writes to you, you pass the letter over to me to deal with. If you see her in town, you cross the road and pass by on the other side. If she throws herself off the bloody cliff, you don't conduct her funeral!'

Her malice was implacable. Every blow was like a nail driving through his flesh. He was shuddering from head to foot, but he could not, would not weep. His very soul now was dry. Because with the unerring aim of a diviner she had discovered the well-spring of his life, and cut it off.

Truly the spirits of darkness and destruction were at large in Brightstone that night. The spite of the heart-sick watchers and waiters, the furious hate and envy of the lonely ones lurking in the shadows which fall from the brightness of others' happiness, was no longer to be contained. The poison of resentment, of love insulted, love denied, had gathered to a head and was bursting, its corruption spreading even to the innocent and dragging them down.

All Paul Everard ever knew of the start of that evening in all the long years that followed was a feeling of restlessness that drove him from his mother's house, where he might have spent a peaceful, unremarkable evening and gone innocently enough to bed as he had done a thousand times before. It drove him also from the pub, where he could likewise have passed a night without event and without consequence, again as he had done countless times in the past. It prevented him from looking up any one of a number of girlfriends on whose willing bodies he might have vented the inexplicable frustration he felt. And it drove him to his car, where he started up the Dodge and automatically turned the wheels in the direction of Ally Calder's house.

Why did he keep hanging round a girl who had made it perfectly clear that she did not love him, did not care for him at all in that way? On the night of the dance, he had followed her in his car, easily overtaken her in flight, hampered as she was by her stiletto heels, and driven her home. In that short time she had completely refused to confide in him in any way, even as a friend, and his castles in the air – that she would tell him all her troubles, weep on to his manly shoulder and end up melting into his arms – one by one crumbled into rubble at his feet.

She had also put paid to a much bigger, and as he now realised, deeper dream, blast her! She had told him point-blank that she did not want to see him again, even as a friend. She did not love him – she could not love him – she could not even imagine the circumstances in which she might ever love him. Or any other man in Brightstone, she had said under her breath – but he had paid no attention to that; that was cold comfort in the ruin of his own hopes.

For he *had* hoped, he acknowledged now. He had hoped to win her, to make her love him. He'd planned a little house, neat and clean, a loving, sparkling welcome from those eyes – those, and no others in the world – when he came bounding in from work to sweep the little thing off her feet and cover her with kisses, then tumble her upstairs for the first of however many bouts of loving it took to exhaust them both for that night. And if children came along, which he knew they would, all the boys would be as big, bold and black-eyed as him, and all the girls as sweet, slim and fair as her . . .

What a dream . . .

What a beautiful dream . . .

How could he give up that dream, that hope? And even without the dream, how could he suddenly now stop caring about her, worrying about her, alone as she was and abandoned to the mercy of that bastard Calder? Mrs C. must have had a lot to put up with, he reflected grimly, but had she ever thought when she pushed off that she was simply condemning her little girl to suffer in her turn all the miseries she was so keen to escape herself?

Oh, Calder was a drunk, a bully and a wind-bag all right, with more piss and wind in him than a prize bull on Show Day. He'd always think twice, even when he was full of beer, before taking on a bloke in a fair fight. But a girl? And a little tiny thing like Ally, lean as a whip, muscles softer than satin? What hope did she have against two hundred pounds of violence coming at her straight from the shoulder?

He turned into her road. Even from the end of it he could see in the distance a scene which brought his darkest fears vividly to life. In the doorway of the Calder bungalow, lit by the light of the overhead porch, a heavy male form was struggling with a much smaller one, whose cries already faintly reached his ears. He ground the accelerator to the floor and the Dodge leaped forward like a stag.

'Let me go! Let me go!'

'Y'not goin' anywhere except back in this house!'

On the driveway outside the front door, the whole scene illuminated by the light from the porch overhead, Ally, clutching madly on to a travelling bag, was fighting off the slaps and pushes of her father as he manhandled her back into the hallway. Paul hurled the car to a halt beside the kerb and threw open the passenger door.

'Ally! Ally! Over here!'

In the moment of surprise and shock that followed Paul's ringing shout, the girl slipped from Calder's grasp and fled down the path. Tearing open the gate, still clinging on to her bag for dear life, she hurled herself through the open door of the car and slammed it shut. 'Go, Paul!' she begged. 'Go! *Go!*'

But Jim Calder had not been a miner for thirty years for nothing. With the lightning reflexes that even years of heavy drinking had not destroyed, he leaped into action. Racing down the path, he cleared the gate and hurled himself in front of Paul's car, towering over the bonnet like an evil genie. 'Goin' anywhere, Everard?' he mocked. Reaching down he grabbed hold of the bumper and began to rock the car violently up and down, jeering and swearing at them as he did so.

Desperately Paul threw the car into reverse. But before he could engage the gear, Calder was at the driver's door. A mammoth fist reached in through the open window and gripped Paul by the throat. 'Take m'daughter from me, would y'Everard? We'll have t'see about that.' Slowly he began to squeeze.

'No! Dad, no!'

Frantically Paul tore at the hand encircling the front of his neck. Calder's iron grip did not falter. From the passenger side, Ally tried vainly to add her help to Paul's, but the murderous angle of the grip and Calder's position outside the car made him impregnable to all attack.

Paul could feel his head swimming, his blood starting to thicken and turn black before his eyes. He knew he could not win, or even survive the struggle much longer. With a last convulsive effort he reached for the handle of the car door and threw it back with as much violence as he could muster against Calder's body. It struck the older man painfully across the shins, and the top of it cut sharply into his lowered chin. With a curse he let go.

Groggily Paul struggled to rise from the driver's seat, and got out of the car. As he did so, Calder caught hold of the door, wrenching it from his grasp, and with calculated brutality slammed it against him, catching his head a cruel blow between the door's edge and the frame. He could feel the blood begin to spring and trickle down his temple as the flesh of his face split open under the impact. He fell back into the car.

'Oh no, y'don't!'

The door opened again, and the great fist reached inside and grabbed his shirt front. 'Y'think the fight's over, do ya, just because y'feel like throwing in the towel

– just because y've had enough? Well, I haven't had enough!'

Dragging Paul from the driver's seat with both hands, he propped the reeling figure against the side of the car and punched him viciously in the face. After the first feeble attempts at self-defence, flailing around with hands and arms which completely refused to obey his brain's garbled commands, Paul made no further effort to defend himself. Not that Calder allowed the prospect of a defenceless enemy to spoil his fun. As systematically as he always conducted his punishments, he beat Paul around the head, face and body, stopping only when his arms were aching and he was hardly able to breathe with the violence of his exertions.

Quite a warm-up, he smirked, and one he had long been promising himself. With a satisfaction too deep for words he looked down at the bruised and bleeding figure lying unconscious on the ground at his feet. Everard had got what was coming to him all right! Nobody took on Jim Calder and lived to get away with it! That'd shut the mouths of the sniggerers down at the pub and wipe the grin off their faces! And talking about faces, wouldn't he have the last laugh when Everard had to show that face of his, his handsome features well rearranged, down at the local!

But this hadn't been more than a starter, really. Now for the main course, the dish of the day. If this wasn't proof, proof positive of what the two of them had been up to behind his back, her and Everard, that bastard sneaking up here in his great stupid car to take her off just when he'd caught her on her way through the door with her bag packed an' all, then he'd never take five bob for half a dollar again. But he'd fixed him – fixed the pair of them.

He flexed his shoulders and coiled and uncoiled his hands like a prize fighter. Now to let the little slut feel the weight of his displeasure, her as well as her bloody boyfriend! A man was entitled to show a daughter like that the error of her ways. With the snuffling pleasurable grunt that always signalled the onset of his worst attacks, he moved round to the passenger side of the car. But when he reached inside for the undutiful daughter who was about to learn the lesson of her life, the car was empty.

Chapter 18

Get away . . .

Get to Robert . . .

He'd have to do something now, he'd have to . . .

Her breath sobbing harshly in her throat, Ally ran like a hunted animal through the night. She was clear of the town now, and the headland road was becoming steeper with every step. Before her the way was so dark that she could hardly see a hand's span in front of her face. Above her the skies seemed to press down upon her defenceless head, so heavy were the clouds that had been massing all day, until now they obliterated the face of the heavens. Without streetlights, without starshine, without pavements, she stumbled often and was in constant terror of falling. But nothing could check her headlong, panicked flight. Get away. Get away. *Must get away*.

Yet even in the midst of her misery, she could feel a strange elation. This was it! Freedom from her father and the right to claim Robert as her own, all in one go! OK, so it hadn't turned out how she thought it would – she hadn't really thought at all, she owned to herself with the honesty of one who has nothing at all to lose. She'd simply cracked when she found herself back home, back in that horrible bungalow, and she just knew she had to get out. Then he'd caught her, and Paul had rolled up . . .

Paul . . . Christ, the mood Jim was in, Paul would be getting the hiding of his life! But better him than me. Almost clinically she dismissed him from her mind. She'd never wanted him, never encouraged him, she'd only ever wanted Robert. Serve Paul right if he just kept

225

hanging around and wouldn't take no for an answer. He ought to've known, better than anyone, that Jim just would not be crossed. And at least he'd made it possible for her to get away.

Get away . . .

Get away to Robert . . .

Because he'd have to come out in the open now, she exulted as she ran, own up to everything that had happened, tell his wife all about it, and then choose to go off with *me!* Me, me, me, Ally! Cold, fear, hope and satisfaction mingled in a grim confusion of emotion which changed her mood by the second. But one thing was clear. Robert just couldn't expect her to stay with her father after this. He'd have to do something – and there was only one thing he *could* do, if she had anything to do with it!

She was climbing the last rise now, and her destination was in sight. Ahead of her, faintly lit by the pale radiance of the light coming off the sea, the solid bulk of the Rectory with the church behind it stood out comfortingly against the thick darkness of the night. From here she could see far out on the horizon the full-bellied clouds beginning to swell ominously and draw towards the land. As she stood for a moment in growing dread, she saw them begin to pitch and toss, the whole mass heaving to a slow, rolling boil. She shivered uncontrollably. God was angry! There was going to be a terrible, terrible storm.

Suddenly she was very afraid. She had to get to Robert. He would know what to do. Weeping, but silently, fighting to control the raw intake of each breath and numb with cold, she slipped across the Rectory lawn and came within sight of the ground-floor rooms. Both the deep bays blazed with light through their uncurtained windows. But the rooms were empty, and the whole house wore a strangely cold and abandoned air as if its guardian angels had moved out, leaving the inmates to an unwelcome fate.

Where was he? She could not feel his presence there at all. But he had said he was going back to the Rectory when they parted earlier, and his car was there, she had seen it as she came up. *Where was he?* Out along the coast a night-bird called, a desolate, screaming cry, and she started uncontrollably.

Come on, Ally, she scolded herself, fighting down the tears that were threatening again. No time for nerves – got to find him, attract his attention! Once he sees me like this, she vowed with a mournful, almost masochistic relish, he'll never let me go again! He'll just take me in his arms, and everything'll be fine, no worries . . . As long as I don't annoy him first. Better be careful, better let him tell his wife, then – and that horrible Joan – he won't want them finding out before he tells them . . . A note! Leave him a note, that was it!

Feverishly she groped in her bag for a pen and something to write on. As she did so she heard a deep rumbling sound far out at sea, and turned in time to see a vivid white flash of lightning split the heavens and strike down to the depths of the ocean. A moment later, rainwater was exploding against her face, her head, and all around her, with all the violence of a tropical storm.

Oh Robert! Robert! Where are you?

She could have screamed with rage. Tears poured down her cheeks, adding to the torrents of the rain the furious overflow of her feelings. Following her instincts, like any wild thing trying to save itself from the savagery of the elements, she crept up the stone steps at the front of the Rectory and sought shelter in the porch.

There, searching in her bag by the light shining through the glass panels, her frozen fingers found what she was looking for. Fumbling with the cold, she seized a pen and a loose envelope, and scrawled a few words, scrawling, as she well knew, for dear life.

The storm was upon them now, all round and everywhere above, releasing all the fury of nature upon her unprotected head. It was a night to wake the dead, a night to bring out the unquiet wanderers of the dark while all good things kept in their caves. Note in hand, she hovered like a lost soul outside the door. She thought of George Everard and his funeral . . . his ghost . . . all the ghosts that walked the headland on a night as bad as this . . .

Abide with me . . .
Robert! . . . Robert! . . . *Where are you?*

What was that? Alone in the sitting-room at the back
of the house Joan raised her head from her Bible,
instantly alert at the slight, unexpected sound from outside. Ears straining, she listened intently for a while,
then relaxed. Nothing to worry about – only the storm.
Well, it'd clear the air, as she'd had to do with Robert.
Calmly she returned to her text.

And it came to pass that the waters of the flood were
upon the earth . . . all the fountains of the great
deep were broken up, and the windows of heaven
opened . . . and the rain was upon the earth forty
days and forty nights . . .

Forty days and forty nights . . . just the length of Jesus'
temptation in the wilderness, Joan noted with clinical
abstraction. Robert's penance, his sojourn in the wilderness, would be longer than that, she knew. But God's
will would be done.

For Noah had done right in the eyes of the Lord,
therefore Noah only remained alive, and they that
were with him in the Ark.

Closing her Bible with a snap, Joan came out of the
dining-room into the hall. Through the glass panel in
the front door she could see the lightning strike and
strike again, and hear the storm rising to even greater
heights of fury now that it could spend its might against
the powerful bulk of the headland instead of rolling
away unchecked out to sea. She hesitated for a moment
outside the study, then pushed open the door and
entered without knocking.

Robert was at his desk, his head in his hands, his
father's Bible and Book of Psalms lying open nearby.
Well, he needed to pray, Joan thought coldly. If he'd
done more praying and less running after that slut, we
wouldn't be in this mess. Pray, Robert, she exhorted

228

him in her heart. That's about the only thing you can do now.

'I'm going to bed.'

He made no reply.

'Everyone makes mistakes, Robert. Don't be too hard on yourself. You've made so few. And remember what the Bible teaches us: "Judge not, that you be not judged: condemn not, and you will not be condemned: forgive, and it shall be forgiven unto you." I forgive you, Robert. I just want you to know that.'

She forgave him. Of all the tortures of mind and soul, thought Robert distantly, he could have done without this. Joan moralising, Joan preaching, Joan – Joan! – forgiving! He struggled to contain his fury.

With all the self-absorption of the blind ego, she mistook his silence for acquiescence. 'It'll all be all right, dear, you'll see. Why don't you go to bed, get a good night's sleep? It'll all look better in the morning.'

He wanted to take her nursery clichés and ram them down her throat. He wanted to take her by the neck and squeeze, squeeze until she choked.

'Go to bed, Joan,' he said.

She turned away. 'I'd better lock the back door, then.'

He sprang to his feet. 'I'll do it!' He had to get rid of her somehow. He could not bear to be with her a second longer. Pushing past her, he strode into the hall. As the light from the central overhead fixture fell on him, illuminating his distinctive form and gait, he heard a soft scratching sound from the porch. A second later a slip of paper floated through the door. He leaped forward and placed his foot on it, whirling round to face Joan as she followed him out of the study.

'What's the matter?'

'Nothing.' Strange, now, how he could lie to her without hesitation and without remorse.

Joan stood immobile, wary and suspicious. 'I thought I heard something.'

'It's the storm.'

She hesitated, then moved off. 'Yeah, sure. Hope it doesn't keep you awake. G'night – dear.'

'Goodnight.'

The note was brief.

CAN'T STAY HERE IM FINISHED IN BRIGHT-
STONE. TRIED TO LEAVE HOME AND DAD
FOUND OUT. CANT GO ON HERE WITHOUT
YOU. MEET ME ON THE HEADLAND ABOVE
BROKEN BAY TONIGHT. A.

He crushed the note in his palm and threw a desperate
glance at the door. Only a moment ago she had been
there, and now – who knows where? Outside, the evil
spirits of the storm were lashing the heavens to a frenzy.
Again and again the forked lightning tore the sky to
tatters as the winds lifted their wild voices in the howling
scream of the elements in torment. Alone in the study,
gazing out on the empty porch, the desolate headland
and the wide wastes beyond, Robert pressed his burning
forehead to the cold glass of the window, and there were
no words to describe the tempest of his soul.

Get help . . .
   Get help . . .
   Must get help . . .
   Desperately Paul held on to the driving wheel as he
peered through the blinding rain ahead. The night outside the car was as thick as soup and the headlights of
the Dodge were pitifully inadequate to the task of lighting his way. Only the long familiarity of a route he had
driven so often that he could have done it in his sleep
kept him on course. Yet he knew quite clearly that if
he did not make it to the Rectory in the shortest possible
time, then he would soon be beyond help, for this night
at least.

   His entire body consisted of so many different sources
of pain that he could not say where one injury ended
and another began. From the agony in his side whenever
he moved or breathed, he guessed that at least one
broken rib testified to the efficiency of Calder's beating.
He could scarcely see through his swollen eyes, one of
which was closing up with every second. But it was his
head, his swimming head, which worried him the most.

It had taken too much punishment for one night, he knew. He felt that he was hanging on to consciousness by the skin of his teeth. Once he got to the Rectory, delivered his message to Robert, he would sing, sink, sink into blissful oblivion and not come back to life for days.

Robert . . . he was the man. He could go down there, gain entrance to the house – even Calder would hardly dare to attack a minister in all the authority of his dog-collar and ecclesiastical dress. Robert'd be able to demand to see Ally, and get her away from there, bring her up to the Rectory, take her in themselves if necessary – whatever it would need to get her away from that hell-hole. Wearily Paul cursed himself that he had not intervened more forcibly before – the bruises he saw under the ruined make-up on the night of the dance had told him then what he had already half guessed, that Calder was beating her up, and badly too. Now, God knows what she was suffering inside that house right now, and himself, beaten to a pulp, feeble as a kitten, unable to lift a finger to do anything.

Except get help.

Get help.

Robert would do it.

His sight was going fast now, too fast. With a groan of relief he saw the headland road level off in his head-lights and the sweep of the Rectory lawn come into view. With difficulty he parked his car behind Robert's on the drive, and straining to open the driver's door against the stab in his ribs, he lost his grip and pitched out on to the wet gravel. For a second he lay there, the rain beating down on his face and body. Then he hauled himself to his hands and knees and with an almighty effort, from there to his feet. A violent wave of nausea swept over him, and he staggered to the flower-bed beside the drive and vomited, the pain in his side slash-ing through his body again and again and again as he voided everything down to the last slimy string of bile.

He felt like death now. Must get to the house. Swivel-ling like a drunk, he made for the front door, and stag-gered up the steps to the porch. On the top step, his hand reaching for the doorbell, he lost his balance. He tried to call out, but his voice would make no sound. At that moment he saw his fate moving towards him with the inexorable tread of an executioner. He swayed and fell headlong over the little wall at the top of the flight of steps into the dense bank of shrubs below, yielding at last to darkness and the demons of the night.

'He's there! He's there! Go faster, God damn ya, *faster!*'

'Steady on, Jim!' urged Mick Ford uneasily. 'I'm going as fast as I can!'

Furtively he shot a glance through the darkness towards his companion in the cab of the van. He didn't like it. It was one thing to be giving his old mate a hand to look for his runaway daughter; it was quite another to find himself engaged in a car chase up the headland road with only one headlight he could rely on, in the worst storm in living memory.

When Jim had burst in on him an hour ago, it'd seemed to be only a storm in a tea-cup. Ally wouldn't be far away, he'd promised Jim over a soothing beer or two. They'd get back to his place in due course and probably find her there, getting the tea or doing the ironing.

Instead they'd arrived back at Jim's place to see the tail-lights of Paul Everard's unmistakeable blue Dodge vanish around the end of Jim's road. Raging, screaming, Jim had insisted that Everard had got his girl, and had howled for instant pursuit. Driving slower and slower, Mick had done his best to lose the car ahead, which normally would have presented no problem to a clapped-out old van following a performance roadster. But the slower Mick drove, the slower the Dodge seemed to go too, hesitating and wavering from side to side in the thickening dark as if the driver could not see which way he was going.

When it became obvious that Paul was taking the headland road up to the coast, insensitive as he was, Mick had known real fear. To go up there, on a road with no lighting, no kerb to distinguish it from the level ground all around, on a night like this when you could as soon as anything drive yourself straight over the cliff like old Reverend Maitland did – no, that was not for Mrs Ford's little boy Mick, who very much wanted to live to see his next birthday. Pulling over to the side of the road at the foot of the headland, he had told Jim that wherever Everard was going, he, Mick, was going no further.

The violence of the ensuing argument had left him still shuddering. Minutes had passed while Jim Calder had ranted and screamed as if he were trying to outdo the fury of the storm outside. There was no withstanding him. Letting in the gear and moving off as carefully as he could, Mick Ford pointed the van up the headland road towards the Rectory, and for the first time in his misspent life, sincerely prayed.

What was that?

Still clutching the torn and crumpled note, his hand reaching for the latch of the front door, Robert froze. Surely he had heard something outside? He waited, his heart pounding, nerves stretched to breaking point. Not Claire coming home yet, please God, not that! He'd had to wait long enough to feel sure that Joan was settled for the night. He had to get away now.

He schooled himself to wait a little longer, the time it took for his thumping heart to subside. Then in one smooth move he opened the front door and slipped out into the dreadful night.

Paul's car! Whatever was it doing here, right by the steps, its keys still in the ignition and door open like that to the driving rain? Don't worry about that now, his overburdened brain instructed him, just get moving! Minutes later, soaked and shivering, when his own car had flatly refused to start or even to spark in the sodden atmosphere, he was racing across the headland in Paul's without another thought in his head except that of dull relief that someone, something, had provided him with what he had to have in his hour of greatest need.

The roar of the enraged sea, its mighty breakers lashed to ungovernable fury by the wildness of the wind, was growing louder now with every minute. The thunder of the rollers spending their violence on the jagged rocks far below reached him even above the howling of the storm. A macabre impulse seized him at random: this would be a good night to die . . .

But to die like this, oh God spare us, no! From the unquiet grave of the past, his father, then his mother rose before him, as vividly as they had lived, their eyes fixed on him as if in reproach. In his conscious mind he knew they were nothing but figments of his overwrought imagination and desperately strained nerve. But it was all he could do not to scream: 'Go away! Leave me alone! GO AWAY!'

Broken Bay – thank God – at last. Somewhere on the clifftop she was here. Stopping the car, he grabbed a coat of Paul's from the back seat, and holding it over his head, ran into the hurricane calling her name. 'Ally! Ally! I'm here!'

God, where was she? As carefully as he could in his frantic haste, he made his way forward, the roar of the sea growing louder every moment. You're getting near, too near! his straining senses warned him, too near the edge of the cliff! Surely she could not be any nearer to the dreadful, almost enticing abyss only a few yards away now. 'Ally! Where are you? ALLY!'

'Robert! M'dad – he's going to kill me! I've got to get away!'

Sobbing hysterically she hurled herself out of the darkness into his arms.

'Ally! What—?'

'I can't go back to that house any more! I'll have to come and stay at the Rectory till you can get us a place – sort things out—'

'Ally, listen! You can't come to the Rectory! My sister knows! *Joan knows!*'

'Knows?' She stared at him in stupefaction, her hair plastered to her head like a drowning woman, her teeth chattering. 'Joan?'

'She knows! She saw us meeting this evening. She's threatening to tell Claire, the church, everybody about us, if I don't give you up.'

'That's it, then.' Her small face set with a mixture of

fear and elation. 'You won't do that – you can't. And if she knows, they'll all know sooner or later. We'll have to go away together. To Sydney!'

She was excited now, he saw, her schoolgirl imagination fired with the idea of eloping lovers, true love crossed yet triumphant and the world well lost. He knew that he was just about to drive a dagger through her heart.

'I can't, Ally. I can't run away like that. And there's no need for you to, either. I'll find you somewhere safe to stay – Molly Everard's – and Joan won't say anything to anyone, I promise you that—'

'*Molly Everard's?*'

She could read what was coming in his face, he knew it.

'Because Ally – I can't see you again – not ever again after tonight. I've wronged you, to think I could love you—'

'*No!*'

'—because I'm not free. I'm tied hand and foot. I have made vows to God, and to the wife I took in the sight of God. There are people here who depend on me – who need me. I can't just walk – or run – away from that.'

'No!' She was hanging on to him now like grim death. 'You can't just dump me like this! What about me? Don't I get any say in it? You're wrong, Robert, you're wrong! You love me, you know you do!'

He could hardly see through the mist of pain. 'And always, always will.' He took her in his arms. 'Goodbye, my love,' he whispered. 'This is goodbye.' He pressed his cold lips to her lips as cold and pale as stone. 'Goodbye.'

'*Everaaaaaaaaaaaard!*'

The howling scream could have come from the throat of a devil in torment. The next second a thundering blow caught Robert on the back of the head and almost sent them both flying. He sprawled forward on to his knees, then scrambled reeling to his feet and faced his assailant.

'You! *You!*' Something snapped in Jim Calder's brain.

'You! All along it was *you*! Jesus Christ! Y'dirty, filthy bastard, I'll kill ya—'

Howling like a banshee he charged straight at Robert out of the night. Instinctively throwing up his arms to defend himself, Robert ducked and dodged, pushing the older man away from him as violently as he could. Jim hurtled past him and saw too late the thinner darkness of space beyond the edge of the cliff where they had been standing.

'*Noooooo!*'

His legs scrabbling like a dog's in the muddy turf, he tried frantically to arrest his headlong forward charge. But his weight was against him. He slipped, fell, and in all the agony of slow motion half slid, half rolled towards the edge.

'No! Noooooooooooo!'

His howl of mortal fear and Ally's scream of terror mingled in a demonic music louder than the storm. Snapping out of his paralysis, Robert threw himself full-length on the cliff edge and made a grab for the older man. His fingers brushed Calder's, and for a second the iron fist closed over his arm, found and grasped his hand. But as the lightning exploded yet again in the labouring sky above the heaving, boiling sea, its livid brilliance lit up Calder's eyes, Calder's face and last of all his vainly clutching hands as the heavy body vanished over the edge of the cliff and plunged in one endless screaming fall all the way down to the final embrace of the cruel black rocks below.

Chapter 19

The scream he gave as he fell echoed in the ears of the two bystanders for the rest of their lives. It seemed to ring through all eternity.

'Dad! Dad! *DAD*!'

He had to hold her back. She was beside herself. In the madness of her hysteria she might almost have thrown herself after the man who, a second before, had been standing there before them in all the pride and fury of life. His mind reeling, Robert saw not only Jim Calder plunging to his death, but a car careering over the headland, an elderly man and woman falling, falling falling . . . all the way down . . .

He threw back his head and howled. 'Ally – *they've gone*! He's gone! They're dead! *All dead*!'

'He can't be dead! He can't be!'

'Help – I must get help—!'

He turned to run. Her scream stopped him in his tracks. '*What about me*?'

He could not think. He could not take her back to the Rectory, entrust her to the tender mercies of Joan. What then?

'Stay here, Ally – under that tree. I'll be back as soon as I can.'

'No!'

'I have to, Ally! He might still be alive! There's a chance, if I raise the alarm quickly.' A chance they never had – Mum and Dad – he thought dully – a chance I might be able to give Jim, if nothing else. 'And I'll be twice as fast on my own. I'll be back for you, I promise.'

He was tearing her fingers away from his arm, her terrified grip from around his neck, as he spoke.

'Don't leave me, Robert! *Don't leave me!*'

Her grief-stricken cry rang in his ears like an echo of her father's, spurring him to action. Instinctively he leapt forward into a sprint, with no thought for the car which had brought him up the headland. Instead he ran off like an animal, close to the ground, darting his head forward this way and that against the lashing rain.

Get help.

Get help.

Must get help.

That was it.

There was no mistaking it this time.

A woman's scream.

Huddled miserably in the cab of his van, Mick Ford knew that he could deceive himself no longer. When they had first arrived at the headland, he had been overwhelmed with secret delight to discover that they could not see Paul Everard's blue Dodge anywhere. 'Sure, he's headed out to Western Point, joyriding or whatever, and it's got nothing t'do with Ally at all, him being out here tonight!' he'd insisted to Jim.

But his relief was short-lived. Jim Calder was not to be thrown off the scent he had followed so avidly for so long. 'He's here, I tell ya,' he snarled. 'I can *smell* him!'

Then the van's headlights, weak as they were, had picked up the unmistakeable metallic blue of the Dodge.

'Told ya!'

With muttered instructions to stay put, keep the headlights on, and don't let the bastard get past you if he comes this way, Jim Calder had vanished into the night. Mick looked at his watch. That had been a good while ago now, and since then—

He couldn't have sworn for sure if the first sound he heard was a human scream. Could'a been a bird. And with the noise of the wind—

Was that it again? It was over before he could train his ears to pick it up and know it for what it was.

But now – there – a woman's voice, raised in agony or terror – but a woman's, no mistake. He shivered with fear. What was he supposed to do?

Suddenly in the outer edge of the dim beam of the headlights he saw what was unmistakably a human form. A man, tall, but huddled low as he ran, cut across Mick's field of vision and was lost to sight, hair plastered darkly to his skull by the pouring rain. Everard! But where was Jim? And Ally! It had to be her screaming, no reason for any other woman to be out here with him. Where was she?

Sicker than he had ever been in his life, he drew down the peak of his cap over his eyes and huddling his waterproof tightly to his chest against the foul weather, he clambered out of the van. Gingerly he ventured to the edge of the weak pool of light cast by the headlights' beam and called, as loudly as he could against the contending elements.

'Ally? Ally!'

How long he stood there he did not know, calling her name over and over again into the wind, the very picture of foolishness. Then in the corner of his eye he saw a flash of movement. He turned. It was Ally, unmistakably Ally, running along the cliff edge parallel with the sea and the dreadful drop below, running as if her life depended on it, taking no heed of the danger she was in.

'Ally!'

Galvanised with fear and relief in equal measure, he jumped forward and sprinted after her. But a handful of paces outside the circle of the headlights was enough for him. The darkness all around was absolute, the velvet blackness only a shade lighter where the cliff ended and the hideous threat of the open space beyond began. Terror gripped him. He could be off here before he knew he had missed one step! And he would not be the first! The spectre of the old Reverend and his wife, the long-dead Maitlands, loomed up before him, and he stopped in his tracks. 'Ally!' he cried again, and 'Ally!' But there was no answer.

No answer from her – no answer from Jim. She might have had her own reasons to run away from him or her father, Mick reasoned, but Jim, never. If Everard had scarpered and Ally had gone as well, there could be only one reason why Jim had not come thundering back to the van demanding instant action from Mick and the resumption of the pursuit. Only one reason, in this world or the next.

With a heart heavier than he had ever thought possible, Mick returned to the van, and turned its nose for Brightstone and the police station. He was parking outside it before he realised that the wailing lamentation that had greeted him halfway down the hill, echoing from the headland right across the town to the twin peak of the headland beyond, was not the sound of his own sorrow but the siren of the mine.

To the ears of anyone raised in a mining town, the ominous wail of the siren signalling a pit disaster had the power to carry over thunder and rain, wind and storm, or any other of the natural elements. Joan had heard it in her sleep, and was up and ready even before the telephone rang.

'Yes? Yes, I heard. Is it bad?' Her grim nod confirmed the news. 'Oh God. God help them, Mr Wilkes. Yes, sure, we'll be down straight away. Robert? Of course, he'll help, I've only got to wake him up, he'll be there in a second. Look, can you send a car? We'll need a hand and some extra transport to get all the blankets and pillows we can lend you down to the mine. You'll send a couple of the junior managers? OK, thanks – what, about ten, twenty minutes? We'll be ready.'

She turned and ran to the foot of the stairs, calling her brother's name. 'Robert! Robert!'

'Here.'

He stood in the hall, the front door swinging behind him. His body was shaking from head to foot and his eyes were staring blackly from a chalk-white face. He was soaked to the skin, and gasping for breath after a long run. 'Help,' he panted. 'Got to get help!'

'Robert! Have you come from the mine? How did you hear about it? Wilkes says it's bad, they don't know how bad till they start digging. But they want you there as fast as you can, they need every able-bodied man they can get to clear the shafts. They won't know the worst till they get the rescue teams down the pit and locate the rock fall—'

'Rescue teams . . . yes . . . get rescue teams . . . up on the headland . . .'

'The headland?' Fear swept through her. 'Robert – *what do you mean?*'

'I – killed Jim Calder,' he forced out. 'Didn't mean to – but I killed him.'

'*Killed Jim Calder?*'

'He wanted to fight.' He was in shock, she noted with almost clinical detachment as a thin shudder wracked the shivering frame. 'He came at me – like a madman. I didn't want to fight him. He fell. He fell over the cliff—'

'*Where?*'

'Broken Bay. He went over – screamed—'

'Robert, listen to me!' She grabbed his hands and shook him as hard as she could. 'You're in shock. You don't know what you're saying. Now listen. You didn't kill him. *You didn't kill him*! You got that?'

He stood before her, shaking his head in disbelief.

'Just pull yourself together, and let's think!' she continued urgently. 'Slowly, slowly now. Did anyone see you? Was anyone with you?' She could read his answer in the newly-washed slate of his face. '*Ally Calder!*'

'Yes!' he breathed. 'I left her there, said I'd get help, get a rescue team, come back for her!'

He was at the phone now, picking up the receiver. With a speed of response she did not know she possessed, she snatched it from him. He faced her across the hall-table, breathing like an all-in wrestler. Then his face lightened a fraction – of course, she was only trying to help him.

'Good idea, Joan,' he forced out in his still-labouring breath. 'You ring for help – I'll get back up there to the headland.'

She slammed the receiver into its rest, backing him up against the door.

'Robert', she said sternly, an evil genius lending her inspiration, 'you can't go up the headland now! They're coming for you! They'll be here any minute!'

'The police?' He nodded. 'Yes, of course. He's dead, I know he is. I'll tell them all about it.'

'No! No! You mustn't do that!'

He shook his head. 'But it's the truth, Joan.'

'Yeah – but – you got to think of her!'

'Of Ally?'

'Yeah, of Ally!' She was improvising freely now, she was on a roll she felt nothing could check. 'If they charge her with being an accessory – you wouldn't want that, Robert, would you, to put her in prison, maybe for years? You got to think of her! She's not smart enough to work these things out for herself! Say nothing for now – say nothing to anybody – d'you understand?'

He shook his head. 'Say nothing – for Ally's sake?'

'Yes! Nothing! Nothing at all!'

'Joan.' Exhaustedly he pushed back a lock of hair out of his eyes. '*What are you talking about*?'

She could hear the low purr of a car approaching up the headland, the crunch of tyres on the gravel outside the front door.

'Look Robert, you don't know what's happened. There's been a terrible, terrible disaster up at the mine, and they need you, there's men trapped down there, men dying, they're sending for all the able-bodied to dig them out, you've got to get there and see what you can do!' She was pushing him towards the door as she spoke, grabbing a coat and warm scarf from the hallstand to thrust into his hands as she did so. 'Look, Calder's dead, and they're alive, some of them anyway. That's where you've got to be.'

Through the doorway, the mine car was waiting for him on the drive, the back door already open to receive him. He saw it and stiffened. She knew what was coming.

'*What about Ally*?'

'Don't you worry, Robert.' She raise her voice, and carolled cheerily to the men in the car. 'He's here, boys! Only half awake! I had to get him up in a rush, so go easy on him, OK? He'll be with you in a second!'

This could be the most important move of the whole game, she told herself. Don't rush it. Stepping close into him, wrapping the scarf around his neck and pushing his hands into the sleeves of his coat as if he were a child, she whispered softly, 'Leave her to me, Robert. She'll be all right. I'll take care of her. You can trust me.'

'Oh God! My God!'

'Here, doctor, over here!'

'Where's my Johnny? Johnny Anderson? Is he safe? Who knows how many men have got out – who's alive?'

The scene at the pit was like a medieval vision of hell. From the great, gaping black hole in the ground flames belched out fifty and a hundred feet high, searing the darkness of the night, mocking the last drizzling downpour of the fading storm. Silhouetted against the garish orange and red of the sky, the huge wheel and crane of the mine workings stood out like a vicious caricature of all that is ugly, dark and dangerous in the restless world of man. In the foreground pygmy figures of men and women scurried around like ants, their puny endeavours powerless to correct the disaster that only man's own insatiable greed and hunger had set in motion.

'Over here! Here!'

'Where's Jim Calder? Or Paul? There's no one to take charge!'

'All the men over here! We've got to get a party down each of the secondary shafts, see if we can strike through to the main workings that way. There's got to be some of the lads still alive down there, if we can just get to them!'

Moving like a zombie, Robert grabbed a helmet from the pile on the ground and fell into line. He scarcely heard the growl from the man behind.

'Where's Paul, blast him? We need men who know what they're doing! This is miners' work, Rev! No place f'amateurs!'

'Ah, shut y'face, Nipper!'

Geordie was in no mood for courtesies. 'Case like this, we need all the help we can get! He may be a Rev, but he's young and strong, and he'll handle a pick-axe as well as any, I'll swear. An' he'll certainly be more use to us workin' than prayin' – though I don't doubt

243

he'll have plenty of that to do when we find out how many of the lads have copped it this time!' He swore violently. 'Over here, Rev.'

Out of the night a woman descended on him, her large and ungainly face contorted with grief. 'Mr Maitland! You've got to help me! Johnny's down there! My son Johnny! I know he's down there! And nobody'll tell me anything!'

'Mrs Anderson!'

Slowly Robert took her in. One of his staunchest parishioners, the woman's whole history was written on her ravaged face. A husband lost to the mine, her one son and only child choosing to follow his father in spite of all her tears and prayers – and now lost too? 'Johnny Anderson,' he rapped out to Geordie, his mind springing to attention under pressure of the mother's need and desperation. 'What news?'

'Main shaft,' Geordie called back. 'That's where he was working. Nothing yet.'

Robert took her hand. 'That's where I'm going down, right now. If I hear anything, anything at all, I'll tell you straightaway. You'll know as soon as I know – that's a promise.'

She clung to his hand, weeping. 'Don't leave me like this, *don't leave me!*'

Leave her . . . don't leave . . . oh Ally . . . His heart was like a stone. 'I must,' he said. 'The men . . . down there . . . I've got to go . . . I'm sorry . . .'

And then it seemed to Robert that they descended into hell. Lowered down the older shafts, long abandoned for active working, by ancient winches and creaking, clanking machinery that had obviously been neither used nor maintained for years, they found themselves stumbling in pitch blackness through rock passages too low to stand upright in, and too narrow even to move through without the visceral dread of being trapped down there and left to die the abandoned soul's long dying. From the neglected roof great hunks of rock and coal had descended to litter and block the floorway beneath, so they could not even move forward without constantly falling foul of obstacles in the way. As they shuffled along like old beggars, knees bent, heads down and backs breaking, they heard through the rocky bowels of the mine all around them the sounds of terror – the screams of the wounded, the shouts of the rescuers, and the greedy roar of the fire, which for all they knew was advancing towards them down this very tunnel to claim them too, even now, this very second. But they heard it all dimly, muffled and far off, like a dream of terror, a nightmare worse than facing the thing itself head on.

It was getting hotter every minute. Like an army of mutes the men marched silently on, each one ready to die before he would give the slightest sign of pain or fear. At the head of the little column Geordie, armed with an old map, directed their course.

'Left here – easy on – shouldn't be long now – *aaaah*!'

A battery of lamps played on the wall of tumbled rock ahead, closing as one on an object that to Robert would not have merited any special notice at all. 'Here! Quick!'

It was the toe of a boot. Its owner was unrecognisable, a boyish figure, bloody and unconscious. Robert's heart leaped. 'Is it Johnny Anderson?'

'Nah.' Geordie had seen too much to entertain any hopes. 'But he's some other poor bloody woman's son, that's for sure. And he's alive. There's others here, too.'

Soon another man's hand appeared, and further away, a helmet. But there was a painful shortage of space – nowhere to work, and nowhere to lay the rescued. Suddenly Robert was aware that Geordie was speaking urgently to him, the miner's light shining harshly into his face.

'Look, Rev, we've got to get this lad out of here – him and the others still in there. And we've got t'get more heavy equipment down here t'get the worst of this shifted, now we've seen how bad it is. Can y'get him back t'the lift, winch him up, and give them the word we're on to something here? I'll send Nipper back with ya.'

'No need.' Robert shook his head. 'You don't want to spare a useful man, Geordie. I can manage.'

* * *

245

O Lord, remember not my sins, rebuke not me in the hour of thine indignation . . . Turn O Lord and deliver my soul, save me for thy mercy's sake.

For in death no man remembereth thee: and who will give thee prayers and thanks from the bottomless pit . . . ?

Back and forth he went, hour by hour, man by unconscious man, sustained only by the snatches of psalms and prayers he shared with each of the mine's victims as he carried them back to safety. Careless of the constant knocks to his head, or the pain in his back and thighs, Robert worked like a machine, one phrase alone in his mind: '*He's dead, Robert, they're alive or could be if you'd just do something* . . .' But he knew there could be no bargaining with death, no cheap and easy trade-off for Calder's life, no matter how many men he saved in this night's work.

On the surface, when he tenderly handed out the first crumpled body from the lift-cradle, he was an instant hero. 'Fantastic, Rev!'; 'Well done!'; 'Never thought a priest'd've had it in him': the sombre compliments came from all sides. He stayed only long enough to deliver the message from Geordie before returning to the life-and-death struggle below, which, as they all knew, would take more than one rescue, however welcome, to win.

All night they laboured like demons, without respite. Towards dawn, when every movement had to be paid for in sheer exhaustion, they broke through to the main shaft, uncovering as they did so the last of the victims of the fall. Almost out on his feet, Robert surveyed the battered form, the features bruised and broken, the hair matted with dried blood and rock-dust, and his heart knocked against his ribs. Surely he knew that poor young face . . . ?

'Is it – is it Johnny?' he said huskily. 'Johnny Anderson?'

Geordie squinted at the unconscious boy with eyes almost as bleared as Robert's.

'Yeah,' he said in wonderment, 'I do believe it is.

And not dead – not yet, anyway. Y'reckon y'can get him up top, Rev, pronto?'

Robert tried a smile through cracking lips. '*Prontissimo!*'

Heaving the slight body onto his back, stooping like an old man, he began the long, tortuous trek back to the lift. The pains across his shoulders, down his thighs, in his forearms, were almost intolerable. But the discovery of Johnny had given him the strength to rise above it all – he felt a new surge of energy, and wave upon wave of joy. 'We'll get you there, Johnny,' he mumbled to the unseeing eyes and deaf ears before him, 'just hang on. Almost there. Your mum's waiting for you, Johnny – hang on. Just hang on.'

As he stumbled along, foot by foot, carefully protecting the boy's head from the side of the shaft, he knew he was making a bargain with himself, too. And not only himself. 'God, hear me!' he prayed. 'Let me save this boy – let me return this son to his mother – and I will face anything, take anything that comes to me for Jim Calder's death.' Already he was regretting allowing Joan to hustle him off down the mine. If he had had time to think about it, he could have found a way to get the cliff rescue tea out to search for Calder's body without getting Ally into trouble at all – and he should have done. Well, he would make it all straight now – just as soon as he came up from the pit . . .

'Y'right, Reverend?'

The winchman running the lift system was waiting for Robert's signal. From his vantage point in the machine house on the platform at the top of the shaft, he peered down into the black depths below. 'Yeah, she's right' floated up to him in a thin parody of Robert's normal voice. 'Just one more. Last one. Ready when you are.'

'You done bloody good tonight, Rev!' called the winchman. 'How many's that you brung out? Seventeen? Eighteen? Good job it's y'last trip, though. I reckon she's just about had it for tonight, this old girl. Been pensioned off years ago anyway, this winch has – and now this. Away y'go!'

The winchman slowly released the lever, and with a

grumbling protest, the wheel began to turn. Flexing his aching shoulders Robert braced himself against the side of the antiquated cradle, gripping the upright cables in each hand to steady himself for the ascent. Propped upright against Robert's knees, his own legs carefully folded in order to fit into the small space at the base of the rickety, basket-like structure, the unconscious Johnny Anderson lolled back in comfort, his body gripped and steadied by Robert as the cradle lurched into the air, then began its creaking rise to the surface.

Up they went, and up, the lift lurching and groaning with every half turn of the wheel. A look of alarm passed across the winchman's face and he peered anxiously into the machine house beside him on the platform. Up, up, up – gently now. With infinite skill he nursed the ascent, turn by turn. At last the cradle drew level with the platform. Heaving the biggest sigh of relief he had ever given in his life, he fixed the brake, locked off the machinery and hurried forward to help lift the injured man out and assist Robert to step on to the platform.

But as the braking mechanism locked on, the final judder as the whole system stopped, then subsided into immobility, proved to be too much for the ancient machine, already overstrained by a night of ceaseless effort. The main hawser passing upwards and over the top of the pulley groaned aloud like a living thing, then slowly, slowly gave way. The winchman leaped forward, scrabbling on his hands and knees to reach the edge of the cradle. 'Jump, Rev!' he howled in terror. 'There's only the side cables now – and they won't hold!'

Robert reached forward. 'Take the boy!' he said. His hands under Johnny's armpits, as if he had all the time in the world, he heaved the dead weight of the unconscious youth, lifted his upper body free of the cradle, and tipped him gently forward on to the platform. The winchman grabbed the slackly-lying arms and furiously struggled to heave the inert figure forward and pull him out of the way. 'Come on, Rev!' he screamed. '*Come on!*'

Robert was poised to follow. But as he moved, the first of the side cables snapped with a retort like a shotgun. With instinctive balance Robert flung himself to the other side, grasping the second cable in firm hands, hurling himself towards the platform in one clean, sure move. But it was too late. The second cable cracked even as he got his hands to the edge. For one endless second he seemed to hang there suspended, then with hideous slowness he fell back, back and down. Threshing like a dying python, the hawser broke free of its moorings and wildly lashed the air in a demented valediction as the cradle, with Robert still aboard, vanished backwards and hurtled down into the heart of darkness below.

Chapter 20

Newly scoured by the storm to a pristine freshness and glory, Broken Bay lay smiling in the early morning sun. All the turbulence of the night before might have been nothing but a bad dream to the innocent sea-birds now whooping and swooping in excitement over all the good things cast up for them from the storm-tossed depths. To the eye of a trained policeman, however, the signs of evil all around were only too plain.

'Here! I told y'sergeant! There it is!'

Triumphantly Mick Ford led the little team of police towards the tell-tale blue Dodge abandoned on the headland above the bay. They circled it like hunters closing in for the kill, checking every detail of its external appearance. Then the senior officer drew on a plastic glove from a sealed packet in his coat-pocket and opened the door.

As he did so, a slip of torn and crumpled paper fluttered from the seat of the car to the floor in the early morning breeze. He picked it up. 'IM FINISHED IN BRIGHTSTONE' he read. 'FOUND OUT . . . CANT GO ON . . . CANT LIVE WITHOUT YOU . . . BROKEN BAY TONIGHT.' Without comment he handed it to his second-in-command.

'It's signed "A",' the sergeant said.

'That's Ally! Ally Calder! An' it sounds like a suicide note to me!' Mick paused, his eyes growing wide with horror. 'Everard done it! He drove her to it, he musta done!'

Mick's entirely superfluous comment was received in silence all round.

'OK, spread out, lads, let's see what we can find,'

251

ordered the Detective-Inspector. 'But carefully, mind. Wet night like last night, there's bound to be footsteps – tracks. I want you all tippy-toeing around here like bloody ballerinas, y'got it?'

Nodding, they slowly fanned out to their task.

'He done it all right, you can bet on that. I seen him!' announced Mick proudly.

The officer stifled a sigh. 'You sure of that, Mick? It was a bad night, pouring with rain an' all—'

'I seen him!' insisted Mick stubbornly. 'Seen him run through the rain like a rat from a trap. Seen his car, seen him drivin' it up here, then I seen him.'

'Yeah, well, identification evidence isn't all—'

'An' it won't be all!' Mick was in no mood to offer the accused the benefit of the doubt. 'You'll find other stuff, you'll only have to look for it. 'Cause he was here! An' you're not tryin' to tell me that I can't identify a man I've known all m'life, been to school with, worked with down the mine—' He came to a halt in sheer disgust at the improbability of it all.

'OK, OK. Well, look, give it me again, what y'saw.'

'I was just—'

'Here, sir! Over here!'

As if in answer to Mick's pronouncement, the first piece of silent evidence had made its appearance. Sodden and abandoned but still undamaged and quite recognisable, a man's anorak lay where it had obviously been dropped, on the grass of the headland away from the car, near the edge of the cliff.

'Seen that too!' Mick crowed in triumph. 'It's Everard's! Seen him wear it. At the pub.'

'This note of hers.' It didn't look good for Everard, reflected the Detective-Inspector, but there's more to a case than a coat and a parked car. 'Why would the girl be writing to him? What was the connection between them?'

'Connection?' Mick stared at the policeman as if he wanted to send him back to school to learn about the birds and the bees. 'He was after 'er! He was hangin' round that milk bar where she worked – you ask Vic,

252

he'll tell you – because he wanted – well, y'know what he wanted!'

'OK, OK. I get the picture.'

'D.I.!'

The young sergeant stood on the edge of the cliff. 'Careful, lad,' called the senior officer only half in jest as he strolled across. 'We don't want you going over.'

'Well, sir – somebody has.'

On the extreme verge of the grassy headland where it dropped away sheer to the rocks below, a raw break in the turf exposing the black soil beneath proclaimed a recent earthfall. Approaching it with extreme care the Detective-Inspector fell on one knee beside it, his experienced eye measuring the circumference of the newly broken edge, noting too, what were almost certainly skid marks of human heels. He stood. It was almost all over now, bar the shouting.

'Better get forensic up here, sarge,' he said heavily. 'Soon as they can.'

'We got this as well, guv.'

Behind him one of the searchers held out a woman's shoe. It was a light summer slip-on, in what had once been a defiant shade of red. They all looked at it. The Detective-Inspector turned to Mick Ford. 'I suppose you recognise this as well, Mick?' he demanded ironically.

To his embarrassment Mick's eyes were filling with tears. 'It's hers!' he muttered thickly. 'Know it anywhere. It's Ally's!' He gripped the policeman's arm in rough, piteous entreaty. 'You don't think – the bastard wouldn't have – not her as well?'

There was nothing to say. Carefully the Detective-Inspector detached himself from Mick's grip and wandered back to the cliff edge, where he remained for a while deep in thought, scanning the restless sea.

'Sarge!' he called finally. 'Better radio for a meat-wagon, and the cliff rescue boys to get out here.'

Below him the surging tide had released a heavy object from a cleft between two rocks, where it had lain wedged and out of sight beneath the surface of the sea. As the D.I. watched, the body of Jim Calder danced drunkenly into view, black and bloated, bobbing and lurching with every little wave. Beside him, keeping pace with his every move, floated the other red shoe.

The sergeant knew the score. 'How many bags, sir?'

'For now – only one. But be on the safe side – you better make it two.'

The Lord is my shepherd: I shall not want . . . Yea though I walk through the valley of the shadow of death, I will fear no evil, for Thou art with me . . .

'Mrs M? Mrs M? It's seven o'clock, Mrs Maitland. Would you like a cup of tea?'

Did they mean morning or evening? Did it matter? 'Yes please.'

'Doctor'll be in later. He said he'd see you if you'd be here.'

'I'll be here.'

'How is he tonight?'

Claire smiled, a brave attempt that struck the young nurse as a thousand times more pitiful than all the weeping and wailing some wives went in for. 'I think he's a bit better. I really do!'

The nurse had seen the brain scan. 'Yes, well, that's nice.'

'I think he could do with another pillow. It's important he's comfortable.'

'Yeah, sure.'

It's better, really, when they can accept the way it is, thought the little nurse as she gently slipped another pillow below the head of the white-clad form lying motionless on the high surgical cot. It's holding out hope that makes it worse in the end. Dr Cook has been trying to tell her for days – weeks. But she doesn't seem to get hold of it somehow.

'Evening, Mrs Maitland.'

'Dr Cook – Nurse said you'd be coming in.'

'Yes.'

With a practised eye the doctor ran through the charts attached to the end of the bed, then checked the levels of the fluids in the containers feeding into the apparently

254

a nice do. Interesting. And so was this. But in a different way.

Stolidly Joan accepted a hymn book and an Order of Service from the sidesman and took her accustomed place in the family pew. Moving from unconscious habit she fell to her knees and prepared herself for her personal devotions. 'Bless me, St Jude, for I have sinned . . .'

She would not pray for Robert. Robert was going to be OK. Robert was going to be fine. From the first moment of the accident Joan had not once wavered from this belief. Her brother could not, would not die. Not after she had herself, through her own actions, saved his life by what she had done earlier that night.

Yes, Joan decided after careful thought, for she was not a vain woman, 'saved his life' was not too strong a term. For Robert to have been allowed to go off with that – that slut – and give up his work, his ministry, the Rectory, everything he had ever wanted and worked for, that would have been death for him. And that poisonous child, that 'Ally', would have been powerless then to give him anything that could in any way compensate for it!

Well, *she* was out of the way now – right out of the reckoning. A small smile curved Joan's lips, and one of her favourite psalms came unbidden to mind. 'We thank thee, Lord, for this deliverance!' she exulted. 'We will rejoice in this thy salvation and the name of God will we set upon our banners!'

If Robert could have seen the little cat as she, Joan, had done that night, standing on the edge of the cliff as if she was going to throw herself over, and only wanted a helping hand . . .

But he was weak. Men were so weak. He would still have loved her, still pitied her, worst of all still wanted her – in that way. She shuddered violently. Yes well, she, Joan, and no one else, had saved him from all that. 'Thank you, St Jude,' she whispered. 'Thank you.'

'I know that my Redeemer liveth . . .'

The pure notes of the first hymn filled the little church. The two coffins were entering now, the foremost unusually heavy, taking six of the strongest miners to manage it, the second small and almost no weight at all. All eyes in the congregation turned in their direction and were as soon shamefacedly redirected to the pages of their hymn-books as all tried not to speculate on what lay within. Jim, everyone knew, had been fished out of Broken Bay hideously black and bloated from the salty sea-water – but what Ally looked like was anybody's guess, since her body had never been found.

And wasn't going to be, thought Joan with a satisfaction too deep for words. Still, the symbolic coffin was a nice idea, very nice. It made the funeral complete somehow – tied it all up, just the way it ought to be.

> Turn thy face again to us, O Lord, and be gracious unto them that do truly serve thee . . . Comfort us again after the time that thou hast plagued us, prosper thou our handiwork, O God, for the day of thy judgement is upon us . . .

Yes, a nice service. Really interesting. She couldn't wait to tell Robert tonight. She'd tell him everything. Because she, too, like Claire, knew that he knew her, that he knew who she was and what she was saying, every morning and evening. He knew. *He knew*.

You knew it would never be easy from the first minute you joined the force, Detective-Inspector Murray reminded himself. And you knew it would never get any better. If you'd wanted a quiet life ending up as little friend to all the world, you should've signed on as a bloody park-keeper! Still an' all, this one was just about fit to beat the band. Bad enough to have to pick up a man who sure looked as guilty as hell, but who you couldn't *feel* was guilty, not in your gut. Where other coppers relied on their nose, after Sherlock Holmes, and concentrated on sniffing out the villains and their crimes, Murray placed an equal importance on the investigative powers of his gut. He'd never found it had given him a wrong steer. And it was most definitely not with him on this. But you can't argue with hard evidence, the Superintendent had insisted. 'Get over there and pick him up – before the bugger gets the bright idea of buggering off!'

And then to have to arrest him in a hospital . . . But if that was where he was, and he certainly wasn't at his home, then that was where the arrest'd have to be . . .

No more stalling. This was it. Checking the handcuffs in his pocket and nodding to the faithful sergeant to stay outside the door unless he was needed, Murray knocked and entered. 'Evening Mrs Maitland, Miss Maitland,' he said respectfully. 'I'm sorry to disturb you.'

As he had hoped, Paul Everard rose immediately from his seat on the other side of the bed and came to the door.

'What's up? You can't come in here. My brother-in-law's been injured terrible bad—' he dropped his voice '—he's dying—'

'It's you we've come to see, sir,' said the D.I. expressionlessly.

'Me?'

'We've got to ask you to come down to the station to answer some more questions.'

'About—?'

'Yes, sir. The Calder murder enquiry.'

Paul sighed with irritation. 'Look, I've told you all I know. He beat me up, I tried t'make it to my sister's, passed out, came round to find my car gone and no one there, and somehow made it back to town to help with the mine disaster.'

'Yeah, well, we'd like to go over it again.'

Paul ran a hand through his hair. 'Well, you'll have to wait till tomorrow! I'll come down to the station when I get off my shift. But I'm not leaving my sister here now.'

'I'm afraid you're going to have to, sir.'

He'd had his chance to come quietly, and rejected the velvet glove. Time for the iron fist.

'Paul – what's up?'

258

Joan had joined him at the door, her face darkening with concern.

'Paul Everard, you are charged with the murder of Jim Calder—'

'*No!*' Even in a hospital inured to grief and suffering, Joan's harsh cry sprang from a new dimension of pain.

'Not me, boys,' Paul was unconcerned. 'You got the wrong bloke.'

They often didn't take it in at first, the sergeant noted, hovering at the door. Took time for the penny to drop. But the woman, the Rev's sister, she'd clocked it all right.

'Officer, listen! It couldn't've been Paul. Because he's got an alibi! He's only been – trying to protect my good name. Because he was with me. On the night of the murder, Paul Everard was with me – all night long!'

Well, well, well, thought the D.I. You never could tell with these spinsters. Looks as if butter wouldn't melt in her mouth, too. But would she stand up and say it in court? Yeah, probably, from the determined look of her. Lucky man, Everard. Plenty of blokes'd give their eye teeth, without anaesthetic, for a witness as good as her to pop up and alibi them for the whole of the time in question.

'No, Joan.' Paul was shaking his head, puzzled but not really worried. 'You don't have to lie for me, Joanie,' he said gently. 'I couldn't take your reputation away like that, in front of the whole of Brightstone. An' I won't need to. It's all a mistake. I'll go with them and they'll sort it all out in a couple of shakes. I'll be back here as soon as I can to run you and Claire home.'

He smiled, and left. The two women stared in consternation at each other across the motionless shrouded form lying between them on the bed. And all the demons of the earth, all the evil spirits of the air and sea, hugged themselves with all the malice of their glee and triumphant joy at a victory that was to reign unabated for a lifetime to come.

BOOK II

1990

Spring

Chapter 21

Seen from high above, beckoning through the infinite emptiness of sea and sky, Sydney unfolds to the newcomer like a giant hand, its fingers uncurling backwards in a timeless gesture of welcome and surrender. When the city was born, its few dwellings provided nothing more than meagre protection from the savagery of life on that fatal shore. But in time the small, huddled settlement, fighting every inch of the way, grew and prospered. Now a great city lies open to all, spreading out on all sides across the plain, its motorways, bridges, buildings and industries flourishing at will. In the city-centre that spring, the tree-lined avenues and squares rioting in their fresh green finery seemed to be giving an extra welcome to the new season and the visitors it would bring. Every day now the sun grew warmer and stronger. A new start. New life. New hope.

From her window-seat the girl looked out on the city below as the plane landed. The airport could have been any airport in the world. But it was the only place in the world for her now. Sydney. The big city. Yes.

As the city reached outwards, so it also grew upwards, each new generation of buildings outclassing those built before, until the low, poor dwellings of the earliest settlers faded from memory. City-centre palaces of concrete and chrome compete in Sydney now with the best of Los Angeles and New York, making London look like a Dickensian afterthought. Sydney skyscrapers have grown bigger and taller every year to form great concrete canyons where the sidewalks are never warmed by the lifeless body through a frightening array of tubes. 'Yes, I like to keep popping in.'

'Doctor?'

He knew what she was asking, what she was desperately craving. 'No change yet,' he said very gently.

'He knew me this morning.'

He had known her every morning, the doctor remembered sadly, without being able to give the slightest sign of it to anyone else, least of all to the highly sensitive machines monitoring his every breath, heartbeat and brain impulse. He repeated what he had said every evening for the past week. 'You should go home.'

She looked at him out of a face grey with exhaustion. 'I'm OK, doctor. I'd like to stay, if you don't mind.'

The doctor exchanged a glance with the nurse. 'We don't mind at all, Mrs Maitland. But it's unlikely that anything will happen overnight. We don't anticipate any change. And if anything happened, nurse would call you.'

He turned to go.

'Doctor . . . ?'

He braced himself for the final part of the nightly routine.

'Doctor, how long – how long will he be like this?'

He paused, then lifted his shoulders helplessly in the time-honoured gesture of indecision.

'But he will – get better? He'll come out of it?'

'I'm not God, Mrs Maitland!'

'Doctor, please say he will – he must!'

He paused, weighing his words. 'I have seen worse cases, Mrs Maitland. Not much worse – but a few. He's young. And his heart is strong. We can but hope. And given your husband's very special place in the hearts of the parish after all he did in the mine rescue, perhaps it is not too much to say – pray?'

She'd never been to a double funeral before.

Double wedding, yes. There was that time when the Warrinder girls, that pair of twins over at Bathurst Bay, had got married together to those fellas they'd met on a holiday trip up to the Great Barrier Reef. That'd been sun, and where the inhabitants, scurrying about their business, resemble nothing so much as worker ants moving at the behest of a higher will than their own.

And is this progress? wondered Claire uneasily as she entered the new Cathedral with Robert, Joan at her side. From where they stood at the top of the Cathedral steps she could see the whole panoply of the city in all its morning splendour, its prize buildings glinting in the sun despite the eternal haze of pollution overhead. She raised her eyes. All around her soared the evidence of man's ingenuity and technological might – the new Cathedral was a living sculpture in glass and steel, striking, uncompromising and bold, a triumph or a disaster in equal measure in the eyes of Sydneysiders. Is this beauty? asked Claire. Or am I just too old to appreciate anything any more?

'All right, darling?' Robert took her hand and brushed her face with a gentle farewell kiss. 'I'll see you later. Hope you enjoy the service – your seats are at the front, the deacon knows where you're sitting.'

''Bye, Robert – and good luck!'

He gave her the sweetest of his crooked smiles. 'You're all the luck I need, darling – you and Joan.' He kissed her again, and was gone. Within a few paces he was being warmly greeted by one worshipper after another, colleagues, supporters and parishioners pressing forward to meet him and shake his hand. Considerate as ever, he had a word and a smile for all as he made his way through the throng to the vestry and the Cathedral offices beyond.

'He's looking well today.' Joan's voice was the most approving she would ever permit herself to be. 'This is a great day, Claire.'

'Yes.'

And one I never thought we'd live to see, Claire reflected sombrely. After Robert's fall, watching and waiting through the long dark nights of despair that followed, Claire had found it in her heart to envy the wives whose husbands had died cleanly in the mine disaster, in one fatal moment. For her, Robert's living death had been far harder, the constant hope springing up only to be as constantly dashed, the prayers that simply repeated themselves ever more hollowly day after day. For Robert's injuries had been terrible. Plummetting backwards down the mine-shaft he had struck his head against the wall in falling, and again when he hit the ground. He had suffered, too, not only from the impact of the fall, but from further dreadful internal injuries caused by the collapsing lift falling on top of him.

There had been no early relief for her after the tragedy of his fall. At first, the glimmer of life in him was so faint that it seemed only a matter of time before he drifted away into death. After weeks of agonising waiting, she was told he would live – but cautioned immediately that with the extent of the injuries to his head, he might never regain consciousness. If he did, she was warned, he could very well be brain-damaged. When at last his eyes flickered open, when later still he looked, spoke, and recognised her and it seemed his mind was intact, his body became the focus for the next wave of intense anxiety – he would have the greatest difficulty in ever walking again, would almost certainly lose the use of his right arm, would be an invalid for the rest of his inevitably foreshortened life.

Without a word of complaint, without even a murmur of pain, with infinite patience, courage, and all the sweetness of his nature, Robert proved them wrong. But even then his recovery, over time, to something remarkably close to what he had been before, never carried for Claire the delight of simple joy. She was never free of the fear – never acknowledged but for that reason ever more insistently there – of seeming to trust in something that might at any moment prove to be a delusion. She had almost lost him once – fate could still snatch him away from her again.

And the near-miracle of his physical recovery – only a few slight weaknesses remaining as a legacy of the closeness of his brush with death – had eclipsed from all, even at first from his doctors, the truth of the hidden damage to his mind: the severity of his concussion had wiped his mind clean, like a slate. To this day Robert had no memory of the night of the disaster, nor of any of the events leading up to it. Then and only then had he cried out in pain, as he stood on the edge of this mental void, looked down into nothing but blackness, and recognised the extent of his loss.

With such terrible injuries needing months, indeed years in the endless cycle of surgery and recovery, more surgery followed by longer recovery, his career in the church had come to a long, painful standstill. But slowly, slowly he had fought back. First had come a transfer to a bigger parish to take up a light job in the diocesan office, then as his gift for paperwork made itself plain, greater administrative responsibility.

Finally had come the move to Sydney, so longed-for in the early days, still welcome now as the opportunity to work on a wider scale, to help those who could not help themselves, to change things for the better as he had always hoped to do. On the Archbishop's staff Robert's success with plans, projects and above all people, had been almost instant. Gradually he worked his way up through the ranks, winning friends and admirers at every stage. And when the new Cathedral was at last given the go-ahead after years of indecision, who better to take charge of it than Robert?

Robert . . . Her face softened into a smile. How wonderful he had been to her – how constant, loving and kind over all these years of grief and disappointment! Never once, in all his own long-drawn-out struggle to recover his health and strength had he ever failed to cherish and support her – never once had he reproached her, as another man might have done, for her failure to give him a much-wanted daughter, or longed-for little son. Instead he had loved her, and gone on loving her with every fibre of his being. To him, she knew, she was still the Claire of their youth, the girl he had loved and won on the beach of Broken Bay.

How far that was from a harsher reality her own mirror told her every single day. For she knew, with her unwavering honesty, that the years had not dealt kindly with Mrs Robert Maitland. But then, they had not been years of kindness. She sometimes thought that that day of their return to Brightstone when she, Robert and

Paul had visited her parents and they had all sat in the sun and laughed, was the last time she had ever been simply, truly happy. She had believed then, truly believed, that they had been sent back to Brightstone for a purpose, the purpose of enabling Robert to come to terms with his continuing grief and guilt over his parents' death – that he would overcome this to build a splendid ministry which would be the stepping-stone to the greater things he so richly deserved – and that everything would then be all right.

If there had been a purpose to all that had followed, God only knew what it was. To preserve her faith, Claire fought off these thoughts when they came, but they came and came again, till she was never without them somewhere in her mind. Could God have wanted Robert to fall from that lift and crash a hundred feet to blackness and destruction? Could He have had a design in making Jim Calder die like that, and his daughter kill herself in such a way as to throw the guilt upon – of all men – her brother Paul?

Paul. The very thought of him brought back the old familiar ache, the sad, silent pain that never went away. 'It's all a mistake,' he'd said, 'they'll sort it out and I'll be back here in a couple of shakes.' From the moment he'd walked out of Robert's hospital room with the two policemen, she had never seen him again outside prison walls: that walk to the police car had been his last as a free man.

How could they have charged, tried, convicted an innocent man? '*Don't ask*!' Joan had said in the end – no, not said – screeched, wearied beyond endurance in those terrible months by Claire's incessant return to the one question no-one could answer. Claire shuddered. Even now she could hardly bear to recall that time.

For Paul's living martyrdom, terrible as it was, had only been part of the cataclysm that had overtaken Brightstone at that same time, overwhelming so many others as well. The rock-fall at the mine had, after days of heart-breaking toil, revealed itself as a virtually total cave-in of the main mine-working, with a loss of 170 lives: the worst mining disaster in the history of Australia.

There was no hope of resuming mining there once the full extent of the destruction was known. Miners' wives and widows alike had been thrown into penury, and mining families of many generations had broken up and dispersed with brutal suddenness as the overnight failure of the mine robbed them of their livelihood or any future hope of survival. With the exodus of its young men and working fathers, Brightstone had died. 'It's only us old women hanging on now,' Molly had remarked with biting accuracy to Claire on one of her daughter's rare visits back to the little mining cottage of her birthplace, now more and more seeming like a ghost town.

Perhaps this year they could at last get Mum to come and live with them in Sydney, thought Claire with a sudden surge of hope. Now the spring was here . . . and now Robert was installed in his new post, or would be after this service . . . maybe Mum could be persuaded to make a new start, too . . . the Dean's mansion, that fantastic new edifice up above the harbour, was certainly big enough for all of them! It'd certainly be worth a try . . .

Absently she followed Joan into the Cathedral. Suddenly she felt a strong hand on her arm. 'Claire! I won't keep you – just wanted to say hello. And Miss Maitland – how are you both?'

'Murray!' Claire welcomed the newcomer with genuine pleasure. 'We're fine, just fine. Excited, of course!'

'So you should be!' Murray Beilby beamed approvingly. 'And how's that brilliant husband of yours?'

Claire laughed. 'You should know! None better! It's thanks to you that he's here at all!'

'I don't know about that.' Murray shook his head. 'Don't forget all his other doctors. I only took over where they left off.'

'Yours was the important part, though,' Joan put in, voicing Claire's thoughts too.

Murray laughed the compliment off. 'Well, I'm here today as his friend, not as his neurologist! I shan't be popping up in the middle of the service to have another

270

look at his head! And I'll tell you one thing – there can't be much wrong with his memory now if the new Dean of the Cathedral is going to take such an important part in his own service of consecration!'

He's right, Claire thought, oddly comforted. Robert is fine now, and he needs me to be fine, too. He needs all his strength now, because he has so much to do. And it all looks good, all wonderfully good. Perhaps – after all – even now – it's going to be all right?

At the airport the girl disembarked from the British Airways Boeing 747, and waited along with all the other passengers for the baggage to be offloaded. In spite of the air-conditioning, the atmosphere felt oddly sticky against her pale golden skin, and the voices of all the people around her rang with a strange music to her un-Australian ears. She collected her one battered piece of luggage and moved towards Immigration.

It's going to be all right.

It's going to be all right!

Seated next to Claire, Joan could hardly keep from standing up and turning round to shout out the joyful tidings to the whole of the assembled congregation of Sydney's finest, all the civic dignitaries and leaders of commerce and industry, the ecclesiastical bigwigs and representatives of the founding families, a cross-section of the great and the good of the capital and hence of the whole of the island. To be here! – on this occasion! – Joan thought her heart would burst. Robert now Dean Maitland! It was the high point of her life.

But no more than he deserved. And it was not to be supposed that even as Dean, his career would now stay still. After Dean, Bishop . . . even Archbishop . . . why not?

It was amazing the way things worked out. Robert had been so worried all those years ago that he'd get stuck in Brightstone, bogged down in the routine of a small-town ministry with no scope or future for his talents. In the event he had been there for less than a year before the events of that terrible night had taken him

271

out of it. Then as he grew better, the Bishop, impressed by the vigour and success of his fight to get well, partly, too, bowing to the force of circumstances as Robert's congregation died under him with the closure of the mine, promoted him to a much bigger parish in a thriving town far enough away from Brightstone for the change itself to play a part in Robert's recovery.

And where Robert had gone, Joan had gone too, without question part of the team now on every level. For Joan had been a tower of strength through every trauma. She had taken her turn at nursing the patient along with Claire when he was finally allowed home, neither flagging nor complaining even when weeks melted into months, and months into over a year, before he could even be left alone at night to deal with his nightmares. She had continued with his parish administration during his illness, indeed some unworthy souls were even heard to grumble that she had taken over the parish and made herself, without so much as a by-your-leave, the first woman priest in Australia.

Now he could not manage without her, Joan knew that. Her position as her brother's right hand had been formally ratified with the move to Sydney when she had been taken on the diocesan payroll as his executive assistant. It gave her a deeper satisfaction than anything else in her life, anything else that she had ever known.

For she never once thought of relationships, marriage, men, now. There was no other man in her mind, in her heart but Robert. She'd only ever really thought of one, and he – he'd proved himself unworthy. How unworthy, she wondered, if even now, he'd ever know. She could have, would have forgiven him falling for that tart, especially once she knew that he'd never touched her, that the little slut's love, such as it was, had been reserved exclusively for Robert, Paul's successful rival in sex. But when she, Joan Maitland, had thrown him that lifeline – had offered her name, her reputation, her love to him right there, in that hospital room, in front of the half-cynical, half-contemptuous stare of the two policemen, when she had done all that for him, and he had turned her down – had refused to countenance the possibility that he, the great Paul Everard, could have spent the night with her – *even to save his life* – then – then –

She shook her head, conscious that a familiar ugly flush was mottling her neck and creeping up her cheeks as it always did when she allowed herself to be taken over by these thoughts. He had got what was coming to him. He did not trouble her conscience or keep her awake at nights. He was in the best place. Best for him, and best for all of them.

For while he was there, the secret slept. Robert's guardian angel had wiped his memory clean of all recollection – he had forgotten not only the night of the cave-in, Jim Calder's death and his own terrible fall, but the events of the weeks immediately before that, too. That meant that he had no memory of any connection with a girl called Ally Calder.

There had been many anxious weeks and months for Joan before she was able to establish that to her own satisfaction. When she was finally sure, she had made a special visit to the church to thank God and St Jude for his goodness. She did not know how she would manage Robert if, when he came round, he had insisted on making a clean breast of it, cleansing his soul by the act of confession, and ruining not only his own future but everyone else's as well by his quixotic gesture.

For nothing could bring the three of them back from the dead: Calder, Ally, and it had to be said, Paul, buried alive as he was in the state prison. Who wanted to, anyway? They were better off dead. Good riddance to bad rubbish. The Lord giveth, and the Lord taketh away. Blessed be the name of the Lord. For the righteous shall triumph and the last trace of the unworthy perish. These are the words of the Lord. Yes!

> 'Let all the world
> In every corner sing
> My God and King!'

The high, pure voice of the trebles led the choir into the processional hymn. The Service of Dedication, of the new Cathedral and of its first spiritual leader, was about to begin. And she was going to enjoy it more than any other service of her life! Fortified by her Christian thoughts and newly dedicated to the strength of her purpose, Joan rose with the rest of the congregation to greet the incumbent Dean. It was all right. It was more than all right. It was fantastic!

At Immigration the girl had quite a hard time convincing the officers to let her in. Too many of you English sheilahs think you can just walk in here, get a job, or pick up some dumb bloke, marry him and stay here, said the hard-faced man in Immigration. Just travelling around, she said. And why would anyone *want* to get married? Finally they let her through. Picking up her suitcase, she went out of the airport terminal into the bright spring sunshine, and the city swallowed her up at once in its restless, heaving crowd.

'This day we are gathered together to celebrate the completion of a mighty task – the building of this magnificent Cathedral, for me, for so long, simply an idea, a dream, and it must be confessed, at times a nightmare.'

Dean or no Dean, Claire thought, he was still the same old Robert, his integrity, like his physical beauty, quite undiminished by time. He had to tell the truth. Not for him the soft-soap speech of empty nothings, calculated to soothe and please, in his first-ever address from the fine new pulpit. But Robert's way of speaking, his manner, his smile, all as honest and warm as ever, drew the sting from what might otherwise have been seen as an unwarranted attack on the Cathedral labour force whose constant strikes and unreliability had brought the work to a standstill time and time again.

'Now, thanks to all who worked here, all who believed in our vision, all who donated, all who cared, we are able to be together in faith, love and hope in the newest, and some of us feel the most beautiful of God's houses to grace our beloved city and to enrich our sunburned land.'

He was good, you had to give him that. Seated

towards the back with a block of men whose solid build and unimpressed demeanour betrayed them as the union labour whose delays Robert had just touched on, Mick Ford had to admire a professional operator. Well, we've both come on, Reverend, come a long way, you and me both. For Mick, his new post as national organiser for the Union of Labour beat twenty Deanships into a cocked hat. Still, if that's what he wanted – or rather, what Miss Joan wanted – then fair enough. Wonder how long it'd take to get used to calling him 'Dean'?

'I greet this day with great humility, honoured simply to be here to play my part, privileged to be able to conduct the ceremony which will consecrate for us all – for all of Sydney – this place of worship. This house of God is more than a physical reality. It is a symbol of our faith, of the importance of God in our lives. May it give heart to all who suffer and are in need – all who seek, and are in despair of finding. Like a beacon of light in our long night of darkness, may it shine through us and in us for all to see.'

He bowed his head and fell to his knees for a moment of silent prayer. The organ music surged up to terminate the service. Already the female members of the congregation were getting ready, Mick could see, to flutter round Robert like a flock of swallows and bask in the kindness of his smile. And there was his little wife, too, still in good shape, and his sister – Mick sat up with a quickening of interest, and only just remembered in time not to let out an approving whistle. Joan Maitland had turned into a real cracker – even now, after all these years, she was better looking than she had ever been! Not bad to have all that around you at your beck and call!

Nice work, Rev, thought Mick. Nice work. You just can't put a foot wrong, can you? Wonder what it'd take to make your charmed luck run out?

Chapter 22

It never got any easier.

How could it?

And why did he expect it to?

Shivering a little in the still-wintry wind off the low, level plain around the state prison, Robert took Claire's arm to help her through the gates, across the inner yard, and into the prison visiting-room. She hated these visits so much, he could hardly bear to see it. Yet she also lived for them, spending every month winding up to see Paul again, and leaving every time as if she had just left her brother behind in the prison cemetery, instead of alive and as well as could reasonably be expected under the circumstances.

'Paul! You're looking good!'

It was true. Paul smiled, a worn smile, but still somehow, miraculously, the same old Paul.

'Paul!'

Claire always had to struggle hard not to cry when Paul was first brought in, a prison officer on either side of him like the convict he was. Knowing this, the men tried hard to keep the conversation light for the difficult opening moments.

'Hello, kid. Don't know why you bring your wife here for her outings, Rob. Helluva long way to come, and not much to see at the end of it!'

'I wouldn't say that,' countered Robert in the same bantering vein. 'You're always worth a once-over. You never look a day older. How've you been?'

'Better than you, by the look of it!'

Claire smiled tremulously. 'Robert's been so busy!' she put in. 'Consecrating the new Cathedral, being inducted as Dean—'

'Inducted? What's that? Sounds painful!'

Robert nodded. 'Formally inaugurated. Quite an ordeal. Big do.'

'I know.' Paul smiled. 'Saw you on TV. Good stuff!'

'What did you think of it?' queried Claire eagerly.

'The Cathedral?' Paul still liked to tease, Robert noted wryly. 'Be all right for growing tomatoes, I suppose, all that glass. You thinking of going into the fruit and veg business, Dean?' Suddenly he was deadly serious. 'You've heard about the mine?'

'No! What!' Their reactions came in unison.

'Well, it's only a rumour so far. One of the screws, his brother used to be a miner, still lives in Brightstone, he told me. He says they haven't fixed a date yet, nothing's been agreed. But I believe it! It's just the sort of thing those bastards'd do!'

'What is it, Paul?' Robert demanded. 'Tell us!'

Paul's expression took on the hard and violent look of banked-down fury that he usually tried to keep out of his face when they came. 'They're re-opening the mine. They've got new technology; they can cut through now where we couldn't go before, by-pass the cave-in, and get to the seam underneath.'

They looked at him, unable to read his reaction and in dread of what he might be feeling.

Then his mood changed again with the wild, free-swinging emotion of a man with too little to absorb his still-vital animal energy and spirits. 'Still, maybe they're just fixing to re-open the mine so they can give me a job again when I get out. My parole's coming up again, did I tell you? And I'd better get it – this time, I'd bloody better!'

He paused, and drew a trembling breath. 'Because there's ghosts – miners' ghosts – going to walk when they take the lid off that grave and let them out, you mark my words! And I'm damned sure I'm going to be there to see it! Got some scores of my own to settle, haven't I? Because somewhere – somewhere out there – is the man who's robbed me of the last twenty years, and I'm going to find him! And when I find him, *I'm going to make him pay*!'

* * *

'If only he didn't seem so . . . so bitter every time.'

As ever, Claire was leaving the prison feeling totally defeated by the horror of it all.

'Oh, Claire.' They had had this conversation a thousand times. 'How do you expect him to feel? He does pretty well, considering everything, to keep his spirits up the way he does.'

'Oh God, please let him get parole this time!'

Robert reached for her hand and gave it a loving squeeze. 'Don't let's ask God for what may not be in His power to give,' he said gently.

'But they have to! This time! They *have* to!'

He did not have it in his heart to crush such passionate hope. But she read his silence. 'Well – maybe this new lawyer – the one from the Law Centre who's agreed to look over the papers one more time – maybe he'll come up with something. Who knows?' she demanded with a forced laugh.

After twenty years, Claire? he wanted to ask. Her loyalty was wonderful, he thought. But her persistence in hoping against hope conflicted sharply with his greater sense of realism. Without his constant sympathy and understanding, they could have been in serious conflict about Paul's chances. But he loved her too much to argue. He nodded gravely. 'Who knows?' he agreed.

'There *must* be something they've missed,' Claire continued urgently. She had said this before, too – he couldn't remember how many times. 'There's a missing link. Something we don't know.'

He had to speak. 'Claire – darling – what more do you think you can do? When does it end? After all the lawyers, petitions, appeals—'

'Didn't work, though, did it!' Her sweet face was harsh with anger. 'Didn't get him out!'

The headache that had troubled Robert on and off since his accident began to throb quietly in his temple. Ever attentive, Claire saw the colour drain from Robert's handsome, life-conditioned face. 'Never mind me, darling!' she said with a quick, false brightness. 'One day. We'll do it one day!'

He forced a smile. 'Never give up, you Everards, do you?'

She threw her head up, proudly and unafraid. 'Not when we're right! And not when it's something worth fighting for!'

'I know. And you're right about this. Poor old Paul.' Suddenly he felt exhausted at the thought of the long overland drive back to Sydney, then that social function afterwards at the residential centre . . . oh God . . .

Claire was there, as always. 'Look, darling, you don't seem to be in the mood for a party.'

'Are you?'

She slipped her arm encouragingly through his. 'No, but I will be by the time we get there. I'll drive the first part of the way back. You can refresh my memory of all the folks we're going to meet tonight, with a few of those celebrated Maitland thumbnail sketches of yours, then I'll know exactly who I've got to be nice to when we get to the Allambie!'

The venerable 'Allambie' had once, long ago, seen better days as a house grand enough to be owned by a big Sydney merchant and the pride of his large family. But when the Second World War had put paid to the availability of servants ready to labour all hours for a pittance a week, the descendants of the dead tycoon had been happy enough to sell up to the Civic Trust, a body guaranteed to preserve the old beauties of Sydney and put them to good use. So the Church had entered into a fruitful relationship with the Trust to take over the old mansion and restore it to life as a residential hostel and day-care centre for the elderly and retired of Sydney.

Allambie had become one of Robert's favourite places in Sydney from the moment of his arrival in the city. The Allambie residents had been the first to give him a warm and unconditional welcome, without any of the critical stand-offishness that usually greets any newcomer in what are considered to be more sophisticated circles. And only at the Allambie was he assured on every visit of smiling faces, innocent gossip, and the sense of leisure which was more and more a luxury in his highly pressured life.

Today's occasion was the 'Allambie Birthday Party', the annual celebration of the occasion, forty years before, when the house had been opened to provide live-in accommodation for a favoured few, and day-care, endless food and drink, conversation and company for the rest of the over-sixties of the city. If the house was quite a bit more shabby than in its days of glory under the merchant's regime, no one was inclined to complain. For the warmth and comfort in the worn, battered chairs, the cheery old rugs and low, inviting sofas made it more homely and welcoming than a king's palace. As a final touch of sprightly gaiety, someone had slung a rough, homemade banner reading 'Good On Yer, Allambie – Happy Birthday!' across the large, communal living-room which took up almost all of the ground floor. Robert could feel his spirits rising as soon as he walked through the door.

The heart of this evening's entertainment was centred on the piano, where a group composed of residents and staff were gathered around one old-timer resolutely plodding through his entire repertoire of pre-World-War-II popular songs. 'Who's sorry now?' he sang in a high, clear, buzzing voice like a bee up a chimney.

> 'Who's sorry now?
> Whose heart is aching
> For breaking
> Each vow . . .'

Smiling warmly, Robert crossed to the piano and clapped the elderly crooner on the back. 'Hello, Arthur! Why, you're in good voice. We'll be seeing you on television next!'

'Robert!'

Joan was there as ever, a huge, institutional-sized teapot in her hands, a ready greeting on her lips for all the Allambie regulars who knew her as well as anyone in Sydney.

'Glad t'see ya, Miss Maitland – how about a wet?'

281

'Hang on a minute, Timbo. I've just got to have a word with the Dean.'

Robert twinkled at her. 'You don't have to give me my title every time you talk to me, you know! I'm still the same old Robert Maitland underneath!'

Or am I? he wondered suddenly. An old Spanish proverb flashed unbidden into his mind: 'Take what you want – *and pay for it*, says God.' He had wanted this – yes, he had wanted promotion, recognition, favour, distinction, since he joined the church. Before that, too, if he was honest enough to admit it. The thought of being just Robert Maitland, plain Robert Maitland, ordinary Robert Maitland, had always been impossible for him. Dean Maitland . . . yes. It was good. It felt good. But not at the price of losing his sister's love, becoming an ecclesiastical eminence to her instead of a real, fallible, flesh-and-blood brother.

'Oh, Robert!' Surreptitiously Joan nodded at Claire across the room, where she was greeting two of her octogenarian admirers. 'How did it go – the visit?'

'Like always.'

His tone made it perfectly clear that he had no more to say on the subject. Obediently Joan took her cue to move on. 'Well, there's a couple of things I've got to tell you about who's here. You know old Arthur, he's the one you just spoke to, singing by the piano? Turns out it's his birthday on Tuesday: he's seventy-six. Thought you might just bring it in when you say a word about the hostel. It sort of personalises things – he's very popular.'

Robert nodded.

'Something else – it's a bit worrying. Some of the old folk have got hold of the idea that Allambie's closing down – that it's being sold to developers.'

'It can't be.' Robert's response was automatic. 'It's a listed building, protected by city bye-laws. And it belongs to the Civic Trust. They'd never sell out for development.'

'That's what I said!' Joan smiled. 'But they're feeling upset about it all the same. Will you have a word where you can around the room to calm them down?'

'I'll do more than that.' Robert made a mental note. 'I'll look into it, the first chance I get. I'll have a word with the chairman of the Civic Trust; we'll nip this rumour in the bud. It'll only get the residents all worked up for nothing.'

Joan smiled her gratitude. 'One last thing. The new curate's wife is here, Patsy – you know the Reverend Wright, he's just taken over the parish, he'll be joining us in a while, as soon as he's finished his evening calls. You should just say hello to her when you can. She's a nice girl. Turned up early to give us a hand with the teas. Seems very willing.'

Joan would have been very much less pleased with the willing little Mrs Wright, the young woman she had already targeted as another useful pair of female hands around the Cathedral, if she could have overheard the conversation taking place between her new-found paragon and one of the Allambie's care assistants in the privacy of the kitchen.

'What? Mrs Maitland's *brother*?' Patsy's eyes were like saucers. 'Is it true?'

The attendant shrugged. 'True as I'm standing here.'

'And then the girl he was after, the one he killed her father for, she killed herself after all that?'

'Found her things in the water. Shoes and that. Never found her. Not even bits of her.'

'Ooo-er!'

Mum had said she'd have more excitement in Sydney, Patsy thought. But she couldn't have meant anything as exciting as this!

'Wow! Only found her shoes? Ugh, how horrible!' Then the ghost of suspicion crossed Patsy's mind. 'If it's true, how come I haven't heard about it before? How come they don't talk about it?'

Where do they find them, thought the care assistant, stolidly washing up. And when they find them, where've they been all their lives? She shook the water from a cup and fixed Patsy with a withering stare. 'Think about it, sunshine. Would you?'

'But the Dean – if he was such a big hero that night, down the mine and all, why doesn't he talk about it?'

'Can't, can he?'

'Why not?'

The care assistant laid down her washing-up sponge. 'Amnesia!' she said impressively. 'Complete memory loss! Like a baby! His mind's gone! He can't remember a thing!'

Patsy had in fact been rather impressed by the Dean's recent conduct of the very long and complex service of inauguration without recourse at any stage to Bible, book or script, not to mention his ability to remember kindly almost every person in the parish. But she was not about to spoil a good story. 'Go on!' she breathed.

'Well, that's it! The family taint! The dirty secret!'

'Taint! Secret! Yes . . .' Patsy was in her seventh heaven. Mom would love this.

'So next time y'see that Miss Maitland with her nose in the air—'

'What's that, Ellen?'

Joan stood behind them, her eyes glittering like a snake's. But the assistant was not abashed. 'Just talking about the Brightstone murder,' she said defiantly. 'Nothing wrong with that. It's common knowledge.'

Joan drew herself up to her considerable height and fixed the transgressor with a look that would have lasered processed steel.

'For common people, Ellen – common people.' She turned on her heel. 'Come with me, Patsy. If you're going to be happy here – if you're really going to fit into the diocese and learn how to be one of us – I think you and I had better have a little talk.'

That was nice. Abstractedly Robert noticed Joan and the new little wife of the curate deep in conversation across the living-room and felt his usual sense of gratitude for Joan's incessant care. She'd put the girl at ease all right, he thought. Help her to find her feet.

By now the party was in full swing and all around him the old people were having a great time. Robert smiled, his pleasure almost too deep for words. Quietly he drifted off into a corner of the room where in the shelter of a big bay window, shielded by heavy drapes from the world outside, he found the solitude he sought.

Why was it that a deep sense of happiness, a certain kind of peace within himself, always brought with it a feeling he could never quite identify, like the echo of a voice he had never heard or the presence of a person he had never known? Quite often now, especially around twilight, he found himself pleasurably tormented by things he could not explain, things so vague he could not even conceive of trying to share them with anyone else.

For how could you discuss or even describe a half-recalled wisp of scent – the ghost of a memory – a sudden stirring of desire – a fleeting feeling that just over your shoulder, almost in reach, but always fading even as you turned, was the spirit of someone – someone so important – a face you were doomed never to see, a hand forever slipping from your grasp like the dream that dissolves even as you wake? Someone you did not know – but yet knew, had known, better than anyone else in the whole wide world? How could you say that a sound, a scent, a colour, seemed to trigger – not a memory, for that was gone, but an echo – of something – of something yet unknown?

He shook his head. Too much of this – and lately there had been far too much of this – left him trembling with a strange kind of elation, a happiness he could neither speak about nor share. He could lose himself in this feeling, he knew, lose his grasp, his control. He was imagining things. He had been working too hard, with the opening of the Cathedral. And now, with the long, debilitating trip to see Paul on top of everything, he was exhausted. Even Paul had noticed how tired he looked.

Time to go home. He must find Claire. Locating her, he reached her side. As he did so, she turned up her soft, smiling face to greet him. 'Hello, Robert. Is it time to—'

The sudden run of chords on the piano went through him like an electric shock. The song it introduced floated across to him and hung in the crowded air.

> I'll be loving you,
> Always.

With a love that's true,
Always.
Not for just an hour,
Not for just a day . . .

He was floating with the music; he *was* the music; like the music itself he was spinning through time. Then the sense of losing himself which had been troubling him before returned to him sharply and he felt the need to steady himself against something solid, a wall, a door. Beside him Claire's face swam into view, looking up at him with a smile that seemed to say 'Our song – remember?'

Wisps of – of what? – drifted across the edges of his mind, plucking at his memory. A large room, like this, and like this, too, full of people. Claire beside him, as now, and that song – that song . . .

And something else. Something else, more important than all of these. A memory of – of what? A place? A person? A special gathering? Or all of these, and more? He felt it, knocking at the door of his mind, longing to be let in. But the door would not yet open. And until he could let it in, he would not see its face . . .

When the things you've planned,
Need a helping hand,
I will understand,
Always . . .
Always . . .

'Always, Arthur?' he murmured in the quietness of his soul. 'How long is always?'

The next morning dawned with the promise of one of the pearly spring days that can be even sweeter than summer. Slipping quietly out of the house in the still-grey light of dawn, Robert drove musingly to the Cathedral.

He had not slept well last night – yet he had not suffered the miseries of insomnia either. Coming home with that feeling – he hardly knew how to describe it, even to himself – suffusing his mind, his being, he had taken Claire with an unexpected passion, loving her long and ardently, riding on that emotion, going with its every swell and flow, till he had brought them both to the explosion of release not once, but again and again. Afterwards Claire had dropped heavily, instantly, into a deep sleep, while he had lain awake, still reaching out, still floating, till dream met desire in some white realm neither of sleep nor wakefulness.

A white night, then. But he did not feel tired. On the contrary some of that strange excitement, that exultation, still clung around him and he revelled in its touch. He knew that the feeling would not leave him now, but would at least persist throughout the service he was about to take. Calmly he focused his mind on the task that lay ahead.

He had always loved early morning Communion almost more than any other service, even including the happy family occasions of weddings and christenings. He robed himself that morning in a mental state of almost perfect happiness, at ease with his life, himself and his God. As he prepared, the beloved and well-worn phrases of the service slipped sweetly and easily through his mind, like antique ivory counters long shaped into smooth currency by their owner's loving caress.

Almighty and ever-loving God, unto whom all hearts be open, all desires known, and from whom no secrets are hid, cleanse the thought of our hearts by the inspiration of your holy spirit . . .

It was time. His heart overflowing, he moved forward to begin.

The service was going well, he felt it. Not that his services ever went badly – he cared too much about every word, every hymn, every reading, to allow that to happen. But occasionally, as now, something special happened and the people were with him, he knew, at a deeper, more meaningful level than he usually achieved. Bible in hand, he ascended the pulpit and began to read.

' "Now it is high time for all sinners, and all who sleep

through the bounty of the Lord, to awake out of their sleep. For now is our salvation nearer than we thought possible in the days of our darkness. For the night of our darkness, is spent, the day is at hand, the fair day breaks around us on either side . . ."'

He raised his eyes to the congregation. Below him the communicants knelt in rows, heads lowered in prayer, a kaleidoscope of brown, fair, grey, some hatted, most uncovered before God. What was that? Towards the back of the church? He looked down the aisle. No, there was nothing. His imagination again – or was it his eyesight? Strengthening his voice, he continued. ' "Let us therefore cast off the works of darkness, and put on the armour of light." '

Light . . . Suddenly he caught sight of the crown of an oval head, the hair as fair and flaxen as a child's, the kneeling body lithe, girlish and slim, clearly that of a young woman. Robert stopped in his tracks. That head . . . that hair . . .

What was he thinking? Everything . . . nothing. From somewhere far away the feeling of happiness he had known last night at Allambie grew and flourished inside him until he felt his heart singing with joy. Shaking, a little alarmed, he struggled to pull himself together again. Smoothly but speedily he moved through the service to begin Holy Communion itself. Standing at the altar, the bread and wine in his hands, he felt good again, steady and capable. Rejoicing as he always did in this supreme moment, he took the bread in his hands and blessed it.

'The body of our Lord Jesus Christ who died for thee: take, eat, do this in remembrance of Christ's love, and feed on him in thy heart with thanksgiving . . .'

One by one the communicants shuffled quietly up to the far end of the altar rail and kneeling before him, heads bowed in prayer, patiently awaited his approach.

'The blood of our Lord Jesus Christ which was shed for thee, preserve thy body and soul unto everlasting life. Drink this in remembrance that Christ died for thee, and live in thankfulness . . .'

He had reached the end of the row of kneeling

worshippers. Turning to the altar, his back to the congregation, he replenished the chalice with the thick, sweet, blood-red communion wine and took up the paten to begin again. Behind him the new line of communicants had replaced the first. He turned back towards them.

Before him, kneeling at the altar rail, was a young girl, her long, pale hair falling from the crown of her perfect oval head forward over her praying hands. A shadow passed over his mind, something he could not explain. He stepped towards her.

'Take – eat—'

As he spoke, she lifted her head and raised her eyes to his face. The look she gave him was pregnant with meaning, expressive of some strange, secret purpose he could not begin to understand.

'The body of our Lord Jesus Christ . . .'

Her eyes were as blue as slate, and they lifted with what seemed to be their own hidden smile at the corners. He was floating now, drifting, almost lost. She stared into his eyes, willing him to look at her, commanding him to respond. She was calling him to her, claiming his very soul, as it seemed, for her own. It was more than he could bear. As she looked up at him, looked into him and through him, the blackness surged over him, clouding his thought, his soul, his sight, until he lost consciousness, slipping away into the welcome, waiting darkness all around.

Chapter 23

'No, I'm sure it's nothing serious. Just strain, most probably. It's only to be expected, the way the Dean's been working lately. Yes, you can leave him to me now. Yes, I'll call if I need any help. Thank you.'

Robert could hear the sound of the vestry door closing, then male feet returning to his side where he was lying on the vestry's ancient couch. He opened his eyes and looked up into the smiling face of Murray Beilby. 'Good Lord!' he said in wonderment. 'What are you doing here?'

Murray laughed. 'Your sub-deacon – officiating with you this morning – remembered me from your inauguration service. So when you staged your rather spectacular collapse right at the altar, I got the call to come to the rescue.'

'Oh God!' Robert groaned, and his pale face coloured a little. 'Did I really pass out? God, I feel such a fool!'

'Now that is a fool thing to say and no mistake!' returned Murray crisply. 'You're only human, you know, Robert – and human bodies like to call a halt every now and then – especially if we overdo things. Tell me what happened this morning,'

'Nothing,' said Robert slowly. 'I was giving Communion. I felt fine, honestly, absolutely fine, even—' he broke off.

'Even what?' prompted Murray.

'Well . . .' Robert gave an embarrassed laugh. 'Even good – in fact, I felt particularly good last night and today.'

Murray's keen eyes registered this, but he made no comment.

'Then at the altar – God, this sounds so ridiculous – you'll laugh . . .'

'Just try me, Robert. I'm your doctor, remember.'

'I saw this girl – a girl I'd never seen before in my life. She looked at me – she gave me such a strange look – that I passed out.'

Murray did not laugh. 'And you didn't feel tired? Or sick?' he probed.

'No.'

'And no recurrence of your old trouble – from the injury?'

'Just the odd headache from time to time – nothing unusual.'

There was something unusual going on here, Murray decided, or he didn't know a cortex from a thalamus. But there was no point in alarming a patient unnecessarily. 'Well, why don't we run a few of the old tests again, just to make sure?' he said casually. 'And in the meantime, whatever you say, Robert, don't overdo it. There'll be no point in your great new appointment if you're going to crock yourself up trying to move mountains! Now you take the rest of the day off, spend it peacefully at home with that nice little wife of yours! And that,' he finished firmly, cutting off Robert's protests before they could be made, 'is doctors' orders, right?'

Of course, he needed a holiday. Or a bit of a break. Soon be as right as rain. Be himself again in a few shakes of a kanga's tail. He'd be fine.

With the comforting platitudes she had heard on all sides still ringing in her ears, Claire walked along the beach a few paces behind Robert, lost in thought. Of course she was glad that Murray had been called to the Cathedral as soon as he fell ill, but not even Sydney's best consultant, backed up by a fresh battery of neurological tests, could come up with any convincing explanation as to why Robert had passed out so suddenly and unexpectedly that morning at Communion. Claire did not know either. All she knew was that this strange turn of events left her feeling very vulnerable, and very afraid.

A pace in front, Robert turned towards her, lifting his face to catch the warmth of the spring sun. 'Come on, Claire!' he called happily. 'We're supposed to be taking a gentle walk together, enjoying the scenery and the spring weather, and here I am all on my own!'

She hesitated to catch him up. He gave her a shrewd glance. 'Something on your mind? Penny for them!'

'Oh . . .' What could she say? 'I'm glad we came out here. The wind – the sea – it always reminds me of home.'

Brightstone was still home to her, he had always known that. And she was such a homebody, it was hard to see how she could be expected to feel homely about the grand new Deanery he had been given as his official residence, as impressive as it was. Brightstone. Yes, he thought gently, Brightstone will always be home to her . . .

'Will you go, Robert?'

'Mmmmn?'

'Back home. To Brightstone. To take the service, now it's definite that they're re-opening the mine.'

'Oh yes.' He paused, fishing in his pocket for the official letter of invitation that had reached him that morning. 'It's not just a service, apparently. They're planning a whole lot of things to mark the official re-opening. Including' – he smiled ruefully – 'a tribute to the heroes of the mine disaster.' Claire smiled back sympathetically. She knew how much it embarrassed him to be praised for his part in saving Johnny Anderson and the others, or even reminded of it. 'So I don't know. I honestly don't know.'

'They've got to have a service, or some form of commemoration, as a mark of respect. After all, it's not just a disused mine. If there isn't some recognition of the fact that it's the grave of so many of Brightstone's men, the whole re-opening will just be unbelievably sordid.'

'I can see that.' She saw his fingers fly unconsciously to his temple. 'I think it's a fine idea. I just wish it hadn't come from Mick Ford.'

A quick flush rose on her still-delicate face. 'I didn't know it had!' As the man who had put her brother behind bars, Mick Ford was anathema to Claire, Robert knew. But she had to be told.

'Apparently, yes. And I don't trust him, Claire.'

'You don't say!'

Her flashes of sarcasm and bitterness never failed to surprise Robert. 'Look, I don't mean about – his evidence against Paul,' he said levelly. 'We've agreed – he wasn't lying at the trial. Whoever he saw, he genuinely believed it was Paul that night on the cliff.'

She shook her head violently. 'He had it in for Paul, you know he did!'

'True. But he wasn't making the whole thing up.'

'But if only he'd even been willing to admit that he might have been mistaken, Paul'd've had a chance. As it was, he was determined to put him away – for good!'

'That's not the only problem. If Mick Ford's behind this suggestion for a grand service to re-dedicate the mine and pay our dues of respect to the men who died there, I can't help suspecting a stunt of some kind. But it's very hard for any minister to refuse an invitation to conduct a service of worship. And if I don't go, they'll only get someone else. But the main problem is the usual old one – pressure of work here. Now the new Cathedral's officially open, there's a huge fund-raising and new building programme to be planned and co-ordinated. I really can't afford the time.'

'And there's Allambie – don't forget Allambie, Robert, and the old people.'

'No, I haven't forgotten. That's certainly another thing on the list here. I just haven't been able to get hold of the Civic Trust boys yet. But that's another good reason not to leave the city right now. I'm just going to have to decide where my duty lies – here or in Brightstone. At the moment, I honestly don't know.'

Deep in thought, he covered the sand in light, easy strides, obviously welcoming the respite from his daily concerns. At last Claire broke the silence. 'Robert,' she said frowning, 'the invitation came to you from the people of Brightstone, didn't it?'

294

'Yes.'

'So even if it was Mick Ford's idea, all the Brightstonians were behind it, they really wanted to see you back again?'

'Yes, I suppose so.'

Oh God, thought Claire, we have been here before. Once again Robert is being called back, back to Brightstone . . . to Brightstone, of all places . . .

Robert seemed to pick up effortlessly on her train of thought. 'God moves in mysterious ways, darling' he said quizzically.

'Yes.'

'Truthfully, Claire – how do you feel?'

'The truth? It'd be good to see Brightstone again.'

'Truly?'

'Good and bad. But mostly good. It's ages since we've been home . . .'

Home . . .

That word, and way she said it, the little ache in her voice that accompanied it, decided him. 'Right then, I'll do it. It'll be great to see all the old-timers again. And nice for Molly to have us there with her instead of having to come up to Sydney to see us all the time.'

She nodded. 'I sometimes wonder—' She paused, threw him a look, then pressed on, ' – if it hadn't all happened – the way it did – if we'd have still been in Brightstone, in the old Rectory, still living there now . . .'

He looked at her in complete surprise. She could see that the idea, even the possibility, had never crossed his mind before.

'In *Brightstone*?'

She hastened to retract. 'Oh, I know it wouldn't have suited you – not really. You were meant for bigger things – bigger places. But we were young there – life was very precious then, it was so good – I sometimes think—'

He cut her off with unusual abruptness, as if he did not even want to think about it. 'No brooding, darling. No looking back. You know we agreed – God's will be done.'

They walked back to the car in silence. I sometimes

think we would have been happier there! her inner voice protested. And there – if we'd stayed – I might have had children, I might have been a mother . . .

'Robert?'

But he was miles away, lost in some bleak recesses of his mind. What had she said to drive him so far away, so distant from her, so shut off that it hurt her like a physical pain?

'Robert?'

No answer.

We might have been closer, a small, defeated voice whispered in her ear. And when that night in bed he unexpectedly refused her timid overtures of love, she had to listen to its sad refrain over and over through the long dark reaches of a cold and sleepless night.

'Ladies and gentlemen, the modern Church has to move with the times! With your encouragement – your support – and if you'll forgive my being blunt, your money – we can build for a future that will make Australia the leader of the world in this field of ours.'

A hearty approving ripple of laughter and applause greeted the opening remarks of Robert's speech. Flashing a delighted smile, beginning to enjoy himself as he got into his stride, Robert warmed to his theme. Clustered around a scale model of a low-level, sympathetically designed office-block complex, a handful of Sydney's wealthiest dignitaries listened in respectful silence as Robert explained its purpose and design. They knew that the Church was after their money in inviting them to this presentation on its newest construction site, for at their level of wealth, someone always was. But when it was done with such humour, such style and grace, the new Dean wouldn't only get my cheque, vowed the oldest, crustiest and richest of them all – he can have my vote, too, any time he wants to run for President!

At the back of the gathering, Joan glowed with the kind of wordless pride she always felt on these occasions. Robert was in fine form today! Firmly she dismissed the last of her anxiety about his collapse in the Cathedral the other day. Of course, they'd been right to be concerned at first, she and Claire – it was so unlike him to be ill. But really, there was nothing wrong with him, you only had to look at him to see that. And to watch him in action like this – he was so natural. She didn't know how he did it, but the truth was that he had these people eating out of his hand. He was so good at what he did! There was no one to touch him, no one!

'Shall we go outside?'

Smiling, chatting, working the party, Robert led the way out of the building-works office and on to the construction site itself. Before them stood a huge glossy sign proclaiming 'St Matthew's House – By Order of the Diocesan Council'. In the distance a mammoth crane indicated the start of the excavations, a gaping hole in the ground apparently big enough to bury the new building, and the Cathedral with it.

'It's going to be a big do, then, Dean Maitland?' asked one of the dignitaries, an industrialist named Phillips, impressed.

'I think it's a mark of the Church's current success that we need the space!' responded Robert. 'The office accommodation on the lower floors will be rented out, of course – to carefully selected tenants. Then the top area will be occupied by Church functionaries, for Church business.'

'Nearer to God, eh?' cracked Phillips.

There was general laughter.

Robert smiled his easy, pleasant smile. 'Too true, sir. Wish I'd thought of that!'

It was going well, Joan thought. As it had to. For Robert had not been made Dean as an empty honour. He owed his promotion to the fact that in his previous job he had proved himself to be not just an able administrator and a highly efficient, even visionary planner, but so good with people that he really could win over anyone and everyone to his side. Given the Church's endless problems, his was a unique gift. And his ecclesiastical masters had made it very plain that they expected to exploit it to the full. And then, Robert, and then . . . Joan exulted again. Then Bishop . . . and then . . .

Phillips would put his hand in his pocket, Joan

decided. Robert had convinced him of the value of the project and its sound commercial sense. She could almost see herself counting the Phillips dollars when the cheque came in. Not so sure about Mrs Maddox, though. Her wealthy husband had given very freely towards the building of the Cathedral, which was how they had got to know her. But it was Joan who had pointed out that as the only surviving descendant of Sydney's biggest brewer, silly, flustered, middle-aged Bessie Maddox had money in her own right and was well worth cultivating. Now the lady herself moved tentatively up to Robert's elbow and made the point she had been trying to get out for the past half hour.

'But do they have to build these things so big, Dean Maitland? I used to like the old houses that were here before. There's not so much of the old Sydney left. We don't want to go tearing down what we've got just to make more and more skyscrapers.'

'It's always a difficult problem, Mrs Maddox,' responded Robert gravely. 'But the church can't live in the past. We have huge needs now – we spend millions a year on community welfare, and that all has to be administered somehow. And I hope you'll agree that the design we commissioned was as sympathetic as possible to the city's architecture and the feel of the surrounding buildings.'

As they walked forward Mrs Maddox, struggling with her court shoes over the broken surface of the building site, had imperceptibly lagged further and further behind. Robert turned back to assist her, then turned again in haste, springing forward with the intention of catching up with his other guests. Without warning came the site engineer's call.

'Hey Dean – Dean Maitland!'

He turned. Without warning, it seemed, they had come to the edge of the excavation. A massive gaping hole opened before his feet and the blood rushed to his head. He swayed, fighting for control.

Get a grip, man, for God's sake! he raged. Determinedly he stared into the void, forcing himself to try to focus on the reality of it. His senses began to swim.

From far off there came a sound like the sea, then a roaring in his ears like a tidal wave. He found himself looking not into the sunlit excavation, but into darkness, the blackness of a bottomless pit.

It was a waking nightmare – the torment of the survivor. Sweating, he faced again the ordeal he had endured for so long after the fall, when he had been condemned to relive that endless, suffering plunge, the extreme mental agony before the body's pain took over, night after night after night. Not that – not now – surely not . . . ?

Or *was* it a pit? Was the blackness not the terrible sightless black of the darkness below the earth, but the thinner darkness of night – the hole not a tunnel indoors or underground but a much bigger chasm gaping to receive him – and higher up too?

For he was high up, too high, too near the edge . . . too near to eternity . . . someone would die, someone would be killed . . . ! Why did he hear, smell the sea, and hear a woman's voice screaming, screaming, screaming . . .

'You all right?'

He opened his eyes. A foot from his face the concerned eyes of the site engineer gazed into his, on his forearm the steely grip of a work-strengthened fist supported him and held him back from falling. Again the man looked him in the eye, his anxiety plain. 'Thought you were going to take a dive for a minute there, Dean.'

Robert tried a laugh. 'If I had – that would have spoiled the party and put the schedule back a bit, wouldn't it?'

A flurry of laughter ran through the group. No one had noticed anything much out of the way. But when they all dispersed, satisfied with a good day and generously translating that satisfaction into sizeable donations to the church, there remained an odd sense of unease in the two Maitland minds – yet neither of them, least of all Joan Maitland, could have said what the reason for their concern had been.

In here – it must be in here somewhere.

Methodically yet feverishly, too, Robert pulled yet another yellowing file from the bottom of the filing-cabinet and began to sort through its contents. He did not know what he was looking for. He did not even know why he was looking. All he knew was that there was something – something he had to find, had to know – and that it must come from the time of his accident, the start of the great void in his mind.

Check the archives, Murray had said when reporting to him what they both had already suspected, that the new set of neurological tests had revealed nothing untoward. Scout around, see if you can find out who that girl in the Cathedral reminded you of. There must have been a pretty powerful trigger there, to cause you to pass out. Track that down, and you'll be on the way to understanding what this is all about.

A trigger – a pretty powerful trigger. Something of the sort had happened to him again on the seashore when he had been walking with Claire. Something she had said about Brightstone – he could not even remember what it was. But it had brought on again that strange feeling, that floating, happy, lost sensation that he could neither own up to nor control.

And now this semi-blackout on the edge of the excavation at the building site! That could have been danger-ous – he had so nearly fallen in! Why should he be thinking of the fall in the mine again now, after twenty years? Why had he suddenly become vulnerable to these random associations, these inexplicable attacks of dizzi-ness and vertigo? Or *were* they random? Was there some connection, if only he could find it? If there was, it all had to do with Brightstone, and the time before his fall. He had to know. And there was only one way to find out.

When they had moved to Sydney, he knew, everything had moved with them. Systematically he began searching through all the files and folders in the room which was now Joan's office, her records having long ago outgrown the battered old cupboard in the corner of his study where they used to be kept. Wearily he stretched his shoulders, and rubbed the ache at the back of his neck.

He had been searching for more than an hour now. But when you can't sleep, what else is there to do?

He opened another battered folder, dusty and worn with age. Disintegrating newspaper cuttings, brown and tattered round the edges, fluttered to the floor round his feet. He bent to pick them up. The headlines seemed to leap up at him off the page. TERROR IN MINING TOWN, he read. BRIGHTSTONE DISASTER – 170 DEAD. His own face, improbably young and unmarked, smiled up at him from another front page: MINE HERO IN COMA: CLOSE TO DEATH. He threw it aside, and reached for the next.

SCANDAL IN MINING TOWN, he read. His skin prickled. TRAGEDY STALKS FAMILY: TWO DEAD. The face smiling beneath was that of a girl he had never seen before. He stared at it, beginning to shake. For he recognised it. It was the face he had seen two days before in the Cathedral, the face of the girl, whose sudden appearance had made him black out. But she had died twenty years ago! She . . . *who*—?

The harsh central light burst over him like an explosion.

'What's all this?'

Closely wrapped up against the night in her thick dressing-gown, Joan stood before him, string-lipped, tense and watchful.

'The old files,' he said, waving a hand. 'From the Brightstone days. I couldn't sleep – the nights are getting so warm – I just thought I'd have a look at them.'

'Why?' Her voice was high and harsh.

'I don't know.'

'You don't know?'

'I don't know why I wanted to bring them all out again. I was just thinking—'

'Thinking?'

If only she would not repeat everything he said, pouncing on his words like a cat with a mouse.

'Yes.'

'About what?'

'About – this morning.'

'What about it?'

The tension between them was palpable now – they might have been playing a fencing match whose object was not to strike, but to kill. He tried again.

'Look, Joan, it's nothing to get worked up about, really. It's just that this morning – at the building site – I wanted to know what happened.'

Joan sighed a little, and seemed to relax.

'Robert, I was there – I saw what happened. Nothing happened!'

'What do you mean?'

'Look, you had a little dizzy turn, that's all. You got too close to the edge of the hole – it could happen to anyone. Probably your blood pressure.'

He stared at her in amazement. 'Joan, you know perfectly well that my blood pressure is about the only thing in this crock of a body that never suffered any damage from the accident!'

Her eyes flashed. 'OK then, remember those blackouts you used to have? The doctor said you might still get them from time to time.'

He shook his head. 'No,' he said firmly. 'It was like falling . . .'

'Mmmn?' She tried to conceal her eagerness to know.

'Into the dark – a great gaping void—'

She jumped in to interrupt him. 'That was your accident – the fall down the mine-shaft. The lift-cradle fell down when the cable broke. You know all this – you were told all about it afterwards. You lost your memory of it through the concussion, of course – but you're bound to remember it somewhere in your mind.'

'But in the lift – I was on my own when I fell, wasn't I?'

She narrowed her eyes. She would have denied it if she could. But he could so easily find out the truth from someone else. 'Well, the winchman was there – and Johnny Anderson . . . but you were the only one that fell, yes.'

'Well, yesterday – that feeling of falling – there was someone else there . . . a woman . . . screaming . . .'

'Robert!'

Her brittle laugh jangled his nerves as nothing else

could have done. 'You've got to stop this! You're just beating your brains for nothing. It's not good for you. Why torture yourself?'

'Because . . .'

He had no answer he was prepared to give. Suddenly he had had enough of the discussion, and of Joan. He shrugged. 'OK, Joan. I guess you're right.'

'I always am!' Bustling like a mother hen, she tidied around him, gathering up the cuttings and sweeping them carelessly into the folder. 'Leave all this to me,' she said busily. 'I'll sort it out – you should get your beauty sleep.'

'OK, OK.'

She came towards him for a sisterly kiss. As she did so he laid the cutting he had been holding out on the table. The face of Ally Calder smiled up at them both with the smile of the girl at the Cathedral rail. 'Joan,' he said. 'Who's this girl?'

Chapter 24

Look – look – there's a ship out there, way out on the horizon . . . Where's it gone?

If the earth is round as they say it is, why does it look like a straight line out there, where the edge is?

Once, I came up here on my own at dead of night, and I could see lights out there, hanging above the water, like fairy-lights on a Christmas tree – miles away, miles out to sea. And music – the most beautiful music – like magic – so beautiful . . .

The night was glorious, soft and spring-like, and already rich with the promise of a wonderful summer. The encounter with Joan had left Robert more restless than ever, and abandoning all thought of sleep for the night, he came to rest in his new and palatial study with its commanding views over Sydney harbour and the wide waters beyond. There, reclining at ease, half dreaming, half dozing, he gave himself up to what he what he knew was becoming a gathering obsession: thinking about the girl.

If thinking was the right word . . . because he seemed to be hearing her, too. Alone now and at peace, he surrendered himself to whatever came into his head, and let himself flow with it. But was he hearing these words, or dreaming them? Where were they coming from? For a moment a chill finger of fear touched his heart. Was he going mad, hearing things, imagining things? As coolly as he could, he considered the possibility, and rejected it. His pulse, when he tested it, was rock-calm, his mood peaceful, even dreamy, and that strange sense of bliss was on him again – no, whatever else he was, he was not mad.

Think about the girl, he urged his dreaming mind. Somehow, she is the key. Although the newspaper picture of her was now lying face-down on his desk, Robert did not need to have it before him to see her face. His back to the room, he rose to his feet in the window of his study gazing out over the night-time harbour palely glimmering under a perfect ripening spring moon. As a resident of one of Sydney's much-prized waterside locations, Robert knew he was privileged to possess a twenty-four-hour grandstand view of what was universally acknowledged to be the finest natural harbour in the world. But he felt now, for the first time, that for all its magic, it could never quite compare with the rough, wild nobility of the headland at Brightstone. Still, the sea soothed him, and the overwhelming sense of calm concentrated his thoughts. Think about the girl, yes. But which girl? The girl in the Cathedral or her ghostly double, the girl in the newspaper cutting?

And whose voice was he dreaming now? Was he really remembering these phrases, these fragments of conversation, or was he, as Joan said, hallucinating them? With unseeing eyes he stared out at the horizon where the night melted away in tones of blue, black and gold out over the sea. And why were they somehow, on some dim fringe of his mind, seemingly connected with the girl Ally Calder?

Joan had explained who she was, of course – a girl from the parish, who came to church once with her father for George Everard's funeral – he'd met her then, Joan said; he couldn't remember. She was the girl Paul was supposed to have gone to the headland about, on the night he was arrested – he was keen on her at the time – but as Robert had been too ill to know anything about the trial, he wouldn't have remembered any of that either.

And then she had killed herself. Joan said. No one knew why. At least they hadn't charged Paul with that death as well. But a young girl, Robert pondered sombrely . . . to die like that, in such despair that her life did not seem worth living – somebody should have saved her.

He should have saved her.

A subtle thrill ran through him, like an electric shock. Should he have saved her? Could he have? How could he even have known her, let alone helped her, if she had not been a parishioner, would not come to church? Because church had been the last thing on her mind, Joan said, in such a way as to make very clear what the first thing had been. She wasn't much good, Joan had said. Not much hope for that one there.

Yet even more reason why a girl who had strayed should have been able to turn to her priest for the help and guidance she needed. Had he failed her, then? He must have done! It was no excuse that he had not known her. That, especially in a town the size of Brightstone, was the first failure, the failure of knowledge, of attention, from which the other inevitably grew.

Just as with his parents. The need, the cry for help, had been there, all along, right under his nose. And he had missed it. Why had he been so blind?

God, no! When would he be free of this infernal guilt constantly plaguing him, constantly dragging him down? He groaned and turned sharply, knocking over the chair at the side of the desk as he did so. A moment later there came a swift knock at the door, and Claire came in. 'Oh Robert!' she murmured, confused. 'I'm so sorry, I didn't realise you were here, it's so late. I thought I heard a noise, that's all.'

It's the sound of a soul in torment, he wanted to say – help me, Claire! But how could he trouble Claire with his problems now? She was desperately anxious about Paul as the question of his parole approached again. And she was worried about her mother, too. Molly's bad circulation was now affecting not only her legs, but her heart, and the strain of waiting to know about Paul was taking a heavy toll. Above all then, Claire needed no extra worries about Robert's health, physical or mental. Stifling a sigh, he got up. 'I'm all right, Claire. No problem.'

'What happened?'

She was not placated, he knew. 'Just clumsiness. Knocked over a chair, that's all.'

She hovered by the door, unsatisfied, but not knowing how to penetrate his defences. 'There's something else you ought to know, Robert. Patsy Wright, the curate's wife, called earlier and left a message. They're closing down Allambie!'

'Allambie?'

'The old people's centre – you know!'

'But they can't! It's a protected building, it belongs to the Civic Trust.'

'I thought it belonged to the Church.'

He shook his head. 'The Church just has it on a permanent lease.'

Claire's face was pale with determination and the strength of her feeling. 'Well, it's definite now – it's been announced, it's going to be in all the papers, Patsy says. I thought you were looking into it – going to do something?'

'I was,' he murmured, overcome with guilt. 'I – I still am.'

'Well, you'd better do something fast! Because you've got to get round it somehow, Robert. Think of all those poor old people, kicked out of the only home they know, out on the street!'

His pulse quickened. 'Not if I can help it! I'll call the Archdeacon and the management committee first thing in the morning. And I'll organise a meeting – assemble a few of the interested parties and see what we can hammer out. It won't hurt to put the pressure on. I'm afraid we'll have to play politics a little if we're to save the house. We'll certainly have to try.'

He spoke firmly enough, for sure. But it did not seem to come from the heart, Claire thought with sadness. She turned to go, then hesitated at the door. 'Look, darling, it's very late. Will you be long?'

'Not long. Just got a bit of work to finish. You go on up to bed, I'll be up later. As soon as I can.' He turned away from the look she gave him, from the recognition of how often now he was saying this to her. 'I won't be long, Claire!' he insisted stubbornly. 'Go on up, I won't be long.'

She departed quietly, as she always did. He moved

again to the window, and stood for a long while over-looking the cold wastes of the unresponsive sea, wondering if he had told the truth, asking himself – how long will this be?

Even in the winter, Sydney's elegant city squares, protected by trees in the European fashion, are still warm enough to sit out in. Truly we live in the most congenial climate in the world, thought Robert thankfully as he threaded his way through the lunchtime groups around the fountain below the diocesan offices where he spent most afternoons of his working week. Why don't I try to put in at least one good afternoon's work, instead of chasing these ghosts and will-o'-the-wisps he asked himself? Newly invigorated, he hastened upstairs determined to throw himself into his work and continue without mercy until he had achieved everything he had set himself to do.

'Afternoon, Miss Pritchard.'

'Oh – g'day, Dean!'

'Miss McCarthy.'

'Dean!'

Oh, those eyes! thought Miss Pritchard dreamily, if only he wanted someone to take dictation more often! At the other desk, Miss McCarthy, a devout Christian and pillar of the Cathedral community, had just mentally murdered Mrs Maitland and was proceeding down the Cathedral aisle on her father's arm towards a newly widowed but happily not inconsolable Dean. Oblivious to any promptings of masculine vanity that might have been generated by the obvious adoration of the women behind him, Robert entered his office and prepared for work.

There was a huge pile in his in-tray, all carefully docketed in Miss Pritchard's meticulous script with instructions as to what kind of attention from him it would require. Slipping off his jacket, he hung it up behind the door and began to roll up his sleeves. Work! Great! Just what he needed to stop all this self-indulgence and get himself back to normality. He stretched like a wrestler, threw one last glance out of the window at the sunlit crowd below, and returned to the desk.

Below . . . below, there in the square! Galvanised, he leaped back to the window and looked out. A flash of flaxen hair, the top of a perfectly formed small round head . . .

The floor of his office seemed to be coming up to meet him. As he stood there, the scene at the Communion rail of the Cathedral passed again before his eyes – a fall of bright hair, seen from above lowered in prayer, a round, childlike head set above a young, womanly body . . .

She raised her head and looked up directly at his office window. She seemed to be looking straight at him, straight into him, and there was the same challenge, the same sense of purpose, of demand, in that hard, unflinching gaze. Yet it was a perfect oval spring flower of a face, with wide, dark blue eyes, golden skin, and an expression of cat-like concentration. Arched eyebrows and a slender nose, with perfect teeth in a full, moulded mouth which seemed older, more experienced than the rest of the honey-coloured body . . .

It was the face of the girl in the Cathedral. But beyond that, above and beyond, it was the face in the cutting . . . it was the face of the girl dead now over twenty years ago . . .

'Dean! Dean Maitland! Why, whatever is the matter?'

But as Miss Pritchard was later to tell the Archbishop when he appeared for an appointment with the Dean only to be greeted by an empty office and neither explanation nor apology, when the Dean ran out in his shirtsleeves, it was if he had suddenly gone completely deaf – and she would have added had she not been a sincerely Christian woman, perfectly, totally mad, too.

In the grip of a compulsion he could not have begun to explain, Robert tore down the stairs and hurled himself out into the square. The seat where she had been sitting was vacant. There was no one there. His mind refused to accept it. He stared blankly at the empty bench, as if he could somehow will her back into existence through the overwhelming power of his need. Then he glanced wildly around.

At the top of the square, where it joined the main thoroughfare, he caught another flash of the distinctive fair head. She turned right and was lost to view. But in a moment he had reached the corner and had her once again in his sights. A moment of caution made him slow his headlong pace to a walk – he could not simply run up to her, after all. Breathing heavily, he settled back in the crowd to follow her.

It was not easy. The sheer volume of people, the number of Sydneysiders happily taking advantage of the spring sunshine, gave his task all the dimensions of a nightmare: the endless chase, the hopelessness of pursuit when the quarry seemed so often lost, and the constant torment of the inner cry, 'Why am I doing this?' which dogged his every step. He felt it was madness – that he had gone mad.

Once she plunged into a subway running under the street, and he thought she was gone for good. Then she took the underground train and he lost her, saw her, lost her again. Doggedly he searched the length of the train as it ploughed on through Sydney's endless miles of suburbs. He caught up with her as she was disembarking at a remote station and as she emerged into the main street, lost her again.

This time she was not to be found. He scoured the long main street of the suburb, substantial enough to be almost a small town, peering into every shop, returning again to the station to make sure that he had not somehow missed her there. In the window of a smart gentleman's outfitters he caught sight of his reflection and saw for the first time what a figure he must cut, flushed and jacketless, his hair on end, and excitement and despair written over his face and body.

Collecting himself, he tried to decide what to do. In the absence of any idea, he turned into a café beside the station, hoping to sit down and collect his thoughts. It was a typical down-at-heel refreshment bar, plastic flowers on plastic tables and a television set permanently flickering away up on the wall above a few depressed-looking customers. As he entered, a young girl came in from the door at the back behind the coffee bar, tying

311

on her apron and preparing for work. The flaxen head was bowed in concentration, the two white wings of hair falling forwards across her face. It was the girl he had been chasing – the girl from the Cathedral.

'Get you anything?' Her smile seemed very knowing – almost self-congratulatory.

He was suddenly angry with himself, and with her. Why was he chasing this girl? And why was she looking at him like that?

'Yes? What would you like?'

He tried his voice. 'I don't know. I mean – what do you recommend?'

'The fish is always nice here. Bream fillets are the special today. Very good value, too.'

Her voice was English. How could that be? He decided not to ask. How old was she? Nineteen? Twenty?

'Bream fillets, then. Thank you.'

'Anything to drink?'

'Drink?'

'Yes, you know—' She tapped her pencil on her pad with a flash of impatience and recited, 'Beer, mineral water, milk, tea, coffee . . .'

'No, thank you.'

She raised her perfect eyebrows in a 'suit yourself!' expression and departed. The speed with which the bream made their appearance on his table suggested why they were being pushed as the special of the day. But it did not matter. He could not eat, or think of eating. He seized his moment as she turned to go.

'Excuse me – please don't think this is strange – but I know you, don't I?'

The cool blue eyes skewered him through to the backbone. 'Where from?'

'From the Cathedral. I'm the Dean there. I saw you at Holy Communion recently, didn't I?'

'Salad and chips?'

'I – I beg your pardon?'

'With your bream. I forgot to ask before. I haven't been doing this very long. I keep making mistakes. You want them? No extra charge for them. They come with bream.'

'Er – yes – I suppose so . . .'

But by the time the salad and chips made its appearance, he had gone. Only a dollar note of a large denomination tucked under the plate of untouched bream gave any indication that he had ever been there at all.

The meeting to save the Allambie hostel had got off to a bad start when Robert had hastily tried to assemble at short notice a group of influential people, many of whom had been unable to come. Then he had decided that to give everyone dinner would help to break the ice, create a good working atmosphere, but despite the best of Joan's exertions in the kitchen, the atmosphere all evening had remained stiff and cold. Now, he felt, they were making no headway at all. Looking round the table of unconvinced faces, Robert acknowledged to himself that he should have acted before – that he had probably missed the chance to save the hostel by being too slow, too involved in his own affairs, too obsessed, it had to be said, with the mystery of the elusive girl.

Or was it worth all the trouble anyway? Feeling deeply depressed, he allowed himself to wonder if it had ever been good idea, or if he had just been responding emotionally and not very intelligently to Claire's first appeal. Claire herself, who could have been such a valuable advocate for keeping the hostel, its principal champion and defender, was nowhere to be seen. She had not recovered from Robert's announcement that he had asked Mick Ford to join the lavish dinner at the Deanery where he hoped to sway enough influential people to overturn the decision to develop the site.

'*Mick Ford*? Why'd'you have to ask *him*?'

Robert was all too aware of the hatred Claire had never ceased to cherish for the man who had put her brother away with a life sentence. But Mick Ford could not be left out of this meeting.

'Because I needed him, Claire. Or rather, the Allambie residents do.'

'We needed him twenty years ago. Look what we got!'

He pushed on. 'If I can get Mick on our side, if the unions can be convinced that this is wrong so they'll refuse to touch a project that will cause so much unhappiness to the elderly, to the people least able to defend themselves, then the developers will never get the thing built.'

'It's a big "if"! Too big for a selfish pig like Ford, you'll see! He'll only be interested in something that helps himself. He doesn't give a damn for anyone else! Well, you'll see. Just don't expect me to be there, that's all!'

Now, as Mick Ford pushed back his plate, wiped his greasy lips on one of Claire's best napkins and accepted another glass of wine with an ingratiating smirk, Robert was beginning to have a horrible sinking feeling that she was right. 'That's it, then, is it, Dean?' queried Mick. 'Apart from a sumptuous meal from Miss Maitland here?' And he raised his glass to Joan across the table in a coarse, leering parody of courtesy.

'Well, I hope I've convinced you of our case, Mick. As Dean I naturally feel that the interests of the old people of Allambie would best be served by allowing them to remain together in what is, after all, a very old-established community—'

Mick cut in expansively. 'I'm just an ignorant working man, Dean. Give it to me in plain English. Here we all are' – he waved his glass again around the table – 'we've had good food, good wine, and the best of beaut company!' Another wave at Joan, augmented this time with a drunken wink. His hot little eyes swivelled suddenly from Joan to Robert and just as suddenly hardened like stones. 'So what's the price of the ticket?'

Robert threw a glance round his other guests, thinking fast. Mrs Maddox was on his side, he knew – so were the Archdeacon, the new curate Geoffrey Wright, and the chairman of the Civic Trust whose supposedly watertight permanent lease with the Church had been torn to shreds by the developers' sharp lawyers. He decided to go for a home run.

'OK, Mick, this is it. I want this development stopped. To do that, I need the support of the unions. What can you do?'

Mick pursed his lips and whistled. 'Not a lot.'

Robert persisted. 'I know that there was a union ban on a similar development not so long ago.'

Mick stared at the ceiling. 'Might have been.'

'So?'

'So what?'

'So can you do that again – for us? For Allambie?'

Mick returned to his perusal of the ceiling. 'That was then, Dean. This is now. You know, I got good feelings about that new development there, up at Allambie. I think it'll go through.'

He's already been bought off, Robert realised – bought and paid for. We got there too late – and empty-handed too. Didn't have a prayer.

'More coffee, anyone? More dessert, Mrs Maddox? Or a mint?'

Ever the perfect hostess, Joan was on hand to cover the embarrassing silence with a flurry of after-dinner attentions. As she withdrew to the kitchen to replenish the coffee-pot, Mick Ford ambled out to lend her a hand. 'Hello, Joanie,' he leered. 'All on your own? That's not nice.' And when the Maitlands, brother and sister, alone and comfortless in their separate isolation reviewed the humiliations of that night, it was to be doubted whether Robert's signal public defeat at Mick's hands had been any harder to endure than Joan's ordeal in the kitchen when the union boss, flowing in wine and self-satisfaction, had repeatedly tried to convey his life-long admiration of the parson's daughter and claim his just reward of a hot and greasy embrace.

Chapter 25

The atmosphere next morning at breakfast was as dull
as the day. After a run of fine spring mornings they had
woken to a canopy of thick grey clouds half eclipsing
the low, menacing bowl of the sky. But to Robert's
current cast of mind the greyness of the world outside
seemed to harmonise with his inner state and bring him
an obscure relief he would not expect to find under the
pitiless eye of the Australian sun on any normal day.

For the mood in the Deanery at large was far from
happy. Claire could not forgive him, Robert knew, for
neglecting the cause of Allambie until now, when it
looked as if it could well be too late. Worse, he could
not confide in her what he was going through – for what
was he going through? He could hardly say himself.
Even Joan, normally bright and brisk however early in
the morning, was nowhere to be seen. Murmuring a
goodbye, he left the house.

Driving into the city centre, he parked some distance
away from the old established professional quarter, and
began slowly to pace towards his destination. Twice he
passed the door on which he was due to knock and only
on the third occasion did he conquer his resistance,
knock and enter. A few minutes later the quiet-spoken
receptionist came forward to usher him into the inner
sanctum. 'Dean Maitland? Dr Beilby will see you now.'

'Robert!'

'Murray, how've you been? Good of you to see me
now, without an appointment like this!'

The vigorous handshakes between the two men testified to the warmth of their personal regard. But Murray
Beilby's response to Robert's question left no doubt as

to the professional nature of his concern. 'How've I been? Seems to me that that's the question I should be asking you. Here, have a seat. What's the problem? Thought we'd cleared up any worries about that blackout of yours with that last round of neurological tests. Any new difficulties?'

Robert sighed. 'Well, yes and no. I don't know. Oh God, Murray, I just don't know!'

'Mmm . . . ?' Murray paused, head cocked like the wise old bird that he was, eyes glinting in sympathy, knowing better than to interrupt as his patient rushed on.

'It's not physical. At least, I still get the occasional headache – sometimes worse than ever in fact – but it's not only physical. And it's a lot of new stuff – yet I'm sure, I'm completely convinced, that it's somehow all tied up with the old.' Robert paused, and a wry smile shaped his lips. 'You reckon we could look at all that again? After all this time? You're the head expert. D'you think there's any chance you could still crack it open, this defective nut of mine?'

'Crack it open?' Murray paused to consider the implications of the question. 'Do you mean recover your memory of the fall? Of all that happened to you then?'

'Partly, yes.'

'What's the other part, then, Robert?' Murray probed. 'And why do you want to get back into all this now, when you've lived with it for twenty years?'

Robert took his time over the answer. 'There are things – in my life—' he said slowly, 'I just don't understand. And I don't like—'

Murray smiled. 'That happens to a lot of blokes, Robert. It's called a mid-life crisis. It doesn't mean there's anything wrong with your head. It just means you have to look hard at your life, the way you're living it, your career. Everything OK' – he trod carefully – 'in that department?'

Robert shifted restlessly in his chair. 'Since you ask, Murray, that's another thing. I'm the blue-eyed boy in the Church all right, but I've never felt further away from what I really want to do! I didn't become a priest to spend my life sucking up to rich people! Even if it's all in a good cause!'

'And Claire?' Murray's voice was very low. 'Things at home?'

'Oh . . .'

God, Robert thought, that's the worst of all. We're growing apart, why try to deny it? And I don't know why . . . or where to start to put it right . . .

He met Murray's kind, questioning gaze and gave a crooked grin. 'Where shall we begin?'

'At the beginning!' Murray had established all he needed to know for now. 'And I'll tell you, Robert, if you want to do it, I think we can. As far as the recovery of your memory goes, there are things we didn't try before – newer drugs, newer therapies, all sorts of stuff that has been developed since. I've learned some new techniques, too – hypnotic regression, for instance. And you're stronger, of course, much stronger. We had to tread very carefully before when you were still in the worst throes of post-trauma.' He paused, and fixed Robert with his bright eyes before he went on. 'Tell me one thing, though.'

'What?'

'What makes you think you're going to find anything in there you didn't find before – that you don't already know?'

'That's just the point!' Robert's frustration, his fury with himself, were brimming up to danger point, Murray could see. And you don't have to be a qualified psychiatrist he told himself quietly, to know that this man on a short fuse is capable of a terrible explosion.

'How do I know? How can I?'

Robert was almost shouting now, his anger at what had happened to him surging up once again to the boil. 'All I'm left with is a scrapbook instead of a memory, and a head full of holes! Even the things that happen to me I don't understand!'

'Calm down, Robert.' Murray's voice was as soothing as honey. 'There's only one decision. Of course I'll help you. But you've got to help me! I've got to know where to begin.'

'I want to start with trying to get my memory back. I know if I could only just remember . . .'

'No, Robert.' Murray's tone had all the grave authority of his long experience and deep compassion for human suffering. 'No – wrong way round. We start with what has happened to you in the last few days that makes you want to remember this – this whatever it is – all over again. After all, you've been happy enough with the memory you had, the memory you'd managed to regain, for the last twenty years. And I must warn you of one thing. Ever since the days of Freud, we've known that when something is forgotten – so deeply repressed that the conscious mind will not admit its existence – then there's usually been a very good reason for the psyche to have done so. Are you sure – one hundred per cent sure – that you are ready for whatever we manage to dig up?'

'Mrs Maddox?' With practised skill, Joan concealed her irritation. She'd known this would happen, the moment she realised that Robert had gone out without saying where he was going. Normally she knew his every move, for every moment of the day, so that she could at least tell callers when he could be expected to phone them back. But today – and the phone had never stopped! 'I'm sorry, no, he's not available just now, can I take a message? Oh, it's urgent? Allambie? Well, I'm hoping he'll phone in before lunch . . . or after, anyway . . . and I'll get him to call you the minute he gets in touch . . .'

He had to know. Frowning with concentration Robert reached his car, unlocked it, and slid into the driver's seat where he remained for a while deep in thought. Whatever this was going to cost him, he now knew, either in time, money, effort or personal pain, he had to get to grips with it. If the first session with Murray had given him anything to go on, it was that. He couldn't simply sweep his life under the corner of the carpet any longer. He had to find out everything, as soon as he could. And that meant asking questions, Murray had said, asking all the questions he'd been sleeping on for so long. Asking everybody. Might as well begin at the beginning then. No time like the present. Flexing his shoulders, he set his course due west, switched on the engine, and began to drive.

'We weren't expecting you today, sir . . . we do like to have notice, you know, especially for the Category A prisoners . . . regulations . . .'

The prison officer was going through the motions, Robert saw, just to say he'd gone by the book. But he knew that they would be as helpful as they could. 'Yes indeed, officer,' he agreed, then concentrated on deploying all his best powers of persuasion. 'Rather unusual circumstances . . . found myself passing . . . wondered if it might be possible . . .'

'We can but ask, sir, we can but ask . . . would you take a seat . . . ?'

'Robert! Great to see you! What a surprise!'

Paul looked thinner, Robert noted even in the midst of his own preoccupation, and strained. But his ebullient spirits threatened to go over the top with excitement at this unscheduled addition to his meagre ration of one visit per month. Suddenly his face darkened. 'It's not Mum? She's not—?'

'No, no.'

'Claire then?' His anxiety was painful.

'No problem, she's fine, we all are. It's just that I found myself—' He could not say 'passing' to Paul as easily as he had said it to the prison officer, for Paul knew his pattern of life, his routine and his heavy commitments, and you knew, too, that few people 'just passed' a maximum security prison located for even greater safety in a remote position many miles from the nearest human habitation. 'I was – in the region,' he concluded lamely, 'and I – wanted to see you – man to man.'

'Yeah, I get you!' Paul's still-handsome face distorted again with concern. 'You're worried about this parole business – worried about Mum and Claire, I guess, how they'll take it – if the news is bad. Well, so am I, mate – so am I! They've slapped me down so many times before! I'll give it to you straight, I don't know what my chances are.'

His sympathy instantly stirred by a more pressing anxiety than his own. Robert let Paul take the lead. 'You reckon you'll get it this time?'

'Get it? I've only just been told they've allowed it to go forward to the review board! The governors stopped it at first, the bastards!' Furiously he kneaded one sinewy fist in the palm of the other. 'They've got it in for me here – or someone has!'

How could he argue with that? Disturbed by the open signs of rage and despair that Paul usually succeeded in concealing from him and Claire on visiting days, Robert trod with care. 'What are the chances?'

'The case against, you mean?' With a sardonic laugh Paul flung his fingers in the air in a gesture of explosive rage, and began counting off the reasons he was sure his parole appeal would fail. 'Attempting to escape, one. Trying again a year later, two.'

'That was over ten years ago!'

'And I've been a such a good boy since – they don't think!' Remorselessly the catalogue continued. 'Refusing to attend chapel on Sundays – sorry, Rob, I never told you about that. It's just that I thought I didn't have too much to thank Him upstairs for – and I thought I'd feel a right bloody hypocrite going along there every week just to get a few lousy privileges.'

'But surely they wouldn't hold that against you?'

'Wouldn't you – if you thought it betrayed a bad attitude, showed me up as a real wrong 'un? And last, but not least, don't forget the cream of the collection – "Inciting to violence".'

'You were trying to stop that fight!' protested Robert in anger.

Paul shrugged, his black eyes hard as adamant. 'I was there. The screw got killed. And it was me leading the strike that set it all off.'

'Years ago now – years!'

'The past never dies, Robert. It's got a way of coming back to haunt us.'

'But these are men of the world – experienced people!'

Paul grinned mirthlessly. 'Long memories, these boys. Like me. I don't forget.'

Forget . . . forget to remember . . . Robert leaned forward purposefully. 'Paul, I'd like to talk to you about that. That night, the night of the tragedy, do you remember—'

'Do I remember? Christ, Robert, what are you talking about? D'you think I can *forget?* Could ever forget?' The violence flashed out again, only just below the surface. 'And when I get out – however long it takes – my first job, and I've been promising myself this for years – my first job is to get hold of Mr Mick Ford and give him a few lessons in how to remember. I've had a lot of fun working out the precise ways I'll be teaching him what he should have remembered about that night!'

'Paul!'

Robert reached across the table and gripped him by the shoulders. 'Look, this revenge thing – that's not the answer. For God's sake, let it go! Concentrate on what really happened. We all need to know what really happened that night. How much of it do you really remember? After all, you got a knock of the head that night, too, just like I did.'

'Oh no, mate, not me!'

The words were coming fast and furious now as Paul fought back. 'You can't pin that one on me! I got done up by Jim Calder, and I hit the deck for a while, right enough. But there's only been one head-case in the family through all this, and that's you! You're the candidate for the giggle-house, brother-in-law, not me! Whatever I did, I knew what I was doing, right enough – and I know I didn't kill Jim Calder, bastard though he was!'

With difficulty Robert held on to his temper. 'Paul,' he said, as evenly as he could, 'tell me, then. If you remember that night – if you remember everything that happened to you – do you remember anything, anything at all – about what happened to me?'

* * *

Nothing.

He might have expected that.

But he had hoped, however dimly, that Paul might have known something, might have been able to give him some clue . . .

It was a long, exhausting drive back to Sydney, hour after hour of pounding the freeway with the sensation of grit in his eyes, gravel in his joints, a vague depression like mildew in his soul. He did not have to turn his thoughts to the girl to cheer himself up – his mind simply gravitated to her as if he were coming home, and he made no attempt to resist it. Approaching the city, he found himself deciding without conscious volition where he wanted to go. Turning off the freeway at the first exit for outer Sydney he threaded his way through the endless suburbs and found the café.

A young man was leaving it as he approached, turning with a smile to wave goodbye to someone inside as he came out through the door. Robert's interest quickened and he hastened forward. Was the boy waving to her? To the girl? He caught himself up. What if he was? She was entitled to have boyfriends, for heaven's sake! Was he – surely not – jealous? The boy sauntered away whistling, his youth and happiness expressed in every joint of his long, rangy body.

She was serving a customer right by the door as he entered. She did not look even faintly surprised to see him.

'Hello,' he said with a smile.

'Hello yourself. Table for one? Coming up!'

She found him a table and made a great play of dusting off, none to efficiently, the previous occupant's generous legacy of crumbs. 'Get you anything?'

'A beer, please.'

'Nothing to eat?'

Again that English voice. Where did it come from?

'Nothing – thanks,' he mumbled.

She looked at him straight-faced. 'Can't tempt you to another pair of nice bream fillets then?'

He laughed. 'Sorry to walk out on you before. Didn't mean to insult the cuisine. Just remembered – an urgent appointment.'

'Ah yes. An urgent appointment.' She was smiling at him now, the almond lilt at the corner of her eyes setting her whole face alight. It was odd how easy he felt with her all at once – as if he had known her before . . .

'Mmmn,' he smiled back. 'Sorry about that!'

'You left a whacking dollar note. I kept the change.'

'You were meant to.'

She laughed openly this time. 'No, silly. I mean I kept it for you – for when you came back. I've got it behind the counter. I'll get it now.' She went off in the direction of the bar.

A tiny frond of discomfort brushed him. How did she know he would be back? What made her so confident of his return?

She was back again, a sizeable collection of notes and coins clutched in her small hand. 'Here you are.'

He shook his head. 'I meant what I said before. It was for you to keep. I wanted you to have it.'

Her eyes were like globes. 'For a tip? But it's far too much! Anyway, you didn't have anything! So you didn't get any service.'

He grinned, looking suddenly years younger and happier, she thought. 'Well, how about if I have some now! Then you can keep the money, and we'll both feel OK. How's that?'

She considered for a moment, head on one side like a child. 'OK. What'll you have?'

'What've you got?' He was enjoying this game.

'Depends.' She grinned at him, delighted to play, too. 'On what?'

'On what you want.'

'Let me see . . .'

'I'll let you see a menu, then you'll get an even better idea!' She vanished again, returning this time with the café's one and only battered menu in her hand. He opened it and burst out laughing. 'Whatever's this?'

Offended, she poked her head nearer the menu to track down the source of his amusement. ' "Special snippets à la maison",' she read. 'Nothing funny about that. It's just toasted sandwich – with special interesting bits in it.'

'Not interesting bits of bream, by any chance? Left-over bits not required by customers?'

He could not remember the last time he had laughed and joked liked this. But there was something about her – something which called to him so deeply. He had to know more about her. When she was bringing his food, he made the obvious comment. 'You're English?'

'You can tell from the accent. Yeah.'

'Born in England? English family?'

She gave him a curious stare. 'Yeah, of course. Can't you tell? Why?'

'No reason,' he said lamely. 'It's just – I wondered if you'd ever had any connection with Australia before. You're a long way from home.'

'Oh, I don't know. Home is where your backpack is.'

'First visit to Australia then?'

'Sure. And the last stop on a round-the-world trail.'

'You're travelling around?'

'You could say so.'

'What do your parents think of that?'

She shrugged her small golden shoulders. 'With so many other kids at home, they don't miss me. Glad to get some off their hands to make a bit more room for the others.'

'You seem – very young – to be out in the world on your own.'

'You're as old as you feel – and I feel a hundred most times.'

'But haven't you thought of staying on at school – maybe going to college—?'

'Oh, where have you *been* all your life?' The violence of her reaction was shocking after the freedom of their shared humour immediately before. 'It's all right for you! – for people like you! But you've got to have money to stay on at school, let alone go to college, at least in England. And I can't imagine it's much different here – except maybe for families like yours – for the children of a Dean!'

Angrily she flung away and disappeared into the kitchen. Puzzled, he remained seated over the cold remains of his toasted sandwich, but she did not reappear. At last he approached the greasy proprietor who had emerged from the kitchen not long after the girl had gone out.

No, he was brusquely told, he could not see the waitress. She'd had to go off, an hour ago, with a sick headache. No, he couldn't take a message – what is this, a café or a post office? No, he couldn't have the phone number – the girl came here to work, not to take telephone calls.

The hostile stare and brutal tone of the rebuffs were beginning to make Robert feel uncomfortable. Slowly the penny dropped. He thinks I'm after her – he thinks I'm a dirty old man, he thought with slow amusement. But before he had even stepped out into the street, he had seen just how unfunny that really was. And as he made the long, dismal drive back to the Deanery through the endless, unforgiving suburbs, he realised with an even greater sense of irritation that he hadn't even asked the girl her name.

SUMMER

Chapter 26

By the time he got back to the house – somehow he still could not think of it as 'home' – it was so late that everything was in darkness. Slipping thankfully into bed he lay for a long time beside Claire's heavily inert form until sleep came, and woke late the next morning, feeling dull and unrefreshed. No one was in the breakfast-room, and the pot of coffee, stone cold, betrayed how long it was since the girls had breakfasted. Well, he wasn't really hungry. Time to begin the day.

He could hear the sound of the photocopier from Joan's room. As he opened the door she greeted him with a face of fierce accusation that indicated far louder than any words that she was furiously angry with him. Not that Joan was in any mood to dispense with or indeed mince any of the words of reproach she had obviously been storing up to heap on Robert's head.

'Where were you? Yesterday? All day yesterday!'

He was startled by her sudden attack, the complete lack of preamble. 'I just – felt like a day off, that's all.'

'But Robert – to take off like that – without a word! To disappear for the whole day – and all night too! Whatever were you playing at?'

He was not about to get into a fight with Joan, whatever else. 'Look, I'm sorry!' he said brusquely, and turned to go.

But Joan's fury would not be contained, 'You're sorry!' she exploded. 'You don't give a damn! Or you couldn't have dropped us in it the way you did!'

'Dropped you in what?'

She could not resist a cruel barb of sarcasm. 'Don't tell

me you've forgotten! Your memory giving you trouble again?'

He could feel his anger rising. 'Joan, why don't you just tell me what you mean?'

'Yesterday.' She was breathing heavily, like a wrestler. 'Yesterday, you had a meeting at eleven-thirty – the Estimates Committee, remember? And at three you were supposed to be seeing the Bishop for your regular Wednesday afternoon get-together—'

Had he forgotten? He could not think back to yesterday morning when he had decided to go to the prison.

'Robert? Oh, you're here.' Claire's face, drawn and troubled, came round the door. 'Has Joan told you how worried we were abut you yesterday?'

'I – got up early to go to early morning Communion in the Cathedral. Then it was such a lovely day – I thought I'd go for a drive. I went to the prison – to visit Paul.'

'Paul?'

He had to tell them. Claire would find out anyway, and he had to account for the length of his absence. Two pairs of eyes were locked on to his face.

'I was – concerned about him. His parole coming up – the possibility of failure . . .'

It sounded limp, and he knew it. But he also knew that they would both be reluctant to challenge him about it.

'But even so . . .' Claire's doubt was heart-rending. Why didn't he feel guilty – about abandoning them, about neglecting to let them know where he was, about lying to them now? 'Even so, Robert, shouldn't you have been back by evening?'

'Yes!' Joan was almost triumphant as she returned to the attack. She's enjoying this! he thought with a sudden sense of shock, then a dull, growing anger. 'Because it wasn't just me, you know, Robert, sitting waiting for you in the Estimates Committee meeting with egg all over my face. You dropped Claire in it as well!'

'Claire?'

'Oh Robert – had you forgotten we'd fixed another meeting last night? Here at home – about Allambie?

332

You'd arranged to see Mrs Maddox again – she's really keen on this, she hates to think all the old houses are coming down. And you'd got that reporter coming to give you some publicity? From the *Sydney Star?*'

He cursed himself furiously. All true. And it had all been as unreal to him as his – his – what should he call it? – his fantasy life, his obsession with the past, with the girl – or girls – had been real, true and compelling. How could he make it up to Claire and Joan now?

'God, I'm sorry,' he said explosively. 'I'll contact them all first thing, and apologise.'

'Well, you'd better put the Archbishop on your list as well!' cut in Joan with sadistic satisfaction.

'The Archbishop? Why?'

'It was him you ran out on the other afternoon – the day you were supposed to see him at the diocesan offices in town – the day you ran out into the street without your jacket, Miss Pritchard says, and never came back, not even to say where you'd been—'

'Joan, enough!' One glance at his face and she fell silent. 'I've said I'm sorry about this. You can rely on me to deal with the consequences. Now let's leave it, OK!'

It was over. But not quite. Even as he had his hand on the doorknob of the welcome refuge of his study, Joan was behind him. 'Just one thing, Robert,' she hissed into his ear, throwing a glance over her shoulder at the retreating figure of Claire.

His stomach knotted. 'Yes?'

'I know who was at early morning Communion at the Cathedral yesterday morning – and who wasn't! Patsy Wright, the curate's wife, was there, she goes most mornings. And it didn't take Sherlock Holmes to get out of her the fact that the Dean was nowhere in the place!'

He turned to look at her. He knew what he would see, the dry fury burning in her eyes.

'So don't lie to me, Robert. You can say what you like to Claire, she doesn't see through you. But I can read you like a book. And I don't like what I'm reading at the moment. You'd better sort things out – Dean. Or you won't be Dean much longer! And that is a fact!'

The late evening glimmered over the city like a pall as
Robert pulled up in the mean suburban street outside
the café. Only a sliver of a waning moon rode in the
troubled night sky, a few rags of clouds tossing fretfully
in the light, cutting wind. Summer had come coldly this
year, Robert thought. Even inside the relative protection of his car, he found himself shivering. But he would
not switch on the car engine to enable the heater to
provide a little warmth: he preferred to be cold. It kept
the brain alert – and he wanted to know – whatever the
cost – what had brought him here.

Was he just in the grip of an inexplicable obsession –
a fascination with a girl he did not know and another,
long dead, whom he had never known, hardly ever met?
Or was he, as he believed, simply obeying both Murray's
instructions and his own deepest instincts in going with
this thing, allowing it to lead him to whatever he needed
to know? Either way, all the threads he was trying to
unravel seemed to lead back to the girl. He knew, with
all the force of inner conviction, that she held the key
to some door, somewhere, that he had to unlock. Only
by being with her, questioning her, getting to know her,
would he find the answer.

Clear now in his mind, he went to get out of the car.
But as he did so, a movement from the door caught his
attention. Someone was coming out of the café. It was
the boy he had seen leaving the café once before, the
lanky youth with the cheerful smile. Behind him, and
obviously with him, was the girl.

He caught his breath and watched narrowly as the
young couple turned out of the café and made their way
past the underground station and on down the street.
They were deep in conversation and seemed on familiar
terms, laughing and fooling like young people anywhere.
When they had gone past, he started the engine of the
car and followed them.

They were almost alone in the deserted night-time
streets, with all the shops and offices closed and only
the odd late-nighter hurrying home to bed. Their route

took them on a long walk, which they seemed to have no inclination to hurry, all the length of the main road, along a side road and finally through twisting back streets until they fetched up outside what was obviously a cheap rooming-house. From the porch where they had come to rest their conversation reached him clearly through the still night air.

'How about asking us in for a coffee then?'

'Have a heart, Gary! I've been on my feet all day.'

'Y're not the only one that works for a living, y'know.'

'Well, in that case you need your beauty sleep too!' He laughed. 'I could spare an hour or two of it for you.'

'No chance. Time for all good boys to be tucked up in bed.'

'That's what I was thinking . . .'

He moved closer to her and tried to take her in his arms. But she was ready for him. With a swift side-step and a sharp but playful punch to his chest she was away, and up the low flight of stone steps to her front door, key in hand. 'I'll call you, Gary,' she called over her shoulder as she vanished inside. 'Don't call me – I'll call you!'

He smiled, waved, shrugged and slowly ambled off down the road. His mind racing, Robert sat in the car and waited for what seemed like an age until the boy turned the corner at the end of the road and eventually wandered out of view. So the girl lived here – and not with him. Who with, then,? Surely not all alone, at her age? But how old was she, anyway? That was another of the great unanswered questions. Eighteen? Twenty?

Well, no reason not to ask. He looked at his watch. It was only just gone nine – not too late. He left the car and approached the house. It was an old, four-storey tenement building like a New York brownstone, which like so many of those had seen better days and better tenants, too. He let himself through the low wrought-iron gate in front and mounted the steps.

The list of tenants' names beside the old run of bells by the front door was no help at all. Many of the bells had no name beside them; others were just as clearly years out of date. Segal, Jackson, Metakis, Irwin – which was she? He peered at the faded, fly-blown scrawls with mounting frustration.

And from the battered and useless-looking bell-pushes, too, there could be no guarantee that they would ring out in the rooms in question, even if he had been able to identify which bell was which. And was he really going to pay her a call like this, so late in the evening? Just passing? It sounded weaker every time he said it. He decided to call it a day, and return to the café during daylight hours.

Retracing his steps he regained the ground level, and turned towards his car. As he did so, he collided with an unnoticed dustbin standing against the fence right behind him, and sent it flying. The clatter was indescribable in the quiet of the suburban night. A muslin curtain flashed back up above, and her head appeared like a jack-in-the-box from a second-floor window.

'Who's there?'

He was too surprised to answer.

'Who's there!'

It was not a question now, but a challenge. The cry came again. 'If you don't show yourself – this minute – I'm calling the police!'

'Hey, hang on!' Laughing, he found his voice. 'No need for that!' He stepped forward into the light shining from the window so that she could see him.

'You! What on earth are you doing here?'

'I didn't mean to frighten you. I just—' Just what? What could he say?

She laughed. 'You'd better come in. You can't go all the way home without even a cup of coffee. Just push the front door and it's all the way up to the second floor – the big room at the front.'

Her bedsit was small, shabby and none too clean. But she moved about it with confidence, obviously well at home. 'Have a seat,' she said, directing him to the one easy chair. 'Make yourself at home. Coffee?' Picking up the kettle, she crossed to the sink, filled it, then put it on the electric ring.

Fascinated, he looked about him. On the walls were

bright posters of Australia: Perth, Alice Springs, the Great Barrier Reef. Three pairs of shoes, brightly coloured slip-ons, were tucked neatly side-by-side under the wardrobe. On the mantelpiece above the boarded-in fire were her few girlish treasures – a little box open to reveal a tangle of beads, some earrings and a couple of inexpensive bangles, a china cat and a postcard of a rural scene, somewhere in England, by the look of it.

'Your home town?' he asked when she brought him his coffee.

She threw it a dismissive glance. 'If you can call it a town. It was pretty dead. Sydney's better.' She turned back to him with a harder glint in her eye. 'Forget that. Why don't you tell me what you're doing here? That's what I asked you up to find out.'

He grinned at her. 'Well, that's the question!' He felt as if he were a million million miles away, and yet never more intensely present. 'I just wanted to know where you live.' He wanted to add 'and how', but was not ready for the questions that that might bring.

'So you followed me from the café.' It was not a question. 'Why?'

'Well, for one thing, I didn't think we'd finished our conversation at the café when you ran out on me last time!'

'Yeah, well.' She made no attempt to excuse or explain. 'I went, didn't I? I just came home.'

'Well, I wanted to see you again. To talk to you.'

'*Why?*'

This was it. He drew a deep breath. 'You remind me – of a girl I think I used to know.'

Her laugh was harsh. 'Don't you *know?*'

'No.'

'Who was she, then?'

'A girl who lived in the town where I first began. I didn't know her, though.'

'I thought you said you did. What was she called?'

'Alison. Alison Calder. They called her Ally. You're so like her, it's uncanny. You could be her sister. But she never had any relations, it seems. All I really know about her is her name.' A chord began to echo somewhere at the back of his mind. 'By the way, you haven't told me yours.'

An oblique flash of emotion passed across her face and was instantly gone. 'It's Emma.'

Emma. Another echo down the dark halls of time. 'Emma. That was my mother's name.'

She was not interested. 'This girl – the one I remind you of – what happened to her?'

'She died.'

'Died, huh?'

Again he caught the trace of a strange emotion, instantly subdued. What was it? Anger? Resentment? She gave him no time to consider. 'So you're hanging round me because I remind you of a dead girl you never knew you knew?'

How could he defend himself? 'It's just that you look so much like her . . .'

'Pretty stupid reason!'

'I can't help it.'

'Well, I can't help looking like her, either! It's not my fault!'

She was angry again. He wanted more than anything to calm her and make her happy. 'I know, I know. I can't expect you to, especially when I can't even understand it myself. But I'm working on it. And when I get there, I promise you, you'll be the first to know!'

'So you followed her in your car from the café?' Murray Beilby's voice was grave.

'Yes.'

'And she caught you snooping round the front of her house—'

'Not snooping, Murray, for God's sake!'

Murray privately thought that a jury of twelve good men and true might consider 'snooping' a pretty accurate description of the activity in which his patient had been detected, but he was not inclined to argue. 'No, no, of course. Then she asked you in . . . asked you up to her room . . . Did you get the impression that she . . . made a habit of asking men in to her room?'

He had put it as delicately as he could. But Robert

flushed with furious anger, and leaned forward as if to do violence with his bare hands. 'Certainly not! She's not a prostitute, if that's what you're thinking! My God, Murray, she's only a child! She can't be more than eighteen or twenty!'

Take a walk down the dockside, Robert, Murray thought. You can have your pick of prostitutes there at any age from nine to ninety. What are we going to do with you? A nagging concern, the kind of anxiety he was not used to feeling about his patients, closed in on him as Robert plunged on.

'Oh, I know I'm talking rubbish, Murray! Of course she could be a girl like that. I just know she's not, that's all. And I know something else, something that bothers me far more. I'm in a mess, Murray, and I know it. Last night – listen, I'm not so far gone that I can't see how it would look – for me of all men! – to be caught in a situation like that! Hanging round a young girl – going to see her alone in her room . . . And even though I know it's all above board, I have to think of Claire and Joan. I'm not a free agent. Any disgrace of mine would be a terrible shame for them.'

Murray nodded. 'And for you, too, Robert, don't forget that! It wouldn't do you much good around the Cathedral, that's for sure.' He paused. 'Have you thought – have you ever considered what you would do if you could no longer work as a priest, for instance?'

In the silence that followed, both men sensed, far away, the distant surge of events passing beyond their control.

'No!' Robert's cry was harsh and uncompromising. 'But I've got to see this girl again!'

'Got to?'

'Yes! And I've got to get back into the blank in my memory, find out why she reminds me of a girl I never knew. *Can you help me?* I'm begging, Murray.'

Murray's medical and professional training made it impossible for him to refuse the cry of a soul in pain. But with a more primitive part of himself he became aware of a dark sense of dread, a fear of untoward events which he could feel were coming, but which he was powerless to avert. Like a sacrificial victim he bowed his head to fate. 'We could try hypnosis, Robert – it's a technique called regression. It could take you back to that night – to that time . . . track down – whatever it is . . .'

'Let's do it! *When can we start?*'

Chapter 27

A light, warm breeze heady with the scent of summer was blowing off the harbour, rifling the papers on the desk through the open window of the study. But the news Robert was hearing obliterated all considerations of the beauty of the day. He gripped the telephone receiver in fury as he spoke. '*Today?* I don't believe it! There must be some mistake.'

'No mistake, believe you me! They got a legal thing, a "quick process of execution", it's called. Means they can expedite any decision that's already received legal assent. They stole a march on us, Dean.'

Bessie Maddox's was the voice of a child who had been set on in the playground by the school bully. She had really cared about Allambie. She had done her best to save the old hostel. And now . . .

Silently but fiercely Robert cursed his recent self-absorption in his own affairs. God, he should have taken care of this! Instead of . . . instead of . . .

'But they can't be bringing in the demolition crew today. Not as fast as that! They just can't!'

His protest sounded feeble even to his own ears. Bessie Maddox's tone crisped up. 'They can and they will! They'll be starting any minute now.'

'But what about the residents? The old people?'

'Evicted.'

'On to the street?'

'Well, I don't suppose the Church has had time to arrange any alternative accommodation for them, have you?'

Through the window he could see the tiny curling wavelets dancing away out of sight across the surface of the water. Such a beautiful world . . . a world to be happy in, not to let this sort of thing take place . . . Again the hammer-blows of conscience smote him, keeping perfect time with the hammering inside his head. 'Well, I asked my curate, Geoffrey Wright, to look into it, take the initiative. Allambie's in his parish . . .'

Her silence made very plain what Mrs Maddox thought of the Church's initiative in all this. But she was not a woman to rely on subtle silences. 'You said you'd do something, Dean. People took you at your word.'

He could not speak. Those old people . . . so aged, so defenceless . . .

'I know.'

'So what you going to do?'

'Contact Mick Ford. Oh I know he's already been bought off by the developers. But we've still got a lot of clout in terms of what the Church is building in Sydney. And he promised to get back to me. If I can pick up with him where we left off, do some kind of deal with him, we could still get the unions on our side and stop the whole thing in its tracks . . .'

'Mick Ford? When I saw the report this morning on breakfast TV – the only notification we've had in the whole thing about what's really happening – Mick Ford was there, right there, bang in the front, leading the delegation for the topping-in!'

'Topping-in?'

'First move into the site. First strike. For heaven's sake, Dean, he let you down! He doesn't give a damn about Allambie! All he's concerned about is himself!'

Mick Ford. Yes. He fought down his anger. 'Look, Mrs Maddox, it may not be too late. I've let this slip, it's clear, and I'm desperately sorry. But I'll get right over there now. We may still be able to do something – even at this late hour.'

In the country of the mad, where everything is upside down, early is late enough. Even though it was only eight o'clock when Robert arrived at the Allambie hostel, the heavy machinery was all drawn up on the pavements as if for battle, simply awaiting the signal for the carnage and destruction to begin. On the pavement outside the poor old house stood an even poorer huddle of Allambie's distraught residents. Prominent among them, as Robert immediately saw, was Arthur, the vocalist of the group at the recent entertainment, looking bewildered and clutching a pathetic bundle of his meagre possessions. Who's sorry now, Arthur? he wondered, the pain in his head and heart keeping perfect harmony. Who's sorry now?

Next to Arthur sat an old man in a wheelchair, his head turning wildly from side to side, his fingers plucking compulsively at the threadbare tartan blanket across his knees. Moving sturdily among their distracted charges, the care assistants were doing their professional best to soothe and console their grown-up complement of terrified children. Across the pavement, drawn up in a solid phalanx of expensive suits, well-shaven jowls and clipboards, were the representatives of the developers. Power against weakness, thought Robert, strength against vulnerability, and the might of terror against all. It was like a scene from the holocaust.

'Dean Maitland!'

It was the reporter from the *Sydney Star*, young, keen and even more eager for having missed the evening meeting with the Dean which he had been promised before this story broke. "Morning sir! Do you have any comment on these proceedings?'

'Any comment?'

Robert looked at the poised pencil quivering over the notebook and felt sick to his soul. 'The real question is, do I have a comment that would be legal, decent, honest and printable. This is a terrible occasion for everyone here – and most of all for the developers!'

'Can I quote you on that, Dean?'

'Quote away. Plenty more where that came from!'

'The Civic Trust seem to have caved in, sir. They say that in view of what they've now been offered for the site, the cost of keeping Allambie going as an old people's home simply couldn't be considered viable . . .'

'Cost! Cost! What's the cost of a human life?'

The reporter wavered a moment, but stuck to his guns.

'The cost, Dean. How can you justify it when to so many people today, especially to the young people, the Church and its services are simply irrelevant?'

The next moment an iron grip descended on the reporter's shoulder and he was forcibly wheeled round ninety degrees. 'You see that old man clutching all his worldly belongings, the accumulation of a whole lifetime, in one rotten little bag?' the Dean's furious voice raged in his ear. 'You see that poor old soul in the wheelchair, just ripped out of the only place his confused mind knows as home? Now do you think that Allambie, and what the Church has done for all these people, is "irrelevant"? If you think so, why not tell them? I'm sure they'd be very interested to learn!'

The *Sydney Star*'s finest was not their chief cub reporter for nothing. 'But with so many homeless around today, sir,' he persisted, surreptitiously, freeing his bruised shoulder from the vice of the Dean's grip, 'wouldn't that money also have been needed for the young? The teenage mothers? Single parents? Drug addicts in rehabilitation?'

Robert groaned, unnerving the boy more than anything else he managed to say or do. 'It's a world of evil now!' he said passionately. 'We live in terrible times! But you've got a rocky coast – treacherous waters. What do you do?'

Silence.

Robert roared again, leaning forward. '*What do you do?*'

'I don't know, sir!' gabbled the cub, terrified by the intensity in his eyes. 'What do you do?'

'You build a lighthouse, boy. *That's what you do.*'

The atmosphere was hotting up now, with the arrival of camera crews and outside broadcast vans from Sydney's various television networks. A small, very decorous and as yet well-behaved demonstration had begun to foregather under the direction of a vigorous young female student who looked so much like Mrs Maddox that it had to be her daughter. Good on you, Bessie, thought Robert with a surge of interest. Like mother, like daughter! Glad to see someone's ready to carry war into the enemy camp!

He started to cross the road to give the demonstrators a word of greeting and welcome. As he did so a car screeched to a halt at the kerbside, and Joan came hurrying towards him with a face like thunder. She gripped his arm, forcing him back on to the pavement. 'Robert, what are you doing here? What the hell do you think you are doing?'

Her anger awoke his own in swift response. 'Joan, they're closing the hostel down, about to demolish it, right now! And I only found out this morning!'

Joan did not tell him that at least part of her fury had been produced by the discovery that he had simply left the house on receiving the call, without consulting or even informing her. Only a follow-up call from Bessie Maddox had given her a clue to where Robert was. 'I'm afraid that you missed your chance to save the day a lot earlier than this morning!' she snapped, her eyes as hard as stones. 'You should have thought of Allambie when you kept going walkabout all the time, pushing off on your magical mystery tours without telling anybody where you were going! Bit late now for heroics!'

'It's not "heroics", Joan.' He determined not to rise to her taunts like a fish to the bait. 'I owe it to these people to—'

'To what?'

'To make our protest heard – and if possible, felt. If I can organise these demonstrators into a human chain against the demolition machines—'

'Robert, will you *think?* Will you just use your head for a minute?'

He stared. 'What do you mean?'

'This new development – who d'you think is funding it?'

He frowned, and tried to recall. 'The Plaza Corporation, aren't they?'

'And who's the CEO of the Plaza?'

He shook his head.

'Remember Phillips? The big man you were trying to interest in the St Matthew's project? Who's on the verge of giving us millions of dollars?'

'Yes . . . what about him?'

Joan could have howled with frustration. 'He runs the Plaza Corp, that's what about him! And if you get up his nose about this development, you can kiss goodbye to St Matthew's, that's what!'

A chasm seemed to open in his soul. 'So I have to be nice to Phillips no matter what he does, eh?'

The sarcasm floated straight over Joan's head. Dear God, Robert was so stupid sometimes. 'Yeah!' she flashed back with her own turn of sarcasm. 'It would help!'

He felt a dangerous impulse to raise the stakes. 'Shall I beatify him now, or would that look out of place?' She glared at him, her mind going into overdrive as she wrestled with his meaning. 'And when does he get to kiss my ring? Or is that what I'm supposed to do to him – in gratitude to him for destroying Allambie?'

In true Joan style she cut straight through finer considerations above her head, and went for the jugular. 'Look at me, Robert,' she ordered.

He held on to his temper. 'I'm looking.'

'*Y'want to be Bishop, don't you?*'

He thought about it for all of half a second. 'Not half as much as you want it for me – or for yourself?'

She laughed savagely. 'You're talking rubbish! I know what you want – what you've always wanted.'

He felt very calm, and very sad. 'I think that's been part of the problem, Joan. And I think a man must know what he wants – for himself.'

She brushed him aside. 'Believe me, I know you. I know you'll be happier as a Bishop – or even—'

'As Pope? Why not? First Anglican bishop to be made head of the Roman Catholic Church. Maitland for Supreme Pontiff! What a great idea!'

He had gone too far. If there were two subjects on which Joan, never famous for her sense of humour at the best of times, could permit no jest, they were her religion and her brother. No matter who was making the joke – this was beyond the pale. 'Very funny!' she hissed, pale with fury, and turned on her heels and left him.

He did not remain unaccompanied for long.

'Dean Maitland?'

It was the leader of the demonstrators, a young woman with an open, strong face and a look of determination written all over her. 'It would help us a lot, sir, if you'd come over to be seen with us, give us a bit of moral support – a man like you!' she said boldly.

Joan never forgave herself afterwards for not having been there to head off the little pinko rabble-rouser before she got anywhere near Robert. Because when the demonstrators were finally lifted bodily from their positions lying down on the pavement in front of the demolition gang, and carried to the police vans in full view of the press and television cameras to be arrested for disturbing the peace, most prominent among them, and plastered all over the chief media of Australia, was the Dean of the Cathedral, the Very Reverend Robert Maitland himself.

What was the matter with him?

If only she could find out!

If only she knew – if only he knew himself!

Her thoughts twisting and turning like rats in a trap, Joan did her best to observe the agreement she had made with Claire not to keep going over the same old ground as they went through the motions of preparing the evening meal together in the kitchen of the Deanery. By common consent they had not spoken since they had returned from the court, where they had stood surety for Robert to bail him out. But it was more than Joan, twitching and jumping like a fly-bitten mare, could endure to remain silent.

'Why, I'll never know!' she muttered viciously, as much to herself as to her companion. 'Why he had to do it – to risk everything, all the work we've been putting in for years – and for what?'

'Joan! Joan, please!'

Claire's plea changed halfway through to a rebuke.

But Joan was not to be silenced. 'For a rotten demonstration! To get himself into this mess!'

'Joan.' Claire's tone was tougher than Joan had ever heard it. 'It's bad enough as it is. Why don't you just leave it?'

'And now to be called up before the Archbishop to answer for himself – that shows how serious it is!' Joan worried on relentlessly. 'Dear God, the shame of it! I can't believe it! I can't—'

'Joan!'

Where does Robert get the love he has for her, after all this? wondered Claire in amazement. He has the patience of a saint! Determinedly she returned to the attack. 'Joan, let's remember what Robert said. He hasn't broken the law, he's been told the charges will most likely be dismissed. He hasn't hurt anyone. And in my eyes at least, he hasn't disgraced himself or his calling.' She tried to smile. 'And who's the Archbishop and his wretched little committee anyway? He's only a man, just like Robert, after all!'

But however well-meant, if Claire's remarks had been designed to soothe and console Joan, they were having precisely the opposite effect. Joan was on the verge of hysteria, Claire could see. She was almost spitting with fury and frustration.

'He's not just a man! He's the head of the Church!'

Claire laid down her knife with final emphasis. 'Well, at least Robert will be dealing with the man at the top then, won't he? And we'll just have to trust to God and his own good judgement that he'll be able to get himself out of it!'

'Dean Maitland, sir? The Archbishop is ready for you now. This way, please.'

From his seat in the ante-room of the Archbishop's palace, Robert rose to follow the usher. Church intelligence was still a pretty powerful thing, he reflected wrily, even if the great wars of religion were a thing of the past. From the speed with which he had received the summons to appear before the Church's highest disciplinary committee, the Archbishop must have spies on every street corner, just as in the bad old days.

What was he going to say to them? How would he account for himself? As he pondered, the pain in his head, growing more frequent these days, he noticed, stirred lazily in his right temple and uncoiled itself for action. I really must get Murray to give me something for this head, Robert told himself. I know I told him no drugs before we tried the hypnosis – must have my mind clear – but for something like this I need to be on the ball, not operating with only half of my brain!

'Robert – do come in!'

The Archbishop came forward to greet him with the *bonhomie* for which he was famous. 'Thank you for coming. How are you? Are you well?'

'Fine, thank you.'

'Good, good – that's what we like to hear.' He gestured to the three men seated in a semi-circle in the great room's big bay window. 'Shall we join the others? I just thought they might be helpful to our . . . deliberations. Now, you know the Prebendary, don't you? And Canon Wishart? And I hardly need to introduce you to your own Bishop!'

A little general ecclesiastical laughter greeted this sally. But the atmosphere was not, Robert noted sharply, either warm or relaxed, however hard the Archbishop tried. 'Take a seat, take a seat!' he said with what seemed like a forced joviality. 'This isn't an inquisition!'

'Gentlemen'. Robert bowed his acknowledgements.

'Well, let's see.' The Archbishop kicked off by right of his rank. 'The problem seems to be that you've been . . . dabbling in politics?'

'You could call it that.'

The Bishop leaned forward. 'Robert,' he said earnestly, 'do you think it's wise?'

'Something had to be done. I promised—'

'But getting yourself arrested?' This was clearly more than the dapper, fussy-looking Canon could tolerate. 'On *television*?'

'You saw it?'

'Thousands – probably millions – saw it!' sniffed the little man.

Robert stared him in the eye. 'It made its point, then. Made an impact.'

'Look, Robert.' The Archbishop wanted to get back to basics. 'A man of your standing – a public figure – our official spokesman – how do you think that all this is going to reflect on the Church?'

Frightened men, thought Robert, frightened men. 'You tell me. You're obviously more worried about it than I am.'

'Young man.'

This was the first intervention the Prebendary had seen fit to make, and he was determined to make it good. 'Young man, this is hardly the attitude we have the right to expect. You don't seem to realise that you're speaking to the head of the Church!'

'The head of the Church.' Robert paused. He had never felt more in control. 'Forgive me. I seem to have got something seriously wrong here. As far as I'm concerned, there's only one head of the Church, Prebendary – and I'll answer to Him soon enough – in my own time – and in my own way.'

He could tell at a glance that he had made an enemy of the Prebendary for life. Obviously no one had ever spoken to the corpulent, self-satisfied dignitary like this before, and it was an outrage that he would neither overlook nor forgive. But Robert felt unconcerned, above all such petty considerations. It could not have mattered less that to him that the self-important cleric was hissing like a cobra about to strike. 'Mr Maitland – I repeat – consider your attitude! This behaviour is hardly likely to endear you either to your congregation, or to your superiors. And from one of such promise – one from whom the highest has been expected – and from whom, in the course of time, not even the highest would be withheld . . .'

Why can't they speak plain English, thought Robert. Why doesn't he say, we had you in mind for Bishop when John here goes, only you've got to be a good boy and play ball?

'Look, Robert,' the Archbishop intervened heartily, 'we're not here to threaten or punish you. I'd just ask you to look at some of the implications of making this kind of gesture, and getting people's backs up like this. These are difficult times for the Church. We very much need friends in high places – not to mention their contributions to our coffers!' He laughed heartily, an ingratiating man-to-man chuckle. 'And Phillips, you know Phillips through the interest he's taken in the St Matthew's project – well, you know he's the head of the Plaza Corporation and not a man to cross in Sydney – I think you get my point, Robert, eh?'

'Oh yes. I get the point. I just don't happen to agree with it, that's all. What are we talking about – people, or profits? What's it worth, an old man's peace of mind in the hostel he's lived in all his life? And how does it rate against the chance to make a fast buck? Jesus Christ—' he paused, and transfixed the Prebendary with a look '—Jesus himself, the head of the Church, never cared about the opinions of the land-owners, the rich men, the Pharisees. He drove the money-lenders out of the temple without a backward glance over His shoulder to see who He ought to keep in with. There's a lesson in there somewhere.'

He pushed back his chair, and rose to his feet.

'I'm sorry, gentlemen,' he said distinctly. 'I did what I thought was right. If it's not good enough for you, I have to say I think that's your loss, not mine. I did my best, but I'm only human. Not fit for "the highest", it seems. Better find someone else.'

He turned and walked out, leaving a silence no one felt inclined to fill. It fell to the waspish Canon to write the obituary. ' "How are the mighty fallen",' he quoted, with scarcely suppressed satisfaction. 'Or should we say, "How to ruin a career in one easy move"?'

Chapter 28

'G'night, Emma.'

'G'night, Mr Gazouli.'

He wasn't a bad old stick, as bosses go, old Gazouli, the girl thought. Shouldering her laden bag, she slammed the café door behind her, and set off on the long walk home. It'd been good of him to give her a job with no qualifications, no cards, and not much idea of waitressing, even though she'd said she'd done it before at home. He'd seen through that straight away, surprise surprise. Still, he hadn't minded. And at her age, how much did they expect her to know anyway?

And there were advantages to working in a café. If she wasn't, if she'd been in a shop or something, she'd never have seen that fantastic thing on the lunchtime news. Working there all day, the television always drivelling away in the background, you couldn't be constantly looking at it, or you'd never get anything done. Most of it was boring, anyway. But that thing today . . .

Her eyes sparkled with excitement at the memory and unconsciously she quickened her step. Who'd have thought he had it in him? She could never tell anyone – anyone – the shock she'd had when hearing all that confused racket of shouting and protest, she'd lifted her eyes to the television set on the wall and seen him – him of all people! – leading the demonstration to save that old hostel. In front of all those people too! Television crews and police and people from the company that owned the place and all the rest of the God Squad from the Cathedral. And there he'd been, out in front of all of them, rallying the demo through a loud-hailer. Fragments of his speech floated back to her memory.

353

'Is this the price of progress? Is this the cost? The cost to those with no money, no power, without even youth on their side any more – are they the ones who have to pay?'

Yeah! Great stuff! She gave a little skip of excitement, and punched the air with her fist. Tell 'em, Dean! And what was it he said after that?

'Stand up and be counted, all of you! Don't let this happen to those who are too old to fight any longer – too weary to fight for themselves. They need our help!'

That was about as far as he'd got before the coppers jumped on him. Not too hard, of course, and not so's you'd notice, because after all, he was a Dean. The soft girlish mouth hardened imperceptibly. Pity, that. A bit of rough treatment's the one thing he's never had in all his life. And wouldn't that give him a much-needed idea of how the other half have to live! Still, Dean or no Dean, they'd carted him off in the paddy-waggon with all the rest of the common riff-raff just the same. Wonder how he felt about being inside a prison – even if they were only booking him for breach of the peace!

And it's not over yet. Not by a long chalk. What she'd seen today didn't change anything for her – it certainly didn't change her plan, not in the slightest. But having a bit more respect for him – that would certainly make it more interesting.

The whole of the young face had hardened now, and a strange gleam of purpose shone in the slate-blue eyes. No, it's not over. In fact, you could say it's only just begun.

Home, and safety – from unwanted questions, from prying eyes. Gaining the privacy of her room, she unpacked her bag. Carefully she laid out upon the table copies of the *Sydney Star* and as many other daily and evening papers as she had managed to secure from the news-stand at the underground station.

From every one of them, under an assortment of banner headlines, the face that looked up to her was that of Dean Maitland. She stared at it for a long time with an almost vengeful satisfaction. Then she reached for a pair of scissors and began cutting out.

354

Some time later, among the remains of the cannibalised newspapers, lay a sizeable pile of Maitland cuttings. All were carefully inserted into a battered folder to take their place alongside a small collection of old snapshots, and an even smaller number of certificates issued for birth and death (one birth, one death). What filled the folder was not this pathetic clutch of documents but a bundle of much-handled newspaper clippings, yellowed and dog-eared souvenirs which were nevertheless still clearly the most treasured possession of any young girl in Sydney, if not on the whole island.

All those bloody old newspaper cuttings! Who cared about the old days in Brightstone anyway, let alone the mine disaster and the death of those good-for-nothing Calders, especially after all this time? They'd have to go! Should have gone ages ago! Clutching a black plastic bin-bag in her hand, Joan surged into her office and heading straight for the filing cabinets, located the files she sought. Bloody rubbish. Bloody rubbish! Time it went! Overdue!

Joan Maitland had never sworn in her life. More and more these days though, foul words came bubbling up to her mouth along with the foul thoughts of her mind, and she seemed powerless to stop them. She'd prayed, of course, as she did every day of her life. But that, too, her daily communion with God, seemed out of kilter now, out of true. What was going on?

That something was going on – something evil, something very dangerous – Joan was in no doubt. She'd find out what it was, she had no doubt of that either. And when she did, the least doubt in her mind was that she would know what to do, and when and how to do it. Brightstone – and now Sydney! – had not regarded Miss Maitland as 'capable' all her life for nothing. Oh yes. Miss Maitland was capable of anything, and that was another thing that Joan was perfectly sure of.

Yet how to act, decisively and successfully, when she could not be sure of what the trouble was, or where it was coming from, was the conundrum that now plagued her days and tormented her nights. A big part of it was Robert's health, she knew that. It could only be a recurrence of his old trouble, the damage caused by the injury to his head in that terrible fall – it could only be that that was making him behave so erratically, go off on his own for hours without saying where he'd been, and get involved in stupid things like the demonstration about the Allambie.

Well, she could do something about that. So far he had brushed aside all her questions, refused all her entreaties to go back to the hospital, to the surgeon who had operated on him immediately after the accident, who must still have all the old X-rays and tests. But after that dreadful scene at the demonstration, when he'd got so carried away he'd even managed to get himself arrested, then he just couldn't go on pretending that he was absolutely fine. He would have to see a doctor now.

So that was number one – that would sort itself out, she was sure. And the dizzy turn he'd had outside the Archbishop's reception room – even though he said it was only a bad headache, the usher had seen him leaning against the wall and had been concerned enough to report it to everyone – well, as it turned out, that wasn't such a terrible thing either. At least it would have cancelled out – to some extent anyway – Robert's insane folly in more or less inviting the highest echelons of the church to forget any thought of promoting him – he wasn't interested!

Joan had thought she would have an apoplectic fit when she first heard what had transpired in the Archbishop's inner sanctum. But she had controlled her fury, then got on the phone straight away to the Archbishop. Half her work had been done for her already, she found, by the knowledge that he hadn't been well when he faced the disciplinary committee. Of course the Dean wasn't himself – no, naturally, nobody placed the slightest weight upon what he had said in the meeting, and of course also, if he had been feeling ill, under the pressure from the launch of the new Cathedral and all the worry of overseeing the St Matthew's development too, then clearly that excused the lapse of judgement in getting drawn into the demonstration outside the Allam-bie, especially as the Bishop understood now that there was no intention on the part of the police to press any charges . . .

She permitted herself a thin smile. Looked as if Robert Maitland might once again have fallen into the proverbial, and come up smelling of roses. Just as long as she could get a grip now, make sure there were no more demonstrations or unfortunate incidents or rapid exits sans jacket from church premises . . .

She frowned. That was the missing link. The thing, whatever it was, that had triggered all this off. It was something to do with the mine tragedy back in Bright-stone – somehow connected with his loss of memory, or his worries about that . . .

Well, that was one place to start. Those sleeping dogs were going to be left to lie, if Joan had anything to do with it. She moved to the filing cabinet and attacked the lowest drawer with venomous determination. Inside lay all the folders of cuttings from the Brightstone days, all the historical material assembled for the Centenary carefully labelled in neat, schoolgirl writing. The Cen-tenary! God, that could have been a hundred years ago, not twenty! Joan thought furiously. Frowning, she dug deeper. Below it was all the information about the mine disaster, the murder and the trial, this collection – post-Ally Calder, she of the schoolgirl script, Joan noticed with a smile of savage satisfaction – spikily annotated in Claire's unhappy hand. Without a backward glance she shovelled the lot into the black plastic bin-bag and tied off the label. Good riddance to bad rubbish, she thought. Blessed be the warriors of the cause of the righteous, the soldiers of the Lord.

Outside in the square the sun was blistering the pave-ments, frazzling the leaves on the trees, roasting the passers-by. Inside all was cool, ordered and as it ought to be. Alone in the Cathedral in the rare moment of peace and complete stillness between early Communion and morning service, Robert wandered at will, his soul at peace.

How mistaken even the best-intentioned of outsiders could be! he reflected. They all seemed to think that he had spurned the Church dignitaries and destroyed his chances of promotion during that ill-starred meeting a few days ago now, in a random moment of illness, or temporary insanity, or both. If only that were true. He smiled ironically. The truth was – and how marvellous to admit the truth, if only to himself for the time being – the truth was that he had no desire to be a bishop, and no certainty any longer that he even wished to continue as Dean.

His lips twitched with amusement, instantly suppressed, as he thought of how this would appear to Joan, how she would take the news of his dereliction, as she would surely see it. How would he even begin to explain it to her? I just don't feel like deaning it any longer, sister dear. So I'll just do us both out of a job, and the whole family out of a home, through sheer perversity. Yes, do continue to call me Father, my parishioners. I am still a minister after all!

In spite of himself, he felt an enormous temptation to laugh. Dropping into a pew, he fell to his knees and buried his face in his hands as he struggled to pull himself together. Suddenly to his total surprise, a stealthy hand dropped on his shoulder and a voice whispered in his ear, 'You all right?'

Smothering a start of fear, he whipped round.

It was the girl. Did he detect a faint flash of malice in the perfect Madonna countenance as she informed him, straight-faced, that she was just passing, thought she might find him here, didn't mean to make him jump? But how could he suspect her of anything? In the morning sunlight pouring through the glass walls of the chrome and concrete palace, she looked like a nymph of the summer. And who better to see on a glorious summer day like this?

He was enormously pleased to see her. He was only just beginning to realise how important she was to him. He felt sure that by working with Murray he would get to the bottom of the mystery of the other girl, the unknown Ally Calder, whose face he now knew so well that he no longer needed to consult the faded cuttings he had abstracted some time ago from the folders in Joan's office and had since kept securely under lock and key in his own desk. But the purpose of working with Murray was not only to uncover the past. Now it seemed to him that all his anxieties about this plan, digging into the past to find the way ahead, the next step, were so much self-oppression, so much hot air. For here she was, flesh and blood, bathed in sunlight and smiling like an angel.

'Hello,' he said quietly.

'Hello yourself!'

Where did it come from, this easy humour, this sense of belonging? Lightly she dropped down beside him in the pew. 'I really was hoping you'd be here. I wanted to talk to you – properly. I've been thinking about what happened the night you called round.'

His lean, handsome face took on an attentive look. 'Oh yes?' he murmured.

'I just want to say I'm sorry about the way I was with you at first, shouting about the police and all. It was just that I was so frightened.'

'Ah yes, the police . . .' He gave a rueful smile.

She shot him a sly grin in answer. 'You've been having a spot of bother with them on your own account since I saw you, haven't you?'

'Just a bit. A piece of folly . . . or wisdom . . .'

'I'm sorry.'

'No need to be sorry for me.'

She laughed. 'Well, you don't have to worry. I won't tell a soul about you coming to call on me! I know you've got your respectability to worry about.'

'Mmmn – my respectability.' He looked at her, she thought, with a kind of quizzical amusement. 'I'm not sure that I care so much about that these days. Anyway, I think you can leave me to worry about that. That's not your problem.'

'No,' she agreed.

Was there once again a strange look in her eye? God, he'd better pull himself together, or he'd be imagining a strange look in the eye of the Virgin Mary in the Lady

Chapel! 'Anyway,' he asserted, making an effort to get on top of the conversation, 'I should be apologising to you, for the fright and the inconvenience.'

'All right, then. So now we're even.'

'I guess so.'

His smile was fantastic, she thought. He could've been a film star when he was younger, before he got so old. Must be at least forty now. But still great-looking. Wonder if he knew? Probably not. Pretty unworldly, ministers. They certainly wouldn't go round trying to work out who fancied them!

She spoke on impulse. 'She must have been something really special, that girl I remind you of.'

'Yes.'

Why did the very mention of Ally Calder now seem to connect with that deep, untranslatable feeling of happiness, the odd sense of drifting, floating, losing himself in some wordless, nameless joy? 'She was very beautiful, and very young,' he said slowly. 'I know that from her picture. And in the end, very lost. I know that from the way she died. But that's all I can tell you.'

'That's all, huh?'

She was looking away down the aisle, as if losing interest. Following her glance, he saw a party of Cathedral visitors enter with one of the junior clerics for the first of the day's guided tours round what had immediately established itself as a new architectural wonder of the world, rivalled only by the internationally celebrated Sydney Opera House.

''Bye, then.'

She was leaving. He did not want to let her go. The words were out of his mouth before his brain was aware of forming them. 'Look, if you're not doing anything, I'd like the chance to make up to you for the fright I gave you that night. What say we take a day off – do the sights of Sydney? Could be fun, yes?'

It was – and more than fun. He could not remember when he had had such a good time for years. First stop, he assured her, had to be Sydney's zoo, where the special creatures of the island – koalas, kangas and others – lived happily together in conditions like those of the wild, expressly for the benefit of young lady visitors Down Under.

'Or isn't it a visit?' he probed gently as he bought the tickets. 'How do you like it here? Think you'll be staying?'

'Depends.'

Her odd moments of reserve and the unfailingly English voice never let him forget how foreign she really was. He longed to ask her, too, about the boy he had seen her with at the café, and then again the night he had followed her home, but he did not want to endanger the fragile trust between them.

But once inside the zoo, she became like any other kid out on a treat. 'I've wanted to come here ever since I arrived,' she announced happily.

'Oh . . .' He tried to sound casual. 'How long ago was that?'

'Oh . . .' She echoed his sound – mockingly? 'Six months or more now.'

'As long as that?' He was not sure that she was telling the truth. But he was not inclined to argue.

'Hey!' She had just caught sight of a sign. 'Do they really have pandas here?'

He smiled. 'Of course. Miles away, though, over the other side of the park.'

'I've got time.'

'Good.'

'Have you, though?'

He looked at the deep, thoughtful, rather guarded eyes in the beautiful oval face, and resisted the sudden, inexplicable urge to give her a hug of simple joy. 'Yes, actually, I have.' He grinned, like a teenager deciding to play hookey. 'I've got time. I've got all the time in the world.'

Chapter 29

In Murray Beilby's consulting room the golden sun poured through the blinds to create a warm, somnolent atmosphere broken only by a calm, murmuring voice. 'Think, Robert. Let your mind float away, float freely. What do you see? What is all around you? What is that feeling of happiness you can't explain?'

Floating . . . floating away . . . into the night, velvet, blue and black . . . the stars . . . the end of a wonderful summer, the best summer of my life . . . then the touch of a hand . . .

And the moon and the music and you!

With savage derision Robert snapped the train of his thought, and his mind flinched away from wherever it had been leading him. Free association, Murray had said. Just allow your mind to drift, and see whatever it comes up with. Yet how free could a man be who had spent his life in chains ? It was so hard, impossibly hard. But nothing had ever been so important.

'It's in there – somewhere – I'm sure of that, Murray,' he insisted, tapping his forehead.

'Maybe so,' agreed Murray. 'But we'll never get it out until you learn to relax!'

'Sorry.' Obediently Robert stretched his long legs out on Murray's comfortable black leather couch, and closed his eyes again. 'Where were we?'

'We – you – were free-associating.'

'Oh – yes. Not very successfully.'

'OK, let's back-track. You've seen the girl again, properly now, for a considerable period of time, and in daylight. Do you still think she's the image of the girl who died?'

'No . . .' admitted Robert reluctantly. 'She's got the same shaped head, the same fair hair.'

'A lot of young girls have got fair hair, Robert.'

'And the shape of her face is the same, too,' persisted Robert stubbornly. 'At least from the old newspaper photograph I've got. But there's something about her eyes – the look in her eyes, not the colour , or the way they go up at the corners – that's different. And the way she is – English, for starters – no, she's a very different girl.'

'And how do you feel when you're with her?'

Robert pondered. 'Confused, mainly. And wary . . .'

'What of?'

'Of her – a bit, anyway. Because there's something about her I can't pin down—'

'You keep saying that. Try to pin it down.'

'Well . . . there's a kind of watchfulness about her. She's always on guard. And something more. Anger? She seems very uptight about something. The first night I talked to her in the café she just walked out on me in the middle of a simple conversation, and didn't come back.'

'Did you ask her why?'

'Yes.'

'And?'

'And she refused to say anything about it.'

'Was she angry yesterday – when you took her to the zoo?'

'No, not at all. She was happy.'

'How did that make you feel?'

'Happy too. Yes – so happy!'

Murray created a pause. Then he slipped into it the question he had been preparing for some time. 'Did you feel like that when you were with Ally Calder?' he asked casually.

'I never was with—'

Lying on the couch, Robert had changed colour, Murray's shrewd eyes could see. His expression had changed, too, his whole being apparently suffused by the strongest emotion.

'How do you feel now?' he pressed softly.

364

'Oh . . . *happy* . . . So happy . . .'

'In what way happy?'

'God, Murray!' Robert's explosion was somewhere between a groan and a howl of rage. 'You're a man, too! Do I have to spell it out for you?'

There was a long silence. His face buried in his hands, Robert lay on the couch like a knight crusader on a tomb, completely immobile. But the tension written in every line of the long, lean form proved that this man was not made of marble.

'You knew that Ally girl, Robert,' Murray said very quietly at last. 'Your body and your emotions remember what your brain has decided to forget. You knew her, and you knew her – pretty well.'

The tormented figure on the couch moved, uncovering his face, but the eyes remained firmly closed.

'Don't play with me, Murray. What does that mean?'

'What does it mean? That you were close to her emotionally . . . and my guess would be physically and sexually too.'

'But how could I – how would I . . . ?'

Smiling ruefully, Murray returned his own words back to him. 'You're a man, Robert. Do I have to spell it out for you?'

Robert was in shock now, his face white and glistening. 'But a parishioner of mine – and such a young girl—'

'Like Emma?'

Murray's quiet question threw him completely, seemed to scramble his brain. 'Wha-at?'

Murray leaned forward intently. 'This is not a cheap crack, Robert, but I want you to think about it. You're a man – still in the prime of life. A man like any other, underneath the black coat and dog-collar. You wouldn't be the first – especially at this stage of your life – to have your head turned by a lovely young girl – especially one who, lonely in Sydney or whatever she is, seems to be taking an interest in you.'

Disgust seized him. 'You think I've got the hots for the kid! Oh my God!'

'Tell me, Robert. Convince me you haven't.'
'Because it's different!'
'Different from when you were with Ally?'

With Ally . . .
When I was with Ally . . .
Why did he feel he was falling? Taking deep breaths, he fought down the impulse to sit upright, swing his legs over the side of the couch and return to normal everyday life. Go with it, he heard Murray's soft stern voice inside his head, go with it.

With Ally. What was that? A smell, sweet as innocence, like babies, something about babies. A small, firm hand . . . That immortal fine rain of hair, yes, that definitely. And her eyes . . . the stars shining down on them . . . the sea . . . falling . . . the sea . . .

The sea! Panic broke over him like tidal wave. He sat bolt upright, fighting for control. 'Murray, the sea!' he muttered, 'the sea!' He swung off the couch and stumbled to his feet, clutching the desk for support as he went forward.

'Calmly, Robert.' Murray's voice was calmness itself. 'You've done very well for one day, Robert, very well indeed. I think we'll stop there for today. Now I want you to go away, and try not to think about all this. Don't vex your poor old brain by trying to make it work overtime between sessions – it's having a hard enough time right now as it is – I'll give you something for those headaches of yours before you go, by the way. But it's going to tell you everything you want to know, in it's own good time, if you'll just give it a chance – *everything*!'

Ally – Emma – Emma – Ally.
Where did one end and the other begin?
He did not know. But he did know that they were different – that the feeling of happiness that finding Emma had given him, as he had described it to Murray, was also different. Yet undoubtedly meeting Emma was somehow like a second chance – a chance to make it up to her. Make what up? And to which of them? He shook

366

his head. It was like the worst kind of jigsaw – the one where you know from the start that some pieces are missing, and you don't know how many, or where from.

Musing deeply, he drove back to the Dean's residence blind to the route he was taking or the traffic all around him. Slowly he parked and went in to the house. At Brightstone, he thought, his whole being attuned to that past time after his session with Murray, I always used to come into the Rectory and call, as soon as I walked through the door: Claire! Joan! We were always so keen to see each other then. Now, everyone seems to stay in their own rooms, and we creep around this mansion avoiding each other. His heart too heavy for a sigh, he closed the front door and made for his study.

As he did so, he was surprised to see Claire come out of her sitting-room at the back of the house. 'Hello,' she said quietly.

'Claire! But I thought you were at – I thought this was your day for—'

Claire's resigned smile tacitly challenged him to tell her the last time he had shown any interest in her movements, or indeed had the faintest idea what she did with herself from one day's end to the next. 'It's Tuesday, Robert,' she said. 'You haven't forgotten?'

'Tuesday?'

'Tuesday. First in the month. Our day to visit Paul?'

'Oh God.'

She was not angry, just painfully matter-of-fact. 'We can still make it, if we drive like mad. I've got the sandwiches I'd made all packed up – we can eat on the way.' Only when he continued to stand there like a pole-axed bull did she reveal even a flash of the tension she was under. 'Come on, Robert, *please!* You've obviously got something on your mind. But whatever it is, you can tell me on the way!'

A journey of almost three hundred miles each way, would seem as good an opportunity for conversation as any. But as Robert hurtled the car through the traffic and out on to the freeway in a determined effort to make up for lost time, speech between him and Claire was painfully stilted when it did not dry up outright.

If he had loved the girl Ally – *if*, thought Robert, for his conscious mind was once again shrinking back from what had seemed so clear in the seclusion of Murray's consulting rooms, then how had he any right to sit in this car with Claire as her husband? To break his marriage vows, vows promised not just to her but to God, was a terrible thing!

And for a priest to fall that way, not merely an ordinary man, but a man who had promised his life to God, in the image of God – had he so tripped? So fallen? So betrayed this quiet, sweet woman, now rather pitifully worn and defeated by life – so betrayed himself – betrayed his every trust? He thought suddenly of the fall of Lucifer, the brightest and the best, of whom only the best had been expected!

The best expected . . .

Could he really have been so interested in becoming Bishop that he had allowed Joan to push him along all these years with that one aim in view? That seemed almost impossible now. Might as well ask him if he wanted to paint a Picasso, or lead the next mission to the moon. These ecclesiastical fancies had been the ambitions of another time, another man. Surely he owed it to Claire to share at least some of this with her?

'Claire,' he began diffidently. Where to begin? 'This business about the Allambie – did it upset you very much?'

'Are you serious?' Even out of the corner of his eye as he concentrated on the road ahead, he could see her look of distress. 'It almost broke my heart! To see all those poor old souls turned out of the only home they knew – and that lovely old family house reduced to rubble – yeah, it upset me!'

How easy it was to get off on the wrong foot! God, he was stupid! 'No, I meant my part in it. The demonstration, my getting arrested – the harm it might all have done to my career . . .'

'Oh . . .'

She didn't exactly say 'Oh, that'. But she might almost

as well have done, he felt. 'Don't you care?' he demanded.

'Oh, Robert.' Conversation with him in this mood was like jumping from ice-floe to melting ice-floe, in a river in full spate. 'If I didn't care,' she said as evenly as she could, 'I don't think you'd be where you are today.'

His mood changed at once. 'Of course – you're right, of course. God, I'm sorry, Claire.'

But she was launched now, and not to be diverted from what she had to say. 'Where *are* you today, though, Robert? And where are we in all this? You've achieved your ambition – one of them, anyway, a grand position on the Cathedral staff. And where's it got you?'

He gripped the wheel, willing her to continue.

'You're not a happy man, I can tell. And I know you're involved in something – something you don't want to share with me. I only hope it works out for you, that's all.'

So do I, Claire, so do I, he thought fervently.

'Whatever it is, I don't think it's got anything to do with the Church. You can take this as you like, Robert, but I think your heart has gone right out of the ministry these days. You don't want to be a Bishop, no matter what Joan thinks. You wouldn't have handled that interview with the Archbishop the way you did otherwise, I don't care how ill you were. What you did was the action of a man who had come to the end of the road.'

He hardly dared breathe for fear of interrupting the flow. How long had she been thinking like this?

'Well, that's you. You'll have to sort it all out. You'll have to do it on your own if you won't turn to anyone else for help or advice – but that's you, too, that's the way you've always been, and you'll do it – whatever it costs you – in the end.'

She paused, as if gathering her forces for the final thrust.

'But that still doesn't do anything for us. Us, Robert, you and me. I may have lost my brother, but I'm not ready to lose my husband, too. What's happening to us? When was the last time we talked?' She stared out of the window, blinking back angry tears. 'And when was

369

the last time we made love? Oh, you may think I got used to not having a baby years ago, just because we stopped talking about it. Well, let me tell you something! I didn't! Every time I see a baby in another woman's arms, I'm crying inside. Every month I still live in hope. Only a glimmer these days, but it's still there. I'm not much over forty, it's not impossible. But there's one thing you don't have to be clairvoyant to know – you can't get a baby without making love first, no way!'

They always tried to arrive as cheerfully as possible at the state prison, to avoid depressing Paul still further in his already miserable surroundings. But this time, with the weight of so much unresolved unhappiness between them, it was simply not possible. And with the sensitivity of those who have too much time on their hands for watching and studying the reactions of others, Paul seemed to pick up instantly on their mood, as soon as they walked into the prison visiting-room. But one look at Claire's face checked whatever he was about to say, and he contented himself with waving a hand to embrace all the other occupants grouped around separate tables in the room, then throwing an arm around his other visitor to draw her into the conversation.

'Better late than never, you two! Just as well Mum fancied an outing and turned up unexpectedly, or I'd have been left on my own here like a virgin at a wake, with no one but these other old lags for company!'

'Sorry, darling,' said Claire anxiously, trying to smile. 'We got held up. Good to see you! Hello Mum!' And she folded the elderly woman in her arms with a big, loving hug.

'Hello, mate!'

Robert gripped Paul's hand with a wealth of feeling. He had never ceased to admire his brother-in-law for the courage with which he had borne what Robert passionately believed to be a miscarriage of justice. But even as he did so, he felt the tension in the man. Paul had endured an enormous amount. Could he simply go on indefinitely?

'Robert.'

'Hello, Molly.'

Molly smiled. 'Looking well, isn't he?'

'Fighting fit.'

'Ah, that's nothing! He'll be even better when we get him home. There's still plums on the tree in the back yard,' she said, turning to Paul with all her loving, suffering mother's heart in her eyes. 'You can have the picking of them, son.'

'I'll have other things to do when I get back besides picking plums, Mum,' said Paul heavily. 'An old score or two to settle – couple of debts to pay. That's what I'm looking forward to.'

Claire's face was suddenly irradiated, transfigured with joy. Robert was startled to see how beautiful she was. 'Is it settled then – Paul's parole?' she breathed.

'Not yet, love,' said Molly stoutly. 'But it will be. I know he's going t'get it this time. I can feel it in my bones.'

Claire's face fell, and she shot an anguished look at Robert. Help them! her look commanded. Don't let them get up false hopes. It's a fool's paradise! And we've all been here before . . .

Claire was right, he thought, with his infinitely swift and sympathetic awareness of the sufferings of others. He had to have a word with Molly, warn her privately that there was no future in building up hopes if they were likely to be disappointed. Praying for inspiration, Robert leaned towards the work-and-care-worn figure perched so indomitably on the hard prison chair, and took one of the arthritic hands. 'Can I get you something, Molly?' he inquired gently. 'Cup of tea or coffee? Let me take you over to the refreshment bar and we'll organise tea and biscuits all round . . .'

Chapter 30

Few of the customers came to Gazouli's café by the underground station to sample the cuisine, and fewer still for the comfort and elegance of the interior design. But more and more now, just as he had calculated when he employed her, were drawn to drop in at the Jacaranda for the pleasure of being served by the pretty young waitress, however little she put herself out to attract them. One of her admirers was pleading now for rather more than the cup of coffee she had brought him some time ago, and which he had slowly been eking out down to its last cold dregs ever since.

'Oh go on, Emma. Just say you'll see us later and I'll hang on for as long as you like!'

'I don't like for you to hang on at all, Gary!' came the smart rejoinder. 'And there's no point. I'm not free when I get off my shift here. I've got another appointment.'

'It's not him, is it?' demanded the boy, his brows darkening. 'That old guy, the parson I saw hanging around here the other day?'

'None of your business.'

'Aw, come on, Emma! You can't prefer him to me! He's an antique!'

'It's none of your business, Gary! Now will you get out of here before you get me into trouble with Mr Gazouli?'

'He can't get cross with you. I'm a paying customer.'

'Only when you pay! Now will you give me the money for that coffee and clear out!'

It was not a question any longer, but an order. He scrambled to his feet. 'OK, OK! I'm going! But don't forget you said you'd meet me in the park on Saturday. If the sun's right, I really want to take those pictures of you – should get some marvellous effects of light on your hair. And I bet that's more than your old God-botherer could do for you, any day of the week!'

'Less of the "old God-bother", thank you!' said Emma, her smooth face shadowing with sudden thought. 'You know, I bet he'd take a pretty good picture himself. Gary, I think you just gave me a very good idea . . .'

Was he really an old God-botherer? Emma quizzed herself when he collected her later. He didn't look like one. Secretly she surveyed him as they walked from the café to his car. He didn't look that ancient, to start with. A few lines, but they made him look more attractive really, just like Clint Eastwood. And that ash-blond-coloured hair never seemed to show grey, even supposing he'd got any to show. As to God – he never ever mentioned the Lord's name. Though if he had, it would have been in vain to her! She giggled irreverently at her own schoolgirl joke.

'Something funny?'

He looked so nice when he crinkled at her like that. She caught herself up. What could she be doing, thinking like this? Of course he could be nice. Any man could be nice when he felt like it. It was all right for them to be nice!

Not for the first time Robert caught the swiftly changing kaleidoscope of emotions as they passed across her smooth young face and wondered if he would ever be able to know what she was thinking. Yet how could he expect to know that when he did not know what he was thinking himself half the time? He smiled at his own folly. Stop thinking. Just go with it, Murray had said. And that was all he wanted to do, after all.

'I thought we'd just go for a drive, see if we can locate your nearest beach,' he said as he helped her into the car. 'I'm sorry I've only got an hour, otherwise I'd take you out for a meal. And I thought you'd be glad to know where the sea is, so you can go there on your day off.'

'Sure.'

Robert's discovery that Emma had never been to even one of Sydney's thirty-odd beaches confirmed his impression that she had not been in the city for the six months that she claimed. But he always had to tread carefully when pumping her for information about herself. Other times, though, she would chatter freely about her life in England, and why she had been happy to get away. Tonight the beauty of the little bay they found, along with the outsize ice-cream he bought her from a providential kerbside van, seemed to put her in a reminiscent mood.

'Ooh, I'd love to show this off back home!'

'Who to?'

She veiled her eyes. 'All the – all the family in England! They'd all want to come!'

'Why don't they?'

She thought about it. 'Well, let's see. My . . . my sister's only a couple of years older than me, but she's married, with a baby already. They tie you down, kids, don't they?' She gave him a hard, inexplicable stare. 'Then my brother . . . he could do what he likes, go all over the world if he wanted to – not bad, being born a man, free to do what you please and never mind the consequences.'

Another curious stare. He had the feeling he was missing the point of the conversation. 'So he could come out here? But he won't?'

'Nah. Too conventional. It's all "get a good job, settle down, fiddle your income tax and save up for double glazing" with him!'

'And after all—' he smiled at her '—after all, *you're* here, and that's the point, isn't it?'

'The point. I dunno. What *is* the point?'

He laughed at her candour. 'I don't know either!' he admitted. 'When you're young, you really believe you'll discover the secret of life, you feel sure that you'll get to a stage when you've got all the answers. But it simply doesn't come. In fact it keeps drawing away from you, and as you get older you seem to know less and less.'

He paused – was he boring her? But she was watching

him narrowly with that cat-like concentration of hers, following his every word.

'So here I am now, at my age, still wondering, still searching. Recently—'

Should he be telling her this? Was it fair to burden someone so young with the miserable complexities of adult life? And was this really the appropriate behaviour for a Dean of the Church? The clear certainty that it was not encouraged him to go on.

'Recently I've been asking myself more and more, is this all there is? Is this what I've given my life for? The same mistakes, over and over again. The same vices – stumbling over the same sins. Always searching, always looking for that special something – that feeling of "yes, this is it! This is what makes it all worthwhile".'

'I know what you mean.'

The ice-cream had been unceremoniously dumped as she listened to him with the utmost attention. 'It's the same for me. I thought it would get better.'

'Some things do'.

She stared him out. 'Not that many, according to you. And where's the fun of it all? Life should be fun! You're only here once. Most people give up before they get anywhere near it – and forget what it's like to be alive. Alive! Alive!'

How was it that almost everything she said seemed to be laden with bitter-sweet meaning for him? He felt touched by her, touched in his heart as nothing, no one had touched him before. Yet he was also filled with an absurd and quite unreasonable desire to look after her, to protect her – absurd, because she could so clearly take care of herself. Perhaps if Claire and I had had a child, he thought, unwilling to be forced to tread again even in his mind that particular path of pain. Or if Joan had married and made an aunt and uncle of us, then we might have known this – this special joy . . .

He smiled down at her. 'Some people are just more alive than others, always.'

'What about you?'

'Oh . . . alive days and dead days, I guess – like most people.'

She squinted at him with a shrewd curiosity. 'What's today?'

He didn't have to wait for the answer. 'Alive,' he said, grinning broadly. 'Today, very definitely alive!'

'This is it, love!'

Beaming broadly, Molly Everard came struggling heavily towards them as soon as she saw them approaching the prison gate.

'Oh, Mum!'

Claire and Robert exchanged glances of deep concern. Robert's attempt at their last visit to the state prison to take the edge off Molly's conviction that this time Paul would get the parole they all longed for, simply had not worked. Molly wanted it so much, believed in it so much, that in her mind it was as good as here. Robert had been sincerely praying, every day since they had last talked, that she might be right.

'How y'doing, yous two?'

She was clearly in high spirits, despite her difficulty in getting around. Claire frowned with concern. The heat was oppressive, and outside the prison gates there had been nowhere for her to find shade or shelter, nowhere to sit down. 'Mum, you shouldn't be standing here like this waiting for us! You should be sitting down.'

'Ah, I'll be resting long enough when I pop off!' Molly laughed. 'And I couldn't miss this afternoon! He'll have heard by now. They were due to hear this morning. I'll take it easy later.'

Claire was not placated. 'How was your trip?'

'Doesn't get any shorter. And that overland train from Brightstone, it doesn't get any more comfortable. Especially at my weight! I could do with a wet, and a bite to eat.'

'As soon as we get inside,' Robert promised. 'Biggest cuppa the canteen'll rise to, and a slab of cake besides.'

They turned towards the prison. Molly's progress was painfully slow. But Claire knew better than to offer her mother her arm. 'You all right, Mum?'

'Fine, love, fine,' said Molly breathlessly. 'It's just my poor old knees. Not much spring left in them these days.

Still, after nearly eighty years' wear and tear, what can you expect? But they've kept me going. And they'll get me the last mile or two. Just long enough to see my Pauly walk out of here, and that's the only thing that counts!'

'Mum, we've talked about this! You know they've knocked him back before – lots of times!'

'Not this time, love.' She turned to Robert, and abandoning all pretence of being able to manage unaided, grasped at his arm for support. 'Y'husband'll understand better than you do,' she said with a knowing grin. 'I've been goin' up t'St Jude's. Not that it's a patch on the way it used t'be when you were there – but I've been having a regular word with Him Upstairs. I reckon I've swung it this time! Because I haven't got much more time, I reckon, to swing it in!'

Once again Robert marvelled at her high spirits. If only we could all approach life with this courage, this gaiety, he thought. Carefully he shepherded her over the last few yards to the prison visiting-room.

''Course, yous two wouldn't know Brightstone these days,' Molly battled on despite her very obvious shortage of breath, 'what with the mine starting up again after so long, and all. The old place'll never be the same again, you don't need me to tell yous, but it's something, f'the younger people anyway.' She fixed Robert with her tiny, boot-button eyes. 'Y'll be coming down, will ya? F'the service? The commemmoration?'

Claire looked at Robert. 'I don't know. Will we?'

'Not sure, Molly.' They hadn't talked about it for ages. And the earlier decision that they would go seemed to have got lost a long way back down the line.

The old woman tossed her head wearily. 'Ah Robert, they'll be counting on you. It's only right y'should come. People think a lot of y'in Brightstone, remember. They don't forget. Specially Johnny Anderson's Mum! Remember Johnny? The one you saved from the pit? He married, did I tell you? Two little kids now. It's a lot t'be thankful for.'

'Yes.'

'And when Pauly's home as well . . .'

378

Robert came to his decision. 'We'll be there, Molly, never fear.'

'Oh darling!'

Claire's face was glowing, too. He'd forgotten how dearly Brightstone had always been home for her. And he could not remember the last time he'd done anything to make her call him 'darling'.

They were in the visiting-room now, ahead of time. Around them the representatives of other families sat quietly grouped round their respective tables, but they all had eyes for nothing but the door through which Paul would come. Molly's excitement had mounted now to a new, and Robert thought uneasily, dangerous pitch. She was panting heavily after the exertion of what had after all been a fairly short walk on level ground, and her face had taken on a strange, puttyish hue. Anxiously Claire took her mother's hand. They waited.

Afterwards Robert thought that the length of time they waited might have told them everything they needed to know. But they were still not prepared for the news when it came. The door opened, and Paul stood on the threshold, his face as black as fire. Molly took one look at him, rose to her feet and let out a high, unnatural scream.

'Paul – *no!*'

'No it is, Mum.' His voice was thick with rage. 'No parole.'

Clumsily braced on her uncertain legs, Molly made one last sound – 'Oh, son!' Then she fell heavily forward on to her knees, and pitched over on to her side. By the time Paul reached her, she could only manage a flutter of her lips to show that she knew he was there. By the time the prison doctor appeared, she was gone.

Autumn

Chapter 31

Many times in his dreams Robert had returned to Bright-stone again – and it had never been like this. Of course, it had been marvellous of the Archbishop to suggest he flew up here, and with all the pressures on him now, it was about the only thing that made it possible for him to be here to conduct Molly's funeral. Yet he knew he would have done it somehow, if only for Claire. And to arrive by plane, only to fly out again an hour or so later, made him feel like an alien beaming in from another world.

Poor Claire . . . there were no words to comfort her in this double blow. All he could do for her now was to make sure that the funeral he was about to take did full justice to Molly and to her memory. Leaving Claire at home in her mother's now pathetically empty little house, in the company of Geordie and his wife, with a few other neighbours and friends too old to be driven away when the mine collapsed, he set out to walk up from the town to the church to prepare for the service.

Deep in thought he strode through the town and on up the headland road. At last he breasted the rise and came out on top of the great bluff. Before him stood the Rectory, looking exactly as it had almost twenty years ago when he had turned the key in the lock for the last time and handed it over to the churchwarden before joining Claire and Joan at the overland station. Passing by, he made for the church and turned aside into the cemetery. Treading reverently among the silent sleepers, he came to the grave of his parents.

'SACRED TO THE MEMORY OF ROBERT GEORGE MAITLAND AND OF EMMA LAVINIA

HIS WIFE', he read. Would he and Claire rest here like this one day, the trials of their life forgotten in the bliss of eternal peace? Nearby was the grave of 'GEORGE EVERARD, BELOVED HUSBAND AND FATHER', newly opened to admit 'HIS FAITHFUL WIFE MOLLY' in a last union from which they would never be divided. The cemetery was fuller, much fuller, than in the old days, and he cast around at a loss among all the new gravestones. Finally he found the one he sought. 'IN MEMORIAM . . .' he read. 'JIM CALDER, MINER OF THIS PARISH, AND HIS DAUGHTER ALISON' . . . Eagerly he leaned forward, as if he could force the quiet earth to yield up its secrets to him. Was she here? Or had she risen again to haunt him?

The air was curiously muggy, not fresh and clear as it ought to be here, so high up above both the sea and the town. His head was spinning. So many questions – and the answers? How would he – when would he – ever know the truth?

The service was drawing to its close. For the final moments Robert gave himself up to the sadness of loss, the deep, harrowing lamentation of the organ, and the power of the occasion.

'This journey, our final journey, is one, it seems, which we must all make alone. Molly Everard died, as so many of us must pray that we will, among her family, in the arms of her son. But that last step – the step into the darkness of the undiscovered country beyond death – we take alone.'

Below him Claire was weeping freely now, alone and unsupported in the family pew. At the back Paul, flanked by two prison officers, returned his every glance of commiseration with an iron stare.

'Yet we are never quite alone. In the darkest night there is someone with us, One who only asks us to put our trust in Him, our hand in His, and He will light our way. In your own darkest hours, never forget the promise that Jesus made to every one of us: "Lo, I am with you always, even unto the end of the world".'

384

'Y'can have five minutes with him, Reverend, if y'want, before we take him back.'

At a con's mother's funeral, no matter what his crime, you had to make it as easy on him as you could, the officer's manner implied.

'Thank you, officer.'

A petulant wind whipping his surplice around his legs, Robert strode from the church precinct and across the headland to where Paul waited, his rigid body and forbidding back a study in desolation and resistance. He searched for something to say. 'I'm sorry,' he said.

Paul turned to face him, and the iron regard Robert had seen in church now pervaded his whole body. 'Don't be.' His voice was metallic, harsh. 'She knew there was no point in sticking around any longer. She had the right idea. You come to the end of your rope. Only one thing to do then.' He looked away, staring out over the sea to the far horizon.

With a sick lurch of horror Robert saw that Paul had stationed himself within easy reach of the cliff edge. Would he – was he thinking of—?

'A man can't hang on for ever, mate. Comes the time when you've got to take your own life into your hands.' Paul's voice, like his expression, was completely calm. Whatever he had decided to do, his mind was made up.

Should he shout for help? Or grab Paul now, before he jumped, and wrestle him to the ground? What did Paul mean to do? The breeze had died and the atmosphere all around was stifling again. He could not think straight. His dog-collar, always a trial in the heat, seemed to be choking him. His eyes followed Paul's to the edge of the cliff. There was a macabre compulsion in that view, in the great void beyond . . . so easy to imagine falling, falling, crashing down to the rocks below . . .

The sea roared in his ears. He was falling, he was falling . . . before him a shout, a man's shouting call, behind him a woman's scream, on and on and on.

'Hey mate – you all right?'

He felt a strong arm around his waist, bearing him up. Paul's face, shaken by concern, swam into view. As

Robert focused his eyes, Paul immediately resumed his hard demeanour, loosed his supportive hold and stepped back.

'Five minutes up, Everard!' called the prison officer, starting to walk across to them.

Paul straightened and shrugged. 'Gotta go.' A pace or two away, he turned back to Robert. 'But if I was you, mate, I'd see a doctor! Because I don't know what was happening to you when you almost blacked out there, but I tell you, you looked as if you'd seen a ghost!'

In Murray Beilby's consulting-room, the blinds were drawn against the cool autumn sun, filling the whole space with a muted grey-green glow, like light striking through deep water. Robert lay on the couch, his long body as relaxed now, Murray judged, as it was possible for him to be. Out of sight behind his patient's head, Murray silently threaded his fingers and flexed them back against his palms. This was it. After all the preliminary work to clear the ground, he was about to take Robert into the depths of his unconscious mind through the medium of hypnosis. Please God, he thought, his or mine, it doesn't matter – make this work!

'OK, Robert.'

The voice in Robert's ears began to take on a soothing, incantatory rhythm quite unlike Murray's everyday speech. 'I want you to roll your eyes right up to the ceiling, up to the ceiling as high as you can, and fix them on a real or imaginary spot above you, high above your head . . . take a deep breath now, breathe in, fill up your lungs and hold it, hold it to a count of five . . . and as you breathe out, just let your eyelids close, let those eyelids become loose and heavy and sink to a close . . . breathe out, close those eyes, and sleep now . . .'

Sleep now . . .
  Sleep now . . .
  Sleep . . .

As the voice which was Murray's – and yet not Murray's – rolled round and round in the caverns of his mind, Robert felt a heaviness creep over him that he could not resist. He did not want to resist it – it was such an irresistible warmth, a beguiling languor, a seductive sense of freedom and floating like nothing in the world, nothing he had ever felt before. 'Sleep now,' came the irresistible, murmuring command, like the purring call of a dove, '*sleep* . . .' With the sigh of a man downing for the first time a burden dragged behind him for far too long, Robert slept.

'We're going back now, Robert, way back in time . . . back to Brightstone . . . you're a young priest again, and you're meeting a girl . . . a lovely young girl, for the first time, at George Everard's funeral . . .'

'No . . .'

'Tell me . . .'

' "There's only one carton of crisps left in the store-room, Vic." ' He spoke in a light voice not his own. Murray held his breath. ' "I know who you are – Reverend . . ."'

' "Call me Robert." '

' "Reverend . . . Robert . . ."'

Another voice now, older, deeper, but still a woman's intonation. 'She's no relation of Vic's! She's Ally Calder, daughter of the old union boss . . . Everyone calls her Ally . . .' The voice tailed away.

Silence.

'And then . . .' murmured Murray almost sound-lessly.

'In church . . . George's funeral. The most beautiful girl. With that swine, that hateful swine!'

Nothing that came out under hypnosis surprised Murray.

'Her father?'

'Bastard!'

'You hated him.'

'Yes! She came to us. Came to work for us. Claire loved her, like a – like a baby.'

'And you loved her . . .'

'Yes! Yes! Yes!'

'But not . . . like a baby?'

The fine ivory face warmed with colour and the

apparently sleeping form on the couch was suddenly suffused with what looked like an extraordinary wave of happiness. More accustomed to human misery, Murray was shocked to find himself overtaken by a surge of envy. Whatever it was, this had been no ordinary relationship! Was he justified in prying into the heart of this dream? He gritted his teeth.

'Tell me.'

'Loved to teach her things . . . driving . . . she had so much to learn . . . no one to teach her . . . no one to love her . . .' He was showing signs of distress.

'You're going deeper now, ever deeper,' Murray murmured. 'You're floating, you're free . . . you're where you wish to be, where you long to be more than anywhere else in the world.'

Silence.

Then the light, soft voice came again. ' "Look! There's a ship out there, way out on the horizon. Where's it gone?" '

' "To England." '

' "Are priests – like other men?" '

' "Yes. Just like other men." '

'Now you're going deeper, Robert, ever deeper, with every easy breath you take. On the night that the mine caved in . . .'

He was fighting it, every inch of the way. 'No! No!'

'You're there, Robert. You're there. Tell me. Where are you?'

'Dark – oh God!' His whole frame shuddered. 'Long way down!'

'Down – the shaft? Inside the mine?'

'A shout – shouting. And crying . . .'

'Where are you?'

'Watching.'

'What can you see?'

'Dark.'

'It's dark, Robert, and you're a long way down, you're deep down in the mine—'

'Up.'

Murray started in surprise. 'Up?'

'High up.'

'High? You're high up? *Where*?' He had hit him too hard, and he knew it. The quiescent form on the couch began to twitch with agitation. Clenching his fists, Murray moved to relax both himself and his patient. 'Deeper now, ever deeper. Slowly, slowly, let everything go . . .'

But it was some time before he felt it safe to resume.

'You're going back again now. It's dark, it's a long way up, you're high up, and somebody's crying . . .'

'Screaming . . .'

Murray knew the answer to his next question before he asked it. 'Is it Ally?'

'She's there! She's on the cliff with me! We're on the edge! Danger! Terrible danger!'

'Danger? Who from? Or what?'

'*He wants to kill me*!'

He was shaking violently now, moaning and shouting, and trying to raise his fists as if to defend himself, but feebly, because of the hypnosis, like a man fighting a nightmare. He had remembered the danger, Murray observed, but not the whole story – above all, not the outcome. He could not leave him like this. But at the same time, he could not push him any further today. One more question then – and that had to be the last. But again he felt that he already knew the answer.

'Where is he, Robert?'

'Gone! Gone! He's gone!' He screamed aloud. 'Ally! *He's dead*!'

Silence – a long silence.

'OK, OK, don't upset yourself, calmly now, calmly, breathing deeply, deep breaths, that's it, there now, there's nothing to distress you, you're safe, you're here. Now in a little while I'm going to bring you back to full consciousness and you'll be yourself again in every way, refreshed, relaxed, fuller, freer, no more anxiety now, no pain.'

Slowly Robert's agitated frame subsided. But the quiet voice murmuring into his ear had not quite finished.

'In a moment we'll be counting back down to full consciousness again, ten, nine, eight, just as I told you. But when you come out of your hypnotic trance, Robert, this time you will not forget.' He leaned forward to make sure that every syllable he was uttering travelled straight into the mind of the sleeping man. 'Everything that you have recalled under hypnosis now, *you will remember*.'

With the nearest thing to a smile that she ever managed these days, Joan let herself into Robert's study and moved over to the desk. Complacently she surveyed the memo she had prepared for his return.

'*Re: Service of Commemoration and Rededication, St Jude's, Brightstone*. This is an unusual and interesting service in view of the tragedy that overtook the mine, and especially so when a cleric of your eminence, who was also a hero of the original mine disaster, is about to undertake it. It would make a very nice "human interest" story for the newspapers and television, too, so I will be releasing a press release in the next few days to inform all the media. Make a note in your diary to be available for interviews as soon as the story gets out.'

There. That ought to do it. A bit of good, warm-hearted publicity should go a long way towards repairing the damage caused by that nonsense at the Allambie demonstration. That was the first good thing.

The second was that the Archbishop and his cohorts had all quite forgiven Robert for his indiscretion on that occasion. Indeed, the added flurry of concern about his health, plus Robert's steadfast refusal to take the excuse it provided to drop any of his workload or commitments, had made him even more special to them all, and he was their blue-eyed boy again with a vengeance.

And then Robert had been behaving himself. He was still up to something, she could tell that. But as long as it was something quiet and furtive, she didn't give a damn. All he had to do was to keep his nose clean in public. And he was doing that just fine right now.

Best of all, though, was the news about Paul Everard. She hadn't really thought he would get his parole. But even the possibility of his release, even worse, his embarking on a quest for truth or a trail of retribution had cost her some anxious moments and more than one sleepless night. But that possibility was off the worry list as well now. Too bad for him – as if anybody cared!

She dropped the memo on Robert's desk and turned to go. As she did so, something caught her eye. It was Robert's diary, not the official version bound in dark blue which never left her own desk, but the tiny little pocket version which normally he always carried with him. Curiously she picked it up, and turned to the day's entries. One word leaped at her off the page: 'Murray'.

Murray Beilby! The neurologist – psychiatrist too! – the man Robert had been referred to when he had first lost his memory after the fall! When she and Claire had run into him at the Cathedral for Robert's service of inauguration, he was there as a friend, not as a doctor. Why was Robert consulting him again? *Why*?

Fear, as physical as a great winged creature from a nightmare landscape of prehistory, clattered across her mental horizon. No, Robert, no! Why was he determined to open this can of worms? To ruin them all? Shaking with anger and apprehension, she reached for the phone.

He was exhausted. God, he was getting too old for this game!

Feeling completely wrung out, Murray Beilby escorted an equally drained-looking Robert to the door of his consulting-room, then showed him across the outer office. Wordlessly the two men shook hands, sharing the satisfaction of a session that had gone better than could have been expected. Then with a murmured 'Thursday, then?', Robert was gone.

'Excuse me, Dr Beilby.' It was Janet, his ever-reliable and resourceful secretary. She was holding the phone in one hand, the other firmly clamped over the receiver. 'Can you take a call now?'

'God, no, Janet,' he groaned. 'Put them off for me, will you? I don't care if it's the Prime Minister! I'll call back later.'

'I think you'd better take this one, doctor, if you can.' Janet's expression was serious. 'She's already rung several times this morning. And I'm sure you'd prefer to deal with it yourself.' She nodded towards the inner office. 'I'll transfer the call through.'

'Yes, yes, of course I remember you, Miss Maitland – Joan – we met in the Cathedral last spring, at Robert's inauguration. Yes, it's been a good few years. What can I do for you now?'

Joan's voice was throatier than he remembered, but nothing had changed that passionate concern for her brother. 'It's Robert.'

'Yes?' Without knowing why, Murray was instantly on guard.

'I know he's been seeing you. Has he told you about his . . . blackouts . . . or anything?'

Murray sighed. 'Miss Maitland, you must know that I can't discuss a patient – even your own brother – with you or anyone else.'

'Yes, yes, but—'

'There's no "but", I'm afraid. I know how much you care about Robert, but the trust between a patient and his psychiatrist is sacrosanct.'

He could almost hear her mind whirring as she worked out her next move.

'Don't think I want to interfere, Doctor. I'm just so worried about him, that's all.'

'I can understand that.'

'And I thought – I thought that perhaps there must be some way I can help him. I mean, what if something else comes up to trouble him? A crisis at home?'

She was improvising now, Murray felt. But even so, what crisis? 'If there is,' he said crisply, 'call me at once. Robert must not have any undue excitement right now.'

'You mean you're getting close to something important in your sessions with him?'

'I didn't say that.' But he had, and he knew it.

'Like what?' She was gabbling now, overcome by some rapid emotion. 'What sort of thing? About his accident? About – that night?'

'You two have always been close,' said Murray slowly, feeling his way forward. 'I know he depends on you for almost everything—'

'Like what?' she cried again. 'What has he said? He doesn't know! He didn't know what he was doing! And it was all for him – everything I did, everything I've ever done – all for him!'

There was a deep silence.

'Why do you say that, Joan?' he asked casually – too casually.

What had she said? And why? Trembling more violently than ever, she put the phone down.

Some time later, as the heavy eastern clouds began to gather in the louring sky, she put on her coat and left the house.

'Now let's get this straight.'

Mick Ford prided himself that he had learned the art of the deal. And rule one was to find out what you had to do for what you were going to get.

'This Beilby bloke – this shrink – you want him out of the way, right? And you're asking me to set it up?'

Joan's bold front and iron composure did not entirely conceal her nervousness. She shook imperceptibly now as she replied. 'Just a minor accident. Nothing serious. Just enough to take him off work for a little while. Give him something else to think about.'

Mick Ford had not looked too attractive last time she'd seen him at the 'Save Allambie' meeting, even by the flattering glow of an evening dining-table. Now, in uncertain daylight, with a watery, overcast sun casting a grey sheen through the filthy windows of the union's city-centre office headquarters, he looked what he was – greasy and unkempt. His charm was not increased by the pious look of innocence he affected for his next utterance. 'Violence? Corruption? What makes you think I'd be into anything like that?'

You had to admire her, though, he grinned to himself. She wasn't easily put off.

'You've got your contacts. Mick, everyone knows that.'

'Me?' he rolled his eyes ridiculously. 'A man in my position?'

She was not inclined to play games. 'Oh, come on, Mick. I know you. Corruption's been your middle name since the day you were born!'

'Now Joan—'

' "Your position" – that would've been Paul Everard's position now if it hadn't been for your evidence, and you know it!'

'It was him. I saw him.'

'So you said. Swore to it, in fact.'

'What are you trying to say?' His small eyes narrowed with suspicion.

What was she trying to say? Get a grip, Joan, she warned herself. Use your head! Just because you know he's a lying bastard simply determined to fix Paul Everard with the evidence he gave at the trial, doesn't mean you can use that against him. Because the only person who knows that he was lying – you! – can't reveal that without betraying everything else! Think!

'What are you trying to say? You saying I made it all up, just to get rid of him? Perjured myself? Risked going to jail?'

She gripped on to her handbag like a drowning woman. 'Will you do it, or not?'

'Depends.'

'On what?' She did not like his grin.

'On what y'r offering me.'

'What you always want, Mick – money. How much?'

But his mind had wandered. 'This bloke – this Beilby – he hasn't got something on you, by any chance?'

'Of course not! Look, I'm offering you a very good deal, Mick . . .'

Still he stared at her from behind his desk, the little eyes fixed apparently vacantly upon her face. A terrible thought dawned on her. He wasn't going to take the bribe! He was going to turn her down! What a humiliation, to come crawling to Mick Ford for a favour and have him kick you in the teeth! Furious with herself for even thinking of it, she turned to go. As she did so he rose casually, and sauntered across the tiny crowded office to block her path to the door.

'Where d'y'get all this stuff, Joanie? "Little accident – nothing serious?" '

The hairs on the back of her neck began to prickle. 'My name is Joan.'

'Y'know, y'haven't changed a bit in twenty years, have you?'

She fought to contain her fear. 'Neither have you.'

He patted his gross belly complacently. 'Ah, I've put on a few pounds. Still pretty fit, though.'

He was unpleasantly close. She could smell him, a nauseous combination of old sweat, old beer, and something worse.

'Y'got a nice place there, up at the Deanery. But you always knew how t'make a place nice. Always kept y'self nice too. Y'done all right for yourself, Joanie, one way anyway.' He leaned an arm casually against the wall beside her head. 'Another way, not so good. Y'never married, did ya? Some poor bloke missed out there.'

'Neither did you. Some poor woman had a lucky escape!'

It was her last throw, and it failed. He chuckled delightedly, opening his piggy eyes wide. 'I've always admired y'spirit, Joanie. And now this! A nice girl like you – an' you a parson's daughter, an' all. Oh, we used t'talk, us lads back in Brightstone. You'd be OK if y'could crack on t'her, we'd say, she'd see you right.'

His hand had descended on the side of her face, and he was stroking her neck and shoulder absently, as if his mind had no connection with what his hand was doing. 'Not that any of us had even half a chance with Miss Maitland, eh? Not unless we'd lined up behind Paul Everard!'

Paul – oh Paul! She let out a moan and flung her head away from the loathsome grasp. He chuckled in his throat, a horrible, snuffling sound, and gripping her face in fingers like steel subjected her to a wet, slobbering kiss. He was pressing her to the wall now, his fingers wandering down her neck, and down and down. Fumbling at her buttons, he laid open the front of her dress, and with sadistic slowness, slid her bra strap off her shoulder, exposing her breast.

'Well, whaddya know?' he murmured with interest, gazing at the nipple already erect to his touch. 'Now ain't that nice? And the other one, too?'

She stood there, stripped to his gaze, eyes closed, burning with pain and shame.

'Your first time is it, Joanie?' he mouthed into her neck. 'Don't worry, I'll make it easy on you. Y'can trust me . . . now we got us a deal . . .'

Chapter 32

In the seven circles of hell that make up prison life, it is well known that the seventh is reserved for those condemned to the long-drawn-out torment of waiting for parole, and then being refused it. However much the prisoner has boasted his indifference to his chances or tried to anticipate his disappointment, in reality no man can ever strangle hope, which springs unseen and eternal in even the most hardened breast. The death, therefore, of hope and the enforced acceptance of despair, bring the cruellest suffering and a hardening that even the best of men cannot avoid. Nor do they choose to, since to go on feeling is only to go on feeling pain.

All this Claire could read in her brother's face as she sat opposite him at her next prison visit. All her loving greetings died in her throat as she watched him walk in, and for the first time in all these years, she felt she did not know what to say.

Paul's greeting was brusque and abstracted as if he, too, could hardly make the effort to speak. 'No Robert?' he demanded.

'No.' I won't lie for him, thought Claire, I won't come out with all those wifely excuses, too much work, couldn't get away . . . 'He had too much work,' she said. 'He couldn't get away.'

'Well, there's not much here to tear him away from the big city!' said Paul savagely, throwing a glance around the cramped and meagre visiting-room with its cheap, tacky furniture and inadequate canteen struggling away in one corner. 'And there's not much to say for the company, either!' He flung himself sideways in his chair and gazed away across the room as if his eyes were raking some far horizon instead of the blank wall only twenty feet away.

'Paul—' She could hardly bring out his name, let alone any more coherent speech. She felt as if some evil spirit must be hanging weights upon her tongue. But she had to speak. 'Paul, what are you going to do?'

'Do?'

He threw back his head and let out a hectic laugh, so loud that it turned all heads to look at him. 'Do? Well, I thought I'd go up to the mountains for a bit of skiing, then take a trip to England – always wanted to see where the Poms come from, work out how they make 'em that way. Then with winter coming up, I'll have the planting on the estate to see to against the next season, and I thought I'd put a few new trees in round the boundary fence. And, of course, there's always my stocks and shares to see to. It's a full life being an international playboy an' businessman!'

Claire bowed her head. 'I didn't mean that,' she said in a low voice.

'Well, what did you mean?' he returned truculently. 'What d'you think I'm going to do, stuck here for another ten-to-fifteen years?' His voice had risen again in what would probably have been taken for hysteria in a woman. '*Fifteen years*, sis, think of that!'

'I can't.'

'Well, I can! I've bloody well got to, haven't I?' His face was working now, like an animal's. She half feared he might turn on her, sink his teeth into her – or into himself.

'Haven't they – haven't they given you any help with this?' she faltered.

'Oh, sure! 'Cause they only want all their boys to be happy, after all! I got the routine homily from the Governor – "Ours not to reason why, Everard. A law unto themselves, the parole board. Can't always see the reason for their decisions, but believe me, they're usually right in the end." Laugh? I thought I should've died!' And again he loosed off the manic, frightening, humourless laughter that she had heard before.

What was there to say? In the face of Paul's wounded hope, his raging sarcasm, his justifiable frenzy, all comfort could only inflame, all consolation merely insult. She sat there like a schoolgirl, staring at her hands and racking her brains for something, anything to break the terrible silence.

Then his mood changed as suddenly as the wind swings about without warning out at sea. 'There was one thing, though . . .'

'Yes?' Anything, Paul, anything.

'Got a new chaplain here – arrived the day I got turned down. Came to see me that night, said he'd heard I'd been a bit – knocked back by the decision and he wanted to help. I wasn't too friendly at first. Gave him a couple of home truths about the great Governor in the Sky.'

Claire did not need much imagination to work out how much of the milk of human kindness, or simple saintliness, the new chaplain must have needed to persevere. Paul in that state would have been like a gored bull. Trying to reach him, even attempting a conversation with him must have been like inviting yourself on to his horns.

'He talked to me for a bit and he asked me what were my chances of getting out without parole. I told him the appeal'd gone cold, no new evidence, and with so much of the old circumstantial evidence against me, the chances of re-opening the case were nil. Then he asked me if we'd be prepared to adopt another tack?'

'What did he mean?' Claire breathed.

Paul threw her an aggressive look. 'Turns out he's seen your husband making a fool of himself on television, leading a demonstration or something. Says he's known in Sydney and beyond now as a man who takes up the cudgels for the weak and oppressed. He says why doesn't Robert get up a campaign for me – appealing not on legal but human grounds for my release. He says Robert has got the clout to embarrass the hell out of the prison service, the parole board tossers, the lot!'

'Yes!' Claire's face flamed with enthusiasm. 'If only we'd thought of it before!'

'He wasn't famous enough before,' said Paul sardonically, 'And he might not be famous enough now. What d'you think, though? Worth a try?'

His studied casualness wrung her heart. 'Of course, darling,' she said unsteadily. 'Anything's worth a try – anything.'

'Would he do it?'

'Of course he would . . .'

Horrified, she found her voice petering out. Would he? A year ago, even a month ago she could have given Robert's answer without question. Now – God! – she didn't know! Her mind flew back to that morning when she'd awoken, as she almost always did these days, to an empty bed – a bed that had been equally empty when she'd climbed into it alone last night and the night before. She didn't even know where he was right now, this minute, why he wasn't with her or where he'd gone off to without even leaving her a note, so that she'd eventually had to set out for the prison on her own, or risk being late and even missing the visit. She blushed with anger and shame. This wouldn't do, Robert, this wouldn't do! She was going to have to do something about it.

Supersensitive as ever, especially in his highly irritated state, Paul caught her hesitation instantly. 'He wouldn't, huh?' he demanded, an ugly hostility disfiguring his face. 'What's his problem?' he jeered, rage covering his disappointment. 'Is he worried about his bloody career? Why don't you ask him what kind of career he thinks I'm having buried alive in here while he ponces around the Cathedral in his bloody frock?'

She could no longer hold back the tears that had been building; building, it seemed, for twenty years. Horrified, Paul gripped her hand.

'Hey, sis,' he cried in a voice thick with emotion, 'You all right?' Then a thought struck him, horrible but completely convincing in its simplicity. 'Hey – everything is all right between the two of you, isn't it?'

'Cup of tea? Coffee? Have a seat. Oh, don't look at the

mess, I had a couple of the girls over and we made a bit of a night of it.'

Standing on the threshold of Emma's room, Robert gazed in amazement at the debris. To his eyes, accustomed as he was to the neat, clean, orderly regime of Claire, the present clutter of Coke cans piled up with the odd lager bottle, a malodorous heap of cigarette butts and the remains of a Chinese takeaway for four, looked like the aftermath of an orgy. 'A couple of the girls?' he said humorously 'Some night!'

He managed to find a seat. Around him Emma busied about, tidying up none too efficiently and sticking the kettle on. In the middle of all this activity she took time to size him up. 'You look tired,' she said. 'Anything wrong?'

He smiled, evading the question. He knew he looked drawn and drained – so many people had commented on it – but how could he tell them he'd never felt better, too? The strong sense he had now of coming close to whatever it was he sought, the feeling that the veil over the last twenty years of his life was about to be drawn aside, was so exhilarating that he had to keep a fierce control over his emotions, keep banking down the excitement welling up every moment inside him.

There was fear there, too; he knew that. What had really happened that night? What night was it even, and when had it taken place, the night that Murray had called up from the buried depths of his subconscious? Still too many pieces to fit together, he thought. But I'm getting there. And when I do, she'll be there, she'll be part of it somehow, I know. He fixed his eyes on the girl as she made the tea, absorbed in the preparations. More strongly than ever he felt that she could throw light into his darkness, no matter what she said, if only she would – or if only she knew what it was he needed to know.

Above all, though, he recognised with great clarity, he simply wanted to see her. He wanted to be with her, to get to know her, to talk to her, more than anything in the world. Getting up that morning, slipping out quietly to avoid waking Claire, his one urge had been to be alone, to work through all the thoughts and fears that the session with Murray had brought up, then to make contact with her, to be with her in the easy, simple togetherness that had grown up between them now. She knew that, too; he felt sure. And she didn't mind. His visits were expected now, expected and welcomed. She was never surprised to see him when she opened the door. And not because she had no other callers either, as today's scene made plain. He smiled again. 'Good to know you've made a couple of girlfriends, then.' Yes, it was good. She was entitled to a normal life, the happy, carefree life of the average young girl. You're only young once! a voice cried inside him. And not for very long!

'Yes, I met them through work,' she smiled back. 'One of them's the other waitress, the other's her girl-friend. They're not really my type, but you get a bit lonely sometimes when you're on your own.'

It was the first time she had made any admission of the kind to him, or compromised her usual attitude of sturdy independence in any way.

'Well, when you settle in, you'll get to know more people.' He paused, and gave her a questioning glance. 'D'you think you'll settle here? Stay for good?' He was astonished to realise how important the answer to this question had become to him.

She seemed even more casual about it than he was attempting to be. 'Dunno. 'Spose I'd have to apply. Depends.'

'On – what?'

She rounded on him savagely. 'You ask a lot of questions, Mr Nosey!'

'Sorry.' He backed off at once. But the damage was done.

'Why d'you keep asking me these questions?'

'Just – curious.'

'About me?'

'About you – and everything.'

She wasn't fooled. Her derisive look called his bluff. 'Ask me, then. Go on. Ask me what you want to know.' Violently she sloshed the boiling water on to the teabags in the pot, and poked them about with a spoon. 'Go on!'

'Er – where do you keep the cups?'

They sipped their tea companionably, her bad mood blown over. But she had not done with the conversation. 'If you won't ask me things, I'll ask you,' she announced.

He tensed a little. But he did not want to stop her.

'That girl – Ally. The one you say I remind you of. Did you love her?'

He felt as if he were opening something up inside himself, revealing something infinitely fragile and more precious than words could say. 'Very, very much.'

'Why didn't you marry her?'

'I told you. She died.'

'Before that.'

'I was – I was already married.'

Now the contempt in her eyes was open and unmasked. 'Just a fling, was it then? A bit on the side?' He did not know whether the pain lay in hearing Ally described in this way, or in realising that Emma was thinking such a thing. She read his face. 'Well, I don't know! Don't blame me! Just give me the truth.'

'The truth?'

'Yeah, the truth! Did you really love her? Would you have married her if you could?'

He could not speak. His memories of Ally, so new, so raw, so precious, and only just restored to him by Murray after lying in the dark abyss of time and oblivion for so many years, could not stand up to this relentless inquisition. But even to talk of her was an exquisite release and torment, a cruel kind of bliss. 'Oh yes! Yes!' He was being torn apart by the warring of his emotions, memories, sensations. 'I loved her more than all the world – I can't begin to tell you how much . . .' He closed his eyes, and her face at once rose before him. He could see her, just as she was, as if she were here, right here, here with him – Ally smiling, Ally laughing, Ally looking at him with that sideways look of hers, Ally holding him, loving him . . . The world began to dissolve around him and he longed to fade away too, to melt into nothingness, to be with her . . .

'Hey!' Emma's voice, subdued and changed, reached him from a great distance. 'What's wrong?'

'Nothing . . .'

'Here.' Small hands guided him firmly to the bed, where he stretched out with thankfulness. Soon a cool, wet face-cloth was lying on his forehead, quickly soothing the pain inside his temple. When she spoke again, her tone had completely changed. 'What's the matter. You ill?'

He shook his head. 'An accident. A long time ago. Injured my head. I was in a coma for months, convalescent for two years. When I woke up, I didn't remember anything.' He set his face against the sudden, fierce pain that had awoken now not in his head, but in his heart. She could see the pulse beating behind his closed eyelids. 'And then – when I came round – she was gone.'

There was a long silence. Then he heard her shift a little in the chair beside the bed. 'Did you ever get your memory back?'

'No. Not till recently.'

'Didn't you try?'

He gave an angry laugh. 'It's not that easy.'

'So what happened recently?'

'I met you.'

'And that was it, bingo, like in the films, it all came flooding back?'

'No. Because there's only some things about you that remind me of her. Your hair. The shape of your head. Your hands. And oddly enough, your voice. Oh, I know you're English, and I couldn't say you really sound as she used to. But in a funny way, she never sounded quite Australian. Her voice had a lilt in it – she had a way of speaking – she was never as Aussie as you'd expect her to be. And when she spoke—'

She interrupted him harshly, as if she could not bear to hear the other girl discussed. 'For someone who forgot everything, seems to me that you remember quite a lot!'

He smiled. 'You take me back. And it seems like yesterday.'

'Ah, you men! You're all the same.' For the umpteenth time he wondered on what experience of men she based her almost universal disapproval. She sounded like a forty-year-old, jaded and abandoned, not a lovely young girl on the brink of life and love. She drew near to him and removed the face-cloth from his forehead. 'I'll just cool this off for you again.'

He looked up at her, into the clear, cold eyes. 'Thank you. This is so good of you. I shan't forget.'

She burst out laughing. 'You! You're the great forgetter of all time! If what you say is true, you've forgotten more experiences than most men have in a whole lifetime!' She paused. 'Wonder if you'll forget me.'

'Never.' He spoke with a strange purity of conviction. How could he be so sure?

Something equally strange flitted across the Madonna face above him 'Well, we'll see.'

'Yes.' He smiled at her. He spoke as he thought, without weight, without particular meaning, and with no idea that the simple monosyllable could cause offence. But she flew off the handle all the same.

'You think I'm too young to know what I'm talking about! You think I haven't got the faintest idea about this great lost love of yours! Well, let me tell you something, Dean Robert Maitland! I may be nothing to you, just a no-account kid! But I know what it is to want someone you can never have – to long for someone to come back and love you who never will, and never can. I know! I know! I know!'

It was very late when he reached home. He and Emma had talked for hours, he trying to convince her in every way he knew of his care and concern, she circling warily round him, longing to open up and confide in him, he knew, yet refusing to follow up or even explain her passionate outburst of earlier in the evening.

Now as he pulled up outside the Deanery and wearily uncoiled limbs stiff with tension and the long drive home, he suddenly became aware that it was well past midnight, and into the small hours of the morning. How absurd – and how suspicious – for a married man, a respected dignitary of the church, to be coming home at this time! What would he say to Claire? Any wife could be forgiven for suspecting a husband who disappears on 'business' early in the day and does not return until almost two in the morning. How could he defend himself? After all, he had been with a young girl – and no relation of his – alone in her room for hours upon end! Innocently of course – yet why should he expect anyone to believe that?

Rehearsing a variety of approaches he opened the front door and let himself into the house. Immediately he knew that he could have saved himself the trouble. Claire was awaiting him in the hall with news which drove any question of where he had been out of his head.

'Thank God you're back!' she said dully. 'I think Joan's ill. I found her here when I got back, shaking all over in the bathroom, trying to wash herself, God knows why. She was freezing cold. I managed to get her to bed, but she was still shivering so badly, I thought she'd have convulsions.'

'Oh, poor Joan! Did you get the doctor?'

'Yes, of course. He says he thinks it must be a virus, there's a lot of it about.'

'Can I see her, talk to her?'

'Probably better not. The doctor gave her something. It took ages to work, but she's sleeping now.' She saw his concern in his eyes. 'I'm sure you could just look in on her, though. That couldn't hurt.'

Relieved, he started up the stairs. 'That's not all, though,' came Claire's voice behind him. 'There's something else you ought to know.'

He turned. Claire was standing there with an expression, he noticed for the first time, of complete exhaustion.

'Rather sad news really, although I know you haven't seen much of him in recent years. It's Murray Beilby. There's been an accident – a car crash. Murray was driving. I'm afraid he's dead.'

Chapter 33

Everything dies in the autumn. But Murray?

No, it couldn't be.

'Murray? *No!* He *can't* be dead! I only saw him yesterday – I only just saw him—'

He was taking it as a terrible shock, she could see that. But what was Robert on about? He hadn't seen Murray for years except as a friend, and on the odd social occasion. What was the matter with him? He always seemed to be getting things out of proportion these days! Claire could not hold back the angry response that rose to her lips. 'You just saw him? Would you expect "just seeing you" to keep him alive?'

He looked at her, wounded to the quick. 'No, but I—'

She turned aside. He saw her small shoulders drooping with exhaustion, signalling, as clearly as any words, her feeling of alienation from him. 'You only seem to be able to think of yourself these days, Robert. What about his wife? And family? Or all his patients?' She paused and turned back. 'And what about Paul? I've driven all the way to the prison today on my own, because you were too wrapped up in yourself to remember it was Paul's visiting day. What about that poor man practically going mad, locked up in there without a hope of getting out now? Do you ever think of him?' She shot him a farewell look of burning reproach and anger. 'Or is the great Dean Maitland the only consideration in all this?'

The great Dean Maitland . . .

Claire's words, and even more the final shrug with

407

which she turned away, seemed to cut into the core of his very being. Taken with the news of Murray's death, it was almost more than he could bear. And he had to bear it alone, Claire's retreating back, already halfway up the stairs, betraying her indifference. You're on your own now, Robert, her attitude said more clearly than words. Sort yourself out. Like a wounded bull he held his ground while the pain soaked through him like blood.

In the study he gave himself up at last to the full horror of his feelings. Murray gone . . . Murray, who had offered him his one chance of piercing this darkness. Murray, who had already restored to him the most precious and most painful piece of knowledge of his whole life, the remembrance of Ally. Murray, who alone had held the key to his mind, that box with a broken hinge whose contents were yet so vital to his hopes of peace, his future, his sanity.

And Murray – in all this terrible time his one friend – the one soul in the world in whom he had dared to confide, dared to be himself, dared to stop being the great Dean Maitland and make an attempt on the far harder task of thinking and living like Robert, an ordinary, sinful man . . .

Murray gone.

He bowed his head on his arms, and wept.

The Deanery next day was a house of mourning in a gloomy world, the sadness within a perfect mirror of the heavy grey skies outside. Overhead clouds of gun-metal gloom brooded with a fearful expectancy, threatening every moment to open up and deluge the world below, then as if changing their minds, wallowing off in elephantine flirtatiousness at the behest of every mean and ragged mare's tail of a wind. It was a day to be unhappy in. And nothing else was on offer to all three inmates of the Deanery now.

In the early morning light filtering through the kitchen window, Claire's petal-soft face was grey with fatigue, not simply tiredness but the nausea of complete exhaustion. It had been almost dawn before she had felt it would be all right to leave Joan – before the troubled whimperings, the heavings of her body and feverish gestures of her hands had subsided into an apparently dreamless sleep. Her own sleep when it came had been patchy and troubled, and hours too short. Now she desperately needed a cup, or more likely a pot of good strong coffee to help her face the day. She reached for the percolator, and did not hear the soft approaching footsteps coming down the stairs.

'Morning, Claire.'

Claire started violently. 'Joan! What are you doing down here? You should be in bed!'

'I'm all right.'

Claire looked at her anxiously 'I was going to come up and peep at you as soon as I'd had a cup of coffee. Surely you ought to be back upstairs? Go on – I'll make you a breakfast tray and bring it up.'

'I'm all right.'

Amazingly, thought Claire with relief, it seemed to be true. Joan stood before her fully dressed and although pale, was looking once again as if she were in control. Only now did Claire acknowledge to herself how frightening it had been to see Joan, Joan of all people, grovelling over the bidet as she punished her thighs, her stomach, her breasts with violent scrubbing. But today the fever had obviously subsided – no more vomiting like last night either, or I'd have heard her, Claire told herself, ticking Joan's complaints off her mental checklist – and the sleep she's had must really have done her good. Also, the stuff from the doctor probably helped – just fantastic, what they can do with drugs these days!

Marvelling and thankful, Claire busied about the newly recovered patient. 'Coffee? And could you fancy a plain piece of toast, just something to put into your stomach? It'd be a good idea to take the edge off your hunger, but you don't want to overload yourself . . .'

White but composed, Joan lowered herself carefully into a chair beside the kitchen-table, and accepted a cup of coffee. Tactfully accepting that her sister-in-law did not want to talk, Claire concentrated on trying to make cheerful conversation and ministering to her needs. As she served up the slices of toast, Claire caught sight of the clock. 'Look at the time! Almost nine o'clock! I must get dressed. I've got a meeting at ten, then another at twelve about the Charity Gala tonight – God help us if it doesn't live up to its expectations in raising funds, they're all counting on that! – and I've got all the minutes to see to first . . .' Housecoat flapping, she rushed out of the kitchen. As she did so, the telephone rang in the hall. 'Could you get that, Joan?' she called. 'If I have to stop and take it, I'm going to make myself late, I know I am!'

Stiffly Joan pushed herself up from her seat and made her way into the hall. She picked up the receiver, then turned from it in a violent spasm as she realised who the caller was.

'Hello, Joanie.'

She could not speak.

'Just called t'see how you're doing this morning. You looked a bit peaky after – after last night.' He chuckled, a gross, greasy sound. 'It gets better, y'know.'

'Mick—' It killed her to say his name. But she had to know. 'What went wrong?'

'What went wrong?' She could almost see his mock-mystification, the piggy eyes rolling in affected innocence. 'Why, nothing. Nothing went wrong. Not as far as I can see.'

'But—' Words and reproaches were bubbling in her throat too fast for her to get them out. 'It's not what I wanted! Not what – we agreed!' Frantically she cast a glance up the stairs. But she could hear that Claire was safely out of earshot in the shower. 'I didn't want him dead! Not killed! Just – out of circulation for a bit! Time – that's all I asked you for, a bit of time – a breathing space . . .'

'Yeah, well, y'got a bit more than you bargained for all round, eh, Joanie?' Again the glugging laugh. She was burning inside, in the deep core of her sex and in her soul.

'Time—'

'Got plenty now. All you want.'

'If I'd had any idea—'

'Oh come on, Miss Maitland! I think you got what

410

you really wanted. In every sense of the word . . .' His every intonation was like a groping hand. What could she say? Self-satisfaction oozed from his voice. 'To me, now, it was a nice tidy job. Very professional. Object accomplished, and no loose ends left over to come back and make any trouble. What did you expect? You're playing with the big boys now, Joanie. Big boys' games.'

Her gorge began to heave, and the mouthful of coffee she had taken boiled up biliously at the back of her mouth.

'And y'got yourself a big boy last night, didn't you, Joanie? A nice big one? You liked it really, didn't you, I can tell. An' so did I. I liked it a lot. You know what?'

She knew.

'We're going to have to have ourselves a return match, Joanie. We make a good pair, you and me. What y'doing on Friday night?'

She opened her mouth, but almost nothing emerged. 'Out.'

'Oh, I don't think so, Joanie.' He sounded almost regretful at having to rewrite her social diary. 'I think you'll be free for me. After all, we're – partners now, aren't we? Why don't you hold yourself, as they say, in readiness? I'll see how I'm fixed for time, then I'll call you. See ya, Joan.'

'Who was on the phone?'

Preoccupied with struggling into her cardigan as she ran downstairs, Claire did not notice Joan's face or her demeanour. Before she could pay attention either to her sister-in-law or to the unnatural silence that had followed her question, the doorbell rang.

'Oh, who can that be?' she cried in vexation. 'I can see that I'll never get out this morning!'

She ran to the door and opened it. Wringing her hands on the doorstep, the picture of woe, stood the curate's little wife, Patsy Wright.

'Patsy!'

'Hello, Mrs Maitland.'

'Well, step in a moment, out of the cold. What can we do for you?'

411

'It's about Dr Beilby.' As Patsy stepped through the door, Claire saw to her surprise that she had been crying. 'Geoffrey sent me. He thought we ought to ask the Dean if he thinks there ought to be a memorial service.'

'I don't know – but I expect so,' said Claire, frowning. 'Murray was a very important man in Sydney, and well-known after so many years in practice here – people will want to pay their last respects. But I don't think Robert's had time to think about it yet – he's been so shocked.'

'Well, so were we!' trembled Patsy, her eyes beginning to fill up again. 'You know how much Dr Beilby did for the old people at Allambie, when Geoffrey was first curate there. And afterwards, he kept a lot of them on as private patients for nothing when the hostel was pulled down, wouldn't dump them even after the Church stopped paying him for their treatment.'

'I didn't know that,' said Claire slowly.

'He was a good man. He only wanted to help people. And now this has to happen to him!'

Something – a poisonous cocktail of guilt, grief and disgust – was gnawing away intolerably in Joan's guts. She turned to make her escape.

'Oh, Miss Maitland, I didn't see you there at the back of the hall!' Seeing Joan, Patsy coloured like a schoolgirl. She had never forgotten Joan's stinging rebuke to her on the afternoon of the tea-party at Allambie, when she had been unwise enough to let that Ellen pump her up with all the gossip about the Dean and Mrs Maitland's brother. But even Patsy could see that Miss Maitland had other things on her mind today. 'You don't look very well, Miss Maitland. Are you OK?'

Claire saw the chance to kill two birds with one stone. 'She's had a virus, a very nasty one, and though she's a lot better today, I still think she should take care. Look, Patsy, I've got to get the minutes ready for the Wives' Fellowship at ten; I expect you're on your way there, too. Why don't you slip your coat off and make a cup of tea for yourself and Joan here while I pop off and sort myself out, then we can go to the meeting together, OK?'

Nervously Patsy shepherded the pale and rigid Joan

412

into the kitchen. 'Don't mind about me, Miss Maitland, I'll just make myself at home and have a poke around till I've found everything. Kettle on first anyway, that's easy enough, isn't it?'

Nerves or not, Patsy was one of nature's tea-makers, and the soothing repetition of the eternal ritual soon began to restore her confidence. 'You don't mind me making tea in your kitchen? Well, if you do, you've only got to say. I only just dropped in for a second, didn't mean to invite myself in. Still, a cup of tea's always welcome any time of the day, isn't it?' Garrulity came naturally to Patsy: whatever the occasion, she firmly believed, a bit of chatter always helped to fill the gaps.

Poor old Miss Maitland certainly looked as if she could do with a cup of tea, if not something a great deal stronger. She's obviously taken the news hard, Patsy clucked to herself. 'Terrible about Dr Beilby, isn't it? Do you think they'll have to cancel the Gala now, as a mark of respect? He wasn't in those big society circles though, was he? More of a private person, really.'

'Mmmm.'

'And his poor wife! Did you know they were due to have their thirty-fifth wedding anniversary this Christmas? She's beside herself, they say.'

'Oh . . .'

'And such a pity about all his patients! They all loved him so much. And it's not like an ordinary doctor, is it? You can't just switch yourself over to someone else in the middle of that – that kind of treatment.' She pushed a steaming cup of tea in the direction of Joan's frozen-looking hands. 'How's the Dean going to manage?'

'*The Dean*?'

Patsy coloured violently at the sudden response. Oh God, she panicked, have I put my foot in it again? 'Yes, well, we thought – er, I said to Geoffrey, poor Dean Maitland, right in the middle of his treatment and all—'

Joan's cold hand fell like a claw on her arm. '*How did you know*?'

Patsy trembled. 'I've seen him coming out of Dr Beilby's office! And I didn't know it was supposed to be

413

a secret!' She blinked nervously, and scrabbled for a placatory reply. 'You know I'd never gossip, never let anything personal get around, about the Dean, I mean.'

Silence. The staring figure hanging on to her arm was clearly not convinced. Patsy went into overdrive.

'That's why when I was out the other day with Geoffrey and we saw him with that girl, I said to him, we'd better not let this get about, Geoffrey. I mean I'm sure there wasn't anything in it, but you know how people talk and clergymen are fair game for gossip, I mean, they have to set an example, they should do, anyway, even if they don't, shouldn't they, oh I don't mean the Dean . . . you know what I mean . . . Anyway I said to him, never let me see you driving around like that with a girl, Geoffrey, even if it is all on church business—'

'*What girl*?'

'The girl I saw with the Dean!' Patsy was babbling now, hardly aware of what she said. 'Well, I'm sure she was a friend of the family or something, or a parishioner anyway – she was just a girl, a young girl, I hardly noticed her!'

She's lying! thought Joan in anguish. She must have noticed her, noticed everything about her! A nosey little cow like her could have given me a description of this – this girl that would put Sherlock Holmes to shame! But she won't tell me a word now I've frightened her off like this. New tack, quickly, come on.

'What were they doing?'

'Oh, nothing really, nothing!'

The look of pure hatred that flashed from Joan's eyes at this point galvanised Patsy at least into partial recall.

'Well, they were driving along, out by Double Bay, laughing and . . . and friendly-like, you know,' she finished quickly. 'Like I said to Geoffrey, I'm sure it's all above board, but people can make so much out of nothing, can't they? You have to be so careful. Especially when it's the Dean, such an important person, and so well known, him having been on the telly and all. I said to Geoffrey, you'd better get into the habit of being careful now, my lad, so that when you're as famous as the Dean. . . .'

Sick in heart and mind, Robert had woken that morning as everyone does after a death, to a world grown colder. Slipping out of bed in an ominous grey dawn, he showered quickly and unable to contemplate breakfast, hastened to the refuge of his study. Hours passed, as it seemed, without his awareness, hours of loneliness so bleak and so complete he could scarcely tolerate the company of his own soul. In time he could hear the household begin to stir, normally a welcome and cheery sound to the early, solitary riser. Now he had no desire whatsoever to hurry into the kitchen for a friendly cup of coffee and the comforting ritual of early-morning chat.

Yet what else was he to do? From his vantage point, the day stretched ahead like a desert, arid and unending, one vast emptiness. He forced himself to consult his appointments book. Its days and weeks of times and places, all neatly entered, were nothing to him now, meaningless hieroglyphics, the merest scratchings. He knew that whatever else he was capable of right now, he could not lose himself in a round of mindless busyness – he could hardly even decide which day it was. And how could he face the Charity Gala – was that tonight? How would he force himself to go glad-handing round the leaders of Sydney society, carefully cultivating the rich and charming their wives simply to ensure another boost to the Cathedral coffers?

As ever, his thoughts turned towards the girl without any conscious design, quietly and inevitably. Suddenly it seemed to him that he could get through anything if only he could be cheered by the sight of her face, her bright hair like a beacon in any darkness, or buoyed up by the reassurance of her sturdy common sense and untainted honesty.

As he sat there, the heard voices in the hall.

'Bye then!'

'Goodbye.'

'Bye, Miss Maitland – hope you feel better soon.'

Claire was leaving, going off to her meeting, taking with her Patsy Wright, the early visitor whose incessant babble had reached him even here, in the solitude of the study.

'And you'll go back to bed, Joan? You promise you'll look after yourself?'

'Yes – yes. I promise.'

The door slammed, and Joan's footsteps, heavier than usual, ascended the stairs. Joan had taken herself back to bed to nurse her virus. He was alone. And there was only one thing he wanted to do.

Abstractedly he got into his car, and took the road out of the city to the suburbs. Lost in thought, it never occurred to him to look in his driving-mirror. Already he was looking forward, not behind, already beginning to picture his first sight of Emma, her surprise when she saw him, her readiness, he hoped, for a day out – a treat, a ride, a picnic, or simply just a long, slow, rambling walk talking of everything and nothing. As he thought of her, his face gradually lost its intensity of grief, and began to soften with the healing balm of affection.

What kind of affection? a voice inside him cried. Better get this whole thing sorted out! You're on your own now! But he slammed the door on its demands. He'd think about that tomorrow – he'd have to face up to the whole thing in time, and yes, he knew, on his own, with no more Murray to help him through.

Ally too – he still had to come to terms with the knowledge of that relationship, so long buried that now he seemed to be feeling again in all its primal intensity the love he had first had for her, all its wild delight, all its utter innocence, all its grief, and all the pain of its loss. What kind of a priest must I have been then? he wondered. What kind of a husband? What kind of a *man*? And have I learned from all that? Have I changed? Or did the fact that it all became buried and forgotten by the accident in the mine mean that it all went underground, and taught me nothing?

There was so much still to be done, he knew it.

But not now.

For now it was enough that he would see her, be with her, very soon – soon now, soon.

416

At last, his battered heart reviving under a pure stream of joy, he pulled up outside the café and drawn by a glimpse of the angel hair through the steamed-up glass, hurried inside. At no point during any of this or the day of innocent fun that followed did he ever become aware, even for a moment, of the car that dogged his every move that day, leaving him only just in time to head back for the city in order to arrive before he did, and make it look as if it had never been away.

Chapter 34

Be nice to the people.

It's part of the job.

Because if you don't, they won't give you the money you need.

Wondering how and when, without even noticing it he had become so cynical, Robert glanced unseeing into the dressing-table mirror in the bedroom as he mentally rehearsed the evening ahead. The unsmiling reflection confronting him was that of a very handsome man, his attraction sharpened, not diminished, by the keen, searching look in his eye, the lean, spare, unselfconscious regard with which he bleakly favoured his mirror image. But he was the last man in the world to take any satisfaction from his own appearance. Fastening the stud at the neck of his dress shirt, he began the ritual struggle with his bow tie, and with the never-ending train of his thoughts.

How was Joan? Would she be well enough to make it to the Gala tonight? Uneasily his fingers worried away at the recalcitrant silk, rejecting his first attempt and beginning afresh. And what was the matter with her anyway? She had never, in all their lives together before, been ill – or failed to appear at his side on any important occasion.

And what about Claire? Could he count on her any longer? Like Joan, she had always been there for him, with him, beside him, ready for anything – again, until tonight. But these days somehow, they had grown so apart. Yet for all his concern for Emma, his obsession with her, with the past, and with the lost girl Ally whose mystery double she had turned out to be, he had never,

Robert felt, loved Claire as much as he did now. Where was he going wrong? How – why – was he letting her slip away from him? When would he find his way through this maze? And when – Oh God, when? – would he learn to tie a bow tie? Again and again the slippery silk made a fool of fingers that were beginning to feel like sausages. He fought back a strong temptation to curse.

'You ready?'

Intimidatingly groomed from head to foot, Claire swept into the bedroom and out again. Her swishing, filmy gown was wonderful, the diaphanous matching evening cloak shimmering from her shoulders even more so. What colour would she call it? Blue? Purple? Hyacinth? Whatever it was, it brought out to perfection the colour of her eyes, still the hazy blue of bluebell woods in spring, setting off her porcelain skin just as he first remembered it on the beach at Brightstone. And that rich, rustling sound! Was it silk? Where did she get it? Or when? A confused emotion crept over him as he realised it could well be an outfit that Claire had had for some time, and he had never even noticed it before. Surely not! Oh, Claire, if it is, I'll make it up to you, as soon as this is over, he promised silently. Another wry thought struck him. If it's new, Claire, it looks like a million dollars. Even on a dean's stipend, tell me, darling – how did we afford it?

Money, money, money – he was obsessed with it. That's what comes of having to attend charity galas to raise money for the church, he brooded – nothing was more calculated to make anyone aware of the bottomless pit of human misery that the church was so desperately attempting to bail out. There was just too much, even if all the millionaires in Australia – and there were a lot of millionaires in Australia – put their hands in their pockets. Too much misery. Too much. Too much.

And how hard it was on these occasions, fresh from Allambie as it used to be, from the Single Mothers' Home, or some druggies' last resting-place, to feel any sympathy with the fat cats! They made themselves feel so good, turning out once a year for a big charity do, when they themselves had never had to put up with anything less than total comfort and luxury every moment of their waking lives. And then to be expected to be so charming to them all, expressing gratitude for every crumb that fell from the rich ones' table! Had he really been called to this as the purpose of his life? Or had he come to it by default, through the lack of some other overriding ambition or true vocation? Sooner or later – and let it be soon! he ordered his grimly concentrating double in the mirror – he had to answer these questions, face up to the challenges surfacing every day now from every corner of his mind.

And still the bow tie refused to be tied.

'You ready?' came Claire's call again, from the hall this time.

'I'll be down in a minute,' he replied, wondering how far that was from the truth.

'Need a hand?'

'Suddenly Joan was there, rustling through the door armoured and whaleboned in black satin from head to foot. Her face was very pale, and her eyes seemed unnaturally bright, but she brushed aside all his questions and expressions of concern.

'Me? I'm fine, never felt better.' He did not believe it. But he could see there was no point in arguing.

For Joan was somehow beyond his reach, in a reality all her own. Like Claire, she was wearing clothes he had never seen before. She seemed to prance unnaturally on her high-heeled evening shoes like an overbred mare, and the whiteness of her face shone even through an elaborate formal make-up.

She looked different – she was different. 'Hello, stranger!' she said, flashing him a vivid smile. 'Had a good day?' The simple question was somehow loaded with meaning, if the harsh accompanying stare was anything to go by. But she did not allow him a moment to respond. Her practised fingers pounced on his tie, tore his feeble effort at a bow to pieces and began plaiting and weaving with manic intensity. He wondered briefly if she were completely herself after her illness. Her next

421

words instantly disillusioned him of that possibility. 'I just asked you – *busy day*?'

His stomach contracted a little. He did not want to have to start lying about Emma, about the day he had spent with her. 'So-so.'

Another brilliant smile, from an uncomfortable close-up now. 'I was looking for you.'

What could she mean? 'Were you?'

She adopted a strange, sing-song voice. 'I had the feeling you were avoiding me.'

He could feel the back of his neck beginning to prickle. 'Why should I do that?'

The claws working away at his neck gave a savage tug. 'You tell me, Robert, you tell me.'

He had to get on top of this. 'You nearly done? Claire's waiting. It's time to go.'

The silk round his neck suffered a yank that would have destroyed a weaker fabric. 'Tie's finished. I'm ready. Let's go.' Solicitously she helped him on with his jacket and brushed an imaginary spot or two from his shoulder. 'You're all set, Robert. And don't you look good!' Again the flashing smile, which dropped away like a mask as she drew near to him again. 'But I'm not done yet,' she whispered. 'Some time this evening – *you and I have to have a little talk, OK*?'

'Dean Maitland! So good of you to come!'

'We were delighted, Claire and I – and you know my sister, Miss Joan Maitland?'

'Of course! Delighted! Wonderful! So good of you to come!'

Of course he knew who she was. She was one of the premier hostesses of Sydney. Her parties were spectacular, her galas legendary. She was a personal friend of Nancy Reagan, Elizabeth Taylor and Prince Charles – and although she hadn't seen so much of Imelda Marcos recently since Imelda's unfortunate little spot of bother, she was getting very chummy with the Jaggers now Mick had got so sociable, and especially Jerry Hall. Madonna had promised to be here tonight if she could possibly

422

make it. And Prince was doing the cabaret. At least Prince. Maybe somebody better . . .

Friend and facilitator to the all-celebrity circuit of the great wide world, that's who this woman was. Her house, one of the few of Sydney's legendary old houses still remaining in private hands, was a little palace, its magnificent drawing-room, banqueting hall, reception-rooms and conservatory frequently thrown open for the Church's benefit on charity occasions where he'd often seen her before. So why couldn't he remember her name?

Not that it mattered. Like all such affairs, this was a *bal masqué* – nobody showed their true face. To show your hand would have been regarded as an even worse breach of form, far more dreadful than displaying more intimate parts of the anatomy. He could see that Joan had adopted the rules of the game – she was not going to show her hand. She was simply going to play with him – and wait.

The hostess, resplendent in a bosom's worth of dia-monds and a designer creation of mauve and magenta wild silk was breathing in his ear now. 'Dean Maitland – fantastic effort, best ever! So much money raised by the sale of the tickets alone tonight, and still all the fund-raising activities to come. The Ladies' Committee have really excelled themselves in getting all this together – I'll have to spirit you away to thank them all in person later on – but it looks as if your pet project St Matthew's will be OK now, plus one or two other little things the Church might have set its heart on!'

'Yes, yes. Excellent! Tremendous. Wonderful. Mar-vellous. So grateful.'

He was running out of superlatives. But even at the very beginning, he knew, he did not sound convincing. The hostess swished away. Robert looked round for Claire, detained a moment ago by Bessie Maddox. Nei-ther woman had forgotten or forgiven the destruction of the Allambie hostel for the elderly, and both, he knew, cherished the dream that they could somehow find another house where they could reunite that pathetic, dispersed community of homeless souls once more under one roof. Well, it was far from impossible. He'd have to see what he could do to. Across the room he caught sight of the chairman of the Civic Trust. A word in that direction, now the dust of this last dispute had settled, might be a good idea. Worth a try, anyway.

Before he could make a move, Joan was at his side, and following the line of his gaze. 'Wonder what they'd think?' she remarked conversationally.

He could feel the menace in her voice without even looking at her. He met the challenge head on. 'What are you talking about?'

'What they'd think – if you'd be such a big man, in the Cathedral or anywhere else – such a big hero – if they found out?'

'Joan – don't play games with me! Found out what?'

She smiled at him, the smile of a Gorgon. 'Now wouldn't that be telling!'

The cat plays with the live mouse, it is said, not from sadism, but to soften all the sinews and muscles for greater ease and pleasure of the final consumption. By the end of the evening, Robert thought grimly, he would need all his strength not to be reduced to jelly through tension and fear. He had made every effort to challenge and confront his sister during the rare breaks in his pre-arranged evening's work, meeting and mingling with the people for whose benefit the Gala had been arranged. And still Joan played her game with him, a game whose rules only she appeared to know and whose outcome would be decided only when she tired of it.

All night he pursued her, trying to pin her down. All night she evaded him with a hideous kind of coquettish-ness, alternately beckoning him on and then when he thought he had caught her, slipping the leash to dance with this one, charm that one, or remind the other that his cheque for the St Matthew's project was still awaited.

Only when he gave up the chase did she at last seek him out where he leaned against a pillar in the hall, feeling like Samson in the temple and wondering just how much strength it would take to bring the whole edifice of corruption and indulgence down on to their vain, godless heads. Some of the manic glitter had gone out of her, and when she spoke, she came, like the old Joan, straight to the point.

'You're finished, Robert. It's all up.'

'What are you talking about?'

Joan let a silence pass before she spoke again.

'The girl.'

'OK, Joan – so what?' He could not think of Emma and Joan together, could not speak of them in the same breath.

'I saw you today!'

'Today?'

'I followed you. When you drove out to the café to see her. I watched you go in. I saw everything you did – all day long.' Suddenly her face changed. '*Did Murray know*?'

'For God's sake, Joan – what the hell has that got to do with it?'

'What does she want?' She gripped him by the arm.

'What are you talking about?'

'Is it blackmail?' She was gabbling now, her mouth working with emotion.

He was lost. 'Joan – why on earth should she blackmail me?'

'*I saw her face!* It's Ally Calder's! What's she doing back here? *She's dead! She's dead! She's dead!*'

Fortunately no one around in the crowded ballroom seemed to make out the precise words. But the noise Joan made, a high-pitched scream followed by a moaning which subsided into a kind of swoon, brought several concerned people to his side. 'My sister is not well,' Robert said crisply to the nearest woman. 'Could someone find my wife and ask her to come to us?'

With the help of various good Samaritans, Joan was resting now on a providential chair in an alcove away from the hurly-burly of the ballroom and also out of earshot of the concerned but curious bystanders who had arrived to help at the time of crisis, and now lingered to enjoy it. Carefully Robert shielded her from the rest of the party by leaning over her in apparent concern and blocking her from their view. Nothing could have been further from his thoughts than the desire to talk to her. But he could not prevent her from talking to him. 'Robert, Robert?' she muttered, clutching at the edge of his dinner-jacket, 'Listen to me, Robert! What are you playing at with this girl? We could lose everything!'

'Joan, the exact opposite of that is true. I think we stand to gain everything – everything we need to know.'

'You're making a fool of yourself – God, it's happened so many times before! A man of your age – sniffing round a girl of hers! It's disgusting! Can't you see how it would look? And Robert, you of all men – having an affair with a girl young enough to be your daughter!'

'Not true, Joan – simply not true.'

' – and with a kid who just happens to look like – like someone else —'

'You know that, don't you, Joan? You recognise her, too.'

'No! No! It's not true! It's just a middle-aged fantasy, you're just carried away by sex, you're dreaming it!'

He knelt before her and forced her to look into his eyes. 'Or remembering it, Joan?' he said very slowly.

'No! No! *No*!'

'Robert, whatever's the matter?'

Claire had arrived in a flurry of alarm. 'Darling, what's wrong? Are you ill?'

There was bleak satisfaction, he noted briefly, in the "darling" that had slipped from her when she thought something had happened to him. But there was no time to enjoy it.

'It's Joan, Claire. She's feeling rough. She's going home.'

'Oh, poor Joan!' Claire's attention immediately switched to the rigid figure in the chair, and throwing an arm around Joan's shoulders, she picked up one of the cold hands and began to chafe it. Claire's ready compassion would probably embrace a mass murderer on his way to the electric chair, Robert thought. But not me. She's had enough of me. His heart was burdened with almost more than he could bear. That Joan should have seen Emma – and having seen her, interpreted

426

what she had seen *in that way* . . . no, I can't bear that, he felt, I simply can't allow it to happen – even the chance of it, the danger . . . With difficulty he brought his mind back to Joan. 'I'll get her coat and take her home straight away. Just hold on here a second while I organise all this and get a taxi.'

'I'll drive you back.'

'Don't be silly, Robert.' The moment of warmth had passed. Claire's voice had taken on all the impersonality of a complete stranger. 'You've got to give the major speech before the presentation of the prizes. And there are still masses of people you need to be nice to here tonight. You haven't finished your night's work. I'll see you back home when it's all over.'

When it's all over . . .

All over . . .

It's over, it's over, it's over . . .

Drearily Robert sat in the car outside Emma's lodging-house. It was well past midnight and he should be anywhere but here. Only the knowledge that the light was on in her room kept him still sitting there. But even though he knew she was still awake as he was, he did not want to knock on her door or try to see her so late at night. He had to talk to her. But it could be tomorrow. It would have to be, now. Better go home . . . clear out . . .

Suddenly the big front door of the old house opened and the youth Gary whom he had seen hanging around the café came out from the lighted hall with Emma. With a brief casual goodbye, he was gone. Getting out of his car as slowly as he dared to avoid attracting the attention of the retreating figure, Robert approached the flight of stone steps just as she was closing the door.

'Emma!'

'My God! What are you doing here?' With one glance she took in both his evening dress and the expression of his face and body. 'Party, huh? And not much fun by the look of it?'

427

'What was he doing here? That boy Gary? At this time of night?'

Her face flamed. 'None of your damn business!'

'I saw the way he looked at you.'

'So?'

'He's half my age. Probably younger.'

'What's that got to do with anything? He's just a friend! Nothing more than that. He's been taking pictures of me – he's a photographer – and we're working on – on a project together. Not that I have to account for myself or my friends to you!'

He felt terrible. His head, which had been pounding without mercy ever since Joan had dropped the bombshell of her revelation, rose to a higher level of intensity, like a silent scream. Her face and manner changed abruptly. 'Hey, you look bad. Would you like a cup of tea before you've got to drive back?'

'No – no. I've got to go.'

She took it with the easy casualness of the young. 'OK.' She opened the front door. 'See you, then. My half day's Wednesday this week. If you're around, we could—'

'Emma, I – I'm going away. I – came to say goodbye.'

She jumped to his meaning with the speed of a cat. 'Goodbye? You mean – *for good*?'

He nodded. He didn't trust himself to speak.

'What's wrong with me? We haven't done anything bad! Why shouldn't I see you?' Her voice was raw with tears. He never thought he could have caused her such pain.

'I had – an insight tonight – into how this must look to outsiders. Look at me. I'm old enough to be your father, you're a young girl here on your own, ripe to be – taken advantage of.'

'But it's not like that! And it never would be!'

'We know that. But we can't expect the world to see it.'

'I don't care!'

'Well, I have to care for both of us. And I have other things to worry about, too. My sister knows I've been seeing you. She tackled me with it tonight. She won't tolerate anything she doesn't approve of, or understand. It'll only be a matter of time before she starts threatening me, blackmailing me about it if I don't give you up now, immediately. It's all tied in together – you – me – us . . .'

The words filled his mouth like ashes, and clogged his speech, his thoughts. Did he really mean this? And what of her, this child of his heart, this changeling, this – this – this what? What was she to him? Or he to her? Like a drowning man, he struggled on.

'And I'm a married man. I love my wife, I wouldn't want to expose her to any—'

'That never stopped you before!' She was screaming now, the tears rolling down her cheeks in pain and fury. 'You bastard! You self-satisfied bastard! Is that what you told her, is that what you told Ally Calder, all that lying crap?'

'No!'

'You expect me to believe that?'

'Yes! It was different – with her!'

'Why? What's wrong with me? I wouldn't ever embarrass you. I just want to see you a bit. What's wrong with that?'

'Nothing.'

'I'm not her. I can't help that. Why don't you love me?'

She was crying like a child, but with the bitter defeatism of an adult. He had never felt more of a fool, a fraud and a wrecker of all that was good and beautiful. 'Look, it's my fault. I started this. I should have known better. Just – seeing you brought it all back. But it was wrong. I was wrong, not you. I'm terribly sorry. I'll go now.'

He moved to the door. 'A key to your past, was that all I was to you?' she demanded, her face blistered with tears. 'What about the future, Robert? My future? Don't you care?'

Moving like a condemned man, he let himself out of the door and walked down the steps.

'Don't go!' she cried. 'Please! Don't leave me! Don't walk away from me like this!'

But he kept walking till he reached his car, then he

kept driving all the way back to the house, and never once did he yield to his heart's pulsing command, 'Turn back! *Turn back*!'

Love, love and pain – where did one end and the other begin? Drained of all sensation, empty of all feeling and knowledge, Robert hit the freeway driving fast and carelessly, but even so, even with frequent brushes with danger serious enough to raise the hair on the back of his neck, he could not still the endless punishing rat-race of his thoughts. How blindly he had been coasting along on the thin surface of his recent happiness with Emma! How foolish to think that such a fragile thing could have a long life or growth! And how swiftly, how easily Joan had moved in with her unerring killer instinct to blight it, and to destroy!

Blind . . . blind . . . blind . . .

When – how – would he ever learn? This was the Ally story all over again – with this difference, that this time he was truly innocent before God of any sin, or even the slightest thought of sinning. His feelings for Emma, he would pawn his soul to prove at the bar of almighty judgement even on the day of doom, were all pure, were all protectiveness, all love.

Yet in the end, what difference did that make? He forced himself to try to work it out. Confront your fears, that was the only way. And begin at the beginning. Well, let's start with the basics, then. 'It's all sex, you're just carried away by sex!' Joan had said. He gave a sardonic laugh. That says more about you, Joanie, than me! he thought. He knew he did not desire Emma physically.

You thought that at first about Ally, too, came the cold voice of his conscience.

This *is* – was – different!

How? You loved Ally, you loved Emma, you longed to see them, you wanted to take care of them, yes?

Yes!

So where's the difference, holy man? sneered the chief of his demons. Wouldn't it be only a matter of time before you would be kissing those soft young lips, learning the touch of her small, sweet breasts, her hips, her unawakened thighs . . .

No! No, no, no!

Almost sick with self-disgust, he drove his foot down harder on the accelerator and pushed on. Outside the car window a moonless sky loured over an unhappy world. Ahead of him the clouds clustering on the far horizon were slashed by bars of angry red. Dawn already. But no new dawn for me. The grim refrain of loss and failure played its way into his head, and went round again and again and again.

Heavily he let himself into the house and mounted the stairs to the bedroom. Perhaps he could still snatch an hour or two of sleep before he had to start the day . . . And he would make it a new start, he promised himself, catch up on all the Cathedral duties he had so badly neglected, above all set about making everything come right with Claire . . .

There was a light on in the bedroom as he entered. Across the room Claire sat erect on the upright chair before her dressing-table, regarding him with a cold, fixed stare – of what? Dislike? She had obviously been up for some time, and waiting for him to come in.

'Why don't you tell me what's going on, Robert?' she began without preamble. 'All this time – I could at least have tried to help.'

He groped for something to say. 'It's all under control.'

'Oh, Robert . . .'

At what point, he wondered, had he thrown away the regard she used to have for him, a reverence almost, that used to make her hang on his words, accept all his sayings as gospel and set about implementing them with uncritical enthusiasm? The look she gave him now would have frozen hell.

'You – you've got enough on your plate just now,' he struggled lamely. 'With your mother's death – and Paul . . .'

She did not even bother to answer this. 'You've got someone else, haven't you?' she said quietly.

'No!'

'Robert, don't treat me like a child.' She was terrifyingly calm. 'You both do it, you and Joan. I know that she's concerned about something to do with you. She won't talk about it either. You must both think I'm very stupid.'

'No . . .'

'As if I didn't know! Look, Robert, I'm not going to play the wronged wife. I'm not going to grill you about where you've been till all hours, last night, and the night Murray died – and other times too – you know all this – and it's all too – horrible.'

Only the slight, halting interruptions to her speech gave any hint of the stress she was feeling. Evenly she went on. 'I'll just say one thing. You must have noticed this yourself. Robert, we're getting further and further apart. You're living a separate life—'

'There's no one else!' he interrupted wildly. She ignored him.

'And I'm not prepared to put up with it any longer. You're lying to me, and you're avoiding me, and I can't bear it. I've also come to the point where I've realised that I don't have to. I don't think my marriage vows committed me to going on living in a dead relationship with a man who has stopped even pretending to be a husband to me.'

What was she saying? Furiously he fought to get his mind round her meaning.

'When you come back from Brightstone—' Brightstone! Dear God, he'd completely forgotten he was going down for the service of commemoration for the re-opening of the mine '—we'll have to sit down and work out the arrangements—'

'Arrangements?' Panic seized him, and he began to babble. 'Claire, there's nobody else. Listen to me, I'm telling you the truth! There's nobody but you. There never has been. Believe me! Please!'

'Robert – *I want a divorce*.'

Chapter 35

To Brightstone.

What else did life have to throw at him now?

For Brightstone was the last place in the world he wanted to be.

Everything had begun in Brightstone, the whole story – and everything had started to go wrong there. Everything bad had come from Brightstone, and had happened in Brightstone. And still the bloody place had not finished with him – with them! Still he had to leave Claire at this crisis of their marriage to be back there for the service to commemorate the men who had died and for the celebrations for the re-opening of the mine. After this time, Robert vowed, nothing will ever get me to Brightstone again – wild horses won't drag me there! Yet even as he made this most solemn pledge to himself, somewhere in the silence of his soul a stray thought took root. This was no casual visit. This was his past rearing up to confront his present, forcing him to confront himself, and every truth he had been avoiding or denying all his adult life. If everything had started there in Brightstone – could it all somehow, even now, be ended, made right in Brightstone?

In a tense silence Joan drove him to the station under the uncertain sky of a wretched, overcast day. He felt ragged with anxiety and lack of sleep, for the shock of Claire's demand for a divorce had put any ideas of grabbing an hour or two's rest quite out of court. Yet even in the long discussion that followed he had made no headway against Claire's decision that their marriage was over. All he had wrung from her was the promise not to move out until he got back from Brightstone, and

433

had the chance to talk to her properly. And it's going to have to be good! he told himself sardonically. Because ou'll be fighting for her love, and your life – pretty high stakes!

He threw a sideways glance across the car. It would be useless even to think of sharing any of this with Joan, he thought. How he could bear her presence now, he hardly knew. How had she become so unfamiliar to him, so strange? The thin hands gripping the wheel, bony knuckles protruding, the harsh voice and aggressively staring eyes, the thin, sour stale of distress emanating from her, all these he saw for the first time, and his heart grieved for the girl she had been, for the sister he had lost. Oh Joan – what has happened to you? To us? To us all?

At last they were pulling into the station. Unnervingly Joan affected a false brightness, for all the world as if he were off on a pleasure trip. 'Lucky you! Have a good time! Try and get some fun before the service.'

He hoped his reply did not sound sarcastic. 'I'll try.'

'I'll park and come into the station, get you something to read for the train—'

'Please – don't bother.'

'Not even a magazine?'

She was like a child deprived of a sweet. He leaned forward and looked her in the eye. 'No, Joan,' he said, as levelly as he could. 'Not even a magazine.'

She coloured violently. 'No call for you to get nasty!' she said wildly. 'I haven't done anything! It's you that's got us into this mess!'

He opened the car door. 'Well, I've also got us all out of it as well, you'll be pleased to hear.' He reached for his bag.

Her face flamed with hope. 'You mean . . . ?'

'It's over, that's what I mean.'

'You sure?'

'Joan, for God's sake! . . .'

She could not suppress the wild delight that filled her entire being. 'OK, OK! Well, you'll thank me for this one day!' she exulted. 'You'll be grateful! One day soon! And probably sooner than you think! I was talking to the Archbishop yesterday, and—'

'Joan—' He held the car door. 'Don't. Don't talk to anyone for me, or about me, ever again. I'm making my own decisions from now on. It's quite unlikely that they're going to lead me to become a prince of the Church. And it's more than unlikely that they will ever again feature you.' He closed the car door without violence. 'You're out of a job, Joan,' he said quietly to the white face, the furiously bulging eyes. 'Better start looking for another one.' Then he walked without a backward glance into the station.

Overland, the hard way, it was a long and painful journey. As the train powered forward mile after mile over the level inland plain, Robert knew that every inch of the journey was taking him back in time, back to Brightstone where it had all begun, and yet at the same time forward to the chance, however slight, that he could somehow translate all this into a better future, learn to live more truthfully, more openly, by the light of what he was now going through. No wonder he felt as if he were being peeled raw at every step of the way! A magazine? He did not need a magazine, when he had the whole book of his life to re-read, and so much of it to rewrite.

He dozed, but his sleep was fitful and unrefreshing, filled with phantoms which escaped from him the second he awoke, yet left him with a haunting sense of fear and loss. He knew that he had dreamed something important, yet he could not understand the message or even hang on to its tail. He knew he had to think about Claire – about his marriage – God, not about a divorce, whatever Claire said! – yet his mind constricted around these things like a dry, shrivelled walnut, and he could get no sense from it.

And how to cope with, or even begin on the hollow at his heart, the loss he felt at the idea of never seeing Emma any more? This, echoing the earlier loss of Ally so recently restored to him by Murray, burdened him with a dual weight of grief that he felt was more than flesh and blood could bear. In and out of troubled thought and tormented sleep he passed like a prisoner

435

under interrogation, yet came no nearer to the answers he had to seek.

Never-go-back, never-go-back, never-go-back chattered the wheels of the train. He smiled a grim smile. Wrong. Must go back. The secret of the future lies buried in the past. Without knowledge, without truth, the sins of the fathers are doomed to be visited on the children, world without end, amen.

Lord, I believe.

Help Thou my unbelief.

Grant us Thy peace.

It was not going to be easy. Simply arriving at Brightstone station in a mean autumn wind triggered a flood of painful memories of that earlier arrival in the hopeful spring of so many years ago: the welcoming committee led by the pompous mine boss Wilkes, George and Molly Everard brimming with joy at Claire's return, and Paul, dear Paul, in the pride of his youth and manhood roaring up in his beloved Dodge, the old 'Blue Streak'.

And where are we all now? he reflected with sardonic detachment. Wilkes, broken by the failure of the mine after the cave-in, forced to sell out to an international conglomerate which neither knew nor cared about the people of Brightstone, but was only interested in reopening the pit for pure profit. George and Molly, both gathered before their time to God, Molly's last years darkened by the worst blow a mother could be asked to bear, the living death of her only son. Paul . . . and Claire . . . Joan, too . . . and he had to include himself . . . all leading shadow lives, unreal distortions of what they ought to be, where they ought to be. Why? And could this attempt, however late in the day, to go back to the root of all the trouble, all the unhappiness, stand any chance of success?

'Dean Maitland!' The bright-faced young man in the dog-collar who bounded forward to take his bag was clearly quite overcome by the importance of the occasion and the eminence of his distinguished visitor. 'I'm Lindsay, sir, the circuit minister,' he said nervously. 'Brightstone's one of my parishes. Delighted to welcome you here. We're – we're honoured you could spare the time to come down for our service!'

'I wouldn't have missed it, Mr Lindsay,' Robert responded mechanically as the young man ushered him to his car. 'The old place – ' he caught his breath as the once-familiar scenes of Brightstone began to unroll all around him again ' – the old place used to be very dear to me. And I don't think I've forgotten too much of those times.'

'There's been just a bit of a query about your accommodation, Dean,' said Lindsey nervously. 'We got your request to be put up in the old Rectory, and everything's been made ready. But the Diocesan Council thought you'd be much more comfortable in the hotel. The Rectory's been empty for years now, ever since Brightstone stopped being a separate parish and was combined with the regional circuit.'

'I'm sure it'll be fine.'

'Well, the parish ladies keep it clean, of course, and they've been in this week to make up the bed and get a few supplies in for you. But the phone's not always what it might be up there these days, and the power supply's very dodgy, because we don't maintain those services as well as we used to any more – the expense . . .' frowning, he changed gear as the car began the slow climb up the headland. 'Are you sure you want to stay there, sir?'

'For old time's sake . . .'

At the Rectory, time itself had stood still. Like a dreamer Robert got out of the car, climbed the stone steps, pushed open the heavy door and went in. His escort, clearly relieved by the evidence of recent cleaning, the smell of furniture polish and the neatly made-up bed in the guest-room upstairs, bustled about checking everything that could be checked and finally announced his intention to depart and leave the Dean to his own devices. 'I should think you'll be glad of a rest this afternoon, Dean,' he said. 'There's food in the fridge, of course, and anything you want – my number's on the pad by the phone, just give us a shout. It's good that you were able to come down in advance of the service.

The commemoration Committee were wanting to have a word about the arrangements, but they'll be in touch. In the meantime, enjoy your stay!'

With a smile and a wave, Lindsay departed. Had he ever been that young, Robert wondered, that keen, that *green*? He must have been – more so, probably. And green or not, this young minister Lindsay had clearly not left behind him anything like the trail of wreckage Robert now felt had been his personal, painful legacy to all who had loved him, all whose lives had even touched his, over the last twenty years.

God, he'd better pull himself together or he'd be sounding like the Ancient Mariner, or some other ill-omened creature doomed to roam the seven seas in the torment of eternal self-pity! Time for some fresh air! A stiff, punishing walk down the headland brought him to the main street of Brightstone where the little town unfolded before him in the afternoon sun like a soiled and tattered ribbon, overworn and threadbare. He was perspiring now despite the autumn chill, the first real indication that winter was on its way, its storms and tempests very near at hand. But he was shivering too, a deep chill biting into his bones, into his soul.

His feet knew where he was making for before his mind acknowledged it. At the foot of the main street, in what he grimly recalled had always been 'the poorer part of town', the Paragon café was still open for business, still peddling milk sundaes to the town's disenchanted youth. He hesitated for only a moment outside on the pavement. Then he opened the door and went in.

'Coffee'r what?'

Another Greek held sway behind the counter, not Vic, but almost his clone. Polishing a glass with a greasy cloth he eyed Robert with just the same rank suspicion that his first-ever appearance here had provoked in Vic. The same sunlight streamed through the same window, hitting the same spot in the floor where she had stood . . .

At the back of the shop a young girl stepped into the sunlight and turned towards him. She was short and dark, with an expression of sulky boredom, and her face proclaimed a surly 'take-it-or-leave-it' attitude that she'd obviously had all her life. In her hands she held a dog-eared menu. She looked as if she couldn't care less if all the customers dropped dead there and then. Seeing a stranger, she stared at him as if he were a fool or a freak, or both.

Turning on his heel he left the café and went out into the street. Maybe he was a fool. What was he looking for, hoping for here? Whatever it was, he had better do a little more hard thinking before he went any further!

Suddenly a hard hand clapped him on the back. 'Well, look who's here! If it ain't the Dean himself!'

He turned. It was Mick Ford, attended by a group of cronies, all apparently miners, some of whom Robert recognised though he could not have given their names. 'Mick,' he said sardonically. 'Fancy seeing you here.'

'No surprise in that, Dean. I guess I'm here for the same thing as you. The mine re-opening's official business for me as well as you, you know. Someone's gotta keep an eye on the union side of the new arrangements. And who d'you think handled the negotiations?'

'Yes – of course. Well, it would be you, wouldn't it, Mick?'

Mick surveyed him narrowly, his quick sense of self-importance scenting a put-down. But before he could reply, they were interrupted.

'Hey, Mick—' It was a tall, thin young man standing behind the union boss. 'Introduce us, will you?'

'Sure thing!' Mick hastened to comply. 'Robert, this here's Dave Hastings, he's a TV producer doing a documentary on the re-opening of the mine. This is your man,' he said expansively to Hastings, waving a pudgy fist at Robert. 'This is the guy you want for a bit of drama in your coverage! "Hero of the Disaster", the Dean was. Rescued a load of the men. One of them almost at the cost of his own life – he nearly died down the mine himself, the Dean did. An' he's always on TV. He's a star already! He's the one they call "the Demo dean", remember him?'

'Yeah, sure thing.'

The television producer was looking at him with keen interest. 'No publicity, Mick,' Robert said firmly. 'I've got the service to concern myself with, and—'

'No publicity!' Mick Ford's fat, stubby body shook with derisive laughter. 'The world's press is descending on Brightstone for this jamboree, Dean! They're coming from as far away as Russia, it's such a good story! Your face'll be everywhere again, newspapers, telly, the lot, just the way it was before! You try and stop 'em!'

'Hey, what's the rush?'

Gary Yeats had never deceived himself that Emma cared for him in the slightest. Even so, he was hurt by the speed with which she snatched the package he was carrying from his hand as soon as he walked through the door of the cafe, and turned immediately to the nearest table without even the pretence of a hello. 'Get yourself a coffee if you like, Gary,' she said carelessly. 'I've spoken to Mr Gazouli. He doesn't mind just this once.'

Well, I do! Gary wanted to complain. But he feared her sharp little tongue, and even more he feared that if he ever made the slightest complaint about the way she treated him, that would be the last he would ever see of her. Wretchedly he shuffled off to the counter, grudgingly accepted the cup of unpalatable coffee that was even more grudgingly given, and returned to her side.

'Not bad, not bad, young Gazza!'

Her eyes were shining. He had never seen her in this mood before. Delightedly she raked the array of images spread out in front of her on the table, then her little fingers snaked out and pounced. 'This one, for instance. It's bloody good! How the hell did you get that?'

Somewhat resentfully he took it from her grasp. 'It's not hard to take photographs, you know, Emma. Even when the subject is not supposed to know he's being photographed.'

Emma studied the photograph with the utmost concentration. 'He didn't know,' she said slowly.

'But why couldn't he? What was the big idea? I don't get it.'

'You weren't supposed to "get it", Gary,' she said harshly. 'I asked you if you'd mind taking a few snaps for me as a friend. I offered to pay, and you said not to worry, it'd be fun.'

'I just think it's a funny way to get snaps, that's all,' grumbled Gary. 'Why didn't you just tell him to smile for the camera and let him know he's having his picture taken like anybody else?'

'Because.'

'What does that mean?'

'Because I wanted to surprise him.'

Gary looked down at the countless images of Robert Maitland lying on the table: Robert driving Emma away from the café in his car, Robert buying her an ice-cream, Robert smiling into her eyes. 'He'll be surprised all right.'

'OK, then. Thanks a bunch, Gary.' She was shuffling the pictures together and putting them away. He could feel his dismissal imminent. 'Look, Emma,' he began.

She was immediately on the defensive – aggressive. 'You got a problem, Gary?'

He gathered his courage. 'Look, these pictures. A surprise present, you said. I didn't think much about it at the time. But afterwards – well, why would you give him a present anyway? Who is he? Just some old codger hanging around the café. Why should you want me to follow you all this time and take photos like this?'

'Don't ask questions, Gary, it doesn't suit you. All you had to do was point the camera and shoot. Job over? OK?'

'No, it's not OK.' At his tone Emma threw an anxious glance over her shoulder. Old Gazouli was already watching them like a hawk. She never thought Gary would make any trouble!

'It's my work,' he went on, growing louder every moment. 'And I'm entitled to know what you're going to do with it. I'm not sure I like the way you've been – well, playing with him, teasing him along like this.'

'OK, Gary, you asked for it, and I'll tell you.' Her face was as pale as marble and her eyes like chips of steel. 'You talk about being entitled. Whatever I'm doing, I'm entitled to do, I can promise you that. There's no one in the world more entitled to a bit of Dean Maitland's time and attention than me, and I've come halfway round the world to prove it! And that's what your photos are – proof. Evidence. My evidence. He can't wriggle out of this one, no matter how he'll try. And he'll try, you can bet your bottom dollar on that. Men! They're all the same! But he's not getting out of this – or away from me. Not this time. Not this time. Not again.'

She paused, her eyes far away. 'I won't see you for a bit, Gary. I'm going away. Having a few days – at the seaside. You won't have heard of it, it's a little place called Brightstone. But I've got another place to go to first . . . inland. I'll be calling on someone who's going to be very surprised to see me. And pleased, I hope – because he doesn't get many lady visitors . . .'

Winter

Chapter 36

She felt sick again, sick of everything, sick of life.

Life?

What life?

Wearily Claire gathered her papers together and checked the contents of her bag. Big notepad to get down all the details of the discussion, assorted pens, diary ready to fix the date of the next meeting . . . God, what almighty rubbish! How had she come to find herself on so many committees? How had it happened that she simply acted as an unpaid, unthanked extension of her husband for practically every hour of her waking day? Where was her life in all this?

With a smile of pain, she thought about that. Her life. After twenty years, it was going to be hard. What would she do? She realised she would have to start again from scratch on everything, large and small. Would she go back to her maiden name, for instance? She tried it on for size. 'Claire Everard.'

Claire Everard? No. That had been another woman – another girl, rather – too young, too hopeful, too idealistic, for the way she was now. Yet 'Claire Maitland' was too identified with Robert and the life she was going to have to leave behind. You ought to be able to choose a new surname when you got divorced, she thought, one that was neither your father's nor your husband's but your own free choice as the new woman you were going to be, of the way you wanted to present yourself to the world. Maybe she'd do that. There were some good names around.

If only she didn't feel so – so broken by all this. Oh Robert, Robert, she called to him in her heart, where did we go wrong? I loved you so much . . . so much. And you loved me – once, anyway. We were good together. With the ease of long familiarity she summoned up his image in her mind's eye: the handsome, hawk-like profile, the kind eyes, crinkling with amusement, the long, lean body that had been her own to claim for pleasure, comfort, or deep, deep delight whenever she wanted . . .

Oh Robert . . .

She was groaning, aching for him, for his touch on her breasts, his kiss, himself inside her, his bigness making her feel small, treasured and infinitely safe even as he transported her to the heights of sensation . . .

If he walked through the door right now, she thought with a mixture of anger and shock, for all your protestations and resolutions, you'd be in bed with him in thirty seconds! Yet what would that solve? Or cure?

A hunger, yes . . . she hadn't begun to tell him how much she'd missed the loving, raw, strong and physical, the physical urgency for one another that they'd always had, the closeness that he'd been withholding from her these recent months. But going to bed with him wasn't the answer, it couldn't be. It would be just like putting a sticking plaster on a broken leg, or on a deep, festering, internal wound. And she was sick of it, sick of all the suffering he was imposing on them both, sick to her stomach, sick to her soul!

Passing the mirror on the landing as she came out of the bedroom, she saw in her reflection the disturbing truth of how she really looked and felt. The woman who stared back at her from the glass looked like something out of an isolation ward. Just like Joan, really. She'd probably caught whatever it was that Joan had had, what with caring for her and nursing her when she was sick. Perhaps it was her turn to be cared for now? Trouble was, there was no one available for the job!

'Morning, Claire.'

Making herself smile, Claire raised her head at the familiar curt greeting as Joan came into the kitchen, dressed for work and bearing the morning's post in her hand. 'How are you, Joan?'

'Fine!' The snappy monosyllable was meant as a rebuke, Claire knew. Joan kept insisting she was better now, but she didn't look it, in fact she looked worse. But nothing would stop Joan in her tracks except an elephant gun. 'Letter for you, rest of them for Robert, I'll deal with them when I get back,' she announced mechanically. 'I'm off to the Cathedral office. Lots of requests coming in from the press for interviews with Robert in Brightstone, that'll really do him a bit of good. I'll probably be back late, so don't wait up.'

Stiffly she stalked to the car and began the drive into the city, threading her way through the heavy early morning traffic with her usual meticulous care. It was all going to be all right, she'd decided on that. Robert must be going mad, to think of throwing everything away, everything they'd all worked for all his life! And as for her, "out of a job"! Her eyes glistened with rage. Nobody told her what to do! Nobody did that to Miss Joan Maitland!

And if not Robert – no other man had the right to dictate to her! Especially not – she could not bring herself to frame his name. The familiar wave of sick horror washed over her at the recollection, her gorge rose in her throat, and she had to grip the wheel to fight it down. Don't let him get to you, the filthy, slobbering bastard! she schooled her soul in anguish. You did what you had to do, and it's over! He was over, too; finished, gone, past history!

It wasn't going to be easy to get him to accept that, she knew. She'd only purchased herself a let-out from his insistence on another date by having a tactical Friday-night resurgence of her 'virus'. He knew she was stalling him, but he had enough of the sadist in him to relish the prospect of a game of cat and mouse. He thought she couldn't get away, so he was ready to let her run and squeal as much as she wanted. 'I'll see you when I get back from Brightstone, Joanie,' he'd said with a deceptive mildness. 'An' don't fill up your dance card. I'll be reckonin' on havin' all your dances from now on.'

Him? She heaved with disgust, and too much of a lady even to consider voiding it, forced herself to swallow the stinging bile. Him? 'Dance' with her? He wasn't fit to undo the latchet of her shoe. He wasn't fit to . . . he wasn't fit . . .

He wasn't fit to live.

Other people had accidents.

Murray Beilby, for one. Why not Mick Ford?

Yes, there were ways – if he'd done nothing else for her, Mick had taught her that. But he'd also taught her the danger, and the inconvenience, of relying on a third party. There had to be ways of seeing to – this sort of problem – all by yourself. Then you knew the job would be done. And you knew that you could rely on the only person involved to keep their mouth shut!

It was really just a question of ways and means. Ways . . . there were lots of ways. She'd think of something. Something good . . . and something *soon* . . . and then, goodbye, Mr Ford . . .

That was it, then. With the confident sense of a problem solved and an odd, excited glimmer in her eye, Joan saw a gap in the traffic ahead, changed gear, grabbed her chance, and accelerated away towards the city.

'Look, Everard. I'm not y'bloody messenger boy y'know!'

Prison officers are not appointed for their sweetness of disposition or the kindness of their hearts. Chief Officer Michael Warren already hated Visitors' Days – they always got the cons stirred up, and the sods were hell to handle in the inevitable let-down afterwards. But when he'd got a con refusing to see a visitor, then the visitor refusing to take no for an answer, he came to the end of his rope. 'You either see her or y'don't!' he announced truculently. 'None o'my bloody business! I don't care if you never get another visitor till the day y'die in here, and rot! But I've got to have something t'tell her!'

'Tell her to go and fuck herself in hell!'

Everard was in a dangerous mood all right, Warren knew. Been twitching ever since he got turned down for parole. Last week or two, he'd been spoiling for a fight, boiling up for it. No point in pushing him over the edge.

He mollified his tone. 'She ain't gonna go that easy, son, I'm telling you. An' she's got a right t'know, under prison regulations, why you're refusing.'

'I'm refusing because I don't know her from Adam!'

The officer chuckled. 'Shouldn't think you'd need an introduction to crack on to a smart young bit of knitting like that one out there!' His eyes, hot and lecherous, lingered almost erotically on Paul. 'Well-set-up young bloke like you . . .'

'Ah, shut your face, Warren!'

'Watch it, Everard,' said the screw amiably. 'I could have you for that, if I want to. A slice of solitary for abusin' an officer'd soon put salt on y'tail. Now y'want to see her?'

'I told you, I haven't the faintest fucking idea who she is!' Paul screamed in frenzy. 'I don't know her! And I don't want to know her! So she can sod off back to whatever do-gooding, god-bothering outfit sent her along in the first place!'

'That's funny,' said the puzzled Warren. 'She says you do know her. Used to know her years ago. Says "Just tell him my name. Tell him Ally–" '

'What?'

' "Ally" – yeah, that's it – "Calder." '

'Who are you?'

He was shaking like a leaf, Warren noticed with satisfaction. Musta known her, whatever he said. Hard to work out how – he'd been in here, what, twenty-odd years now, and the kid couldn't be much more than that herself, twenty, twenty-one at most. But he knew her all right, Everard, just from the look on his face. He'd never taken his eyes off her, from the second he walked in. Couldn't blame him either. She was a little cracker, even if she was only a kid. Well, at least she'd be over the age of consent!

'You're Paul Everard.'

She was as cool as a cucumber, he noticed to his fury, while he was trembling like a girl. 'We both know that!'

he said savagely. 'Now tell me something I don't know. Like your real name?'

'Emma.'

'Emma who?'

'Never mind. Look, I can get you out of here.'

'You what?' Shock was followed by outrage. 'What is this? Some kind of stunt?' A fierce suspicion seized him. 'You've been sent by one of the gutter press, is that it? After a sob story, trying to wind me up?'

'No! I'm here on my own.'

'So what are you after?'

She smiled. It made her look very old. 'Oh, would you believe justice? No – how about revenge? It all depends on the way you look at it.'

His short-term fuse began to smoulder dangerously. He didn't have to put up with some evil little witch who walked in off the street to play games. He rose to his feet, almost knocking the chair over behind him. 'Get out!'

'You won't say that to me when I tell you one thing.'

Her calmness arrested him more than the wildest protestations could have done. He paused irresolutely. She leaned forward. 'I know who killed Jim Calder.'

He felt the blow in the pit of his stomach. He could not speak.

'And who put you in here,' she continued calmly. 'Who stitched you up so they'd all be OK – and who's been laughing ever since at how well it turned out.' Her smile called him out once again. '*I know what really happened.* Now throw me out.'

'Look, look . . .' He was gabbling his words, almost speechless with unmanageable emotion. 'Help me . . .'

Another smile. 'That's what I've come for.'

'Why did you say you were Ally Calder? What's it got do with her?'

'Everything. Because she was there, too. That night. And I made a promise . . .'

'Who are you? Straight, now!' But he did not know if he could bear the answer.

'Can't you guess? If you can't, it doesn't matter anyway.'

'What are you trying to tell me?'

He was in anguish now. But her self-possession was total. Could she have rehearsed this scene, planned it, worked out her lines, even the way she would say them?

'What am I trying to tell you? Nothing that you don't already know.'

'Tell me, then!'

'Let me ask you something to begin with. Ally Calder never let you near her, did she? And you respected her. You thought she was a virgin. You never laid a finger on her, did you? Never tried it on? Not even so much as a kiss?'

An age-old burn of masculine shame took him. 'No.'

'Did you never think she might have had another bloke already – at the same time as she was seeing you?'

'Ally? Never!'

'Think about it . . . she was an attractive girl. Plenty of men would have been glad of the chance.' She paused. 'And one in particular.'

'Not Mick Ford!'

'No.' Another pause, followed by a completely unexpected change of direction. 'How d'you get on with your brother-in-law?'

His brain was reeling. Ally? Robert? What could possibly be the connection? But the soft, low voice was allowing him no time to think. 'And Joan? How about Miss Maitland? She visit you often, does she? Or has she been a bit too busy for the last twenty years?'

Her eyes had Ally's odd almond lift to them at the corners. He felt he was drowning in their cold, clear depths.

'And then there's good old Mick Ford. You wouldn't have gone down if it hadn't been for him. All the other evidence was circumstantial. He was the one who tied you in with Ally and Jim – who gave the identification evidence that he saw you there that night – when in fact he saw another man – the man who's walked free in your shoes all these years – who was having your Ally all along under your very nose – who's whiter than white and beloved by all while you're in here, trapped for life . . . They stitched you up, Paul, between them. They were pretty good at getting anyone they didn't want out of the way. You want proof? Here's your proof!'

The newspaper she tossed on the table between them showed two men shaking hands and smiling, the shorter of the two with his arm thrown familiarly around the shoulders of his tall, distinguished-looking companion. 'BRIGHTSTONE REUNION', read the headline. Below it the text seared Paul's brain. 'Two old colleagues-in-arms who were present at the tragic mine cave-in of twenty years ago met again today to celebrate the re-opening of the mine. The Very Reverend Dean Maitland and union boss Mick Ford are well acquainted not only from the old days in Brightstone, but frequently find themselves working together today on construction projects in Sydney, for which the Dean has a special responsibility on behalf of the Church . . .'

Lifting his head, Paul let out a scream like a bull elephant at bay. Then he turned violently on the prison officer Warren, and felled him with one blow. Pausing over Warren for the merest second, he vaulted the little table between the prostrate form on the floor and the door, and raced out into the yard.

Within minutes the prison radio was pulsing its terse commands: 'Runaway – runaway – runaway – all officers red alert. Do not – REPEAT, DO NOT – tackle runaway, he is armed and dangerous. Do not shoot – he has taken a door guard as a hostage. Obey his orders, do not risk lives. Calling all officers, calling all officers, runaway – runaway – runaway . . .'

Chapter 37

What was he doing here?

What had he hoped to find?

And how far could he go now without Murray to help and guide him? Yet he had to try. There could be no turning back now.

As determined as he had ever been about anything in his life, Robert strode remorselessly on through the endless dunes spilling away into infinity beyond Broken Bay. He knew exactly why he had come here – to rediscover the place where he had found that rare and special love, and to recapture that one magical moment of his youth, the only moment he had had, he sometimes thought, of real youth, when without fear or favour he had given himself wholly to something – to somebody – who had seemed to him like the spirit of youth herself.

But he had not found it – nor her, nor the spirit of her, nor even the faintest whiff of the memory of her borne on the harsh, salty breeze. Now he remembered – what a fool he was! too late to save himself this wild goose chase! – that even in the heyday of his love for her, he could not find nor identify the one dune where they first became lovers, that white bowl of sand which had become the chalice of his bliss. They were all alike, the dunes and their seductive hollows, all, all alike. He was flooded with a sudden longing to lie down here, to give up the unequal struggle, to drift away into nothingness. But that would be the coward's way – not his.

On he went and on, his aroused conscience determined to punish his aching limbs, till at last the darkening sky, giving warning of the descending night, made him turn back for the Rectory. At least, he thought ruefully, I'll sleep tonight! Don't count on that, purred the youngest of his demons, as he stirred and stretched himself against what promised to be a good night's work ahead: we have other plans for you, Dean!

Getting dark already?

The nights were still closing in early now. Storms'll soon be here.

It was going to be a long, hard winter.

With this satisfactory reflection Joan Maitland shut the curtains of the study and her mouth like a trap, and took stock of what still remained to be done. Those press calls to return – amazing, and very gratifying, the interest that the Brightstone Commemoration was causing on all sides. You've done yourself a bit of good with this, my lad, she told Robert. She spoke to him in her mind, as she had done all her life, there was nothing new about that. But nowadays, somehow, she often seemed to be surprising herself and other people by doing so openly – when she was in the Church offices, for instance, or even in the kitchen alone with Claire. Inevitably a few words, a sentence or two, would creep out, something urgent she had to tell him or remind him of, or just something she knew she had to share.

And then to see their faces! How stupid of them not to realise that Robert *was always with her* – always had been, always would be, whatever happened to either of them, till the end of the end of the world . . . how stupid people were! How little they knew! She laughed aloud, though how loud these days she never was quite sure.

Mechanically she tidied the perfectly tidy desk. Got to keep it nice till he comes back. Soon have him back, and then everything would be just as it was again. Must remember to tell him that the quarterly meeting of the Estimates Committee had been postponed till Tuesday . . .

Was that the phone? Abstractedly she lifted the receiver. 'Dean Maitland's house?'

Silence. A deep, male silence.

Not – ?

Her thin stomach hurled its contents against the back

454

of her throat. But it was not Mick Ford. The voice when it came conveyed a far sicker terror, a deeper dread.

'Joan?'

After twenty years and more, she had not forgotten his voice. His voice, a voice so dear to her then, that she never even had to name him to herself – the voice that once held more for her than any other voice in the world, even Robert's.

'Joan? I know you're there.'

'How—?'

'Cut the act, Joan, and listen. I found out. *I fucking found out*! Amazing, isn't it? Any poor sap who wasn't as dumb as me might have figured it out years ago, don't you think?'

She was speechless with fear, beyond words, beyond thought. Still the voice rolled on: Paul, yet not her Paul.

'You and your brother! What a double act! Him a pillar of the church, while you could keep ice-cubes in your cunt. Miss Respectable Maitland and the Holy Reverend Robert. Who was going to call you two a pair of liars when you stood up in court – and lied my life away!'

'Paul—'

'Shut your mouth, Joan. After twenty years, I reckon it's my turn to talk. Between you and your blue-eyed boy, a blind man on a galloping horse could work out where the brains lie. You were the boss of the enterprise all right. You always were a smart woman – if only I'd had the sense to know how smart, none of this would have happened. And him – I've found out, too, that minister or no minister, he carried his brains in his cock like any other man! He'd never have had the guts to plan all this and carry it out! You would – and you did!'

'Paul, you're talking rubbish – filthy rubbish—'

'You planned it – but he did it! He did what I've been paying all my life for! He killed Jim Calder, not you. He let you lie and plan and scheme to save him. He caused the whole thing by going after the one woman in the world I ever wanted, when he'd already got a peach of his own, my sister!'

The thick voice changed emphasis now, became almost supportive. 'But you've got nothing to worry about, Joanie. You were only doing it for him, after all. Besides, I don't kill women. I'm after bigger game, the real quarry! I'm on his tail, Joan. I know where he is, and I'm going after him. Tell him – for the last time, the lying hypocrite – to say his prayers!'

The line disconnected. He was gone. She stood for a moment, brain whirring like a dynamo inside the frozen form. Then she turned on her heel and fled from the room.

As soon as Claire entered the house she knew something was wrong.

'Joan?'

She could hear the sound of frantic activity upstairs. As she went up, she heard feet running along the landing from the bathroom, and arrived at the open door of Joan's bedroom to see her sister-in-law violently hurling her toilet-bag into a hold-all she had obviously just grabbed from the cupboard.

'Joan? Are you all right?'

'Going away!' rapped Joan frantically. 'Won't be long!'

'Where on earth—?'

'Got to see Robert! Urgent business!'

'You're going to *Brightstone*? Are you serious?'

'Business!'

'What business? And why don't you just ring him up, if it's that urgent?'

Joan had finished her packing, such as it was. 'Got to go! Nothing for you to worry about! Stay here! We'll call you!'

She was down the stairs by now and halfway across the hall. This is madness, thought Claire, the very face and voice of madness itself. She grabbed her sister-in-law's arm. 'Joan,' she said as soothingly as she could. 'I think we should go together. We can share the driving. And whatever it is, I can help you. If there's a problem for Robert, I should be with him too.'

'No! No!'

She doesn't know me, thought Claire in terror. She doesn't know who I am. She's looking at me as if she's never seen me before in the whole of her life – as if I'm her mortal enemy – as if I'm a monster . . . oh God, dear God, help her . . . help us . . .

'What's wrong, Joan?'

But Joan was mouthing at her like an animal now, beyond human speech. Carefully Claire approached the writhing, distorted shape.

'Joan – dear Joan—'

A stunning blow caught her on the side of the head and sent her sprawling. Stumbling to her feet, she made for the door in the wake of the flying feet. Only the brake-lights of the car burning a furious reproach as it hurtled down the drive and round the bend into the roadway answered her feeble cries. Her hand to her throbbing head, she withdrew into the hall, then climbed the stairs as fast as she could to pack in her turn.

Free.

He was free.

It was going to take a bit of getting used to, this freedom.

Grimly Paul smiled to himself as he struggled with the unfamiliar controls of the car. You're a far cry from the old Dodge, the fabulous Blue Streak, he told the little Datsun reprovingly. You don't handle like a man's car, and you're too full of fancy new gadgets for a man to get his mind round – specially in the first few hours of being out in the great wide world . . .

Whewheeee . . . !

Free!

Gripping the wheel as he bowled along, he howled with joy and exhilaration. Free! To make it out of the prison like that – and to find a car waiting at the door for him as well! He patted the wheel. A bit unfair to run down the little motor when there it had been parked slap-bang ready for him, keys in the ignition and all! Guess the owners thought it was a safe enough place to park a car, right outside a state prison in the middle of nowhere. Well, they'd learned a valuable lesson for the future then, hadn't they? You simply can't trust anyone these days. Least of all an escaped con, a man on the run! He laughed aloud with glee.

Now where? Only one place. Wouldn't take too long to get there, he wouldn't exactly be stopping for any sightseeing along the way. If he needed petrol, he had something that he reckoned would do just as well as money, or even better. Tenderly he patted the gun lying beside him and ready to his hand on the passenger seat. So the petrol station would report him to the police? They'd know where he was making for already, if he knew Joan Maitland. And he didn't care.

He shivered with a sudden chill. It was cold in the car – how did these blasted new car heaters work? Around him the bleak and wintry landscape, desolate as it was, could have been the most wonderful thing a man locked away from the world for twenty years could ever hope to see. Even the clouds swelling and gathering black and huge on the horizon were ripe with the promise of nature at her fiercest. But Paul was dead to the outside world, lost in the kingdom of his mind, exploring and mapping the country of his revenge. Beyond that, he saw nothing. Just as long as he made it, he pledged himself grimly, in time to pump even one of the revolver's six bullets into the treacherous heart of the Reverend stinking Robert, they could pay him the same compliment back in his own weight of lead, for all he cared. See you in Brightstone! And after that, in hell! he telegraphed ahead. Say your prayers, Dean!

You have to keep your spirits up on a long journey. And there's nothing wrong with talking to yourself. Some of the most famous people in the world have done it, people like . . . like . . .

Well, it's a well-known thing. Anyone can talk to themselves. But how do you stop the talking? And how do you silence all the other talkers, when the car is full of voices?

'Shut up!' Joan screamed. She was hoarse and shivering from screaming at them. But the car was suddenly, blissfully quiet. That shut them up all right! For a bit, anyway. That was telling them! If only it wasn't so cold. Once again she reached over to switch up the heater, and discovered to her surprise that it was already on maximum. It obviously wasn't working properly. She'd get it fixed as soon as she got back to Sydney.

Brightstone – how many miles, what was that sign? She didn't catch it. She hadn't caught the others on the way either, somehow, but what did it matter? She knew where she was going, and she didn't need to stop. Just get there. That was the important thing. Get there, save Robert – I'll protect you, she told him, you've got no need to worry! – then get the police to round up that mad dog Everard, and it's all going to be all right.

The police. A moment of objective clarity shone through the last working regions of Joan's decaying brain. Should she have rung them before she left the house, alerted them to be on the look-out in Brightstone in advance of the killer's arrival?

A moment's reflection showed her how silly that was. The police could do nothing that she could not do. Her powers were infinitely greater than theirs, her knowledge of Robert, of the enemy Everard, of Brightstone – in fact of everything in the world – was so much vaster than theirs. For they were petty where she was infinite . . . no, forget the police, it was true of the whole of the human race – little tiny creatures crawling between heaven and earth while she and Robert soared far above them in the blue of endless space, supreme creatures, above law, above death, above reproach . . .

How many miles to Brightstone now? It was getting dark, and cold, still so cold. Winter was here again when it should be spring; the seasons were rolling back at her command! Yes! She laughed in triumph. As if on cue, the mean, cold wind that had trailed her since Sydney grew and blustered, began to ruffle all the countryside around, and the heavy clouds gathering overhead presaged a fearful storm. Let it come on! she exulted, let it come down! And all the voices in her head awoke and leaped about and howled and wailed and screamed their encouragement.

459

It was getting dark and the furious sky, pregnant with thunder, was holding the whole region to ransom. Thank God she'd managed to make it to shelter before the skies opened and the storm broke. Shivering, she paid off the taxi and hefted her bag into the dingy back-street hotel. The taxi-driver at the station had known at once what she wanted, and by the look of the dump had actually managed to find her the only place to stay even in this hole of a town that she could in fact afford. But what a town! Brightstone? Emma could hardly believe it. What was bright about it? Even the name was just a sick joke. The sooner she was out of here, the better. 'Not long now,' she promised herself. 'Not long!'

The owner, versed as he was in the seedy, the sordid and the unexpected, still cast more than a curious glance over this odd customer. 'A room? F'one?'

'Yeah, just for one.' God, he wasn't going to be a pain in the neck, was he?

'F'how long?'

'Not long.'

'How long's not long?'

Dickhead, she thought, her tolerance at breaking point. Like to play games, do you? Aloud she said sweetly, 'One night anyway. Maybe two or three.' And what's your problem, sunshine, finding me a room in a flea-pit where you're obviously not exactly overbooked?

'OK, then. I'll put you in number five. Have to ask y'for one night in advance, o'course. And if y'll sign the book, Miss—'

'Sure thing.' She took the pen from his hand as he turned the register towards her. 'And the name's Calder – Miss Ally Calder.'

'AND HIS DAUGHTER ALLY' . . .

Head bowed, Robert stood silently before the double grave of Jim Calder and his daughter and gave himself up to heavy, racking grief. All the losses of all his life seemed to melt and merge into the sorrow he felt for Ally: the loss of hope he had to suffer as a boy, when all the spontaneity, all the fun had been beaten out of him by parents, teachers and a sister who knew all too

460

well what he wanted, before he'd had a chance to know it for himself. Then the loss of his parents, the first cause of all this sorrow and remorse, the original sin for which all this, all this must in some way be a punishment.

One after another, the losses racked up. The loss of his youth, which had ended with their lives, on that very day. The loss of his life, when he had thrown away his own free right of choice, his truth to himself, his decision about a career, in his determination to serve the Church as a way of making restitution for his father's death. Slowly, slowly, he raked through the audit, though it ripped apart the very fibres of his soul to do so. There was his loss of integrity, which had inevitably come from doing a job in which he had slowly ceased to believe, then his loss of faith and with it the growing loss of face, and not least, oh no, the most, the worst, the last, the loss of Claire.

Ally – Claire – where did one now end and the other begin? Or had Ally all along been a fantasy, a phantom, a midsummer night's dream, the briefest episode in a long lifetime of love with Claire? Vividly Claire's face rose before him in the gathering gloom, her little pansy face, too pale of late, her dark hair brushed back from her forehead with one impatient hand, the softness of her skin, the feel of her womanly body . . . she was so real he almost felt he could reach out in the dark and clasp her to his side.

Ally, though, his other love – where was she? He had sought her, oh, how he had sought her all the length of these last, lonely, empty days – in the milk bar where they had first met, in the church when he saw her at George Everard's funeral, in the Brightstone town hall when she had danced with Paul on that last night when they had all still been free, happy and alive.

And he could face the truth now – she was not there. She was gone. She had been restored to him by Murray, he began to see, so that however belatedly, he could now say goodbye. And against the background of a rising, wailing wind heavy with the tears of the universe, he lifted up his voice in salutation, and made her a full farewell.

Far out to sea, the storm was moving in on the headland now like a hostile army racing toward an undefended land. Recklessly he stood his ground – no reason now to dodge and weave, to run or try to hide. From the very arc of the heavens the first shaft of lightning split the world beneath, plunging into the heart of an ocean already boiling with fire – then another, then another. It was a spectacular show, cosmic fireworks on a scale he had never seen before. With it the first huge splashes of rain, harbingers of the deluge to come, broke over his unprotected head. Within seconds he was soaked to the skin.

At last he tore himself away. He was reluctant to go in – he felt completely at home with the wildness of the world outside, at one with the elements, at one with himself. Purged and strengthened, prepared for anything, he moved towards the Rectory. Claire filled his thoughts and floated before his eyes. How much he loved her, he felt, he had only just begun to know. He had to be able to convince her of that – to regain her love and with it rebuild their marriage and their life together. At last Ally Calder and her poor, sad little ghost had been laid to rest. The past was buried. Time to face the future and move on.

At last he gained the Rectory porch, and feeling for the lock in the pitch darkness, opened the front door. Thankfully he stepped forward over the threshold into the warmth and light of the comforting, sandalwood-scented hall, closed the door behind him, and began to make his way upstairs to strip off his wet clothes. As he did so, a tiny noise from the porch caught his ear. He turned to see a slip of paper flutter through the door.

Before he picked it up, he knew at once what it would say. 'I CANT STAY HERE, IM FINISHED IN BRIGHTSTONE . . . MEET ME ON THE HEADLAND ABOVE BROKEN BAY TONIGHT – A.' He tore open the door, but there was no one to be seen, nothing but the raving of the storm and the wild, wicked dance of the unleashed wind. Without pause, without thought, he set his face into the driving elements and raced out once again into the darkness of the night.

Chapter 38

Out into the night . . .

Should've brought a coat . . .

Wouldn't make any difference now anyway . . .

His brain numbed to the driving rhythm of his pounding feet, Robert ploughed on down a headland road awash with sheeting rain, half expecting any moment that one of the thunderbolts screaming round the sky would make him its target and strike down without mercy on his undefended head. But he felt no fear. He knew that events were moving to their pre-ordained climax without the need of any intervention from him – which, given the elemental nature of the powerful forces at work, could in any case be no more than a puny and pathetic show on his part, like an angry child railing at the mighty gods.

At the foot of the bluff, the lights of the town pub beckoned like a good deed in a naughty world. Secure in their warm fug of friendship, conversation and booze, the Brightstone drinkers were shocked to see the wind-lashed stranger suddenly erupting into their midst from the howling storm outside, like a refugee from another world. Only the publican, who prided himself on keeping abreast of local affairs, recognised the town's recent distinguished visitor in tonight's scarecrow, his hair plastered to his head with the rain, his wet clothes clinging around his limbs in a way that exaggerated their length and leanness. 'Evening, Dean,' he said in wonderment. 'What can we do for you?'

Exhaustion rather than rudeness made Robert skip his normal preamble. But he feared his demand sounded unacceptably abrupt. 'Do you have a car I could borrow?'

'Well . . .' As a publican in towns large and small, Bill Price had built a successful career on the old Shakespearean adage, 'Neither a borrower nor a lender be'. But there was something so compelling, so unnerving about the deep, burning regard in the hollow eyes fixed on his that it overthrew a lifetime of canny self-regard. 'Well, Dean . . .'

As he hesitated, his wife Faye came bustling in from the back with a pile of sandwiches for the bar. The sight of Robert stopped her in her tracks. 'Dear God, what have they done to you?' she demanded, half in disbelief, half dread. 'Haven't you got a coat, or anything?'

'I'm all right, really I am, thank you,' said Robert hoarsely, so far removed from the everyday world of reality that he almost believed it was true.

'But you're soaking! Dripping!'

'I'm so sorry.' Robert looked in disbelief at the water on the carpet which seemed to be leaking from him, from his clothes, his shoes, everywhere. 'I'll get out of your way. Yes. If I could just borrow a car . . .'

Better get him out, thought the publican, before he spoils the night's drinking for my regulars. 'Sure thing, Dean. Take mine.' He fished in his pocket for the driving keys. 'It's the red Ford out the front. Can't miss it.'

'Let me get you some dry clothes, Dean, or you'll catch your death!' urged Faye. 'Step upstairs a minute, I've got some things of my son's'd fit you fair enough. You can't go round like that!'

'I'm fine, thank you, truly I am.' Already he was melting out into the night again like a spirit of darkness.

'At least take a towel to dry your hair! You'll catch your death of cold!'

Softly the door closed as if with the night wind. The publican looked at his wife and shook his head. 'Must be something serious. Some kind of emergency.' Faye nodded. 'I dunno – they're all at it tonight.' With an upward glance he indicated the television set chattering quietly away on the end of the bar. 'Did y'see that?'

'What?' She looked at a face staring blankly out of

the television screen at her. 'Who's he?'

'Will y'listen?'

'. . . escaped this lunchtime from the state prison and made his escape in a stolen Datsun car, colour blue, registration number 336212. Anyone seeing this man is warned not to approach him – he is armed and dangerous. Paul Everard, formerly of Brightstone, a coastal town from the mining region of New South Wales, is serving a life sentence for the murder of a fellow-miner whom he killed and threw off a cliff following a personal vendetta involving a girl. Various sightings of cars similar to the stolen vehicle have as yet left the police with no clear ideas as to where Everard is headed . . .'

Ally . . .

Ally . . .

Where are you, my love? Come back . . . come back to me . . .

His heart brimming with grief and joy, his eyes blinded by tears, his whole being in a revolt of complete confusion, Robert inched the car through the driving wind and rain up the headland road and across the bluff. The note – from Ally? but if not Ally, who could have written it? – had blown his mind away, and with it the clarity and certainty so painfully won in the vigil at her grave. He knew only one thing, that whatever the cost, he must obey her summons – even if it came to him from beyond the grave.

The road to Broken Bay was carved into his soul. The wheels seemed to find their own way forward, and the strange car was like an old friend in his hands. Was everything – against all the odds – about to come right at last? Please God – Ally – Claire – Emma – Ally – Claire – let it be so . . . Father – God – *please* . . .

Moving at a snail's pace, all he dared to risk in conditions so foul that visibility was hardly more than a length or two before his face, Robert felt the drive to Broken Bay would never end. His senses straining, at last he picked up the sound of the sea, the earth-shaking thud of the enraged breakers pounding the shore reaching him even above the howling of the storm, and knew that he had arrived on the crest of the headland. The clifftop could not now be far away, must be in fact dangerously near. He pulled off the road, switched off the engine, and sat for a moment to recover his self-control.

Through the whirling darkness outside, the headlights of the car picked out a level stretch of grassland beneath the blackness of the night ahead, then a paler, vaster vacancy beyond, where the cliff edge fell away into endless space. Almost at the edge stood one lone tree, aged and twisted now by a lifetime's struggle against the cruel winds, but still enduring like time itself. A violent shudder seized him and wrung his shivering frame from head to foot. This spot he knew! He had been here before! And with her! But how? When?

Slowly . . . slowly . . .

With a massive effort he forced his racing heart to still its wild beating, his brain to open its doors to whatever was suddenly clamouring so loudly for admittance. Here. Yes, here! He had stood here, on this point, looking down on Broken Bay, and had seen Ally surf in, her costume white as innocence itself against the jewel-bright blue and green of the waves, herself riding the breakers like a mermaid, like a dolphin, like a nymph of the sea. Yes! His memory returned her face, her body, everything about her, back to him just as she had been on that very afternoon, perfect in her sunlit youth and beauty, perfect in light and grace . . .

But there was something more, something else, something darker coming back to him from this place – something bad had happened here, something he dared not know . . .

A great shadow appeared before him, stretching out its huge black wings to cloud his mental horizon. 'No!' he whispered. 'No!' Ahead of him in the pitchy darkness, something moved. His nerves wound up almost to breaking point, he could have screamed with fear. A slight figure flashed across the headlights wrapped like a bird of the night in the cloak of the rain. 'Who are you?' he cried aloud. 'Ally? Ally? Come to me, come to me!'

The door of the car opened, and she slipped into the

passenger seat beside him. It was Ally – Ally Calder as she had lived – the sideways glance of her almond eyes, the schoolgirl scrape of pink lipstick on her soft peony lips, the thin cotton dress clinging to her slender frame, the string of blue beads he had won for her that last day at the church fête round her neck. She looked at him with a triumphant laugh and opened her mouth to speak. He held his breath, he felt his whole life hanging in suspension for this one moment. 'Surprised?' she said.

His world convulsed. '*Emma*!'

She looked odd, exalted. 'I thought you'd come. Quite like old times, isn't it?'

'What are you doing?'

She gave him her flashing, cat-like smile. 'Oh – just trying to get even!'

His plea came from the depths of his soul. '*For what*?

'For being dumped!' Her eyes sparked with anger. 'For you seeking me out, taking me round the place – then suddenly announcing that you couldn't see me any more when it got embarrassing for you "in your position"! You hypocrite! Well, I've got evidence!' Triumphantly she fished in the bag she was carrying, and threw down a fistful of snaps. Images of himself smiling at her with eyes full of love, walking with her, his arm affectionately round her shoulders, shopping with her, buying her little things, spilled over his lap and tumbled on to the floor of the car. 'Just imagine what the papers'll make of those, you being such a big celebrity, *Dean Maitland*!'

The last two words spattered from her lips like rifle shots. Vengefully she went on. 'Make a nice little scandal, won't it? "The Dean and the Unknown Girl" – with plenty of details from me to help it along! The Dean snooping around my house, looking through my windows like a peeping tom – lurking outside my house at all hours of the day and night – making scenes about my seeing a boyfriend of my own age . . .'

What was she saying? Furiously he groped to make sense of it all. Joan's words came back to him with terrifying immediacy, and he demanded roughly, 'What is this? Blackmail?'

'Blackmail? You don't know anything, do you?'

Suddenly he was aware that his head was throbbing. Unconsciously his fingers flew to the site of the pain in his temple as he fought to think clearly. 'I don't – understand.'

Her harsh laugh hurt him almost more than her words. 'Oh, you've got real problems, haven't you? You don't know, you don't understand, you don't remember! Not a bad excuse, though, is it? And the perfect alibi for everything you've done. You can get away with anything, just by pleading you don't remember!'

'Emma—'

She brushed him aside like a fly. 'Well, let me refresh your memory. You remember Ally? Ally Calder. Your poor old memory's been kind enough to throw her back up again, has it, like something washed up by the sea?'

'Yes . . .'

'You had an affair with her. A bit on the side.'

'It wasn't like that . . .'

'And then when you'd had enough – when you were caught out by your precious sister Joan, you wanted to dump her, just like you wanted to dump me, too.'

'No! I loved her! I loved her so much I risked everything for her!'

'So what happened?'

Nothing could halt the flow of this relentless interrogation. He felt as if he were on trial for his life.

'She was so young . . .'

'Not too young to be screwed!'

His anger flaring, he spoke more roughly than he intended to. 'Emma, you don't know what you're talking about! When I tell you I loved her, that's exactly what I mean! And it was because I loved her that I had to give her up! Joan's reaction when she found out showed me what I should have known all along – that the world has no time for lovers. It only punishes those who break the rules. She would have suffered as much as I would, and more! In a town like Brightstone, to lose her reputation . . . to be at the mercy of her swine of a father – and to be too young, poor, unqualified to have a hope of making it on her own anywhere else . . .'

Her voice coloured with emotion. 'She had to in the end, though, didn't she?'

He stared. 'What do you mean?'

'Make it on her own – young, poor, no job—'

He gripped her by the shoulders. '*What are you talking about*?'

'When you packed her off to England.'

'What?' He could hear his voice rising almost to a scream. '*Who*?'

'Who d'you think? Ally, of course! Ally Calder!'

It was almost beyond him. He could feel the tears of joy springing to his eyes. 'You mean – she didn't die on the cliff?'

'Oh, she died all right – but not then – not there. But what did you care? You and your precious sister? Once you'd got rid of her—'

'*Joan*? How does *she* come into this?'

She turned to face him as if addressing an imbecile. 'That night. When you went down the mine. Joan came up here, to the headland, and found Ally. She wrapped her up in her own clothes, drove her to the next town, gave her some money, and put her on the overnight train with instructions to take herself as far away as she could, and never come back. Then she threw some of her things over the cliff to make sure everyone thought she was dead too, like Jim. A very neat solution! Exit Ally Calder!'

'No! No, no, *no*!'

His howl of rage and grief shook the car. Beside him he could feel the girl tauten with shock.

'My God!' she whispered, losing colour even in the dim light night. 'You didn't know! You really didn't know!'

'No!'

She drew a deep, harsh breath. 'Well then, there's something else you don't know, too. When Ally was sent away, she was pregnant.'

'*Pregnant* . . . ?'

'With her child, Robert. And yours.' She fixed him with eyes that were Ally's and yet her own. 'Me.'

* * *

Inside the pub it was generally agreed that the strange appearance of the Dean, soaking wet and looking as if he'd seen a ghost, had been a sight worth seeing. 'It's a pity you missed, him, Mick,' one of the miners was assuring the union boss. 'Being as y'know him.'

'Not looking like that, I don't,' said Mick, trying first to conjure up from his limited creative resources a convincing picture of the way Robert had looked, and then to marry that to the distinguished churchman of his acquaintance. 'Wonder what was up?' Mick was not an imaginative man. But the story he had just heard rang an alarm bell somewhere deep inside his head, and he could not seem to silence its distant but insistent clamour. 'Looked funny, y'say – kinda weird?'

Preoccupied with this question, Mick, seated with his back to the door, paid no attention to the next entrant to the pub, even though the gust of cold night air from the still-raging storm outside was felt throughout the room. 'Tell me again what you know, Roy, what y'seen. There's something going on – I don't like the feel of it . . .'

At the bar Bill Price and his wife liked even less the look of the newcomer, though he addressed them pleasantly enough.

'Hi there,' he said, smiling. 'I'm looking for the Dean – Dean Maitland. You wouldn't know if he's staying up at the Rectory, would you? Or what he's doing tonight? Wondered if you'd know where he's likely to be.'

'Jesus Christ!' *It's him*, Bill thought wildly, *in my pub*!

'Nah, not quite. Not Jesus Christ in person. Though I guess you could say something about the second coming . . .' His face changed, though the sociable smile remained fixed in place. 'Well, if you know who I am, you know what I've got with me.' Casually he fingered the tell-tale weight of the gun in the side of his jacket. 'I'll ask you again. My old mate Robert Maitland – Dean of the Cathedral – you seen him?'

'He was in here tonight! 'Bout an hour ago!' babbled Faye, in mortal terror lest her normally peaceable husband took it into his head to do something stupid in the

name of heroism and have a go at the night caller. 'He
took the car! Said it was an emergency and he had to
go!'

'Go where?'

'Search me! He didn't say! We don't know anything!
That's all!'

It must be true, Paul thought. The way the woman
was, she'd have told him anything. And she had no
reason to protect Robert, a man who'd been a perfect
stranger to her until this week, even if he was a big
cheese in the Church. With another terrifying smile, he
turned to go. 'You don't know anything, you say? Good
on you. That's a healthy way to be. You don't know
me, for instance – and you don't know I was ever here
tonight, OK?'

'OK, OK!'

Time to go. Still smiling, Paul moved away. But the
atmosphere he carried with him had made its own
announcement of his presence. Heads began to turn.
Feeling their curious glances, Paul tried to school himself
not to rise to them like an animal on the run. From one
corner, though, a low, choking gurgle of fear had him
round on his feet in a split second, his back to the wall
with the gun in his hand.

'Everard!' Mick Ford's face was grey and slack with
fear.

The smile of the killer wolf wreathed Paul's lean jaw.
'Well, Mick! You remembered me! Now ain't that nice!
Nice to know I'm not forgotten. And you've saved me
a journey.'

Mick was incoherent, gobbling his words. 'Everard,
I—'

'Cut it, Mick. You know what you've done, every
mortal part of it. You owe me. A life. Yours for mine.
And guess what? It's the day of reckoning. Yours has
just fallen due.'

'No! NO!' Mick was on the floor, weeping, gibbering,
begging, grovelling with abject terror. 'Don't . . .
don't . . . I never meant to fix you like that, put you
away f' twenty years . . . and getting Murray Beilby put
out of the way like that wasn't my idea, I only made the

471

arrangements . . . Don't kill me! Don't shoot! I'll do anything . . . anything!'

Mick Ford was nothing now but an apology for a man, humiliated, wasted, utterly destroyed. A tell-tale stain had begun to spread across the front of his trousers, and the thin, sharp smell of the fear of death polluted the air around him. But Paul might have been made of marble. Narrowing his eyes and taking careful aim, he raised the gun, and fired once. Then he turned his back on the prostrate form on the floor and calmly left the pub.

Chapter 39

Ally's daughter.

And his.

His daughter!

Bathed in the light of this unexpected, undeserved miracle of joy, Robert still could not come to terms with the jigsaw of darkness and deceit that had encompassed it on all sides. Nor was Emma ready to give up the sense of outrage and grievance that had been the legacy of her birth, of her whole young life. Carefully they traded pieces of information back and forth, but warily, like enemies who have just been told that they must pool their resources rather than continue to fight.

'I was in a coma for weeks, anyone will verify that,' Robert said slowly. 'Even when I came round, the concussion had been so bad that I hardly knew where I was. I had what they call retrograde amnesia. I lost everything that had happened to me in the weeks leading up to the accident. And I'd only known her for those few weeks.' The pain in his voice was unmistakeable.

'So there you were,' she asked, half wondering, half suspicious, 'with no memory of her at all? Everything a blank?'

'Not everything. Most of the rest of my life was still there. And fragments of the memory of her, too. Over the years – a look, a smile, a scent – something would go through me like a knife, and I'd never know why. Or sometimes – ' he shrugged, embarrassed ' – sometimes I'd hear a piece of music or something, and find myself feeling happy for no reason – I loved her so much . . .'

She had to believe him. 'She loved you too,' she said

simply. 'You were the first thing she ever taught me about, the thing we always talked about. She called me after your mother. My middle name's Lavinia. Emma Lavinia Calder, I am. You never knew that.'

'Called you after my mother?' Robert frowned in amazement. 'How did she know my mother's name?'

'Saw it on the gravestone in the church. If I'd have been a boy, I'd have been Robert George, after you and your father.'

'She . . . forgave me then?'

'You were her life. She always lived in hope she'd see you again some day.'

'But how – how could she expect that?'

'She knew you knew where she was.'

'*Knew where she was*? How could I know?'

'Because Joan knew. Joan always knew. Joan knew why she'd chosen to go to England, when she could have gone to America, or anywhere in the world.'

'Why was that?'

'Because her own mother was English.'

'What, the—' He did not want to say 'chorus girl' – it cheapened her somehow. But she picked up his meaning.

'Yes, the dancer. She was touring around Australia when she met Mum's dad, Jim Calder, and they got married. But she was from England in the first place.'

Of course! In a rush he recalled Ally's odd, endearingly un-Australian voice and the way she'd explained to him about her mother. 'So she went back to England to see if she could find her family?'

'Yes. She knew her mother's maiden name, and the town she came from. Her mother had died in Australia years before – she never made it back home. But Mum thought there might be somebody still left.'

'And was there?'

She shook her head. 'No, no luck. She found out a few things, though. They'd been a good family locally, well-to-do. So when their only daughter wanted to go on the stage, they wouldn't hear of it. They wouldn't let her go to stage school and learn how to act. So she ran away with a touring troupe, that was the only thing she could do'.

It was all too pathetically clear. 'And after that,' he said slowly, 'she never managed to make her way into anything better?'

'No. And they never forgave her. She went back home once, to try and make it up. But her father was furious, and wouldn't even talk to her. They kicked her out, and never saw her again. They died not long after. And there weren't any brothers or sisters. But once we were there, Mum thought we might as well stay.'

His heart was heavy with sympathy. He could see why Ally had thought that way. It was the nearest thing to a home – roots – a place of her own – that she was ever likely to find as long as she stayed out of Australia. And as long as Joan knew where she was, she'd have every reason to stay there, for fear of breaking her one connection with Robert. 'So Joan knew where you were?'

'She knew – and she made sure we stayed there! It was Joan who kept telling her that if she stayed put, kept her head down in England, she'd get you to come over and see us. Mum never got over that hope. Neither did I. We always talked about the time when you'd come walking in through the door.'

He could have wept again for their longing, their suffering, their hopeless, lifelong pain.

'In the end, she got fed up. She said she thought Joan was just leading her on, and never intended to let her precious brother anywhere near his by-blow – his little indiscretion.' The age-old bitterness was there again, a lifetime's store. No wonder she had such a low view of human nature – of men! 'That was when she decided to break her promise and get in touch with you.'

'Promise? What promise?'

'Joan had made her promise she'd never try and get in touch with you as long as she lived. Joan said she was the only way they'd ever get you into trouble over the killing, that if she ever came back they'd charge you and send you to prison.'

Another layer of skin was peeling back in his brain.

The pain was unbearable. He could hardly breathe. 'The killing . . . ?'

'Her father. Jim Calder.'

He was facing it now, it was coming, here it was.

'You killed him. He tried to fight you, and you pushed him away. He went over the cliff.'

He could hear his breath rasping in a throat dry with emotion. 'I pushed him over the cliff . . . ?'

'She was the only witness. She saw it all. But she couldn't bear for you to go to prison.'

'So Paul—'

Dear God, let it not be so! *Paul*! The scapegoat for his sins! *Paul*!

'It was him or you, Joan said. Him or you.'

Oh yes, Joan.

He could see it all.

Nice, neat work. Very Joan. Very Miss Maitland. Thank you, Joan.

'But in time – Ally tried to get in touch with me?'

'She wanted to see you. But more than that, she used to say, she wanted you to see me, to have a chance to get to know your own flesh and blood. She wanted me to have a chance of an education – like I'd have had if I'd have been the daughter of a dean, open and acknowledged. She thought I should have gone to college, she really wanted that for me. You remember – we talked about it in the café one time, the time I got so mad, because I'd never had it, never had the chance of it, even.'

'Yes – I remember.'

'And she never stopped feeling bad about Paul. He'd been good to her. She hated what had happened to him. She had all the cuttings about the trial and everything. It was the only thing she left me when she died – that and my birth certificate with your name on, and a couple of snapshots of me and her when I was a baby. She'd got all the newspapers in Sydney before Joan sent her the money to get away. She used to go over and over them and cry.'

476

'So when she decided to try to make contact with me – what did she do?'

'She sent you the letters.'

'Letters! What letters?' God, not more deception, more covering-up, more lies! No more, please God!

'She wrote to you. Twice, in the last year.'

'I never got either of them!'

And why would that be? Because Joan always took in the post! Pure hatred gripped him, shook him like a terrier with a rat. He would kill her. He would have to. He could never forgive her for this.

'She thought you had. And that you were ignoring her. That's what killed her in the end.'

'Killed her?'

'They said it was a virus, a rare virus. But I think it was a broken heart.' She had obviously hardened herself against weeping for her mother's death. But the knuckles of her hands gleamed white with tension. He did not dare to intrude on feelings such as these.

'And then I was on my own. She never married, never even bothered with boyfriends. All she ever wanted was you. She always used to tell me that if anything happened to her, I was to come over here and find you, bring the cuttings, and my birth certificate, and tell you everything. But I didn't know how to do it. And it wasn't as easy as that.'

'No.'

Slowly, simply, it was all becoming clear to him. 'You wanted to get to know me in your own right, is that it? To feel that I would love you for yourself, not just as the by-blow kid foisted on me from England whether I wanted it or not?' At last the pieces were falling into place. Now he knew why she had sought him out at the Cathedral, placed herself in his way, wanted to get to know him on her own territory, on her own terms, in her own time.

'Yeah.' She looked at him frankly. 'I wanted you to know me – as me. And I wanted to know what kind of a man you were. I had to find if you'd just let her down, thrown her away like so much rubbish. I wanted it not

477

to be true. I wanted to be sure you were worthy to be
my dad.'

'And if I wasn't?' He paused, and looked into her
heartachingly defiant eyes. 'Emma – was that all?'

'No'. She returned his look with equal honesty. 'If
you weren't, I wanted my revenge. Mine and hers.'

'Your revenge?'

'Yeah. I knew what I was going to do. I planned it
all. To expose you, humiliate you, lead you on and then
dump you – just like you did to her.'

Brightstone! At last!

Muttering, gripping the wheel, half crazed with tiredness, Joan saw the sign for the outskirts of the little
town and rejoiced in her heart. Here and safe! Now all
she had to do was to find Robert, save him, and he
would love her like he used to do, like he used to do
when they were children here, so long ago . . .

Carefully she threaded her way through the narrow
central street, its bends and potholes even more of a
menace than usual in the sheeting, merciless rain.
Brightstone's antiquated street-lighting seemed even
more pitiful on a night as black as this. But there was
nothing to fear, no one to knock down. On a night like
this, even a rat wouldn't leave its hole, Joan gloated.
Except for one. Except for one. And she was after him
with a knife to cut off his long tail!

The headland now, and the huge old bluff looming
ahead in all its uncaring, immemorial pride. The car
crawled up the hill. As the road began to level out she
could hardly distinguish the shape of the Rectory and
the church against the thick darkness all around. But
the home and the church of her earliest childhood – she
knew they were here, she could feel their welcome –
their welcome home.

Beyond tiredness now, beyond tears, she parked the
car and heaved her frozen frame out of the driver's seat.
She had been driving for hours upon hours, days upon
days, as it seemed. Well, she was here now. She only
had to speak to Robert and it would all be all right.

No lights were on in the front of the house. Maybe

478

he was in the little sitting-room at the back, where Claire always used to read and work. Stalking stiffly up the steps, she tried the door. It was open. He must be in. Breathing deeply, she stepped into the darkness of the hall. The smell of the old building, familiar to her as her own, rose up to meet her. Home. Welcome home.

'Robert!'

No sound. She walked through the hall and pushed open the door to Claire's room. That one, and all the other rooms round the hall were dark and empty. Yet the house had a human feel – it seemed to be waiting, holding its breath for some human activity to begin or resume, some thread from long ago to be picked up as if it had been dropped only yesterday.

So strong was the sense of a masculine presence in the house that she knew Robert must have left here only moments ago, perhaps simply whisked away by the Commemoration committee for a last-minute check that all was well. Wearily she climbed the stairs. I'll just have a little rest in my old room for a minute, she told herself, then I'll get my bag in and sort things out for the night. Her tired feet found their own way, so well did they know every step, every stair in the old house. She did not bother with the lights – she had no need of them. She knew every inch of the way.

On the threshold of her room she could see the shapes of the furniture exactly where everything used to be. Trembling with thankfulness, she took a step towards the bed. Suddenly, without sound or warning, a man's arm came round her waist from behind in a grip like an iron band, and a powerful hand clamped across her mouth and nose, cutting off her breath. She could feel his body, the hard, muscular chest, the long, well-shaped leg rammed viciously up against her from behind. In imagination, if not in memory, this body had once called to her so strongly that she knew every line of it, so strongly that it dominated her every wish, every thought. The scream died in her throat, along with hope. 'Hello, Joanie,' said a pleasant voice with a cutting edge of death. 'What's a nice girl like you doing in a place like this?'

'Paul!'

He felt the breath go out of her like a burst tyre, and had no fear now of relaxing his grip. Easing her body back against his and supporting her with his forward thigh, he slowly drew down his hand from her mouth. 'You come here to meet Robert too?' he murmured into her ear. 'I guess I'm on the right track, then.'

'Let me go!'

'Not so fast. Where's your beloved brother – the sainted Robert?'

'Not here! He had to go! Go away! That's why I came!'

He laughed into her hair, his breath warm on the top of her head. 'You're lying, Joan. But you'd say anything to save him, wouldn't you, anything at all!'

She was intensely conscious of his body, his nearness, his marvellous man's smell. His arm around her waist and across her hips, the other lying lightly across her chest and shoulders seemed to scald her like fire.

'And you lied my life away, Joanie,' he said almost musingly. 'You knew all along it was him killed Jim Calder. And you let me go down for him – for life! A life sentence! You owe me, Joanie.'

'No!' Furiously she wrenched herself round in his grasp. As she did so she could feel the dead weight of the gun in the pocket of his coat. 'I tried to save you, you stupid bastard! When they came for you, I offered you an alibi! I told the police you'd been with me that night. And you turned me down! You threw your own life away, Paul Everard, because you were too proud to say you'd been sleeping with me!'

Fiercely he gripped her arms while he tried to read her face in the glimmering dark. 'Why, so you did,' he said slowly. 'I was a stupid bastard then, wasn't I? Sleeping with you? I wish! Wouldn't that've been something! I always liked you – wasn't a bloke in Brightstone that couldn't have got it on for Miss Maitland. But I dunno . . . somehow I never made the first move . . . and all along, you had your own thing for me!'

Swiftly twisting her arms behind her back he secured her wrists with one powerful hand while with the other he cupped her face almost delicately between his thumb and forefinger. 'You still got it on for me, Joan?' he demanded hoarsely. 'I've been away a long time – haven't had a woman for so long . . .'

Hungrily he claimed her mouth as her body rose towards him shivering in his grip. Like a man who has almost died of thirst before he comes upon water he kissed her again and again, his surging tension building, building, with every move she made. Fumbling like a novice he felt for her breasts, and found the nipples alive and ready for his caress. Roughly he stroked her back, her sides, and pulled the centre of her body into his. From the quivering of her flanks, he knew she was ready for him. Tenderly he lifted her off her feet and carried her over to the bed.

She lay there like marble in the fitful moonlight, but panting lightly from her throat in a way that excited him more than he could bear. Throwing off his jacket and dropping the gun down on the bedside table he laid himself alongside her on the narrow bed and stroked her breasts, unfastening her dress to make contact with her smooth, unblemished skin. Only when she was making the sweet little sounds of joy in her throat did he slip his hand under her skirt and bring it up to the silken triangle at the top of her legs. As he did so, she flung herself violently to one side, and her hands closed on the gun.

He had no time to think. As she brought the gun up between them he struck it violently to one side and throwing himself full-length across her, covered the length of her body with his as he pinned her to the bed.

The explosion when it came echoed in his ears like the last judgement. A dull agony burned through his side. Without releasing her body from the weight of his, he brought his hands to her throat and closed them on her long neck. 'That was very stupid,' he said thickly. 'You've asked for the worst from me now, and by God you're going to get it!'

She did not move.

'You hear me, Joan?'

He shook her violently. She juddered like a rag doll

in his grip, and a dull awareness fought to make itself
felt against the pain. She was loose, too loose, and
made no sound. She made no sound because she had no
breath. Dragging himself from the bed he crossed the
room as fast as he could and threw the light switch.
Illuminated in all the garish brilliance of the electric light
after the deep indigo darkness, Joan lay on the bed,
bathed in blood. Her eyes were open, she was smiling,
and she was quite, quite dead.

'All my life – I thought you didn't care. When all along
– you just *didn't know?*'

This was so new to her, he could see, that she could
not get used to it. And he – how could he assimilate all
this in a moment? 'It'll take us time to get used to all
this – and to each other,' he said slowly, his mind working freely as he stared unseeingly out of the car into the
pouring rain. 'But at last, we've made a start. The truth
is ours now – and the chance to try to right at least some
of all these wrongs is in our hands now, too.' He felt he
could hardly wait to begin. 'Emma,' he began. 'I—'

He got no further. Suddenly the car door was violently
wrenched open. Paul stood there swaying, drenched in
rain, a dark patch of blood spreading across the front
of his shirt and down his side. His face was convulsed
with fury. 'Out!' he ordered, brandishing the gun. 'Get
out!'

'Paul, no!' cried Emma. 'I was wrong! He didn't
know! He didn't mean for you to take the blame for all
this!'

Paul laughed wildly. 'He's got you to believe him now,
has he? What a way with the ladies! Out, you bastard!
Get out of the car – now – or I'll shoot the girl!'

He looked crazed enough to try it. Slowly Robert
climbed out of the car. The wind and rain lashed his
face and body, but he tried not to shiver. He did not
want to show fear.

'Over there!'

They stumbled out across the headland, their feet
dragging in the sodden, slimy grass. With growing horror
Robert realised where they were going. Ahead of them

the cliff edge beckoned only a few yards away. From far below the siren call of the waves breaking on the rocks seemed to invite them to throw himself down into that last savage embrace. He could almost yield to the temptation to surrender to fate, to accept the farewell kiss of this last goodnight. No more distress. No more pain. No more guilt . . .

No. He would not do it. He thought of Ally, then of Emma, then Claire. Calmly he turned and looked into the mouth of the gun. 'Forget it, Paul!' he shouted, his voice rising easily above the howling of the storm. 'You can shoot me if you want to, but you won't make me jump! And if I die, you're killing an innocent man.'

'Die, then!'

'No!'

Furiously Paul levelled the gun at Robert's head, as the first of Emma's screams rang out. Robert bowed his head and closed his eyes. 'Into thy hands, O Lord, I commend my spirit: be with me now in the hour of my death . . .'

'You . . . you . . .' The scream of a mortally wounded man drowned both Emma's cries and the howl of the rising storm. Weeping, Paul tossed the gun aside. 'You set me up, Robert! You set me up! You fucking hypocrite, how could you do it? My own brother-in-law! All these years pretending to pray for me, when it was you who put me away!' The mounting fury of the storm echoed and augmented his screams. 'You! You! All along it was you, you bastard! I'll kill you! I'll kill you!' Madly he reached again for the gun.

'No! No! No!'

The mouth of the gun barrel flamed red against the blackness of the night as Paul fired. With an impact like a blow from a superhuman hand and a searing pain, Robert felt the bullet graze his skull. As the lightning split the sky, so something split in his brain. The storm, the fight, the screaming, furious man, the cry of the girl . . . in a wave of horror the night of Jim Calder's death returned to him – was with him – was here!

He was trembling with dread, his own voice rising now to join the keening chorus of human and superhuman torment as the drama played itself out to its final, terrible climax. his head was bursting, and he knew his strength was running out, his hold on consciousness even now in doubt. Out of the night a man, howling like a banshee, was hurtling towards him as he stood at the edge of the cliff. In terror he braced himself to push his killer away, to fight to the death to defend himself, to save his own life.

It's him or me!

Jim! Jim! For God's sake, *NO*!

As his assailant came abreast he saw in a lightning flash the face not of Jim Calder but Paul. Side-stepping the heavy, hurtling frame, he caught Paul round the waist and throwing him to the ground, checked his furious headlong forward dash. Yet Paul, like Jim before him, was the victim of his own mad fury, his speed too great to be resisted by a slighter man. To Robert's desperation, the heavy frame continued to career helplessly forward towards the cliff's edge under the weight of its own momentum, body, hands and feet weakening now under the loss of blood, scrabbling in vain for a purchase in the mud and grass. With his last ounce of strength Robert hurled himself full-length across the body of his friend and in his last lucid moment vowed to give his life with Paul's, if his strength were not enough. Like lovers they embraced on the edge of death, sliding, rolling in slow motion towards eternity.

'Rob!'

Paul made one last cry and was gone.

'God!' Robert screamed. 'Be with me now – if ever!'

His strength was almost done, he knew he could not hold out much longer. Fighting the storm, his fear and uncontrollable weakness, the wound in his head, the slimy, seductive soil sucking them both to death and destruction and the dead weight of the bleeding, unconscious body of his friend, Robert called on the final dregs of his faith and hope. Below him the cliff edge sloped away into black nothingness. Spreadeagled, Paul was slipping in a hideous slow motion over the edge, his legs and lower torso disappearing even as Robert watched.

A last bolt of lightning, stronger than any of the others, bathed the sky and the earth below in perfect white light. At the point of no return, in one immortal surge he found the force he had prayed for. As Paul slid like a man in love with death over the fatal edge, with a power he did not dream he possessed, Robert reached forward. Inspired by blind fury he found one sinewy arm and then the other, and with a violent, convulsive move, hauled Paul to safety before joining him in merciful oblivion.

Chapter 40

White peace, white calm, and happiness.

More, much more than he deserved.

Had he died and gone to heaven?

He did not want to open his eyes. But the touch of a familiar hand lovingly caressing his own confirmed his opinion. He had died, and this was heaven. For it was a very long time on this earth since Claire had held his hand so, or smoothed his every finger and pressed them to her lips with such melting, trembling love. He slept again, transfigured with silent bliss.

Sleeping, drowsing, waking, he felt himself slipping in and out of the days and nights. Sometimes he felt like speaking, but the effort was just too great. Nor could he understand the words and sentences that floated above him. No problem – deal with it later . . .

Later he awoke to a shaft of sharp, spring-like sunshine slicing across his pillow. Again he felt the warm touch of a well-known, well-loved hand as familiar to him as his own. Slowly he opened his eyes. Claire was sitting close beside his bed, her face a book in which every chapter and verse of total, unconditional love could be read at a glance. As his eyelids fluttered, she broke into a passion of weeping. 'Oh, Robert!' she scolded, laughing through her tears. 'That's two of your deathbeds I've sat through now! Don't ever do that to me again!'

He looked in amazement around the neat, quiet white room, the institutional furniture, the crisp, starched white bedlinen. 'Am I in hospital?' he asked in wonder.

'Yes, darling, and it's the best place for you to be. You've had a head injury, a gunshot wound. It's only superficial, and you'll be up and about later, but you've got to rest for now. So don't bother about a thing. Sleep again, that's best.'

He slept.

At his next waking, he was clearer and stronger. 'How long have I been in here?'

He thought she would say days, even a week. Her answer took him completely by surprise. 'Only since last night. They found you and Paul on the headland. He's in here, too.'

Paul! God, yes, Paul. 'How is he?'

Her face was grave. 'Pretty bad. Seems he's been shot, but the police can't work out where or how.'

'Is he conscious? Has he said anything?'

She shook her head. 'He's lost too much blood, the doctor says. He hasn't come round yet. The police are waiting to interview him. Then they'll take him back, to the prison hospital.'

He took her hand. A fierce sense of purpose seized and strengthened him. 'No, darling, they won't.'

'What?'

'Sssshh. One last question. When we were found last night – was anybody with us?'

She stared at him in amazement. 'Who else would there be?'

'Then how did the police know where we were?'

'Anonymous phone call, I think. Probably from the pub. Paul had been in there earlier in the evening.'

'I don't think so, Claire?'

She was all attentiveness, still not quite reassured that the motionless white form under the sheet she had been greeted with on her arrival in Brightstone was restored to her warm and loving husband again. 'Yes, darling? What is it?'

He took both her hands in his, and gripped them hard. 'Claire, I've made some terrible mistakes, and it's only in the last twenty-four hours that I've found out what they are. The only way forward for me now is complete honesty, acceptance of all that I've done, and a life-long effort to put everything right.' He could see

488

the alarm and mystification in her face. 'Look, I don't want to upset you. But you'll have to know everything, everything that's happened. And if you feel, if you honestly feel, that you can't be expected to live with all this, live through all this – live with me after this – then I'll understand and release you from the vows you made to me, without a murmur. But before you do that, darling – ' he grasped her hands and one by one raised them to his lips in a fervent prayer ' – before you do that I want you to know one thing – that the most important lesson I've learned in these last days, is how much I love you, how unworthy I am of you, and how dearly, passionately I hope and pray that you'll give me another chance – so that I can try again to show you how much you mean to me, and how much I care.'

He closed his eyes in a stern frown to try to hold back the tears. He must not play on her sympathy, or appeal to her through weakness. There was a long silence. He felt his life floating in the air like a feather, waiting to blow this way or that. At last she spoke.

'Robert, I don't know what you're going to tell me, and I'd be foolish to say nothing matters, I forgive you anything just because I thought I might have lost you, and now you're here again. But I know one thing.' Her clear eyes looked through into his soul. 'The way you've spoken to me just now is the most honest conversation we've had for *years*! I'd be just as foolish – even more foolish – to throw that away. Let's just try. You and me together. One step at a time. And see how it goes.'

'I'm afraid that it'll have to go quite fast to begin with,' he said heavily. 'Can you find the nurse and ask her to bring my clothes? Oh, Claire – I have so much to tell you – and there's so much to do!'

Where could he begin but with Emma, the child lost for almost twenty years and now lost again? Why was she missing? Why had the police not picked her up when they came to the rescue of him and Paul last night? And where could she have gone?

To explain Emma, he had to explain his relationship with Ally, how it had ended and the way it had begun.

He felt he had never loved Claire more, even as he knew he was hurting her more and more with every word he said. Her arms round her knees in the unselfconscious girlish gesture which still had the power to tug at his heart, Claire listened in disbelief and distress as he laid the whole story before her, holding back nothing. The shock of learning that the infidelity she suspected now, in the present, had in fact taken place over twenty years before had been for her a kind of reprieve. The object of his love, though, had been a peculiar blow. 'But with Ally, Robert! With Ally!' she murmured again and again. He knew that she would need time to get over that.

Another shock had been the knowledge that the consequence of that liaison was living, was here, and wanted to get to know Robert as her father. 'I can't deny her, Claire,' he said, with a simplicity that struck her to the heart. 'But I don't expect you to put up with it, if you can't.' Claire did not know if she could or couldn't. But she knew that somewhere a child, even a grown-up one, was lost, and the mother in her could not live a moment longer with that. 'Let's just find her, Robert, shall we?' she suggested tremulously. 'Just let me meet her, that's all. Then we'll see. I think – I think – that's all I can do – as far as I can go – right now.'

They began with the police, and immediately drew a blank. No report of any young girl in town anywhere. No one except the two men, both unconscious, found on the headland last night. No accidents reported – no missing persons turned up. No, sorry, can't help you, no.

'She must have stayed somewhere last night!' Robert argued, his anxiety showing in his face. 'Because if she'd been out all night in that storm . . .' He dared not complete the thought. 'Let's try the hotels.'

Brightstone's small size was a bonus for once. There were not so many lodging-houses in the town, and even fewer that she would have been able to afford. It hadn't taken long before they struck lucky. Or not so lucky, Robert realised, his heart sinking. 'Young girl, 'bout nineteen, fair hair? Sure she was here, stayed last night.'

'Where is she now?'

A smile of broken yellow teeth. 'Search me. Checked out.'

He did not say that the young lady had only paid for one night in advance, so that was the end of her legitimate booking as far as he was concerned – nor that she had not slept in the bed during any of the period that she had paid for it – nor that her pathetic possessions were still residing in the mangy room upstairs. None of this needed to be said. A man had a living to make, after all.

Claire was awaiting him in the car, her face pale and set. Robert came out to her, deeply troubled. 'She's gone,' he said shortly.

'Gone where?'

'He didn't have a clue. And neither do I!' he confessed.

They sat for a while in silence. 'Let's think it through, Robert,' Claire urged, anxious in spite of herself. 'Let's try to work it out from her side, where would she go, what would she do? Last night – the last time you saw her before you passed out, she was there. She was up on the headland with the two of you, both collapsed, both, for all she knew, fatally ill or injured. You know her – what would she do?'

'She'd have to get help. That would be her first thought.'

'How would she do it?'

'She couldn't have taken the car. She doesn't drive,' said Robert, piecing it together. 'And the police say that both the cars, Paul's and mine, were still up there anyway when they arrived.'

'So she'd be coming down from Broken Bay on foot. Poor child! In that terrible storm! She must have found a phone somewhere, to call the police and get help as she did. Where's the first place that she'd come to?'

They looked at each other in unison. 'Of course! The Rectory!'

'God in heaven!' snapped Robert. 'What an idiot I

am!' Hurriedly he engaged gear and set course for the headland. Please God, let her be there, he prayed. Let her be safe. Don't give her to me, then take her away again before I have any chance to show what kind of a father I could be to her . . . Lord, Father of All, hear me . . . spare her . . .

They found her under the old oak table in the hall, soaked and shivering, incoherent with distress. At one sight of her, Claire swept to her side and took her in her arms. 'There, there,' she murmured, rocking her on her bosom in the age-old gesture of comfort and mother love. Emma clung to her like a baby, repeating the same muttered sound over and over again. At last Claire raised her head. 'I think she's saying "upstairs", Robert. I don't know what she means, but do you think you could just go up and take a look?'

She was lying in the bedroom on what had been her bed, her eyes closed, her face calm and serene as it had never been in life. She lay there in perfect repose, limbs straight, meticulously neat as she always had been. She might simply have dropped down there for a brief rest. But the deep pool of blood blossoming on the white coverlet under her body showed that her sleep would be eternal. And the hands gently folded across her breast showed that she had not died alone.

A moment later he was downstairs again, his face a mask of control over pain. 'Claire, you'd better get Emma out of here. Take her to the hotel, book some rooms, see what you can do.'
'And you?'
She knew at once that something terrible had occurred.
'Ring me from the hotel as soon as you've got Emma into bed. I'll be here. I'll be . . . waiting for the police.'

The complexity of the story Dean Maitland had to tell caused almost every policeman he saw to refer the matter upwards to his senior officers. From every meeting, every interrogation, wires began to hum, old files were exhumed, investigations re-opened, and blind Justice, the capricious crone with the scales, began slowly, slowly, to swing the right way at last.

Through all this, Paul, shot in the liver and spleen by the bullet which had claimed Joan's life, fought doggedly for his own, sometimes winning, sometimes losing. And through it all either Claire or Robert was at his bedside round the clock, talking, reading, or playing music to the unconscious form, or in the case of Claire, roundly scolding him for not making a greater effort and threatening him with the direst penalties if he failed to make a marked improvement in his state of health right *now*.

It was only justice, therefore, that it was Claire who was rewarded with the heart-stopping moment of unspeakable joy when Paul finally opened his eyes and muttered faintly, 'Hello, sis.'

'Paul! Oh Paul!'

'Hey!' The voice was weak but unmistakeably the old Paul. 'Spare the waterworks . . . or you'll have none left for my funeral!'

The surgeons who had privately despaired of Paul's chances now insisted on quietness and care in the conduct of his recovery, so it was some time before he was strong enough to learn everything that had happened during the weeks while he was ill. The first news Claire could not wait to impart was of his free pardon for the crime he had committed, with an exceptional *ex gratia* compensation award for the length of his imprisonment and the loss of his good name. 'Robert hired the top solicitor for these things to get it for you, Pauly,' she told him earnestly. 'It'll mean you never have to work again. You can be a playboy at last, like you always wanted to!'

He grinned. 'Thank him for me, will you, sis?'

'I will. But he doesn't want thanks. he's determined to do what he thinks is right.'

'What do the police say – about him?'

'They know he had no previous enmity with Jim Calder. And they know, too, what a vicious temper Jim had. They're ready to accept that Jim made an unprovoked attack on him, and met an accidental death in the course of that.' She reached forward and took his hand. 'Something else too. Mick Ford's been put in prison.'

'Yes?' Paul's eyes were bright with interest.

'He's been charged with conspiracy to murder Murray Beilby. What he blurted out when you had him at gunpoint in the pub was overheard by everyone in there. He was arrested almost immediately after. He's confessed to the whole thing. He's sure to get life – even though he says he only fixed it up for someone else.'

'Someone else? Who?'

Claire's voice was heavy with sadness. 'Joan.'

'And what about – Joan – that last night?'

'Her fingers were on the gun, on the trigger. The path of your wound and hers shows clearly that she was trying to shoot you, not the other way around.' She paused. 'Robert thinks . . . he thinks it was better this way. He could never have forgiven her for what she did to you – and what she's done to him all his life.'

'Yeah.' He eyed her curiously. 'She always wanted him to be a Bishop or something. Thing is, I thought he wanted it, too.'

Claire smiled ruefully. 'We all did. We all thought we wanted that and nothing else. But the nearer we got to it, the less we liked it, Robert and I. And the further and further apart we grew. The truth is, he's not really a public person. He can be good at it if he has to, but it's not what he'd choose to be in his heart of hearts.'

'What then? He can't just go back to being a humble parish priest again, can he? I seem to remember he wasn't too happy with that the first time around.'

Claire smiled. She was looking really good these days, he noticed, plump and pretty like she used to be. Happiness agreed with her. And she was not going to let anything spoil it. 'Oh, he'll think of something, never you fret. There's a whole wide world out there for us now. And he's clever enough for anything!'

Her eyes were shining. 'Robert's going to start a new life, for himself and for us – for all of us! After all this time, good has come out of evil and all the bad things are behind us at last. Robert has finally laid the past and all its ghosts to rest, once and for all. There's nothing but a bright future ahead for us now – and I can't wait for it to begin!'

EPILOGUE

Spring 1991

The wind off the sea was wonderful, it made you glad to be alive! Filling her lungs with the raw salt breeze as she made her way forward on the ship, bracing herself against its slow, majestic roll, Claire understood for the first time why invalids used to be prescribed long sea voyages for their health in days gone by. A month of this, she smiled to herself, and I'll be fitter than I've ever been in my life before. And about time too!

Ahead of her, leaning against the rail in the prow, she could see Robert, and next to him Emma, deep in conversation. But as soon as she approached, Robert swung round to greet her with both arms outstretched, and huddled her into the protection of his greatcoat as he read the expression on her face. 'So Paul was in good form?'

Claire brushed back her windblown hair and smiled up at Robert with an air of complete satisfaction. 'Tremendous! He is going to take that skiing holiday after all. And he's planning to catch up with us all wherever we are later in the year. It was fantastic to talk to him! I can't get over being able to talk to Australia from an ocean-going liner in the middle of the Atlantic sea! Best of all, though' – she dimpled at them both – 'you'll never guess!'

'Oh no!' Robert burst out laughing. 'Don't tell me – he's got a new girlfriend!'

'Yes!' Claire laughed, 'He says she's a real cracker! He might even marry her!'

Emma grinned. 'Well, just as long as we can all be there to see it!'

Fondly Claire looked up into Emma's face. Catching

501

her glance, the girl smiled her appreciation. Already she looked years younger, thought Claire happily, yet she was also filling out too her figure looked better, her face less sharp and guarded. All the poor girl really needed was some proper food, and a bit of love and family life, she told herself. And it would be even better when they got their own home!

'What d'you think he'll do – Paul?' pursued Robert. 'Of course he could live off his award. But I can't see him living a life of idleness, somehow.'

'He could always have his old job back!' said Claire mischievously. 'I understand there's a vacancy at the mine, now that Mick Ford's out of circulation! But he won't go back to the mine – he's too clever for that.'

'Like his little sister, eh?' grinned Robert with delight. 'Always knew I was on to something special getting hold of an Everard!'

'It runs,' said Claire impressively, 'in the family. How could I manage you two else?'

'Well, a bit of management is what we need, don't we, Em?' Robert yawned and stretched. 'Better make sure we all get an early night tonight. Big day tomorrow.'

'Oh come on!' protested Emma, laughing. 'We may be making land tomorrow, but it's the last big dance of the whole crossing tonight. We're not going to miss that! I'm going to make sure you two are never off the floor! You know you'll have a great time!'

'Well, we'd better turn out for it then, if only to chaperone you, Miss Emma!' teased Robert. 'If you get as many admirers as this when we're settled in England, we'll have to have special visiting nights for all your gentlemen callers, and dispatch them in bunches of twelve at a time!'

'It's settled then! OK, I'll see you two later. I promised to make up a four for tennis on the lower deck – back in an hour or two.'

In companionable silence they watched her depart. Robert was the first to speak. 'Happy, darling?'

Her smile said it all. 'Oh, yes! What about you? No regrets?'

'None,' he said slowly. 'None at all. Oh, I don't regret

the years I gave to the Church – and I'm sure I did some good along the way. But I know now that I only chose it in the first place as a way of trying to work off the guilt I felt about my father, and the way he died. And once that became clear to me, I knew I had to find a new direction.'

'Oh, Robert, I think it's going to be wonderful!' breathed Claire. 'To have a chance to take over the International Famine Relief work – to co-ordinate that between all the participating countries – it's a marvellous job, Robert, and you'll do it so well!'

'I mean to!' He could hardly explain, even to Claire, how this new post, and the new chance it was bringing, excited him. He felt like a twenty-year-old again, a beginner starting out. 'But I hope there's going to be a lot in it for you and Emmie as well. London's a pretty good place to be, after all – we can make a start there on that "proper education" she's so keen on, bless her. You'll be able to do practically anything you want – the job will take us all over the globe if we want to go – and we'll have all the fun of Europe besides, weekends in Paris, whatever you like!'

'Weekends in Paris! Mmmm!' she mused, her head on one side. 'Oh, I could go for that. Because now I've found you again, Robert, I don't ever want to lose you – lose your love.' She coloured a fraction. 'In that way. You know what I mean!'

'Darling Claire, I know what you mean!' He roared with laughter. 'And I don't think we need to be shy about it after all this time!' Heedless of any other passengers, he pulled her round to face him from where she was snuggling under his arm, and gave her a deep, hungry, adoring kiss. 'Now you just take that as credit on account, Claire Maitland. Because tonight, dance or no dance, I'm going to make glorious, endless, fascinating love to you, and I don't care if the whole boat knows it!'

Tremulously she kissed him back. 'Oh Robert,' she murmured. 'You're so good to me! And honestly, darling,' – she leaned forward and took his hand – 'I hope you don't think I'm being sentimental – but I almost don't want this trip to end. it's been like another honey-moon – and even better than our first!'

'That's not silly, my love.' He held her very close. 'That's the way it ought to be. We're going to need all the love between us for what lies ahead – to face the future together and make it great – to be good parents to Em – to make new lives and careers in a new country, at least for the next few years, till we decide where we're going to settle – and to give Paul the help he needs getting back on his feet. But pulling together – we'll do it.'

'You left something off the agenda, Robert – some-thing very special.'

He looked at her curiously. Her face was pink with excitement and her eyes were very bright. 'We're going to need each other now more than ever in our lives before – because there's going to be somebody who needs us.'

'Somebody – who . . . ?' he said wonderingly. What was this? Claire did not usually play games with him. He searched her face for her meaning. She was brimful of emotion, her lips pressed together as if to hold back the most marvellous piece of news in the world. Slowly he felt his way towards it. 'Darling, no . . . ?' He hardly dared to believe or hope.

'It's true. I saw the ship's doctor this morning, after I called Paul. I'm going to have a baby, Robert. After all these years!' Softly she began to cry the little round tears of true joy. 'New life, Robert – our life, yours and mine!'

'New life! Oh, darling! Wait till we tell Paul! And Emma!' And he folded her in his arms in the knowledge that their new life together, their love, their joy, was only just beginning.